PRAISE FOR
AND *THE PEGASUS SECRET*!

"Fans of Dan Brown's *The Da Vinci Code* are going to love *The Pegasus Secret*, an ecclesiastical thriller that is so action-packed that readers will feel they are on a fast-moving rocket ship. Gregg Loomis writes an amazing thriller with more twists and turns than a maze."

—I Love a Mystery

"*The Pegasus Secret* is a driving thriller that slams the reader from the first page and doesn't let up until the explosive end. A fantastic novel."

—Fresh Fiction

"The international setting and fast-paced action grip... [Readers] looking to repeat the *Da Vinci Code* experience will be satisfied."

—*Publishers Weekly*

"With impressive success Loomis has created a highly entertaining mystery... You won't want to miss *The Pegasus Secret*."

—New Mystery Reader

"[*The Pegasus Secret* has] more intrigue and suspense than *The Da Vinci Code*!"

—Robert J. Randisi, Bestselling Author of *Cold Blooded*

No Accident

Lang customarily parked and retrieved his own car. The temptation for the young carhops to test the acceleration of the Porsche was too great. Tonight, he'd take a chance.

He stood in front of the bank of elevators, shivering from the lobby's aggressive air conditioning. There was a dull thud and the building shuddered, lights blinking off before the condominium's generators cut on. For a second, Lang assumed lightning had struck. Then he heard screams from outside.

Instinctively, he ran for the doors. He was so intent on looking for Gurt that it took him a second and third step to realize he was running on a carpet of shattered glass. A woman was leaning against a dark car, a Mercedes, weeping uncontrollably, and there was the smell of something other than the ozone odor of a close lightning strike.

Still not seeing Gurt, Lang's eyes followed a number of people running toward the parking lot and underground parking entrance. A small crowd had gathered around flames that seemed to be fueled, rather than extinguished, by the sheets of rain. Another flash of lightning showed Gurt, a head above most of the others. There was a scent that had no rational reason to be here, a mixture of transmission fluid, plastic and rubber.

And burned nitrogen sulphate.

He stopped beside Gurt, at first unsure of what he was seeing....

Other *Leisure* books by Gregg Loomis:

THE PEGASUS SECRET

THE JULIAN SECRET

GREGG LOOMIS

LEISURE BOOKS NEW YORK CITY

This book is for Suzanne.

A LEISURE BOOK®

May 2006

Published by

Dorchester Publishing Co., Inc.
200 Madison Avenue
New York, NY 10016

ISBN 0-8439-5691-7

Visit us on the web at www.dorchesterpub.com.

ACKNOWLEDGMENTS

Thank you to:

My agent, Mary Jack Wald, without whose persistence, patience and help I would never have had a book published.

Don D'Auria, Executive Editor, Dorchester Publishing Company, who is always willing to take time to discuss what does or doesn't work, what is or is not believable and what may or may not be commercially viable. He can do all that with such tact I sometimes forget I didn't write this book in a vacuum.

Leah Hultenschmidt, Dorchester's former publicist, now editor, for getting the attention for my last book.

Connie Williams, publicist, who is relentless in seeking maximum exposure in bookstores and the press.

My wife and chief researcher, Suzanne, who loves digging in some of the more remote corners of history.

Any success I may enjoy would not have come my way without the above.

THE JULIAN SECRET

PROLOGUE:
MISCELLANEOUS EVENTS

Rome
Outside the City Wall, South of the Tiber
Month of Julius
A.D. 362

Demetrius did not like being among the dead at night. If the purpose of being here was to visit a tomb, perhaps to lower food to the spirit of someone departed, then it should be done in daylight when the gods could see and note the piety with which the ancestors were treated. The same would be true if this were a funeral procession. Night was the time of evil and the underworld, the time of Pluto or whatever name these Romans had for the master of Hades.

But Demetrius was a Greek, a mere slave, who did not get to choose the time and place of his labors.

Even in the poor light of stuttering torches, though, it was obvious that Sextinus, his master, was unhappy even if he was carrying out a command of the Emperor himself. The other slave, a Gaul whose tongue had been cut out for some minor disrespect, was clearly as unhappy as Demetrius. Not only were the streets between the tombs dark, it was said that at night deadly serpents came out from the Tiber's swamps at the foot of the hill below to devour whatever might remain of the recently deceased.

Demetrius was terrified of snakes, particularly those rumored to be large enough to swallow a man whole.

Ahead, a structure larger than the others blotted out the stars. With whispered curses, Sextinus urged them forward, to carry the burden the two slaves shared next to the foundations of the temple.

Or at least, Demetrius thought of it as a temple.

Actually, it was a palace, the residence of the high priest of that religion the Emperor Constantine had embraced nearly four decades ago, a belief that worshiped a god with no name and his son, a Judean who had been crucified and supposedly risen from the dead.

Rising from the dead was a fairly common trick for gods and goddesses, Demetrius thought. The Egyptians' Isis did it every spring with the flooding of the Nile. There was Orpheus, who went to Hades to retrieve his wife, Mythrin, the subject of Mythrinism, a religion ever popular these days, and any number of Persian gods who jumped up out of their graves as though simply waking from a mortal's sleep.

But there was something different about this religion. Christianity, that was its name. Whatever the difference, it had infuriated the Emperor enough to commence purges that had been unknown for years.

That religion, Demetrius was sure, was why he and the other two men were here tonight, to dig into the underpinning of the temple/palace and place two amphorae there and then replace a part of the foundation itself so that anyone attempting to remove the amphorae would risk bringing the whole structure down on his head.

What was in those clay vessels? Not wine or olive oil. They were far too light for that. It made no sense. But then, emperors didn't have to.

The Vatican
April 1939

Eugenio Pacelli, Pope Pius XII for less than two months, hurried along the dimly lit corridors of the grotto, the name only half-humorously given to the lowest parts of St. Peter's Basilica. Ahead of him, Father Emilio Sargenti turned to wait impatiently for the older man to catch up.

"Slower, Emilio," Pius puffed. "Even if what you think is true, it will not go away."

The young priest stopped, making an unsuccessful effort to hide his impatience. "Of course, Your Holiness."

At a slower pace, they threaded their way between effigies of past pontiffs reclining on marble sarcophagi. Although many might find the company of the dead macabre, Pius often retreated here to pray alone.

To pray and conduct a private, personal exorcism of the demons he was convinced inhabited the soul of Adolph

Hitler, demons he had had an opportunity to witness firsthand as the Papal State's envoy to Berlin only a year or so ago. The man was capable of enormous evil. Swallowing sovereign nations, pogroms, and, if Father Sargenti had found what Pius suspected, doing irreparable damage to the Church itself.

The German dictator was temporarily forgotten as the younger man stooped and directed a flashlight beam at a dark corner. "There, just next to the wall!"

Pius tugged at his white cassock and knelt to see better. This was the niche his predecessor, Pius XI, had chosen for his tomb. In preparing space for it, the discovery had been made.

"Can you see it?" Impatience was creeping back into Father Sargenti's voice. "See the bricks, the dome of the vault underneath this floor?"

Pius saw clearly. He sat back on his haunches. "It's hardly surprising, Emilio. Before Constantine built the first papal palace here on the Vatican Hill, the area had been a cemetery for hundreds of years, first the pagan Romans, then the Christians. In fact, the area was a necropolis, streets running between mausoleums honoring the dead. You've hit the top of one of those, that's all."

Of course, that wasn't all, and both men knew it.

In the Tirol, spring comes slowly and with great caution. It was no surprise to the man riding in the railroad engine's cab that patches of snow lingered along those parts of the track shaded by towering conifers. The breeze whipping through the glassless windows was raw and smelled of the forest rather than cordite, sulfur, and death, odors the man had lived with for so long.

The air was so cold, it burned the lungs.

He smiled. Even though he would not be here for long, it was good to be coming home, to return to his native land, a country he had seen but little in the turbulent last few years. He was delighted to watch the icy streams cascade down verdant hills and through grassy meadows. A doe, pregnant with a fawn to be born soon, stood wide-eyed, watching the train chug along before showing her white flag and disappearing into the shadows. Overhead, an eagle cut endless circles into the cloud-less sky.

Nothing had changed here. The mountains, the trees, the tumbling waters that murmured to themselves as they raced downhill were the same, oblivious to the fact that the entire world was a place far different from when he had last set foot here. In the man's opinion, the changes had not been good.

Ordinarily, a train ride from Budapest to Vienna would take perhaps a half a day or so, perhaps three hundred kilometers. In today's world, the ride wasn't even possible. The tracks, bridges, and tunnels between the two Eastern European capitals had been bombed into so much steel and stone rubble. That was the reason for traveling to a village more than twice the distance from the Hungarian capital, a necessary detour.

At least, that was what he had been told. He didn't believe it.

His disbelief was justified seconds later. Rounding a gentle curve, he saw two American half-tracks across the rails. He recognized the specially mounted fifty-caliber Browning M1 heavy machine guns as the best heavy automatic weapon of the war. The sun twinkled on the brass shells in belts already fed into each breech. On one side was a Sherman tank, the black mouth of its turret cannon turned in the train's direction. On the other was a line of deuce-and-a-halfs, two-and-a-half-ton trucks, canvas covers in place to shield the contents of the beds from curious eyes. About a dozen men in American combat uniforms, some swaddled in great coats, stood around, each carrying a rifle. Even at this distance, he could see the shoulder patches of the 15th Infantry Regiment.

The grade had slowed the train to a near walk. Stopping took little effort.

"Herr *Sturmbahnführer* . . . ?" The engineer asked.

Without taking his eyes off the Americans, the man replied in German, "You are not to refer to me so. I am simply Herr Schmidt."

The engine exhaled deeply, geysers of steam venting into the crisp air, as the man swung down from the cab. He was dressed in Tirolian attire: lederhosen, green wool socks, and a felt hat sporting a brush of mountain goat hair. Though his shirt was short-sleeved, he carried his jacket under one arm and kept his hands visible at all times so there would be no mistake made as to whether he was armed. He walked along the short stretch of track deliberately, as though each step had its own significance. He carried himself ramrod straight, like a soldier marching at attention.

From one of the half-tracks, a man also in American uniform climbed down. His short Eisenhower jacket was adorned with campaign ribbons and his shoulder straps bore two stars each, the rank of major general. Instead of advancing to meet the man from the train, he waited calmly where he stood, as if high-ranking Allied officers met German-gauge freight trains in secluded woodlands all the time.

A few paces from the American, the man from the train stopped, touching the brim of his hat in what might have been either a salute or a civilian greeting. "Herr General!"

The American didn't bother to return the gesture, whatever its significance. "You are right on time, Mr. Smith."

The other man smiled, an expression that emphasized the scar running the length of one cheek. "Punctuality is a virtue of my people."

His accent was almost nonexistent other than the "v" sounding slightly more like an "f."

"Only fuckin' one," the general grumbled. "You have the list?"

The other man produced a sheaf of papers from inside the bib of his short pants and extended them. "Not only a complete inventory, but a car-by-car list."

Without reply, the general motioned to a man with sergeant chevrons on his sleeves. The sergeant gave the man a suspicious look, one that said he wasn't overly certain the surrender of all German forces just eight days earlier applied here. He said something to two other men who followed him as he walked alongside the still-wheezing locomotive.

The man from the train watched appreciatively. American soldiers slumped as they walked, like old men. They also cared little about the condition of their uniforms and less about the polish on their boots. Sloppy. Sloppy and deceiving. How could such slovenly men be such fierce fighters? If someone had suggested five years ago that American auto mechanics and shoe salesmen could be trained to beat the finest army the world had ever seen, they would have been considered mad.

"That one." The general was walking behind the three enlisted men.

With a screech of metal on metal, the three American enlisted men pulled the door of the first freight car open. Even the cool air could not disguise the faint sour odor that wafted out.

The general made a face. "I'm afraid to ask what I'm smelling."

Without a trace of apology, the other man replied, "This train has been moving for nearly three months now, collecting art and treasure from both Hungarian and Austrian museums who wished to prevent it from being taken by the Russians. Many of the crew lived in these cars without benefit of modern conveniences such as soap and running water. Also, a number of these cars were used in the resettlement program, moving Hungarian Jews to the camps."

The general gave the other man a glance, the same sort of look he might have reserved for a child molester.

Without seeming to notice, the man from the train added, "As per our, er, understanding, I took the first cars I could find, Herr General. Since much in these cars comes from those deportees, I had no idea of your, er, sensibilities on the subject."

The general inhaled deeply; whether to mix as much clean air with the smell or because he was without answer was impossible to tell. He looked inside the first car. Rolls of cloth were stacked upon each other. "Rugs?"

"Rugs and tapestries. A few fine tablecloths as well."

And so it went: art, silverware, fine porcelain, antiques, coin collections, even boxes of gold wedding rings that spoke more than other items about what had happened to their prior owners.

At the end of the train, the general dismissed the three enlisted men, indicating he and the other man should take a brief walk along a narrow deer trail.

The general brandished the list. "This inventory, it is complete?"

The other man, his hands clasped behind his back, shook his head. "Oh, no, Herr General."

The man in uniform stopped in his tracks so suddenly he might have hit an invisible barrier. "No? What the hell d'ya mean? Our agreement clearly specified *all*."

"Of course, Herr General," the other man said amicably. "You wanted the entire Reich stores of goods confiscated from deported Jews. You were quite clear."

The general's frustration level was clearly growing. He was not someone used to having explicit directions ignored. "Then what the hell . . . ?"

From the direction of the train came a ragged series of gunshots, their echoes bouncing like pinballs from hill to hill.

Undismayed, the man in civilian clothes nodded toward the sound. "A little insurance to make sure I don't join our poor friend, the engineer, and his crew."

"Exactly how much . . . ?" The general was too flustered to finish his sentences.

The civilian turned to go back up the path. "Enough. Michelangelo's Virgin, a Van Eyck, some trinkets. No furniture. Too bulky. All in all, probably fifteen to twenty million or so of your dollars."

"You sum'bitch!" the general exploded. "I shudda known better than to parley with some goddamn Kraut!"

The other man was unperturbed. "I might remind you, General, that a number of your superiors would be . . . shall we say 'interested' in what you're doing? I'm aware you have the power to requisition furnishings for your headquarters, but seventeenth-century boulle desks and Flemish rugs? Not to mention a half-ton or so of wedding rings plus jewels both set and loose."

The general's hand went to the holster on his belt. "I oughta . . ." He grimaced, fighting for self-control. "For your information, all this property is going to a warehouse in Salzburg until the legitimate owners can be identified."

The man in lederhosen met the other man's eyes with his own blue stare. "Of course, Herr General. I'm certain your men shot an unarmed engineer and two crew members trying to escape. All you have to do is live up to the bargain we made and the rest is yours."

"How do I know that?"

The civilian gave him a smile that was as cold as the mountain air. "You don't. You *do* know that without me, you'll never see the rest." He glanced up the hill and extended a hand to rest on the other man's shoulder, two old comrades returning from a walk. "Now, shall we go back to your men?"

West Berlin, Germany
Templehof Flughof (Airport)
December 1988

The U.S. Army version of the Beech King Air A300 bucked like a rodeo bull. The pilot, a career major, muttered into his headset while the copilot, a first lieutenant, shifted his gaze between the instruments and the open book of Jepps approach plates on his lap.

"Look at that," the major observed, staring into the snow-filled sky. "Like flyin' in a fuckin' bedsheet. We'll be damned lucky not to cut this one short."

The lieutenant nodded his agreement. With short runways and surrounded by apartment buildings, Templehof was not a place anyone wanted to miss an approach and go around, to reach the minimum published descent altitude, have no sight of the runway or its environs, and have to climb steeply out to regain approach altitude.

He returned to the Jepps. "Five hundred, sir."

The major liked to have the altitude read to him, the distance between the plane's height and the missed approach point. That way he could keep an uninterrupted lookout for the first light, the runway "rabbit," or anything else that would visually establish the approach.

"Four hundred, sir."

The major kept a steady, sweeping stare in front. "You check on our passenger?"

The lieutenant nodded. "Yes, sir. Just before we were handed off by Center. He was sound asleep."

"Asleep? In this turbulence? He's either an idiot not to be scared shitless, drunk, or just doesn't give a damn."

"Yessir. Three hundred."

"Berlin Approach, we have runway three six," the major announced gleefully into the headset's microphone.

It took the lieutenant another thirty seconds before he could make out a series of dim white lights delineating the runway. "You have the aircraft, sir?"

"I have it, Lieutenant. Give me full props, rest of the flaps. I have the power."

The lieutenant had been only slightly happier to get his first promotion than he was to see Templehof's massively hideous fascist architecture through the blowing snow. The Allies had built a bigger, modern, joint civilian-military field to the west of Berlin, but Templehof was much closer to the center of the city. The lieutenant supposed the older facility still operated, because no one wanted to shut down a living monument to those who had flown those months of 1948–49, landing an aircraft every sixty-three seconds, night or day, fair weather or foul, to bring food and fuel to the besieged city. Although he couldn't see it, he knew that on the edge of the field stood a three-pronged monument to those men, a modern sculpture the ever-irreverent locals dubbed "the Hunger

Finger." Templehof would, the lieutenant supposed, remain as long as anyone remembered the Berlin Airlift.

The buildings needed paint, and the tarmac could use paving. The field reminded the lieutenant of one of those movie stars from the 1940s now down on her luck, living on charity and Social Security.

The lighted wands of the line personnel were the only signs of life outside the aircraft as the turboprops spooled down. As the major completed the shutdown checklist, the lieutenant stooped through the cramped division between cockpit and passenger compartment.

The passenger was rubbing his eyes, clearly awakened only by a landing somewhat more rough than the flight crew would have wished. He smiled sleepily at the lieutenant and looked out of the window. Squatting to follow his gaze, the lieutenant was impressed, if not surprised, to see a black limousine pull up beside the airplane and douse its lights.

The passenger stood and stretched as high as the cabin's low ceiling allowed. "That's for me, I think. Thanks for the lift."

"Our pleasure," the lieutenant muttered, edging past. He twisted the latch and the clamshell door's airlock died with a hiss. He stood aside as the passenger went down the stairs. "Enjoy Berlin."

The passenger stopped and turned. "Thanks. But I'm afraid I've made other plans."

The lieutenant noted that the young man had wrapped a scarf around the lower part of his face. To keep warm or avoid the East German spies who frequently photographed arriving passengers?

The major came up behind the lieutenant. "Who the hell was that?"

The lieutenant shrugged. "Name on the manifest is Langford Reilly, some civilian employee from Frankfurt."

The major stooped to watch the car glide off into the white. "Spook, I'll bet."

The lieutenant held up a book. "Mebbe. But he left this, *Winnie Ille Pooh.*"

The major squinted. "What's that? It's a foreign language."

"It appears to be *Winnie the Pooh* in Latin."

Now that he was actually in Berlin, Langford "Lang" Reilly was having trouble appearing composed. He felt the combined urges to vomit, urinate, and open the car door and run. What idiot idea had compelled him to volunteer for this, anyway? When he had been hired by the Agency right out of college, he had envisioned lurking about romantic European cities, Budapest or Prague, perhaps, with a silenced pistol in one hand and a local beauty's arm in the other. As is most often the case, mature reality trumped youthful fantasy. He had taken the standard training at "the Farm," the Agency's facility south of Washington—cryptography, marksmanship, martial arts, psychology, and a number of subjects that, as far as he could see, bore no relationship to the courses' names.

Training complete, he had been assigned to the Third Directorate, Intelligence. He had been disappointed. The Fourth Directorate, Operations, had been his and all his classmates' choice. He had either been too good at the intellectual side of spycraft or insufficient in killing, maiming, and the other activities ascribed to the Fourth Directorate by the fiction industry if not the Agency itself.

Could have been worse, he consoled himself. He could have been First Directorate, Administration, spending his days reviewing budgets, checking expenditures, and generally being the spook equivalent of an accountant. No, he couldn't have been. His math stunk. And he had no engineering background, thereby disqualifying him from the Second Directorate, Material, the Agency's own special version of James Bond's Q, the supplier of poison needles in umbrellas, cameras fitted into belt buckles, and cigarette lighters that fired bullets.

He sat back in the car, staring into the snowy night. So why the hell had he left his Eastern European newspapers, TV transcripts, and comfortable if unglamorous office with the view of the Bahnhof in Frankfurt? Worse, why the hell had he volunteered?

Well, he told himself, this was likely to be one of the very last real ops of the Cold War. The Russkies and their workers' paradise in East Germany were collapsing fast. He had seen the info himself. They were going to be defeated not by superior arms, brighter generals, or better ideology. They were going broke, just plain bust, trying to do the military equivalent of keeping up with the Joneses. Or, in this case, NATO and the United States.

Collapsing or not, he was doing something that could get him killed just for an adventure he could relate to his grandchildren. If he survived to have any.

The car turned onto Friedrichstrasse and slowed to turn into a street the name of which Lang could not see. Stopping in front of a building indistinguishable from its neighbors, the limo waited until a garage door swung open.

Inside was an ancient and battered Opal truck and two men in suits. One stepped forward to open the door next to Lang and extended a hand. "Welcome to Berlin, Lang."

Lang was uncomfortable, because he was unable to exactly place the vaguely familiar face as he climbed out. Being able to instantly recall the circumstances and surroundings of someone was essential to this sort of work. "Thanks."

"We were afraid the weather might scrub the mission," the other man said.

Lang had never seen him before.

The first man handed Lang a suit on a hanger. "We're still running late. See how quickly you can get these on."

In minutes, Lang was attired in a worn but neatly pressed dark suit and highly starched shirt with frayed cuffs. The black tie was a clip-on.

"These, too." The first man handed over a pair of shoes.

Lang noted that they were highly polished but there were holes in the soles.

The next item was a shabby overcoat.

"The only thing that doesn't fit," Lang observed, rolling the sleeves back from over his hands.

"Even in West Berlin," the second man said, "most people can't afford to throw things away, wear hand-me-downs. You'd look suspicious if everything looked tailor-made."

"Okay," the first man said, "here's the plan: You go out of here, turn right onto Friedrichstrasse. Go straight to Checkpoint Charlie. You can't miss it. . . ."

The other man snickered, drawing a glare from his companion.

"Once through the checkpoint, take your second left. At the corner, there'll be a man repairing the chain on a bicycle. He'll get the job done as you arrive. Follow him. The guy you're picking up will direct you back out."

Lang was finishing tying the shoes, noting that the laces had been mended by being spliced. "How do I know I've got the right man—some sort of password?"

The first man pulled a photograph out of his coat

pocket. "We've progressed a little farther than that. This is your man. Be sure you can recognize him."

This was a face Lang was going to be certain he remembered.

The Opal's single wiper only moved the accumulating snow from one side of the windshield to the other. Every few minutes, Lang had to crank down the window and reach outside to maintain a hole of visibility. If the heater had ever worked, it no longer did. Lang was thankful for the overcoat, too large or not.

In two blocks, he saw the reason for the laugh. Checkpoint Charlie's lights would have made an operating room's illumination dim by comparison. A queue of vehicles waited in front of a billboard-size sign announcing, "You are leaving the American Sector," as though the number of armed East German military and Vopo didn't make the fact clear.

When Lang's turn came, a barrier lifted and a man in uniform motioned him forward. A few feet in front of the truck was another barrier, behind which five or six more soldiers paced up and down, trying to keep warm while holding on to AK-47s.

An officer approached, drawing his hand across his throat, a signal to kill the engine. Lang turned the key and shivered as an icy blast of air rushed through the window as he cranked it down.

"Ihre Papier, bitte."

Lang handed the man the several sheets of papers he had been given, along with a West German passport and the requisite amount of deutschmarks, which would be exchanged for worthless DDR currency. The East Germans forbade trading back the other way.

The man retreated to the warmth of the guard hut, while Lang was left shivering. Two enlisted men circled the truck suspiciously while another used a mirror mounted on a pole to inspect the vehicle's underside. It was becoming increasingly obvious that the guards were intentionally delaying their inspection, a form of harassment inflicted on all visitors from the West.

At last, the papers were returned, the barrier lifted, and Lang was on his way. The Opal's meager headlights were as poorly equipped to deal with the snow as the wiper. Even so, Lang could make out the forms of buildings shattered and abandoned in contrast to the shiny new quality of everything he had seen on his brief drive through West Berlin. The DDR, German Democratic Republic, apparently intended to keep ruins as a reminder of World War II.

Lang almost drove by the man, a mere shadow in the car's pale lights, pushing his bicycle erect and pedaling out into the street. The cyclist never looked back until he turned into an alley. About halfway down, he turned into an open shed and waited for Lang to drive the Opal inside. Then he pedaled away.

The interior was lit by a single bulb hanging from the ceiling. Two men in suits even tattier than Lang's waited beside a spade-shaped coffin. One of the men was the one in the photograph.

Gerhardt Fuchs, a ranking member of the East German government. It had been a tribute to Herr Fuchs's durability that he had retained his status even after his daughter, Gurt, had defected to the West. He might not have been so lucky had his comrades been aware she now worked for the Agency. Or perhaps he saw a less-than-prosperous future and that was why he had decided to join her on the other side of the Berlin Wall. He might or might not be of value to the Agency, but it was policy to assist any relative of a defector in departing any Soviet satellite. Policy and good business.

Not being a regular member of the Ops team in Germany, Lang had no idea of Fuchs's value. He did know that Gurt had specifically requested her father be brought out and that no one be involved that could possibly be recognized by the other side. That put the mission up for volunteers, and Gurt had turned the bluest eyes Lang had ever seen on him. He had taken the opportunity more from testosterone than good sense.

The two men lifted the casket onto the bed of the truck wordlessly. Lang understood that the dead were the only ones freely allowed to cross the dividing line between East and West. Even the Communists realized that families geographically separated by politics should be united in death. Transportation of bodies for burial was common.

But this wasn't going to work. What could be more obvious than smuggling someone past the border in a coffin? Surely the Ops guys had more sense than to . . .

The man who was not Fuchs tapped on the window, motioning Lang to open the door.

Fuchs climbed in. *"Guten Abend, mein Herr. Lassen uns fahren."*

Let's go? Fuchs was going to ride up front? What about the coffin? Then the cleverness of the plan dawned. The border guards would be unlikely to think someone would openly try to pass. Instead, they would suspect the body in the back, a false bottom to the casket, or a compartment beneath the truck's bodywork.

Lang backed out into the alley and followed Fuchs's directions.

There was no traffic passing the checkpoint from East to West. Lang handed the same papers to the same bored officer along with those provided by Fuchs. The man retreated again to the guard shack to study the documents, as though he had not seen most of them less than twenty

minutes before. The enlisted men were much more in-
dustrious than they had been previously. Clearly, the
Communists were more concerned about what left than
what came in.

Two of the guards climbed into the truck's bed and,
using a crowbar, opened the casket. In the Opal's rear-
view mirror, Lang watched them recoil in disgust. He
guessed Fuchs had managed to find a very ripe corpse.
Not bothering to reseal the coffin, they jumped to the
ground as the officer emerged from the guard shack,
Lang's and Fuchs's papers in his hand.

He extended them toward Lang, then lowered his
hand, staring intently at Fuchs. The man was making no
effort to disguise the scrutiny he was giving Lang's passenger. Lang's hand crept to the door handle. He could
slam it open into the East German and make a dash for
the border.

There was a yell from the area of the guard shack, ac-
companied by orders shouted in German. Lang, Fuchs,
and the suspicious officer looked as one. An American
officer was struggling with two Vopos, bellowing curses.
The man was clearly drunk. Lang guessed he had been
one of the military personnel who risked crossing the
border to visit the prostitutes that flourished in the Communist sector. Unwilling to admit such a thing existed,
the East German government tacitly allowed the trade
to exist as one of the few ways to bring hard currency
across the wall.

Two white-helmeted U.S. Army MPs were making
their way to the barrier, pistol holsters empty and hands
held up to show they carried no weapons. From the lack
of interest shown by the East Germans, Lang guessed he
was witnessing something that wasn't exactly unknown.
The Germans were dragging the still-cursing American

officer to the westernmost barrier, where the MPs waited patiently.

Suddenly, the American jerked an arm free and took a swing at one of his captors. The East German officer stepped back from the Opal, snatching his pistol loose and shouting commands. Lang prayed the Opal's starter worked better than the rest of its equipment, turned the key, and pressed the old-fashioned starter button. The second the engine turned over, the Communist officer started to swing the hand with the gun in it around. Too late. Lang had already smashed through the western-most barrier and was in West Berlin.

A half an hour later, he was in a small apartment being debriefed over a bottle of scotch by the same two men he had met on arrival.

"That American at Checkpoint Charlie," Lang was saying. "If he hadn't—"

A knock on the door interrupted.

"Any luck at all, that's dinner," one of Lang's inquisitors said.

The other opened the door.

In the hall stood a tall man in a dirty and torn U.S. Army uniform. His right eye was swollen shut by what Lang guessed would be a class A shiner by morning, and his lower lip was still bleeding. It was the guy from Checkpoint Charlie.

He walked into the room as if having drunk military personnel interrupt Agency debriefings were the most normal thing in the world.

"These guys treating you okay?" he asked Lang.

Lang didn't know what else to say. "I guess so."

The American officer eyed the scotch. "You got another glass, or do I have to drink out of the bottle?"

As one of the men got up to look in the kitchen, the new arrival extended a hand. "My name's Don Huff."

CHAPTER ONE

Seville, Spain
Calle Colon 27
9:21 (the present)

The patio seemed an odd place for what was happening. The enclosure was murky, the morning's sun not having yet scaled the enclosing stucco walls. Flashing lights from police cars gave bright hues to water from the thirteenth-century Moorish fountain, and words from crackling radios ricocheted off handmade bricks. In fact, anything modern seemed anachronistic along the narrow streets only a few blocks from the Moorish Mudejar alcazar, where a young sailor from Genoa, according to legend, had convinced a queen to pawn her jewels to finance a voyage. There was nothing merely legendary about the columned and canopied sarcophagus that held the remains of that sailor in the massive cathedral north across the cobblestone Piazza de la Virgen los Reyes.

The huge bells of that cathedral had just chimed the

hour, as they had done for centuries, when the young woman had stopped in front of the ornate ironwork of the gate, inserted a key, and entered to begin her day's work. Inside a wall impressive only because of its height, she crossed a patio still cool from the shadows of the previous night. The fragrance of orange blossoms came from trees lining the street outside, leaves still wet with the morning's dew.

Another key opened a modern dead bolt set into a massive and ornately carved set of double doors. Her rubber soles squeaked on ceramic tile as she made her way across a three-story entrance hall. To her right was a stone staircase that doubled back on itself as it climbed to twin galleries of living quarters. Ahead of her was a massive dining room, its table separating twelve chairs on each side. It was at the end of the table that she stopped, scenting the air like a wary doe in an open meadow.

She did not smell coffee.

Strange.

Every morning for nearly two years now, the American had been in the kitchen drinking freshly brewed coffee when she arrived. Every morning he was in Seville, that is. Many times she would come to work to be greeted only by a note that set forth tasks to be performed in his absence: research some phase of the Franco government, find the address of some aged Falangist he wanted to interview, reduce whatever she had done to a three-by-five card that went into an endless series of filing boxes. It was as if the American did not trust the computers on which they worked.

The American, Donald Huff, or Señor Don, as she called him, had doubled the wage she had been making as an English teacher when he hired her eighteen months ago. There had been other things, too: Wonderful clothes that had arrived from America with the name of the store only, no sender. Of course, had she known her anonymous donor, custom and her reputation would have demanded she return such expensive gifts, presents no single woman could accept from someone not of her family. And the huge American turkey that had crowned last Christmas dinner. Her previously modest salary plus her mother's widow's pension could never have produced such a bird, a monster-sized creature that provided meals for a week. Nor could the two incomes have purchased the train tickets and hotel rooms on the Costa del Sol, a gift Señor Don made to her mother for her birthday.

And now Señor Don would be leaving this magnificent dwelling in a few months, his book all but finished. She would miss him, both as friend and benefactor.

Why wasn't he making his morning coffee?

She pushed the swinging door to the kitchen open. The two fireplaces, one for cooking, the other for baking, were as spotless as ever. As they should be, since they probably hadn't been used for over a hundred years. The actual food preparation was done in a pantry-sized room crammed with the most modern appliances, gas range and oven, refrigerator large enough to hold almost a week's groceries, very large by European standards, and a microwave, the first she had ever seen. A door could be closed, removing these marvels from view and allowing Señor Don to insist to his dinner guests that she had prepared everything bending over the ancient stone hearth.

The coffeemaker had sat where she had left it the day before, empty, silent, and, for some reason, foreboding. She set her purse down beside it.

She retraced her steps and climbed the stairs, walking along the open gallery to the suite of rooms she and Señor Don used as office, research library, filing room, and whatever other purpose needed to be served at the moment.

The door was cracked open.

Señor Don never left the door open. Terrified the cleaning staff would inadvertently toss some irreplaceable bit of research, misplace one of the index cards, or commit some other of what he called Capital Crimes of Negligence, he locked up when work was finished each day.

She opened the door further, just enough to stick her head into the room. "Señor Don?"

No answer.

She felt a chill despite the building's lack of air-conditioning. She forced herself to push the door wider until it bumped against something on the floor. Squeezing between door and frame, she slid fully into the room, looked down to see what was against the door.

Señor Don.

Lifeless eyes seemed to look right through her. His face held an expression of surprise, as though questioning whatever event had taken his life. His head rested in a small pool of blood and a gray jelly she instinctively knew was brains.

From somewhere came screams. It took her a full minute to realize they were hers.

"Señorita?"

Her mind came back to the present and the police cars in the patio like some vibrant nightmare. She was seated at a small, three-legged table in the kitchen, her hands clasped around a long, cold cup of coffee she had brewed because she needed to give herself something to do while the police went through the house.

She looked up into the craggy face of the chief inspector, a man she guessed to be in his mid-fifties. His most prominent feature was a pair of doleful brown eyes that resembled those of a basset hound. It was as though the violence and cruelty he witnessed in his job had given him a permanently sorrowful expression.

"*Sí?* I can go gather up the papers now?"

He shook his head slowly, as though regretting being the bearer of even more bad news. "I am sorry, no. As you saw, papers are scattered everywhere, as though someone, perhaps the killer, were looking for something. We must examine everything."

He sat beside her and shook a cigarette out of a pack, looking for an ashtray. She brought him a small dish, and he raised his eyebrows in a question.

"Go ahead," she said.

He lit up, shaking out a wooden match, and looked at her through a haze of blue smoke before placing a small tape recorder on the table beside a notepad. "You are Sonia Escobia Riveria?"

She nodded, supposing he was asking for the benefit of the recorder. She had given her name as soon as he and the other police had arrived.

He asked her address, employment history, and educational background, questions that, as far as she could tell, had no bearing on the matter at hand.

After asking how long she had worked for Señor Don, he asked, "Any idea why someone would want him dead?"

She shook her head and felt the tears she had given up on brushing away spread across her face. "No."

The inspector stubbed out his cigarette, staring at the ashtray as though ideas for his next question might be there. "This writing he was doing, what was it about?"

She shrugged, aware how silly her answer was going to sound. "I'm not sure. I did specific research for him, most related to Franco or World War Two, but he did the actual writing himself."

"You never asked?" There was a definite note of incredulity in the inspector's voice.

"Of course I did. At first, anyway. He would laugh and say it was nothing I would care about. Then he seemed to get annoyed when I asked, so I quit. I suppose you could access his computer easily enough."

The inspector's eyes narrowed, no longer looking sorrowful. "That would be a good idea had not someone taken it apart and removed the hard drive."

She stared at him in shock, realized her mouth was open, and shut it before speaking. "He was careful about making backups."

He was groping for another cigarette. "On what—disks, CDs? We found none. Apparently, our killer was meticulous in removing whatever research and writing Señor Huff had done."

Sonia stood on legs that did not feel like they wanted to hold her. "Not all of them."

She retrieved her purse. "I have one here, a CD."

The inspector's eyebrows came together. "Why would you have it? The man was so secretive in what he was doing."

She handed it to him. "It was perfectly safe with me. I have no computer at home. Anyway, there are pictures on it, digital pictures he wanted me to take by a photography store and ask if they could lighten some up, enhance others. I was running late, so I planned to take them by this afternoon after the siesta."

He held out his hand. "We will return it when we finish."

Sonia wondered when, if ever, that would be.

CHAPTER TWO

Atlanta, Georgia
Park Place; 2660 Peachtree Road
The next evening

A warm spring breeze gave only a slight hint of the heat and humidity a month or so away. To the two men standing on the twenty-fourth-floor deck, the city below was a handful of jewels stretching to the southern horizon, where aircraft departing and arriving at the airport resembled distant fireflies. Both men took in the scene in silence, each puffing gently on a cigar.

The shorter of the two, a black man wearing a sports shirt open at the neck to display a golden crucifix, rubbed his stomach appreciatively. *"Deorum cibus!"*

The other, also informally dressed, chuckled. "Food for the gods, indeed, Francis. At least you appreciate my cooking. After all, *Ieunus raro stomachus vulgaria temnit."*

"Horace does tell us that an empty stomach rarely declines ordinary food, but that dinner was awesome, anything but ordinary." Father Francis Narumba wrinkled his eyebrows in mock suspicion. "But then, the quality of food around here has improved dramatically since Gurt came along. I don't mean to preach, Lang, but . . ."

Langford Reilly contemplated the ash of his cigar. "Then don't, Francis," he said good-naturedly. "We heretics don't take the same view of living in sin as you papists. Ever heard of *capistrum maritale?*"

It was Francis's turn to chuckle, the sound of a breeze across dry leaves. "As a priest, I've escaped Juvenal's marital muzzle. But your first marriage was a good one. Had Dawn lived . . ."

Realizing he might well have touched a place still raw, Francis puffed on his cigar. Dawn, Lang's wife, had suffered a lingering death from cancer years ago, long before the priest had known his friend.

Francis broke the silence that was threatening to lengthen. "Gurt going to be here indefinitely?"

Judging by Lang's scowl, the priest had made another conversational misstep. "Ask her."

Francis sighed and turned to face his friend. "Look, Lang, everything I say tonight seems to upset you. Maybe it would be better if I—"

Lang moved to put an arm around the priest's shoulder. "*Amicus est tanquam alter idem,* a friend is just like a second self, Francis. I guess I'm a little touchy tonight."

Reassured, Francis smiled, the white teeth doubly brilliant against the dark face. A native of a country among the worst of Africa's pestilential and violent West coast, Francis had gone to seminary and been appointed to minister to the growing numbers of Africans in Atlanta.

Though white, Lang's sister, Janet, had converted to Catholicism and become one of his parishioners.

Lang embraced no particular religion, but he and the black priest had become good friends with more in common than most white Americans and black Africans. Lang described himself as a victim of a liberal arts education, bored by the usual business degree. Ancient history and its languages had been his passion, a neat fit with the priest's knowledge of Latin and medieval history. Swapping Latin aphorisms had begun as a game and become a habit.

"Perhaps you are now ready for dessert and coffee?"

Gurt was silhouetted against the interior of the condominium. Even half in shadow, she could have graced the cover of any number of men's magazines. Or a bottle of St. Pauli Girl beer from her native Germany. Her height, nearly six feet, accentuated a perfectly proportioned figure she seemed to maintain without effort. Sky-blue eyes and shoulder-length hair the color of recently harvested hay could have come straight off a German travel poster. In public, she got more attention than a joint chief of staff on a military base.

"We have also strudel freshly baked," she added with just enough accent to make the mundane sexy.

Francis rolled his eyes at Lang. "Appreciate *your* cooking?"

"Well, I did make the salad," he grunted defensively.

Inside, a small square table occupied that part of the living/dining area of the one-bedroom unit. Before Gurt's arrival, Lang had taken his meals on the open bar that separated the cramped kitchen. The table had been her addition, something she had found in one of the junk shops she haunted. It was one of several additions she had made to the home Lang had bought after Dawn's death.

Under the table, tail wagging furiously, was Grumps, the large, black, and otherwise nondescript mongrel that had belonged to Lang's nephew, Jeff. The dog was the only tangible thing left of the little boy, and Lang had every intention of keeping him despite the regular bribes to the building's concierge staff to ignore the limitations on pet size specified in the condominium's rules.

Gurt's mention of strudel had awakened Grumps, and he was waiting for the handout he knew would be coming from Francis despite Lang's protest that the animal needed no additional food. Lang supposed that had he a child, the priest would be equally ruthless in spoiling the infant, too.

Francis leaned over the table, sniffing appreciatively. "Peach, you've made a peach strudel?"

Gurt nodded. "And why not? In Germany, plentiful are apples, not so much peaches. Here there more peaches than I shake a stick at."

"*Can* shake a stick at," Lang corrected.

She shrugged, despairing of ever really understanding English. "And why would I shake sticks at peaches, anyway?"

Lang rolled his eyes while Francis made no effort to hide a smile.

"If supply's the criterion, I suppose peanut strudel is next," Lang finally quipped, drawing an elbow in the ribs from Gurt.

Ever the diplomat, Francis changed the subject as adroitly as an NFL running back avoiding a linebacker. "You got your work permit?"

Gurt looked up from cutting the pastry. "Yesterday came what you call the green card." A look of puzzlement flickered across her face. "But it was not green."

"It used to be. The name stuck," Francis offered. "So now . . ."

Gurt twisted her face into an expression that told Lang that she was having trouble with the idiom of a name adhering like some sort of glue. The literal nature of her native language made American slang difficult.

"Now," she continued, "I will teach German at the school, Westminster."

Francis gave an appreciative whistle as he accepted a slice that could have been a meal itself. "You started at the top. That's the ritziest prep school in the city."

There was a sudden silence, the interruption of conversation as each person looked into their own thoughts.

Lang spoke. "So the Braves going to do it again?"

Both Lang and the priest were ardent baseball fans.

"If anyone can, Bobby Cox can," Francis said, referring to the manager of the Atlanta team. "Who can be wise, amazed, temperate and furious, loyal and neutral, in a single moment? No man."

Lang thought for a second. "Shakespeare, *Macbeth*?"

"You got it."

"We'll see. It's only April. 'The end crowns all and that old common arbitrator, Time, will one day end it.' "

Francis wrinkled his brow. "Shakespeare?"

"Troilus and Cressida."

Both men were delighted with the new game: Shakespeare on baseball. The possibilities were endless. Lang was thinking of the Roberto Alomar incident of a few years ago, the umpire asking in the words from *King Richard III,* "Why dost thou spit at me?" Francis had in mind the ubiquitous beer ads around the park and *King Henry VI,* Part II, "Make my image but an alehouse sign."

Gurt was standing over them, watching the verbal contest. "And what is next, *Mein Herren,* Goethe and ice hockey?"

"Humor is not a logical part of human behavior," Lang said.

"Shakespeare?" Francis asked.

"Mr. Spock, *Star Trek*."

"Who?" Gurt asked.

Francis started to reply, but was interrupted by the shrill intrusion of the telephone.

Francis looked at Lang. "Somebody's in trouble, I'll bet."

Lang's law practice consisted largely of defending the criminal elite—corporate executives with sticky fingers, or accountants of dubious veracity, tax cheats, those involved in what was referred to as "white-collar crime."

Lang stood, wiping crumbs from his lips with a napkin. "My clientele don't usually get arrested on a Saturday night; they can afford a lawyer who arranges a voluntary surrender during normal business hours." He put the napkin down. "Besides, I'm not taking much new business. Too involved with the foundation."

The foundation. Specifically, the Janet and Jeff Holt Foundation, a charity funded by some European company. Why a commercial venture, one Francis could never find on any stock exchange, would pay an annual ten-figure sum in honor of Lang's late sister and nephew was a question that troubled the priest. Even more mysterious was the fact that Lang had left Atlanta about this time last year to seek the persons responsible for the deaths of Janet and her adopted son, returning some months later as the sole director of an incredibly wealthy charity that spent hundreds of millions of dollars solely to provide medical care to children in Third World countries.

Lang had also returned with Gurt, a woman he had apparently known before his marriage. The specifics of their previous relationship, like the foundation, were quickly established as off conversational limits.

That was one of several areas that puzzled Francis. Among others was the fact Lang had gone to law school in his thirties and had never attempted to explain the intervening years between his practice and college.

All enigmatic; none worth risking a friendship by unwanted inquiry.

Lang returned to the table and sat without a word. He was either deep in thought or stunned by the conversation. Both Francis and Gurt paused, waiting for some explanation, but none was forthcoming.

Francis dabbed at the crumbs on his plate.

"You would like more?" Gurt asked.

The priest held up his hands in surrender. "No, please. It was wonderful, but I've eaten too much."

She stood, taking the platter away. "Then I will wrap it for you to carry with you. Homemade takeoff."

"Takeout," Lang corrected, still thinking.

"Does he not take it off, away?"

Lang didn't reply. He despaired of Gurt's logical mind mastering the American idiom.

While Gurt wrapped the remains of the strudel, Lang brought two glasses and a bottle of single-malt scotch to the table. He set a glass in front of Francis and offered the whiskey.

Francis stood, aware that, whatever its nature, the phone call, not company, was on his friend's mind. "No, thanks. I've gotta drive home, and I don't need a DUI."

Lang gave him a crooked grin. "No papal dispensation for driving under the influence?"

Francis accepted the rest of the strudel from Gurt, nodding thanks. "The police of the apostate cut us true believers no slack." He opened the door to the hallway and elevators, turning to speak over his shoulder. "Although a clerical collar has spared me the occasional speeding ticket."

"Okay, then," Lang said. "But at least let's check the

score. Ought to be somewhere in the middle innings out there in La-La Land."

The Braves were playing a series against Los Angeles, three time zones distant.

"For just a minute," the priest conceded, stepping back inside and closing the door. "But keep that scotch out of reach, my reach."

Both men sat back down at the kitchen table as Lang turned on the small television set on the breakfast bar. No matter how many times he saw it, Lang still regarded the transfer of images across a continent to be every bit as magical as anything the ancient gods might have done.

They had hit the end of an inning, and a car ad began to unfold, the announcer shouting in perpetual excitement. As the shiny new vehicles available at LOW, LOW, UNBELIEVABLY LOW PRICES faded, a familiar figure appeared, a silver-haired man holding a Bible, his ice-blue eyes staring earnestly into the camera.

"My fellow citizens," he began, "it is high time for us to take back our country from the godless courts and those who would crush our Christian heritage. When I am your president, we will work together for these things and to make America, once again, the first among nations . . ."

Both Lang and Francis had heard it before. Harold Straight, candidate for his party's nomination in the upcoming presidential election. His determined face faded to strains of "God Bless America."

"I'm sure the Jews of this country find his message comforting," Lang observed wryly.

"Not to mention Muslims, Buddhists, and everyone else," Francis added. "Also, any country that dares to think it's number one is likely to find the Marines on its national doorstep."

Gurt, abandoning her usual posture that television

was a sure cause of brain rot, moved to look at the fading screen. "This man has a chance to win?"

Lang shrugged at the unpredictability of American politics. "A lot of people believe he can put the Ten Commandments back in courthouses, stop the teaching of evolution, and reverse Roe v. Wade."

"And this is good why?"

Lang glanced at Francis, who smiled back. "I'm sure Francis here would advocate the end to abortion—"

"Not at the price of having Straight in the White House," the priest interjected.

"And," Lang continued, "his message about his dad dying in World War Two to save American values hits home, too."

"This is normal, to get into politics because of what your father did?" Gurt was incredulous.

"There wasn't a war convenient for this guy to get into when he was in the Army," Francis explained.

Gurt turned and went to the sink to wash dishes, a pastime both more interesting and useful than politics.

As the image of Dodger Stadium returned to the screen, Francis said, "After seeing Mr. Straight, perhaps I will accept your kind offer of a little scotch."

In spite of multiple scotches and dinner wine, Lang could not sleep. Instead, he watched shadows of light from the street below form abstract patterns on the ceiling. Finally, he gave up. Moving carefully to avoid waking Gurt, he slipped out of bed and stood on the deck just outside the room. Absently, he observed the golden ribbon of traffic moving along Peachtree Street, his mind miles and years away.

He was startled when an arm encircled his waist from behind.

"The phone call, yes?"

He reached a hand over his shoulder to touch Gurt's face. "Yeah."

"Tell me."

He sighed. "Remember Don Huff?"

There was a pause. "I'm not sure. Should I?"

"Tall, slender fella from somewhere in the Midwest. Passed through the Frankfurt office after coming over to the Third Directorate from Ops. He was the one got my ass out of a sling at Checkpoint Charlie when I was bringing your dad out. We didn't see a lot of Don, 'cause he was older and married."

Gurt shook her head. "There were so many. It is a difficulty to recall even those I was working with last year. Why is he calling you after all this time?"

Lang turned to face her "He didn't. His daughter did. Don was murdered in Spain yesterday."

Even in the dim light from below, he could see her eyes widen. "Was it someone settling an old score?"

Lang shook his head. "I doubt it. Don left about the time I did, took early retirement when the Evil Empire collapsed, the intel budget was getting cut, and anyone not blind could see the main show was moving east, to hot, sandy places where the women hide their faces, scotch is hard to come by, and the fly is the national bird. Last I heard, he was writing a book."

"Perhaps someone did not like what he was writing."

Lang turned back around to stare below without really seeing anything. "Possible, I guess, but I doubt it. Seems a bit of a stretch."

"Then who?"

"That's what his daughter wants me to find out."

"We are going to Spain?"

"*I* are going."

He sensed, rather than felt, her stiffen. "The last time

you left me, ran away, you would have been killed had I not followed."

More true than he was comfortable admitting. "But you have a new job. Besides, all I'm gonna do is look around, see what I can find out. Least I can do for someone who saved my life."

"I also saved your life, and I want to go."

If Lang had learned anything since Gurt had been in Atlanta, it was that he was not going to win this argument. Or any other. At first, he would believe he had won only to discover days later the dispute was far from over. If surrender was inevitable, he might as well hand over his sword as gracefully as possible.

"Okay, I'll do what I can to make sure I have no court dates for the next few days, and you take Grumps to the kennel."

"You can call Sara, your secretary, and she will tell you more about your schedule than you could know. *You* take Grumps to the kennel."

Although Grumps was well-mannered to the point of being docile on most issues, the kennel wasn't one of them.

Lang sighed with his second defeat in as many minutes.

CHAPTER THREE

Seville, Spain
Aeropuerto San Pablo
Five days later

Even with a bedroom in the foundation's Gulfstream V, Lang's basic distrust of anything that flew prevented sleep. There had been a time when he couldn't keep his eyes open on a plane, but somewhere he had come to dislike aviation even if he could not deny its convenience. The flight could have been worse—Atlanta to Madrid by commercial jet, then take Aviaco, the local feeder, to Seville. Lang's view was that if one plane had proved airworthy, it was folly to challenge fortune by changing to another.

That was why he was making one of his rare personal trips on the foundation's airplane. Scrupulous to the point of compulsive, he kept the line between his own life and the foundation's business delineated far clearer than even his battalion of accountants suggested. He had defended too many clients who had let their own needs extend into money they were managing for others.

The irritation caused by lack of sleep was exacerbated by Gurt's deep, regular breathing, which lasted until he got up and went forward to watch one of the movies the plane carried, one described by the critics as a sophisticated, sexy comedy, "two thumbs up." The first twenty minutes went from trite to corny and back again. Lang suspected the leading man, if not the producer, was one of the critics' in-laws.

He never knew if the film got better. He awoke in front of a blank screen when the plane's steward, chef, and majordomo gently shook him with one hand while placing a steaming plate of eggs Benedict on the tray in front of him and announcing that they would be on the ground in an hour.

Having wakened Gurt, Lang showered and shaved. Although minuscule, the Gulfstream's toilet facilities were a vast improvement over the commercial airlines'. So were its storage capabilities. Lang took a sports shirt and slacks from a closet rather than donning attire wrinkled by storage in a suitcase. Minutes after the Gulfstream's tires kissed the runway, the aircraft's clamshell doors wheezed open and Lang and Gurt squinted into brilliant morning sunlight made all the brighter by their confinement aboard the plane.

Leaving the crew to deal with the paperwork generated by international travel, Lang and Gurt carried one suitcase each to the customs area, where a uniformed official spent more time trying not to be obvious in his admiration of Gurt than on his cursory inspection of their luggage. Chagrined at the brevity of the examination of bags, Lang realized he could have easily brought the Sig Sauer P226 automatic that had resided in his bedside table since his retirement. But why? he consoled himself. He was here to nominally investigate a murder while giving such consolation as he could to the bereaved child of a man who had saved his life. What use would he have for a firearm?

None, he hoped.

"Mr. Reilly?"

Both Lang and Gurt turned to look at the young girl. Petite, almost elfin. Her face was longish but with a small nose that looked as though it had been added as an afterthought. Only a closer look told him she was an adult, not a child. There was something in her dark eyes that made Lang think of a small animal about to bolt for its burrow.

"You are Don's daughter?" he asked.

She shook her head slowly. "No," she said in English, "I am Sonia, Mr. Huff's assistant. His daughter is at the house, waiting for you."

The voice had only a trace of the languid Spanish, spoken at a much slower pace than its New World counterparts.

It took a few minutes for Lang to make sure the flight crew had found accommodations and that they would remain in touch with both him and the foundation in case needed by either. He and Gurt followed the woman to the parking lot, where she indicated a sleek, clean Mercedes of recent vintage.

"A beautiful car," Gurt commented, her first words of the morning.

Sonia shook her head sadly. "It is, was, Señor Don's, Mr. Huff's. He was very proud of it." She opened the back door. "Please."

After tossing the bags into the trunk, Lang helped Gurt in, choosing the more informal arrangement of sitting next to Sonia in the front. "Kind of you to meet us. You are taking us to the house?"

The engine started with a purr. "No, Mr. Reilly. Señorita, Miss Huff, has made hotel reservations for you within walking distance."

The ride was through a city virtually indistinguishable from any other in Europe. The greatest difference, Lang thought, was the unhurried pace of traffic. The blaring horns and screeching brakes of Rome and Paris would feel isolated here. If anything, the drivers were courteous, something most cities, including those in America, would find novel. A few minutes more brought them to the sluggish brown waters of the Rio Guadalquivir. Below the *Puente de Isabell II,* foot-powered paddle boats traced lazy S-curves and fishermen stood on the banks.

Once on the eastern side of the river, Sonia turned left on the Paseo de Crisobal Colon and the streets became narrow and twisted. Stuccoed buildings hid behind walls of handmade brick, their orange tiled roofs visible. They were in the old part of the city.

The Hotel Alfonso XII was a structure in an impressive mock-Mudejar style. Its abundance of Moorish flourishes, impeccable service, and lavish accommodations were such that, according to Sonia, the guests to Spain's most recent regal wedding had stayed there, having only to cross Calle San Francisco and the small Plaza de Jerez to the cathedral to watch the eldest royal daughter marry a Spanish nobleman.

But they would have had trouble reaching the venerable church today. The street was filled from curb to curb by men in black robes, peaked hats, masks, and with bare feet. Most dragged wooden crosses.

"What is that—who are those *volk?*" Gurt asked from the backseat.

"Looks like the Ku Klux Klan," Lang observed. "Except they're wearing the wrong color."

"Penitents," Sonia explained. "This is Good Friday,

the Friday before Easter. This is the next-to-last Seana Santa, Holy Week, celebration. The men in the robes seek forgiveness of sins committed the year past."

"Not hard to see where Nathan Bedford Forrest got his idea for the Invisible Empire," Lang muttered.

"Who?" Gurt wanted to know.

If there was anything Lang did not want to have to explain, justify, or apologize for, it was a post–Civil War organization that had morphed into one of America's most famous hate groups. "Nothing. Can we edge by into the parking lot?"

An hour later, the streets were empty of those hoping to clear their souls. Lang and Gurt rode with Sonia down narrow cobblestone streets until huge wrought iron gates opened to admit them to the loveliest patio Lang had ever seen.

Lang got out on the street. "We could have walked."

Sonia nodded in agreement. "I had to bring the car back."

Lang hesitated before entering the enclosure, reaching up to pick a ripe orange from one of a line of trees. He followed the Mercedes into the patio as the gates slowly swung shut, peeling the fruit as he went. The first bite brought such an explosion of sour acid into his mouth that he spat the pulp without thinking.

Sonia, unsuccessful at hiding a grin at his discomfort, said, "*Anglese.* We call those oranges 'English' because only the English buy them."

Lang spat again, but the bitterness remained. "The English eat them?"

Sonia could no longer suppress a laugh. "Eat them? No, Mr. Reilly, they make their beloved marmalade from the rinds."

Lang was wondering if he could ever enjoy that jam on his breakfast toast again when a tall, blond woman came out of the house. Wearing her hair pulled behind her head only emphasized the long, almost equine, face. Her height seemed to give her an awkwardness so that she appeared to walk with disjointed steps, as if her bones had not been properly attached to her body.

She extended a narrow, knobby hand. "Langford Reilly. My dad told me about you. I'm Jessica Huff."

Lang took the hand. "Most likely he told you what a young idiot I was."

She gave a sad smile as she turned to Gurt, just now climbing out of the Mercedes. "And you are Lang's wife?"

Gurt shot a warning look at Lang. "No. I am Gurt Fuchs."

Puzzled, Jessica shook Gurt's hand anyway, waiting for an explanation.

When she realized none was forthcoming, she gestured toward the house. "Let's go in. I appreciate your coming."

Jessica ushered them into a wood-paneled room and indicated they should sit. Lang was surprised at the comfort afforded by the uninviting chair of leather and wood carved in the Spanish fashion.

Sonia appeared with a tray of coffee cups.

"Again," Jessica said, "I appreciate your coming."

Lang accepted a cup, tried to balance it on the narrow arm of his chair, and conceded he would simply have to hold it. "Again, I owed your father big-time and we'll help any way we can. But I don't know what we can do. If Don spoke of me at all, you know I wasn't in Ops. I sure didn't learn anything about criminal investigation."

Jessica nodded, a person not surprised. "You were one of the few of my father's former, er, associates, he ever mentioned. I didn't know who else to turn to."

Gurt's head swiveled, following the conversation.

Lang took an experimental sip of the coffee. It was as bitter as the orange. "Have the local police any idea who . . . ?"

Jessica clasped her hands. Lang noticed they were red, as though she had been doing laundry in strong detergent. "That's just it. They aren't doing anything. I mean, they came to the house, poked around, asked questions. Since Dad wasn't a local, I get the impression his . . . his murder is permanently going on the back burner. They don't have a clue."

"And you do?"

She glanced at the heavy beams in the ceiling as though seeking inspiration. "It had to be because of the book he was writing."

Lang shifted in his chair, uncertain how long he could hold the cup in his hands. "The book—what was it about?"

"Some Nazi. His name sounded Polish or something, not German. After the war he, the Nazi, wound up in Spain. Dad came here to do research."

Lang glanced at Gurt. She was no help. World War II was something intentionally slipping from the German national memory. She would have been more helpful with the Franco-Prussian War of 1870.

Her people won that one.

"But who . . . ?" Lang began.

"Some group of Nazis," Jessica explained. "People who don't want that book published."

Lang finally got up and placed his half-empty cup on a small oak chest with brass edges. He spoke as he returned to his seat. "Jessica, anyone who fought in that war would be nearly or over eighty. I can't see someone that age killing anyone."

"I'm not suggesting they did it personally. Eighty years old or not, no one wants to go to jail. How often do you read in the papers that some retired autoworker is being shipped back to Eastern Europe to stand trial for war crimes or an old man living on a beach in Florida was actually a concentration-camp guard?"

Lang had to admit she was right. Old or not, no former Nazi was going to prison if he could avoid it.

She continued. "I read about a secret organization of SS officers," she said almost crossly. "They didn't hesitate to kill when it suited them."

"Odessa, in popular fiction of a few years back. It *was* fiction."

"The name was, er, fiction," Gurt said, breaking her silence, "but the group was real. *Die Spinne,* the spider. I remember my father of it talking. The Communists wanted such organizations destroyed as much as did the Americans. It was one of the few areas of cooperation."

Jessica was showing an interest in Gurt. "Your father?"

"He was in the East German government," Gurt said, as if that explained everything.

Lang stood again. "I have no idea what I'm looking for, Jessica, but I'd like to see the room where . . ."

She also stood and headed for a staircase. "Daddy used one of the upstairs rooms."

Lang hated talking to the back of someone's head, so he saved further questions until he, Jessica, and Gurt were on a gallery above the first floor. "Who knew about the book?"

Jessica shrugged. "Everybody, I guess. I mean, he hassled his old buddies for a chance to see the files of the old OSS. That was what the Agency was called during the war, Office of Strategic Services. I know he already had a literary agent, and I think she was negotiating with a publisher. The book wasn't a secret. Other than research in Spain and that it was about some Nazi, I didn't really know much about it." She stopped and opened a door. "This is it."

Lang walked into a room equipped as an office might be: two desks, two computers, each with a printer. Government-issue bookshelves, gray metal, lined one wall filled with stacks of papers, books, and a dinner plate with a thriving colony of mold.

"You and Sonia have cleaned up?" Lang wanted to know.

"That's what I was doing while Sonia went to the airport." She nodded to the increasing green on the plate. "As you can see, I haven't finished. That's why I booked you into a hotel. Sonia won't come in here. She's the one who found Daddy when she came to work the day before yesterday. He was lying right here," she pointed, "partially blocking the door."

Lang took a closer look around the room. "If he was blocking the door, how . . . ?"

"The room adjoins another," Jessica said. "In fact, almost all of the bedrooms in the house adjoin each other. It used to be a method of ventilation."

And assignations, Lang thought but did not say. Don Juan's largely boastful memoirs were full of adjoining bedchambers. "Did the police check the other rooms?"

"I—I guess so. You'll have to ask Sonia. I didn't get here until yesterday. I called you before I left. Anyway, Sonia was here when the police inspected the place."

Gurt had been poking through the stacks of papers. She held up several. "These are research notes all. Does anyone have the manu, manu . . ."

"Manuscript," Lang finished.

"Does anyone have a copy of the whole manuscript?"

Jessica shook her head. "According to Sonia, there was only one complete copy, but it is missing along with the computer's hard drive."

So much for the theory Don Huff was killed for something other than the manuscript.

"And this?" Gurt was holding up a small metal filing box full of index cards, a device that reminded Lang of how he wrote term papers in the age before computers.

Jessica shrugged again. "I don't know. I hadn't seen Dad in over two years, had no idea even how he was going about his writing."

Lang took the box from Gurt. Each card had a single name, address, and what Lang gathered to be phone numbers at the top. Under that were one or two words in what looked like German. The rest of the card had handwritten dates, some as recent as two weeks ago.

Lang handed it back to Gurt. "What do you make out of the cards?"

She flipped through slowly. "It is a list of subject matter and people. For instance, here is someone with a reference to the Nuremberg Trials, another with reference to a parachute jump over Crete."

"What does that all have in common?" Lang asked.

No one had an answer.

CHAPTER FOUR

Hotel Alphonso XIII
17:30 (the same day)

A call to the police station from Don Huff's house had informed Lang that Inspector Pedro Mendezo, the investigating officer, observed the usual siesta and would return to duty around 18:00, six o'clock. With nothing better to do and the shops shuttered for the next four hours, Gurt and Lang had returned to the hotel. Before succumbing to jet lag, they had made love, a wild and noisy affair that Lang suspected could be heard all the way down the sumptuous hall.

Neither cared.

Refreshed and sated, they awoke famished.

"Should I telephone the room servicers?" Gurt asked.

"Room *service*. No, let's go out," Lang called back from a shower that far exceeded those in most European hotels.

This one allowed the bather to actually stand rather

than squat in a tub while using a flexible hose with a
nozzle at one end. The normal arrangement reminded
him of the German word for shower, *Dusche*. Stepping
out of the shower, he helped himself to a luxurious robe
and walked into the other room, where Gurt was lighting her first cigarette of the day.

"Do you have to?" he asked.

"You smoke cigars," she replied, shaking out a match.

"Once or twice a month, maybe."

"So your cigars are five or six times larger than my
cigarettes. I smoke one, two cigarettes a day—it is the
same, yes?"

There was a logic error there somewhere, but Lang
wasn't sure where. At least he had gotten her habit down
from over a pack a day. If she didn't quit, she wasn't going to be around long enough to become the next Mrs.
Lang Reilly. So far, though, he had had little luck in per-
suading her into marriage. Instead, she seemed perfectly
content, pointing out that their relationship worked just
fine as is. He had had no success in finding the logic
error there, either.

Minutes later, they were getting out of a taxi in front
of a building with the unmistakable facade common to
1930s-era dictators, a style of architecture Lang referred to as Fascist Modern. After they passed through
metal detectors found in public buildings worldwide, a
uniformed officer directed them to the office of Inspector Mendezo.

Blinds against the still-fierce afternoon sun created an
artificial twilight. Silhouetted by a dim lamp, a thin figure rose to extend a hand and a *"Buenos dias."* A chink
in the blinds behind him allowed sunlight into the two
visitor's chairs in front of the desk, an arrangement that
made it difficult to see the face of whoever was behind
the desk, a setup Lang was certain was intentional.

In Spain, manners required the usual prefatory discussion of the weather, Lang and Gurt's accommodations, their impressions of Seville, and the inspector's recommendations as to local restaurants, a suggestion that was amended when he learned of their arrival by private plane. Lang guessed his potential dinner tab had doubled.

Preliminaries out of the way, the inspector produced a pack of cigarettes and looked at Gurt. She nodded, producing a pack of her own. Lang, unable to say a word, prepared for a double volume of secondhand smoke.

Or double lungful.

The inspector leaned across the desk with a gallant flourish to light Gurt's smoke with a lighter encased in gold. Pushing a cheap glass ashtray across the desk, he asked in heavily accented English, "So how may I help you?"

Although he couldn't see the face because of the light in his eyes, Lang would have bet the policeman was giving Gurt an appraising stare. "The Huff murder," Lang said. "His daughter asked us to look into it."

"Hmmph!" Lang could not tell if the snort was derisive or angry. "Americans. They see too many detective programs on the televisions, believe every crime can be solved in sixty minutes with time for advertising. Even in your country, I think crime is not solved that quickly."

"Of course not," Lang said, "but the woman, Miss Huff, is emotional and cannot understand the diligent efforts you and your department are making. If you would be so gracious as to explain them to me so I may comfort the unmarried daughter of an old friend . . ."

"Diligent?"

"Working very hard," Gurt supplied, flicking an ash into the tray.

Lang made a mental note to keep the language simple. It was difficult enough to carry on a conversation in a tongue not native to all participants. Employing unusual words would only alienate the Spaniard.

"We are working hard," the inspector said. "You see, here in Seville, or all of Spain, for that matter, we have less murder than in, say, your New York. Almost always a *hombre* . . ."

"Man," Gurt supplied.

". . . man killed, it is because he and a friend get drink. A woman, gamble, you know? Narcotics also. Sometime, not many, a . . . man, he bust into house to take, steal, get caught, he kill to get away. Here, Mr. Huff, look like only papers get stealed, yes? Very difficult, this thing, this killing. It was . . . How you say? Like your gangsters."

"Execution?" Lang offered.

"Yes, execution. Bullet to the back of the neck, powder burns on skin. Very intentional."

"Do you have any idea why someone would kill Huff to get his manu . . . his book?" Lang asked.

"I never see before in twenty years," the inspector answered. "To kill for a book . . . ? It is not thinkable. I tell you, Señor, Mr. Reilly, we will not quit until we find man who do it."

The inspector stood, indicating the interview was over. He had demonstrated a talent for packing a maximum number of words into a minimum of information.

Lang remained seated, indicating he was not quite through. "Could we see the papers you took from the house?"

"Ho-kay." The policeman handed a cardboard box across the desk. "If they tell you anything, you call?"

"Sure."

"Ah, I forget." The inspector handed Lang an envelope. "CD. Only one has anything on it, pictures, old pictures, maybe sixty years old."

As Lang and Gurt reached the door, Mendezo said, "One more thing, Mr. Reilly."

Lang turned. "Yes?"

"Any assistance you give your friend's daughter is kindness. Interfering with professional police investigation is something else. You will please leave that job to us."

Lang nodded. "Of course, Inspector. Thank you for your time."

"Amateurs," he muttered to Gurt as they stepped outside the building, "constructed the ark. It was the professionals who built the *Titanic*."

Once back in the old section of town, Gurt led Lang to one of the tapas bars that seemed to occupy every corner. Since the average Spaniard ate dinner after 10:30, the small appetizers at least abated the hunger pangs. From what Lang could see, a couple or a group would enter one of the places, or sit outside if seats were available, have a glass of beer or the sweet, spicy sangria along with two or three tapas, and move along to an identical establishment a few blocks away where they greeted other people.

In the third tapas bar, he noted a pair of men who had been in the other two.

He could feel the old familiar tingling at the back of his neck, the sensation he had whenever danger was close.

He leaned across the small table, using the excuse of refilling Gurt's glass of sangria to get close enough to speak in a whisper. "Did you notice those two guys who came in right behind us?"

He knew she was too well trained to turn around. "You mean the two that have been in each place we have?"

He smiled as though acknowledging a clever remark,

no more than conversation between a man and a woman to any observer. "When did you first pick them up?"

She was rummaging around in the huge purse she carried, one large enough to contain a complete change of clothes for several days. "When we got out of the cab, they from a car got. Everywhere they looked but at us."

She had recognized what they were doing a good thirty minutes before he had. But then, she was still in the spook business. "Why didn't you tell me?"

She retrieved a pack of cigarettes and began further exploration for matches. "You did not notice them until now? You are losing your corner."

"Edge," he corrected tartly. "I'm a lawyer now, not an operative."

She found a book of matches and struck one. "You do not have to be sharp to be a lawyer?"

He filled his own glass, using his hand across the spout of the pitcher to keep the assorted fruit from splattering onto the table. This conversation was going nowhere. "And why, do you suppose, are we being followed?"

She shrugged. "We do not know certainly that we are. There are at least three other couples in this place that were in the first one we went to."

Lang was not about to admit this was a revelation.

Instead, he drained his glass. "We'll soon find out. You know how. Go straight back to the hotel."

Gurt let smoke trickle from her lips. No matter how much Lang wanted her to quit, he found this sexy. "Why do not *you* go back to the hotel? It is you, not I, who is years removed from recurrent Agency training. I resent being treated as though I cannot take care of myself."

"Tell it to Dr. Phil. *You* will go back to the hotel."

If there was one thing a German understood, it was the difference between a request and an order.

He stood, counting out euros, which he tossed on the table. He and Gurt sauntered outside, each taking turns pointing at a number of sights, two tourists discovering one of Europe's more interesting old cities. Suddenly, gestures became angry, voices lowered to keep them from passersby. Tourists had become combatants.

Then they split, each stalking angrily away from the other.

The two men, just exiting the tapas bar, exchanged glances. One followed Lang, the other Gurt.

There was now no doubt.

Lang slowed his pace, the gait of a man perhaps regretting what he had done. A couple of uncertain glances in the direction in which Gurt had departed told him his follower was keeping a consistent distance, not the move of someone intent on a street mugging or picking a pocket, two common crimes in an area with twenty-five-percent unemployment.

Shadows were growing longer. Lang estimated it would be dark in less than a half hour. If there were more of whoever these people were, Lang would prefer to be able to see them.

He studied the flyspecked window of an apparel shop for a few minutes before stepping inside. Clothes, men's suits, ladies' coats, shoes, were dumped in random piles so close together there was little room between them. Lang idly edged between a mountain of cheap cloth handbags and brightly colored sweaters to examine a man's faux-fur overcoat. Why someone would want such a heavy garment in the south of Spain escaped him, but the price was right. Pretending to seek the proprietor, he confirmed that his minder had entered the shop.

Casually, Lang made his way to the rear, brushing aside a curtain that divided the store's public space from the owner's. Dropping the coat, he quickly stepped to the back of the building, gratified to see a door. The dead bolt turned easily, and Lang stood in a narrow alley lined with the rears of buildings.

He waited patiently. Inside, he heard angry voices, no doubt the shopkeeper protesting the invasion of private space by the man following Lang.

Lang moved to the side against which the door would open. For at least a split second, it would shield him from anyone exiting. He thought of the Sig Sauer, useless in his bedside table an ocean away.

The first thing the man did when he stepped into the alley was look in the direction away from Lang. Before he could turn his head the other way, Lang had an arm bent around the man's neck, the elbow directly under his chin so that equal pressure was brought on both carotid arteries. The effect was to starve the brain of blood while allowing oxygen to be sucked into otherwise empty capillaries, causing them to pop like balloons. In four or five seconds, the victim would be unconscious. In twenty, he would be dead.

A trained hand-to-hand fighter would have immediately gone limp, thereby placing his weight against the attacker's arm and lessening the pressure. Instead, the man Lang held struggled briefly to pull the arm away, a near impossibility without substantial height advantage.

In seconds, he was crumpled on the ground. A quick but thorough search of his pockets produced the cell phone without which no European can exist, keys, and a switchblade, which, when open, made a deadly dagger. His wallet held a few euros and a national ID card, which Lang slipped into his pocket along with the phone. The knife he hurled into the gathering dark.

A series of tortured coughs told Lang the man would soon be conscious. He would have liked to question him, but that was not going to happen. All the follower had to do was not speak English, or pretend not to, and interrogation would be impossible. Besides, remaining in an alley rapidly filling with night didn't seem like a good idea.

He looked over his shoulder as he turned back onto the main street. Losing his corner, was he?

Gurt was waiting for him in the hotel room. Her raised eyebrows asked the question.

Lang gave a brief summary of what had happened, finishing with, "I don't know any more than before, but I do have a cell phone and an ID. I suppose it's possible he was just a criminal looking for a score."

"Getting out of a car to follow us?"

She was right, of course.

"Can you think of anyone at the Agency who owes you a favor, can run this ID, maybe find out to whom the number of the cell phone is registered?"

She stood to look out the window. "It is possible."

The equivalent of a Social Security number in Europe would produce not only a credit history but everything from the names of relatives to the date and nature of the holder's last visit to his state-subsidized physician.

Americans would find this intolerable. Fortunately, only a few were aware it was equally possible there.

"And also, see how we can find out to whom this cell phone number belongs."

She cocked an annoyed eyebrow, clicked her heels, and gave him a Nazi salute. "*Jawohl,* Herr Gruppen-fuhrer! Shall I also serve your dinner?"

Maybe she had not forgotten as much of World War II as he had thought.

He played it straight. "That won't be necessary. While you're calling favors due, I'm going to see if the hotel has a computer I can use, check out that CD."

Despite its fourteenth-century Moorish appearance, the hotel had a business center equal to any similar facility in the United States. Lang showed his room key to the attractive young woman at the entrance, and she led him to a cubicle complete with computer and printer.

"Will that be all?" she asked in almost accentless English.

"Yes, er, no." Lang was looking at the keyboard. "I want to print out some photographs on this disk, but I don't read Spanish."

She gave him a very professional smile, one he was sure she lavished on every dullard fortunate enough to be a guest here. "No problem. May I have the disk?"

She inserted it into the computer, pressed a couple of buttons, and stepped back. "That should work. If you have a problem, let me know."

Lang sat in front of the screen as the printer hummed. Why was it technology was less intimidating the younger you were?

The black-and-white pictures were not quite as clear as he might have hoped, either because they were not exactly focused or because of something in the process of transferring ordinary film images to a digital format. The computer had caught the sepia tone of old photographs. Most were different views of the classical facade of the same building, a structure Lang recognized as St. Peter's in Rome. One depicted a man in what might have been a black uniform, with what could have been part of the basilica as background. Lang studied the face. Perhaps mid-thirties, piercing eyes, and, most distinguishing, a scar across the right cheek. Lang looked closer. What was the insignia on the collar of his tunic? Too blurred to be certain. The other pictures seemed to have been taken at night or inside, and depicted the same man, this time in mufti, standing in front of a rock face on which barely distinguishable letters were carved.

Lang stared at the man for a long time. His face was . . . familiar? Impossible. Lang was certain he had never seen the guy before, yet there was something recognizable about him. Perhaps a movie star or other celebrity of years past whose picture Lang had seen?

Hadn't the inspector said the pictures were sixty or so years old? How did he know? The next photo answered the question. In this one, the man's uniform was clearly visible and distinguishable from civilian clothes. He stood in front of the building. Lang looked closer. His attire was either black or very dark, perhaps navy. On the high collar was some sort of . . . Lang held the paper inches from his face and recognized the stylized lightning bolts of the SS, the elite of the Nazi military.

That made sense, Lang supposed, since Don had been writing about some long-dead Nazi. But why would photographs that old be worth killing for, particularly pictures that looked like those some soldier might have had made to send home like any other tourist?

He turned off the computer and headed back to the room.

Gurt was watching what appeared to be a Spanish soap on the room's TV. A man with sideburns that would have rivaled Elvis's was shouting something at a sobbing woman. It was the first time he had seen her watch television.

"I didn't know you spoke Spanish," Lang said.

"I don't, but the story on these programs is much the same everywhere."

Apparently, she was more of a television watcher than she admitted.

Lang put the envelope with the disk in it on the room's desk. "Any luck getting a line on our friend?"

Gurt aimed the remote at the TV. It clicked off. "Luck? No. I intended to get the information. The man is a little-time criminal, has attended prison for purse-snatching, picking pockets, that sort of thing. He has been out less than a month."

"And the cell phone?"

"Someone else's, stolen."

Something Spain and the United States had in common: the effectiveness of the corrective function of their respective penal systems.

Lang sat down on the bed. "Penny-ante crooks can't afford automobiles in Europe. Unless those two stole the one they got out of, somebody hired them to follow us. Or worse."

"Or they wanted to scare us away."

Lang hadn't considered that possibility. "From what?"

Gurt glanced at her purse, no doubt wondering how much grief she'd get if she lit another cigarette. "From whatever they think we are doing. Or whatever they think we might find among your friend's papers."

They looked at each other without speaking for a full minute before Gurt broke the silence. "That knife. He could have intended to kill you."

"And the one that followed you?"

"I on the lighted streets remained. He had no chance to harm me before I walked the two or three blocks back here."

Another pause.

Gurt decided to risk it. She pulled her cigarettes out of the purse. "Lang, what are we doing?"

"I'm not sure I understand the question. What *you* are doing is setting yourself up for cancer, emphysema, and tobacco-stained teeth."

Like her favorite fictional character, Scarlett O'Hara,

Gurt apparently decided she would worry about that to-morrow. "I mean, why are we getting involved in this? Huff may have been a friend, but he was not close. I never heard you mention him before the other day. Besides, what can we do the police cannot?"

As usual, she had looked right in and seen his soul. Or at least part of it. The truth that Lang really didn't want to admit to himself or Gurt was that he had gotten bored. You could defend only so many wealthy embezzlers, stock manipulators, and flimflam artists before they all became the same. Likewise, the ever-growing list of mendicants seeking funds from the foundation were assuming a tedious similarity.

Last year, he had set out to find the killers of his sister and nephew. It had very nearly cost him his life as well. But he had succeeded where the local authorities had failed, and the danger inherent in the enterprise had been exhilarating.

Settling a score for a man who had saved Lang's life was only part of the reason.

And Gurt knew it.

Sometimes he thought he wanted to spend the rest of his life with her only because he dared not have someone who knew him that well on the loose.

"I care more than the police, and I owe it to Don."

Gurt shrugged, not buying it but not willing to argue, either. "As you say. Now what?"

Lang looked at his watch. "We still have a couple of hours before dinnertime—Spanish dinnertime, anyway. I'd like to go back to Don's house, where I can spread out these papers the inspector gave back to us. I'd also like to take another look at those index cards."

It took less than five minutes to walk to the house on Calle Colon. As far as either could tell, no one followed.

"Who is it?" Jessica's voice came through the speaker at the street entrance.

"So, what did you find out at the police station?" she asked as soon as the gates swung open.

"That they don't know zip," Lang said.

"And our help they don't want," Gurt added.

The iron gates closed behind them.

"The inspector, a guy named Mendezo, gave us the CD and the papers he took." He handed her the box with the papers. "I'd like to keep the disk."

She led the way into the house. "Sure. Did you have a chance to download the pictures?"

By unspoken consent, they sat in the same chairs they had that morning.

Lang produced another envelope, this one bulging. "I printed them out. Take a look and see if they mean anything to you."

After Jessica had studied each one, she put them back in the envelope. "Just an old building with some guy in a uniform standing in front. I have no idea what Dad was going to do with them."

Disappointed but not surprised, Lang stood. "In your dad's office or work area, there was a little metal box of index cards. Could we go take another look?"

Jessica also stood. "Sure."

Once back in Don's office, Gurt and Lang divided the cards, A–M, N–Z. They were as enigmatic as before: names, some with addresses and phone numbers. They began reading the names out loud. To each, Jessica shook her head.

"Blake, David. Looks like New York," Lang said, holding up a card.

Again Jessica shook her head. "Never heard of him."

"Blucher, Franz. Heidelberg."

"Him either."

Lang held the card closer to the light to read the notation at the bottom. "Skorzeny?"

She shook her head, then stopped. "Say that again?"

"Skor-zain-nee." Lang pronounced the word slowly. "That's him!"

She had both Lang's and Gurt's attention. "Who?" they asked in unison.

"The man Dad was writing about. One of them, anyway. He was a German, some kinda big deal in the war."

"What about Blucher, Franz?" Lang wanted to know.

Again Jessica shook her head. "Still never heard of him."

Gurt moved to look over Lang's shoulder. "Lang, you said you used cards like that in high school to write papers, put separate facts on each one."

Lang didn't remember telling her, but obviously he had. "Yes, I did. It was before computers made note cards obsolete."

"Suppose your friend Don did his research the same way."

Lang had no idea where she was going. "Okay, let's assume he did."

"What if . . ." She went to her stack of cards and extracted one, reading from it. " 'Skorzeny, Otto.' At the bottom, it says, 'Blucher, Franz.' The reverse of your card, cross-referencing. Suppose this Blucher was Don's authority for whatever he was writing about Skorzeny?"

"Or the other way 'round," Lang said.

This time it was Gurt who shook her head. "I think not. Jessica says he was *writing* about Skorzeny. Besides, there's no address for Skorzeny."

It made sense.

Or at least as much sense as anything else.

"Okay. Would you please call the number on the card?"

Gurt returned the card to the box. "This is your show, Lang. You call."

"Last time I looked, Heidelberg was in Germany. I seem to remember something about you speaking the language."

Gurt sighed theatrically, giving Jessica the same expression she gave Lang when he did something stupid around the house. Like putting laundry detergent in the dishwasher, resulting in a wall of suds taking over the kitchen.

The sort of thing any undomesticated man might do.

Jessica pointed. "There's the phone."

Instead, Gurt fished a cell phone from her bag. Lang recognized it as Agency issue, capable of operating on all but the polar continents. Lang watched as she punched in the three-digit country code and the number. After what he guessed were three or four rings, she gave Don's name, hers, her number, and a request her call be returned. Obviously, Herr Blucher was not in or not answering.

Gurt returned the device to her purse. "What now?"

Lang pointed to the packet of papers the police had returned. "I guess we divide those up and see what we can find."

In less than a minute, Jessica looked up. "These are just lists of stuff. Here's a list of books, and this one's got places on it. Makes no sense."

Lang was already beginning to agree. "This one has only one word on it: Montsegur."

Gurt put her papers down. "That's in France, the Languedoc. I saw a road sign with that on it when we were . . . when we were there last year."

She and Lang exchanged looks. It had been in the

southwest of France that Lang had first confronted the powerful Pegasus organization in the search for the killers of his sister and nephew. The encounter had been very near fatal. It was a region to which he was not eager to return.

Before he could reply, his cell phone chirped. There were only three people who had the number, and two of them were present.

"Yes, Sara?" Lang asked while calculating it was four o'clock in the afternoon back in Atlanta.

The voice was as clear as though it were crossing a room rather than an ocean. "Judge Henderson's put Wiley on next month's trial calendar. Thought you'd like to know."

Lang groaned. Wiley was the civil counterpart to Lang's criminal defense of the originator of a multitiered sales/ financial services scam. Not only was the U.S. Justice Department prosecuting Lang's client for a laundry list of security violations, the SEC was suing to regain investors' money. Mr. Wiley had already been forced to sell his vintage Ferrari and one of his Rolls Royces just to continue his lavish lifestyle. An adverse verdict in the civil case would bankrupt him. Worse, he would be unable to pay the rest of his lawyer's fees. The complexity of the case would require Lang's attention every day between now and the time Mr. Wiley faced a jury of his peers.

Lang snapped the phone shut. "Jessica, I'm afraid something's come up back home. We, Gurt and I, need to leave immediately." He noted the look on her face, that of someone about to lose their last friend. "We can keep trying to contact this guy in Heidelberg. When I finish what I've got to do, I'll be in touch to see if the local cops have made any progress."

From her appearance, Jessica wasn't comforted, but

she gamely extended a hand. "I can't thank you enough for coming all the way to Spain to help."

Lang shook. "I couldn't do enough for your dad. He saved my life. I'll be back if you need me."

Lang left with the dissatisfaction of a job not completed.

CHAPTER FIVE

Southwest France
Montsegur
September 1940

Only ropes and pitons hammered into crevices had allowed the men to climb the mountain's north face. Even so, it had taken over seven hours. All five were close to exhaustion. Had they been mere sport climbers, they would have savored the water in their canteens, smoked a cigarette, and admired the view their efforts had given them.

But they were not amateurs.

A close look would have revealed that, under his Alpine hat, each man's hair was cut so close that the scalp was visible. They all wore identical short-sleeved shirts and lederhosen, which revealed tightly bunched arm and leg muscles.

Although they were dressed the same, one was clearly the leader. A tall, blond man with a scar bisecting his right cheek, he spoke in the accent of his native Austria rather than the harsher German of his companions. While four of the climbers stretched out on the rocky surface, he scanned the countryside a thousand feet below with a pair of binoculars.

He smiled when he saw a cloud of dust moving down the road at the foot of the mountain. The trucks were right on time.

The men groused good-naturedly when he coaxed, rather than ordered, them back onto weary feet. Each man shook off the small pack in which climbing equipment had been stored. It would have no further use, and each man needed to get rid of unnecessary weight. Out of the packs came long lengths of rope, the finest hemp available. Each man stepped into an open harness that fed the rope under one thigh, across the body, and over the opposite shoulder. From each pack came a light grappling hook to which the other end of the rope was secured.

As one, each man jumped into empty space and began to rappel down the sheer southern face of white rock.

About halfway down, the straight drop ended in what to the casual observer appeared to be a mound of rubble and scree. Closer inspection would have shown that the rocks were carved into squares and rectangles, many of which were still in their original position of what had been, centuries ago, the wall of a castle encircling the mouth of a huge cave.

As each man's feet touched the ground, he unclipped his harness and stood, awaiting orders. They came quickly, for there was a sense of urgency. Although they no more believed the fiction of Vichy France's independence from the German conquerors than did the rest of the world, there would be complaints if French historians and archaeologists knew what they were doing.

The men fanned out, searching every square foot of ground before entering the cave. Their leader was the last to leave the sunlight, standing on the edge of the cliff and admiring the location. Perfect for defense, as evidenced by the fact that the place had withstood siege after siege by medieval France's finest armies. The occupants had surrendered only to hunger and left the protection of these walls. The castle itself had never been taken. Its location was largely forgotten, both because memory of its few surviving defenders had dimmed with the centuries and because it was inaccessible since the ancient staircase carved into the rock had disappeared with the exfoliation, the peeling off of layers of rock, caused by changing seasons over the centuries.

Before he had taken a half-dozen steps, excited shouts quickened his pace into the cave. Inside, the inky dark was split by four flashlights concentrated on what might once have been a wooden chest, long since collapsed into a collection of splinters and rusted iron fittings. Also on the cave's floor was a clay vessel of some sort, a cylinder sealed at both ends. Pressed into the clay were a number of letters or symbols that none of the men recognized.

Another shout registered another find. Before long, a stack of earthenware jugs and plates was growing at the cave's mouth. A length of iron was so corroded with rust that it crumbled in one man's hand. Possibly the blade of a sword or the haft of a spear. The leader warned the others to be more careful.

It was by accident that the writing was found, the most significant discovery of the day. One of the men stumbled over a rock, his light flying from his hand as he tried to break his fall. The flashlight fell at an angle, illuminating previously undetected marks carved into the cave wall. The commander, standing in front of the inscription to give it scale, had several photographs taken with flash equipment.

An hour later, crates were being lowered by rope to four trucks waiting below. When the last was loaded, all but the leader rappelled down to the trucks, eager to stretch out among the big boxes and thankful they had nothing more to do today but ride. The leader remained behind for a minute or two, surveying the remains of the walls and the cave's opening, a gaping mouth in the shadows of the setting sun.

Then, as though he had made a decision, he, too, slipped into his harness and began to descend.

CHAPTER SIX

Beneath the Vatican
January 8, 1941

Monsignor Ludwig Kaas was the financial secretary to the Reverenda Fabbrica, the organization charged with the day-to-day administration of the Papal State. Today, instead of pen, paper, and adding machine, he held a kerosene lantern, casting flickering shadows across what, in another setting, could have been the crown frame of a Roman dwelling. Next to it, several more, somewhat less elegant, were visible above the clay.

"Mausoleums," the priest stated, careful in his movements lest he slip in loose soil. "Roman tombs along a street in a necropolis. If we dig, below there should be a road between the buildings."

The lantern's light reflected off Pope Pius XII's glasses, making it appear that the man had fire for eyes. "But that would require the desecration of Christian graves."

"I fear so, Holiness."

The monsignor knew better than to wait for an answer. The Pope carefully weighed even simple decisions. This was far from simple. Easy enough to keep the pontiff unaware that these events were being described daily to Kaas's friends in Rome's German Embassy, difficult to explain to them the delay, friends who were keeping very close track of the events in the Vatican grotto.

"I shall have to seek guidance," the Pope said, "God's advice."

The longer you wait, the monsignor thought, God will have less to do with it than Goebbels' Ministry of Propaganda. The thought of the club-footed cripple made Kaas's skin crawl as did most Nazis, a most un-Christian feeling. Unlikable as they were, though, Hitler and his henchmen knew the real enemies of the Church: the Communists and their Jewish allies.

As a mere functionary in the bureaucracy of the Holy See, Kaas kept his opinions to himself. It was not by advocating politics he had been transferred here from Germany nor would he achieve his purpose by speaking out.

Sometimes, though, silence was difficult.

CHAPTER SEVEN

Atlanta, Georgia
7:42 p.m. (the present)

Lang stepped out of the shower in a swirl of steam and walked into the bedroom. He was surprised to see that Gurt wasn't dressed. Unlike many women, she considered time an absolute, a deadline to be met. Like most Teutonic people, tardiness was a form of disorder, and disorder led to chaos.

And chaos was enjoyed only by Italians.

She was sitting on the bed, reading a text message on her BlackBerry.

Lang rummaged through his underwear drawer. "More spam?"

Gurt had naively given the number of her supposedly totally secure, Agency-issued, state-of-the-art wireless phone to a cosmetic mail-order house to obtain a products list. She had immediately been flooded with solicitations for everything from sex aids to discount baby products. The government's technology was no match for the ad world's. Lang wondered how much e-junk the President would have to go through to receive a message of an impending 9/11-style attack.

Gurt shook her head. "No, Jessica. The police have done nothing."

Lang pulled on a pair of boxer shorts before he responded. He had promised Jessica not to drop the matter, but once back in the States, the futility of trying to solve a murder an ocean away was very clear. "Have you tried that guy in Heidelberg?"

"Blucher? No—not since we got home from Spain two days ago."

Two days and Spain was already a dream, a memory shrinking around the edges, as was Lang's enthusiasm for further involvement. As things had worked out, Mr. Wiley had become anxious to resolve both the criminal and civil cases the day Lang had returned to the office. Sixteen months to serve and a promise of restitution had made both problems go away. Although it was certain Wiley would duly serve his time as a guest at one of the government's more posh Club Feds, giving back the money was dubious at best. Wiley had far too many bank accounts in places Lang had never heard of to voluntarily part with his hard-earned, if ill-gotten, fortune.

In any event, Lang had a lot more time on his hands than he had anticipated. "Should we go back to Spain?"

Gurt slipped a dress over her head, backing up to Lang to operate the zipper. How did women who lived alone get dressed?

"You are the one who wanted to go in the first place."

Hardly a helpful answer.

"Keep trying what's-his-name in Heidelberg. Let's see what he has to say."

Gurt was inspecting her hemline in the mirror. "How

can you 'see' what someone says? I will never completely master this language of yours."

You and several million Americans, Lang thought, but
he said, "You do just fine."

In fact, she was doing better than fine; she was pros-
pering. The American lifestyle, Lang suspected, had
done more than he had to convince her to extend a two-
week visit into a year's leave of absence from the Agency.
She loved the American malls and supermarkets, both of
which were just now emerging in Germany. And she had
made friends, finding an inexplicable commonality with
several of the single women in the building. Lang mentally referred to most of them as "The Wet Cat Society,"
on the theory that nothing is unhappier than a drenched
feline. Divorced, these women's raison d'être was not
the job descriptions of residential real-estate salesperson
or interior decorator. Instead, it was frantic man-hunting,
a desperate seeking for a replacement for the husbands
who had traded them in for newer models. They were
intent on finding men who would relieve them of their
pretense of work. As far as Lang knew, none had succeeded. Each had continued to observe as her personal
Day of Infamy the day an unjust court system had up-
held her prenup, leaving her only the uniformly insufficient alimony and the condominium that had been part
of an unfair and unconscionable settlement.

Lang was as much at a loss to understand Gurt's rela-
tionships with such women as he was to understand why
she could spend hours at a mall purchasing nothing.
Both seemed pleasant, if pointless, activities but were part
of why she was still here.

He hoped she never went back. She represented a
fresh love, the first since the death of his wife, and a chance
at having children of his own. But Gurt had changed the

subject every time the question of a more permanent
arrangement had come up.

Except the one time she had made it clear that marriage presented her with more problems than she wanted.
"If it is not disrepaired, fixing it does not need" was how
she had characterized their relationship.

Inertia, a powerful ally, was on her side.

Gurt was putting on a watch. "What time are we
reserved?"

"Eight, and you recall we're only going across the
street."

Catty-corner across Peachtree was an undistinguished
low-rise condominium. In the basement was La Grotta,
a northern Italian restaurant where the service was almost as good as the food, the geniality of the proprietor
as sunny as his native Tuscany, and the prices almost
reasonable. The convenience was hard to beat, too. Still,
Lang missed the funky surroundings, wretched food,
and collegiate atmosphere of Manuel's Tavern in Atlanta's quirky Virginia-Highland. The gathering place
of such intellectuals, real and imagined, as Atlanta had
to boast, it had been there he and Francis had shared a
dinner twice or so a month, a place a black priest and
a white lawyer speaking in Latin went unnoticed. Gurt
had liked it, and Lang was unsure why they didn't go
there anymore. It was, he supposed, just one of many inexplicable changes that take place in a man's life when a
woman enters it.

"We are driving?" Gurt wanted to know.

"Across the street?"

"My new heels are not so good for walking."

Lang was becoming used to things like expensive foot-
wear that were meant more for display than walking.
Gurt wore clothes that emphasized the curves her height

already magnified. Whatever the practical shortcomings of her wardrobe, entry into La Grotta would be heralded by dropped plates, spilled drinks, and women's catty remarks.

Lang loved it.

He was buttoning on a shirt, having decided he would not be wearing a tie. "So try another pair of shoes. It's a beautiful evening for a walk."

As they went out the door, Lang was conscious of the black fur ball that was Grumps. The dog's resentment at being left alone would be replaced by joyous tail-wagging upon their return, particularly if a tasty morsel personally wrapped in foil by the head chef was tendered as a peace offering.

They had just stepped out from under the building's porte cochere when a streak of lighting split the night, followed by a roll of thunder that Lang could have sworn made the ground tremble.

Gurt gazed up. "I think your beautiful evening may not be so good. I think perhaps we will swim to the restaurant."

As though staged, the skies opened with the comment, drenching Lang. Gurt had ducked back under shelter.

"Shit!" Lang stepped back also. Although exposed to the downpour for only a second, he looked as though he had just gotten out of a bath with all his clothes on. He reached into a pocket and handed Gurt car keys. "Have 'em bring up the Porsche while I change."

Lang customarily parked and retrieved his own car. The temptation for the young carhops to test the acceleration of the Porsche was too great. Lang had heard the protesting squeal of tires as the accelerator of some other resident's auto was pushed to the firewall. Tonight, he'd take a chance. A glance at his watch told him they were already late, and he knew the restaurant's popularity made it difficult for them to hold reservations.

He stood in front of the bank of elevators, shivering from the lobby's aggressive air-conditioning. There was a dull thud and the building shuddered, lights blinking off before the condominium's generators cut on. For a second, Lang assumed lightning had struck. Then he heard screams from outside.

Instinctively, he ran for the doors through which he had just entered. He was so intent on looking for Gurt that it took him a second and third step to realize he was walking on a carpet of shattered glass. A woman was leaning against a dark car, a Mercedes, weeping uncontrollably, and there was the smell of something other than the ozone odor of a close lightning strike.

Still not seeing Gurt, Lang's eyes followed a number of people running from his right to left, toward the parking lot and underground-parking entrance. A small crowd had gathered around flames that seemed to be fueled, rather than extinguished, by the sheets of rain— rain Lang no longer noticed. Another flash of lightning showed Gurt, a head above most of the others, silhouetted by the fire.

Lang was running, his sense of smell telling him there was a scent that had no rational reason to be here, a mixture of transmission fluid, plastic, and rubber.

And burned nitrogen sulfate.

He stopped beside Gurt, at first unsure of what he was seeing. A flaming mass of twisted steel sat on four wheel rims, resembling newsreel footage of Baghdad. Mercifully, whatever was left of the carhop was so burned, so disfigured, that it was indistinguishable from the charred remains of the car. Only by looking closer, seeing the tiny shields imprinted on the wheels, was Lang able to tell that he was looking at what had been a Porsche.

His Porsche.

The Porsche he had always parked and fetched himself.

The Porsche he was supposed to have been in when it blew up.

Without turning around, Gurt slipped an arm around his waist. "They are perhaps back?"

"They" could only mean Pegasus, the international criminal cartel Lang had encountered.

"I don't think so," he said quietly, unable to tear his eyes away from flames that were beginning to diminish as they exhausted the supply of fuel. "They know if anything happens to me, they'll be exposed."

It was the agreement with the devil he had made a year ago. Revelation of Pegasus's secret would have destroyed the organization, but it also would have destroyed a great number of innocents. Extortion to fund a foundation honoring two of its victims had seemed the only reasonable compromise.

The wail of emergency equipment enveloped them as Gurt and Lang turned to go back into the building, dinner forgotten.

Lang was not surprised when the doorbell rang forty-five minutes later. Standing in the hall was a thin black man in a rain-splattered suit.

Lang swung the door wide. "Come in, Detective Rouse. I've been expecting you."

It was the same Atlanta detective who had investigated an attempt on Lang's life the year before. The would-be assassin had jumped from the balcony rather than be captured. Lang remembered the policeman as having a slow, ethnic drawl that belied a very quick mind.

The detective looked around the room, nodding to Gurt. "Evenin', ma'am." Turning back to Lang, he nodded. "I 'spect you was. Ever' time there's death 'n' de-struction 'round here, you seem to be involved, Mr. Reilly. You care to 'splain that?"

"Lucky, I guess."

Rouse shook his head. "Still smart-assin', I see. I swear, I'm 'plyin' for a transfer outta Homicide to Sex Crimes. You a one-man crime wave. Why wasn' I sur-prised that it was your car got blown up?"

"You're good at guessing. Maybe you should try the lottery."

"I hit th' lottery an' I never see you agin, Mr. Reilly. Now, why don' you tell me why somebody want to blow up a 'spensive car like that with you in it."

Lang shrugged. "Maybe I blew the doors off their SL 500 leaving a stoplight."

Rouse looked around and chose a chair. "Sit down, Mr. Reilly. I think I'm gonna be here a while, until I gets some straight answers."

Lang sat. "All I know is that Gurt and I were headed to dinner. I got caught in that frog-strangler of a down-pour and came back to change. Gurt gave the keys to the carhop. Next thing I knew, KA-BOOM!" Lang frowned. "I don't think I even knew the poor kid in the car."

Rouse looked at Gurt for confirmation before turn-ing back to Lang. "Afta we went at it las' year, I did some checkin', Mr. Reilly. You told me you were re-tired Navy SEAL. Turns out you were with some spook organization."

"We spies always lie."

Rouse sighed. "Know what I think, Mr. Reilly? I think some other spook is pissed off at you, tryin' to get even. I was you, I might tell what I knew for protection."

"Protection from whom?"

"Whoever blew your car up with that boy in it."

"And by whom, those Keystone Kops the city calls police? Those same brave lads who literally dragged a hundred-and-twenty-pound woman out of her car and threw her on the pavement for parking too long at the airport's curb? They can't even stop people from getting shot on the street. Great as the amusement value of being protected by the Atlanta Police might be, I'm afraid the mortality rate is greater. A heartfelt and overwhelming 'no, thank you,' Detective. Maybe if you offered me Inspector Clousseau, I'd take you up on it. Except there isn't anything to tell. I don't have a clue."

The detective stood, pointing a finger. "You watch yo'sef, Mr. Reilly. You got away with somethin' las' year. Not this time. Mebbe you're thinkin' 'd be a little clearer, we go downtown."

Lang smiled. "I don't think so, Detective. And I don't think you want to have to explain to a federal judge why you arrested me without a scintilla of probable cause."

Rouse let himself out.

Both Gurt and Lang were staring at the door through which he had exited.

"If not Pegasus," Gurt said, "who?"

Lang clicked the dead bolt. "The same persons who hired those two bullyboys in Seville would be a safe guess."

"But who are they?"

"Good question. See what the man in Heidelberg knows."

There was no longer a question of whether to help find Don Huff's killer. The search was no longer a favor to help the child of an old friend. It had become intensely personal. Whoever had tried to reduce Lang to his composite atoms wasn't going to go away. Twice during the night, he awoke, slipped out of bed, and checked the sophisticated locks on the outer door of his unit, mechanisms that would foil even an expert burglar. But it wasn't the run-of-the-mill felon he feared. For the first time since he could remember, Lang slept with the Sig Sauer out of the drawer and on the table bedside him.

CHAPTER EIGHT

Downtown Atlanta
The next day

Lang was sorting out the correspondence on his desk while trying to prioritize the mound of pink callback slips when Sara buzzed him from her desk in the reception area.

"Gurt, line one."

Lang swiveled his chair to take in the floor-to-ceiling view of Atlanta's downtown skyline. "Yes, ma'am?"

"I contacted Franz Blucher."

For an instant, Lang was puzzled, then remembered. "Great. Can he help us?"

There was a pause for a second, Gurt organizing what she was about to say. "He wouldn't talk to me. I told him I was calling for a friend of Donald Huff and the line died. I called back, and he told me to contact him again never."

Lang stood, absently watching the anthill of pedestrian traffic below. "What did you say to him that—"

"Just as I told you."

"So we only know he doesn't want to help."

"No," Gurt said, "we know who he is. I Googled him."

Lang chuckled. "Really? Or perhaps you had 'enhanced' Google."

"Enhanced" Google. Although implemented after Lang had become a victim of the Peace Dividend and retired from the intelligence community, he was aware of at least part of the Agency's awesome fact-gathering potential. Occasionally, a slip or intentional leak of personal information concerning a current actor on the world's stage would bring such howls of privacy invasion, the same "anonymous source" would attribute the revelation to "Web sites and search engines available to the public." Only if the public had a billion or so for a computer system, the capability of which was so immense it could never be accurately measured. Sort of like the distance to the end of the universe expressed in miles. The data that caused the ruckus usually came from global monitoring of communications. The Agency had the capability to eavesdrop on every electronic, noncable transmission in the world. Telephone, computer, everything. Enhanced Google. Its limitations were only in the manpower necessary to translate, read, and index the information. Lang had little doubt that Gurt still knew how to ascertain the passwords needed to tap into the largest single bank of personal information on earth.

And probably the galaxy.

"Was not needed," she said. "He is a professor at university, has published many papers, books."

An academician who didn't want to talk was an oxymoron. "About what—what is his subject?"

"All about the war, the Second War."

Made sense; that was what Don had been writing about. "What else did you learn?"

"He is retired. His father was a newspaperman, died in Berlin in 1945."

"All that was on Google?"

"Well, perhaps most of it."

Something was playing around the edge of Lang's mind like a moth around a lightbulb.

"He is known to Jacob," Gurt said. "Interviewed him for a book on Auschwitz where Jacob's parents died."

That was it, of course. Holocaust survivors, Jacob Annulewitz.

Jacob had migrated to Israel, chosen Mossad as a profession, then moved to England and obtained British citizenship. In his retirement he had inexplicably chosen to remain in the rain and fog of the UK rather than the balmy sun of the Eastern Mediterranean. In fact, he had begun a second career, the cover for his first, a barrister in London. While he was with the Agency, Lang's path had crossed Jacob's, leaving a trail of friendship as well as professional respect. Jacob, like Gurt, had also been invaluable in Lang's struggle with Pegasus.

"You called Jacob?" Lang asked, slightly jealous Gurt had preempted contacting his old friend.

"I spoke to his wife, Rachel . . ."

"Who no doubt insisted whenever we're in London to come by for dinner."

There was a question in Gurt's response. "Yes. How did you know?"

Rachel's cooking was notorious throughout the intelligence community. Common wisdom held that only the Geneva Conventions prevented the output of her kitchen from being used to intimidate the most tight-lipped enemy into diarrhea of the tongue. The last meal Lang had shared with her and Jacob had left him cramped with flatulence that threatened to be terminal.

"Good guess. Is Jacob calling back?"

"Rachel confirmed Jacob and Blucher knew each other. Not so good, but enough, perhaps. Jacob will call and see if Blucher will see us."

CHAPTER NINE

Atlanta, Georgia
Charlie Brown/Fulton County Airport
At the same time

Burt Sanders loved his job.

Airlines were being forced to count each paper napkin used by passengers or face bankruptcy. Shareholders were routinely calling for the heads of executives. Labor unions were snarling like hyenas over the carcasses of the once-proud air-passenger industry. The companies put the number of pretzels per pack passengers were served with their watered-down and no longer complimentary cocktails ahead of retirement benefits of employees.

And none of that was Burt's problem.

Not anymore.

He had taken the airline's less-than-generous early-retirement offer in what now looked like a vain hope of salvaging his pension. He had taken a job as chief pilot for the Holt Foundation, flying its big Gulfstream V and making sure it was ready to go any time, any place. Oh, the pay wasn't quite as good as the airline's, but the job security sure as hell was. The foundation had about a zillion dollars a year in income and no labor unions. And the head honcho, a lawyer named Reilly, pretty much kept his hands off the flying part of the business, unlike those big-time airline execs who thought they knew more about airplanes than the guys who flew them.

From Burt's point of view, it was an even swap. No more worrying if the airline was going to survive, no more lying to passengers that their flight had been canceled because of weather when the plane was just too empty to make takeoff profitable, no more erosion of benefits and accompanying excuses from management.

Of course, that meant there were times when he had nothing better to do than pretend to be checking on the bird. Truth was, he'd rather be wiping down the leather upholstery on this Gulfstream V than sitting around the house, having his wife think up things for him to do. Besides, the boss appreciated the fact that the man who flew the plane took time to putter around it at no extra charge.

He had just confirmed that the ice maker in the forward galley had been fixed and was descending the steps into the brightly lit and antiseptic private hangar. He was surprised to see a man in mechanic's overalls walking toward the plane. He thought he was the only one with a key to the hangar.

"Excuse me," Burt said, unable to think of anything more original. "Can I help you?"

The mechanic was startled. Obviously, he hadn't known Burt was there. "Yeah, I guess. You the one squawked the . . ." he consulted a sheet of notebook paper, "the digital altimeter readout?"

"Nope, haven't requested any repairs. And I'd be the one to do it."

The mechanic stepped back, taking his time reading the N number along the Gulfstream's fuselage. "Oh shit, says here four-six Alpha, not six-four Alpha. Guess I got the wrong plane. Sorry."

Burt watched him let himself out of the hangar, almost certain he had locked it on the way in. Even more puzzling was the mistake as to aircraft. There were only two other G-5s based here at Charlie Brown, and neither had a number ending in Alpha. Must be a new guy or a transient airplane. Burt had thought he knew all the avionics repairmen.

Strange.

Burt shut the airplane's door and walked across the ballroom-smooth cement to the single door, being careful to lock it behind him. For him, as a pilot, a break in normal routine was disturbing. Anything not readily and satisfactorily explained was to be distrusted. Even so, he wasn't sure what made him pull into an empty parking spot between the airport's exit road and the fixed-base operator's avionics repair building.

Inside, Mary Jo, the receptionist, looked up at him. With pictures of her grandchildren on her desk, she felt safe in flirting with every flyer that came her way. "Well, well, it's Burt Sanders," she cackled. "Come to take me to some deserted isle in his wonderful flying machine. Hold on just a minute, Burt. I gotta go get my contraceptive kit."

Burt smiled sheepishly, still not used to her ribald humor. "Actually, it's something a lot less fun, Mary Jo. You got a G-5 based here or transient with numbers ending in four-six Alpha? Mebbe one with problems with the readout on the digital altimeter?"

She looked at him over the top of rimless glasses. "I

can tell you flat out, we got no such animal. Yours, your foundation's plane, is the only G-5 we service. Other two on the field use someone else, that other FBO." She sniffed as though personally affronted, as indeed she was. "Now, about you 'n' me takin' a little trip . . ."

Burt retreated as gracefully as possible. "I'll ask the boss, Mary Jo. Thanks."

He got back into the Honda, still uncertain what, if anything, he should do. He was already turning onto I-20 when two things jumped out of his memory to hit him like a pair of mental sledgehammers: The man in the hangar had been carrying something resembling a toolbox. Sophisticated avionics weren't repaired like a car, where the mechanic climbed under the hood. The offending equipment was removed from the aircraft and repaired and tested on the bench at the repair facility. Second, the maintenance ladder, the one used during periodic inspections or repairs to reach the higher parts of the aircraft, had been moved across the hangar.

To do what he said he'd come to do, take the altimeter out, the man would only need a couple of Phillips head screwdrivers, not a tool kit.

So, what was in the tool kit?

The digital altimeter was accessible from the instrument panel in the cockpit, which you entered after walking up steps and into the passenger cabin.

So why was the ladder moved?

When in doubt, pass the problem up the line. Burt fumbled his cell phone out of his pocket and punched in a number from memory.

A few minutes later, Lang Reilly was staring at the telephone on his desk as though reproaching it for the problem. The chief pilot had quite possibly prevented someone from tampering with the foundation's G-5. The man had been suspicious initially, enough to return to the hangar, where he found, once again, it was unlocked after he had secured it.

No, there had been no signs anyone had been tinkering with something. But then, an expert would hardly leave smudges of dirty fingerprints on the instrument panel.

Lang sighed as he thumbed through a well-worn personal directory and dialed the number for FAA Security at Charlie Brown. He explained what had happened to a disembodied recording and then touched the number the machine designated to speak with a flesh-and-blood representative of the FAA. The result was as predictable as it was frustrating: canned music interspersed with assurances of his call's importance and the Agency's intent to deal with the problem as soon as someone became available.

Reilly could feel his blood pressure rise. What could he expect from a government who considered general aviation security to be a wire fence with a gate that opened by punching in four digits? Admittedly, most general aviation aircraft weren't going to bring down another World Trade Center, but the Gulfstream was nearly as large as an airliner.

He hung up.

Opening his center desk drawer, he reached in to release the catch on the false back and groped around until he found what he was looking for. He put it on the desk, a disk made to screw into the speaker part of most pay phone receivers. It was one of the few toys he had taken from the Agency, a random modulator that made a voice over a telephone impossible to identify, either by a listener or a voice-wave measuring device. He put it in his pocket and walked out of the office for the elevators.

There were three pay phones in the building's lobby.

Slightly less than a half hour later, Sara stood in the doorway, clearly perplexed. "Lang, there's a man on the phone wants to speak with you, an emergency. Says he's with the Transport Safety Administration. We have any business with . . . ?"

Lang put down the file he had been reading and suppressed a grin. "I'll take it."

The Transport Safety Administration, another of the alphabet-soup bureaus that had sprouted like weeds after 9/11. This one's principal purpose seemed to be to harass commercial air travelers while refusing to conduct politically incorrect searches of profiled persons from places that spawned terrorism. Better to let a bearded, wild-eyed mullah in flowing robes through security and frisk an eighty-year-old grandmother than risk the ire of the liberal media.

The TSA had taken heat lately from the number of fake bombs journalists had slipped by it, incursions into "restricted" areas, and items stolen from baggage.

Like any government entity, Lang figured, this one would catapult itself into an opportunity for favorable publicity.

"Lang Reilly," he said as he picked up the phone. "What might I do for my government today?"

Lang was at the hangar in twenty minutes, watching a swarm of uniformed agents buzz like bees protecting a hive. Each inspection plate was carefully removed by FAA-certified airframe and power-plant mechanics, and the cowling was being removed from both engines. Several ladders rested against various parts of the fuselage.

The chief pilot, Burt Sanders, saw Lang and came over, a worried expression on his face. "I hope they can get the plane back together in time for the next flight."

Lang turned to watch two German shepherd dogs

sniff the landing gear as a uniformed agent stood on tip-toe to peer into a wheel well. "Better to be a little late than take a chance."

Burt was wide-eyed. "I don't understand, Mr. Reilly. If somebody put a bomb on the plane, why would they turn around and make an anonymous call to report it?"

Lang shifted his weight, his hands behind his back. "Oh, I'd guess some organization we turned down for a grant got pissed, and somebody decided a bomb hoax would be a way of getting even."

"But what about the guy who was in the hangar?" Burt was nervous, afraid he'd somehow get blamed for whatever bad might happen. "I mean, I'm careful to lock up every time I leave—honest."

Lang put a reassuring hand on the young man's shoulder. "I'm surprised you don't guard it twenty-four/seven, careful as you are. No doubt in my mind you locked up."

"But how . . ."

A large uniformed black man wearing a TSA windbreaker approached. "Mr. Reilly? Step over here, please."

Lang and Burt followed to the base of a ladder resting against the rear of the aircraft.

The man pointed, looking at Burt. "You might want to take a look."

Lang watched Burt climb the ladder and peer into the small hole created by the removal of an inspection plate. Even from the floor, Lang could see the pilot's face go white. "Oh, shit!"

Lang arched a questioning eyebrow at Burt. The pilot's legs were less than steady as he climbed back down.

"Main control cable, one to the horizontal stabilizer," Burt managed with difficulty. "It's all corroded."

"Logbook shows the aircraft had a hundred-hour inspection less than two months ago," the TSA man said. "That cable couldn't corrode that fast."

Lang was becoming as uncomfortable as his pilot. "Unless?"

The government man shook his head. "Not sure. There was an odor, though, soon as the A & E pulled the plate. That's what made him call me over."

"Give me a swag, some wild-ass guess," Lang said evenly.

The TSA man took one look at the anger burning in Lang's eyes, the threat he seemed to express without words, and decided this was a man who wasn't going to accept the usual government-speak nonsense. He made a most ungovernmentlike decision to exceed his authority. "Can't be sure, but I'd make a personal guess it was some sort of acid."

"Acid?" Lang was puzzled.

Burt, still looking like he might be ill any moment, nodded. "Acid eats almost through the cable. Leaves enough connection to respond to the controls during preflight, then snaps."

"And then?" Lang asked.

"Horizontal stabilizer controls altitude, nose up, nose down. If it went out on takeoff, say, we couldn't lift the nose of the plane to get into the air; we'd crash off the end of the runway."

Lang's knowledge of aeronautics was basic at best. "I thought the air speed controlled when the plane left the ground."

"It does, but unless the plane lifts off, it would just increase velocity until it hit something. Even if the horizontal stabilizer held for takeoff, we'd be unable to climb. For that matter, we couldn't lift the nose on landing, either."

Once again, the TSA man beckoned. "Come with me."

Lang guessed he was used to being obeyed.

Lang spoke to Burt. "Make sure she's properly buttoned up, will you?"

"You can count on it."

Lang followed the man to what he guessed were the airport's administrative offices. In one room, six people were watching a television monitor of Lang's hangar. He had not seen the camera. If there was doubt in Lang's mind that they were all some species of cop, the letters on various windbreakers dispelled them: FBI, ATF, US Marshal, Treasury Department. The only departments missing seemed to be Health and Human Services and the IRS.

A woman, middle-aged and probably once attractive, extended a hand with a badge in it. "Sheila Burns, Special Agent, FBI."

All agents were "Special Agents" unless they were "Special Agent in Charge" or some other derivation. It had been a subject of humor at the Agency. Lang said nothing, waiting for her to continue.

He wasn't disappointed. "An attempt to sabotage your aircraft, Mr. Reilly. That's a federal crime." Her words capitalized the offense. "Just as effective as a bomb, with the added benefit of maybe passing as an accident."

"Any ideas?" a man from the Marshal's Department asked without introduction.

Burns silenced him with a glare. Obviously, she was the chief honcho on the investigation.

She asserted her authority by asking, "Know somebody who'd want you or the executives of your foundation dead?"

"No."

She glanced around the room, making sure she was asking the questions Lang knew they had all agreed upon before he got here. He was well familiar with interrogation by committee. "The Holt Foundation was chartered as a charity a little less than a year ago, right?"

Lang had been wrong. The IRS *was* here, just not in person. That left Health and Human Services.

"That's correct. We fund programs to provide pediatric care in undeveloped countries."

"Do you mind telling us the source of that funding?"

"Our sources are confidential."

Not entirely a lie. The Pegasus organization would hardly want its identity known.

Burns's eyes narrowed, the equivalent of a horse laying its ears back or a dog growling. Law-enforcement agencies assumed that any information withheld was incriminating. Privacy was a bothersome subterfuge of the guilty.

"You know I can find out."

Lang gave her a smile with no humor in it. "Be my guest."

The labyrinth of foreign banks, dummy companies, and assumed identities would take an army of accountants to unravel. Well, a regiment at least.

A half hour of evading further questions left the FBI agent frustrated and Lang mentally fatigued. He could have gone on, however. Agency training included aggressive interrogation, a course its students referred to as "creative obfuscation." This woman was a sweetie compared to the instructors under whom Lang had suffered. His training had also included ascertaining exactly what the person asking the questions did and didn't know from the line of inquiry. Same, similar, and re-asked questions made it clear to him that the Feds suspected the foundation was into something other than charity work. Exactly what, he was fairly certain, they had no idea.

She was clearly winding down, asking, "You're a lawyer, right?"

She made it sound like an accusation.

Lang was tired of standing, but he understood asking to sit would be interpreted as a sign he was weakening. Actually, it was a sign his new toe caps hurt. "That's right."

"No wonder we can't get a straight answer," said an anonymous voice from the back of the room.

Lawyer-bashing, a sport even government bureaucrats could play.

Special Agent Burns sounded like she had just discovered his darkest secret. She pounced. "So you're used to interrogation procedures."

"That's what lawyers do, ask witnesses questions."

There was a snicker from the back of the room that drew a daggerlike stare from the FBI woman.

A few more questions and he was told to go, excused like an unruly child from after-school detention. Since no one had a clue as to the source of the attempted sabotage, he, Lang, was the convenient suspect, he was sure, although it was unclear why an extremely wealthy charitable foundation would want to destroy either a multi-million-dollar aircraft or the executives who flew on it.

Lang did have an idea, though he wasn't about to share it. So far, it had no name, no face. But it was linked to Don Huff. First Lang's car, then his foundation's plane. What was next, the thirty-story building in which he lived? Finding Don's killer had become very personal. Personal and a matter of life and death.

Lang's life and death.

CHAPTER TEN

Atlanta Hartsfield—Jackson International Airport
Delta Crown Room, Concourse B
The next day

Gurt was sipping a beer, her eyes wandering across the crowded room. "Explain again why we are going to Chicago."

Lang was stirring sweetener into a cup of flavorless coffee. "These people, whoever they are, obviously have someone watching."

Gurt waited for the wail of a nearby infant to subside rather than raise her voice. "Obviously?"

Resigned to the fact that he was going to add no taste other than sweet to his beverage, Lang took a sip and grimaced. "First, they know I usually park and pick up the Porsche myself. How many residents you think pay the same fees I do and still fetch their own car?"

Gurt shrugged. "Those who do not need wheelchairs or walkers?"

· The building had a fair percentage of what management euphemistically referred to as "seniors."

Lang was uncertain if Gurt was serious or making a
joke. It was hard to tell with Germans. "Actually, almost
everyone, old or young, uses the valet car service. Whoever planted the bomb knew I didn't. They also knew I
was going to use the Gulfstream for this trip."

Gurt set her glass down. "Or were willing to wait until
your next flight in it."

"Possible," Lang conceded, "but I don't think so. The
acid would have completely eaten through that cable in a
day or two, and then the sabotage would have been detected." He frowned. "Of course, that's why we're flying
commercially now, so the plane can be completely torn
down and inspected, make sure there are no more sur-
prises waiting."

Gurt stood and went to refresh her beer. Admiring
glances from men and jealous ones from women followed her like the wake of a ship.

She returned with a glass in one hand and a paper cup
of snacks in the other. "Did you ever consider that was
what these people wanted you to do, fly the airlines? It
would be much easier to know your whenabouts."

"Whereabouts."

"Whatever."

The implication that he was being manipulated was
disturbing. "Why would they do that? I mean, if the cable had parted, they would have succeeded."

"Only if killing you was what they wanted," Gurt said.
She took a sip and made a face as though she had bit-
ten into something tart. "To call this beer is to advertise
falsely."

"You say that about every American beer."

"It is true with every American beer."

"If they wanted to know where we were going, all they

had to do would be call up the international flight plan that has to be filed with the FAA. I'm pretty sure they're more interested in making sure whatever we found in Spain stays a secret. Problem is, what did we find?"

Falsely advertised or not, she took another drink, this time without the face. "It is also a simple matter, is it not, to chop into the electric files of either the airline or credit-card company and see what your flight reservations are?"

They both knew the answer. Even with the technology available when Lang was with the Agency, obtaining the passenger manifests of any carrier had been simple. In fact, the lists of Iron Curtain airlines were routinely scrutinized.

Cooling had not improved the taste of Lang's coffee. He put the cup down, pushing it away in unconscious rejection. "We can't keep our destination secret, but we can make sure no one is actually following us by taking an indirect route."

Primary instruction at The Farm, the Agency's training facility in the Virginia countryside.

Gurt finished her beer, shot a look at the bar, and decided against another. "Why would they follow us if they know where we are flying?"

Lang leaned across the table. "They might not, but an indirect route might very well make them think we believed we were evading them." He proffered two sets of tickets. "Take a look."

Gurt frowned, squinting at the small type. "But these . . ." She grinned. "The shuffle is on again?"

He nodded.

Lang's eyes felt as though they had sand in them, and his lids weighed a ton each. Sleep had evaded him on the flight from Chicago to Paris. It was as if his subconscious kept him awake in the belief that, should an emergency occur at 35,000 feet, he could do something about it if sufficiently alert. Tired of the novel he had brought along, he tried to get interested in the in-flight movie. A childish comedy sufficiently sanitized by the airline to offend no passenger, it had also been leeched of any entertainment value.

Idly, his mind wandered. How many times had he crossed the ocean? At least once or twice a year while he was with the Agency. Then there had been that trip with his wife, Dawn.

The memory was weighted with sadness. Dawn, bright and çheerful, had been only too happy to work while Lang attended law school after leaving government service. After all, the law practice would mean she would have her husband home at night instead of excuses phoned from undisclosed places. He would succeed, she was certain.

And he had.

An unexplained gap in his résumé between college and law school had made him less than attractive to the big law firms, but he had no intention of spending the rest of his life in stuffy boardrooms, toadying to corporate clients. Instead, he had relied on his Agency contacts for a steady flow of the less reputable part of the practice. Seedy, but able to pay their legal bills. A member of an ambassador's staff involved in a scheme to bribe an official of a foreign government, a national floral chain importing more than roses from Colombia.

His practice had become profitable, and Lang and Dawn had taken the first of a planned series of trips to Europe before beginning a family. Instead, their lives were commandeered by the silver spider, the name he gave the arachnid-like form that appeared in X-rays of his wife's reproductive system. The spider grew while Dawn seemed to shrink, until she was little more than a near-lifeless bag of skin and bone. At her bedside, they planned trips both knew they would never take. Away from the hospital room and the stench of certain death, Lang cursed a god whose eyes might have been on the sparrow but whose back was turned to Dawn.

The end had been anticlimactic and merciful. He had missed her long before.

The empty months spent in an empty house made for an empty life. At first, he dated tentatively, more to please friends than from any desire of his own. The women all had one defect or another, defects he realized were more in his eyes than real. What was missing was that they were not Dawn. He finally sold the house and most of the furnishings and moved to his present high-rise condo.

Even the new place seemed empty. He took on more cases than he could effectively handle, hoping to leave no time for sorrow. That didn't work, either.

In the search for his sister's killers, he had renewed his acquaintance with Gurt, a coworker he had bedded on an irregular basis until he met Dawn. At first he had felt guilty, as though betraying his wife with another woman. The priest, Francis, wise in the way only a man who had never had woman problems could be, had pointed out that Lang did not have to stop loving Dawn to love Gurt, too.

And he had.

The only problem was Gurt's systematic refusal to even discuss a more permanent arrangement. Sooner or later, Lang supposed, she would go back to Germany, back to the Agency, leaving him as bereft of children and family as before. Until then, though, he had intended to savor every moment.

He had almost managed to doze off when the flight attendant announced an imminent landing.

Gurt was bright-eyed and eager for whatever the day held. As always, she had slept soundly from the moment the 757's wheels retracted into their wells.

Lang felt it was one of her most unattractive attributes.

Both retrieved their single bags from the overhead bin. Checked luggage meant a predictable stop at baggage claim as well as the possibility that the suitcases might well take off on an excursion of their own.

Modern travel: breakfast in New York, dinner in Paris, and baggage in Istanbul.

More important, a person standing at a baggage carousel was a fixed target, vulnerable to a point-blank shot or the stab of a knife. The Agency had discouraged any bag that could not be carried aboard.

He had never been in Paris's Charles de Gaulle air terminal when it was not mobbed. Africans in bright-colored cotton robes mixed with the pastel Hindi saris, while mustachioed men in caftans herded their wives and children along. Overhead speakers kept up a stream of unintelligible announcements that blended with a hundred different languages in a re-creation of Babel.

Little had changed since his last visit.

Without further communication, Gurt ducked into the ladies' toilet, leaving Lang to guard her bag. When she reappeared, he headed for the men's while Gurt strained to recognize anyone from their flight. When Lang emerged, he feigned interest in a magazine rack while Gurt disappeared into the crowded exits. Lang kept an unobtrusive surveillance of reflections of passengers scurrying by the glass of the newsstand. He noticed no one purposely hovering nearby. In exactly five minutes, he hurried after Gurt.

At the bottom of a steep escalator, he fed coins into a machine, took a ticket, and boarded a train headed into the city. En route, he changed cars twice and trains once, disembarking just across the Seine from the Ille St. Louis. He was fairly certain he had not been followed, but the sparse foot traffic across the nearby bridge would reveal any tail he had missed.

Across the river, he waited patiently on the narrow Rue St. Louis until he succeeded in getting a cab. The driver mumbled unhappily when Lang gave him the destination, less than a mile away. No one got into the following taxi, and Lang finally gave a sigh of relief despite the cabbie's continuing expression of displeasure at so short a fare.

Oh well, the French were always displeased about something: the wine, the food, or lesser things such as politics or the economy. Lang's pronunciation of the destination must have revealed him as an American, for the cabbie turned to complaints of U.S. involvement in Iraq, although Lang was unable to see why a French citizen would be concerned. France had, after all, opted out.

The French: Our national flag is the tricolor; our battle flag a single color: white.

Minutes later, he was paying the still-protesting driver in front of a pizzeria on the Left Bank along the Quai d'Orsay, one with a view of both Notre Dame and the statue of St. Michael. Gurt was sipping a cup of coffee at one of the tables lining the curb.

Lang took the one other chair at the table. "All clear?"

Gurt looked at him over the rim of her cup. "I saw no one."

In minutes, they were descending another escalator, this one to the St. Germain station. They went directly to Orly, the airport for most of Paris's European flights. Lang used a credit card to buy two one-way tickets on different flights to Frankfurt and used the time before the first to arrange for a car.

"The card is traceable," Gurt said as they sank into seats at his departure gate.

Lang shrugged. "I know, but all my bogus IDs expired years ago. We'll just have to hope if someone's tracking us, they're still looking in Paris or they won't have the resources to meet both Paris–Frankfurt flights."

"They won't have to look, just check the files of your card company."

"Maybe the Agency office in Frankfurt can help, give us some ID we can use."

Gurt shook her head slowly. "Neither of us are actively employed there now."

She was right. Ever fearful of one more wave of un-favorable publicity, the Agency wasn't likely to furnish bogus papers to a former employee and one on an in-definite leave. Lang mentally kicked himself. In an age when teenage hackers were capable of multimillion-dollar identity thefts, it would have been a simple mat-ter to create his own false persona. In spite of the ease of access to information, few government agencies ever bothered to cross-check. The death of someone around the desirable age appeared in the obituaries and, with the readily available date of birth, a request in that name could be made for replacement of a lost Social Security card. The card could be used to obtain a driver's license, and both to obtain a certified copy of a birth certificate to be parlayed into a passport. Assuming the deceased had even modest credit, the banks were only too happy to ship their plastic, one and a half percent interest for the first six months.

Lang consoled himself with the speed at which the bureaucratic wheels turned. Establishing a good false identity with real documents took months. How many more attempts on his and Gurt's lives could be mounted in that time? Lang didn't want to even guess.

They would have to go with what they had.

CHAPTER ELEVEN

Frankfurt Flughof
Three hours later

Miraculously, Lang had napped on the short flight, the first sleep he had gotten on an aircraft since his days with the Agency. He had watched water bead against the adjacent window as the plane descended through clouds dirty with moisture. The runway and taxiway were shiny with rain. Before deplaning the 717, he checked his watch. Gurt should be landing in the next forty-five minutes.

As an arrival from a fellow European Union country, Lang bypassed a line of Japanese tourists at the immigration stations and walked through the nothing-to-declare gate into the terminal. The main area was nowhere as large, mutinational, nor loud as de Gaulle, a fact for which Lang was thankful. It would have been pure luck to find Gurt in the crowded main terminal.

Not that he had to. Knowing the tenuous relation between schedule and reality in the world of the airlines, they had agreed to meet in the city at a small *bierstube* near the Agency's location. Lang was already anticipating a liter of truly fine beer served with the fattest bratwurst he had ever had.

The thought of epicurean delights may have been what momentarily distracted him. He had not noticed the man in the rain-splotched coat who seemed unusually interested in shop displays a regular ten feet from wherever Lang paused.

Lang moved a few feet away, intent on duty-free tobacco products. The man acquired an interest in the ladies' shoes in the window of the adjoining shop. As Lang inspected confectionery, his companion was checking out the spirits and wine next door.

Just because you're paranoid doesn't mean someone's *not* out to get you.

It had taken less time than Lang had hoped for someone to find the credit-card transaction.

Lang made it a point to gaze around randomly, a tourist overawed by one of Europe's least interesting air terminals. He could go to the rental counter, claim his car, and let the man follow as best he could until the opportunity to take action arose. Or he could take evasive action and, unless the guy was a real pro, lose him.

Neither option was satisfactory.

If the man was simply following Lang to learn what he might have stumbled onto in Spain, fine. But blowing up the Porsche was hardly the act of someone merely inquisitive. Besides, there could well be someone waiting for Gurt, too. Lang was not particularly worried at the possibility. Not only was Gurt far more current than he in the more deadly aspects of hand-to-hand combat, she had been the Agency's female champion in four straight women's target competitions, rifle as well as pistol. Not satisfied with this accolade, she had nagged her way into competition with the men. She had beaten them, too. The word around the station was that pissing Gurt Fuchs off was both unwise and unhealthy.

Lang was also certain she would be wary of possible followers. No one who had been with the Agency ever completely forgot to be aware of their surroundings at all times, to know how to reach the nearest exit and where it led, to use available storefront glass to look behind you, to have clearly in mind what fields of fire were usable if gunplay became necessary. Lang used to fantasize the peculiar behavior all that might engender at family gatherings, cocktail parties, or other social events.

Gurt would be fine. The question was, what was Lang going to do?

He looked around with purpose, no longer simply rubbernecking. Across the terminal he spotted what he was looking for, large signs with male and female stick figures, *Damen* and *Herren*, the restrooms. He fought the urge to look over his shoulder as he picked up his gait, the pace of a man uncertain he is going to find relief in time.

He reached the men's room at a near dash. He was not surprised to find it as immaculate as any operating room. He was in Germany, where spotless was the norm and grandmothers on hands and knees scrubbed sidewalks in front of their houses.

He had no time to admire hygiene taken to the max.

He hurried past the rows of crowded urinals to the section with stalls, noting that the area appeared empty. He opened the nearest door, locking it as he set down his bag where it would easily be seen underneath the door. Placing one foot on the commode, he stair-stepped to the tank, reached both arms to the dividing partition, and pulled himself up into the shadows of the low ceiling. Straddling the divider wasn't comfortable, but he didn't intend to be there long. He was pulling his belt from his pants' loops when he heard steps on the ceramic tiles. He flattened himself against the narrow top of the partition.

As Lang had anticipated, the eyes of the man in the raincoat went to the spaces between the floor and door of each stall. He saw Lang's bag immediately. The man in the raincoat bent over to look under the door of each of the other stalls, verifying they were empty, that there was no one other than he and Lang in this part of the facility, before approaching the stall where the bag was visible.

Lang slipped his belt over his head, making a loop. He felt the familiar prickle of neck hair, the familiar sensation of anticipated action. Paranoia or not, that man did not intend him well. Raincoat was gently pushing against the door of the stall with one hand while reaching into a pocket with the other.

Lang moved.

Dropping the loop of the belt over the other man's head, Lang rolled off the partition and into the stall, letting his weight snatch the man up against the other side of the door with a thudding impact. Lang gave a violent tug on the belt and was rewarded with a gurgling, choking sound from the other side of the door. Lang unlatched the door and kicked it outward as hard as he could, sending the nearly strangled stranger sprawling beneath the sinks along the far wall.

Lang was on him before he could recover. He cupped the man's head by the chin and slammed it into a drainpipe under a sink repeatedly, while his other hand patted the raincoat until it found the pocket with the gun in it. A slim-model .28 Beretta automatic, easy to conceal in a suit or coat pocket, even with the bulbous silencer. The weapon of choice of an assassin who intended to fire only one or two shots.

Lang retrieved his belt from the man's neck. The brown eyes that glared back at him with equal parts hate and fear could be Latino, African, Semitic, or European. The skin was stretched tightly over the facial bones, giving the man a cadaverous appearance that was difficult to appraise in terms of age. Lang cocked the slide and pressed the pistol against the man's forehead as he resumed the search of pockets. He was rewarded with a wallet containing cash but no identification. Lang had expected none. He had hoped to find some evidence of carelessness, a matchbook from a restaurant in a specific city, a receipt for a rental car or gas, any of the detritus men leave in suit pockets that might give a clue that this person existed before this instant. Whoever he was, he was a pro. He had even removed the labels from the suit, which could have been purchased off the rack anywhere in the country.

Although certain he would get nowhere, Lang slammed the head against a pipe again. "Who sent you?"

The man gasped for breath, managing to whisper between clenched teeth in clearly understandable English. "Get fucked!"

There was an astonished intake of breath from behind. Flicking a glance to the mirror above the sink, Lang saw a man frozen in the entrance to the row of stalls. Only a closer look noted the crossed white leather straps, the dark uniform.

A cop.

The officer's widened eyes went from the gun in Lang's hand to the wallet in the other.

Lang was up and moving even as the policeman was fumbling the flap of his holster open. Lang swung an elbow against the side of the head of the man in uniform, sending him slamming into the wall. Before he could recover, Lang had an arm around his waist while the other hand removed the pistol and stuck it in his own belt.

"Sorry," Lang said, making for the exit, "but I was just leaving."

Lang walked as fast as he could without drawing attention. He crossed the main terminal building and was heading toward signs that promised exit and ground transportation in three languages. At the foot of the stairs and escalator he would have to take down to the outside exit, three Polizei were listening to the crackling of small radios pinned to their uniforms. Lang did not have to guess the subject of the conversation.

He should have taken the cop's radio as well as his gun.

All three saw Lang at the same time and bounded up the steps. Lang spun around and fled, his ears full of shouts to "Halt!"

He ducked into the first concourse he came to, vaulting over the conveyor belts feeding baggage into the security-check X-ray machines. Open trays went flying, filling the air with briefcases, computers, personal items, and unidentifiable objects.

As he ran, Lang was looking for an exit to the outside. The first one he came to was locked, and he could sense his pursuers gaining. There was no time to try another door.

Instead, he charged into a gate area, shoving boarding passengers aside. He fled down the jetway and into the aircraft. Travelers, many stuffing baggage into overhead racks, stared openmouthed as Lang shouldered his way to the emergency exit with the bullish persistence of a fullback seeking first-down yardage. He could hear the police and the outraged security detail yelling for people to get out of the way. Hoping the instructions he had heard aboard hundreds of aircraft were correct, Lang twisted the semicircular latch on the exit and pushed.

He was surprised at how easily the door opened and fell away.

Sitting on the floor, Lang pushed himself out of the passenger cabin and onto the wing. Eight or nine feet below, two men stopped loading the plane's baggage hold to gape. One pointed and yelled something.

Leaving the baggage handlers openmouthed, Lang slid off the wing, cushioning his contact with the tarmac by bending his knees. He sprinted for the tug and its train of baggage carts. Before anyone was certain what he was doing, he had the little tractor in gear and the accelerator flat to the floor. He crossed a taxiway, headed for what he guessed was the general aviation terminal on the other side of the field, judging by the small aircraft lined up on the ramp.

Security for general aviation tended to be lax, and there should be no police on duty inside the terminal.

First, though, he had to get inside.

A howl of engines overhead made him look up. A jet was clawing its way back into the ragged, cloudy sky. Only then did Lang realize he was in the middle of a runway. The plane was executing an emergency go-around, vortices of moisture whirling from its wing tips like tiny tornadoes.

No sooner had his ears stopped ringing from the jet blast than he heard the pulsating wail of police sirens. He looked over his shoulder to see four cars, side by side, blue lights flashing, in pursuit and gaining fast. The tug was making perhaps half the speed of the police cars, and there wasn't a millimeter of space between the pedal and the floor. They would catch him long before he reached the general aviation terminal.

Unless . . .

Thankful that there were few objects to run into on an airport's surface, Lang drove looking over his shoulder, giving only an occasional glance forward. Just as the police pulled within fifty or so feet, he yanked the wheel so hard he feared one or more of the trailing carts would turn over, taking the tug and the whole train with it. Instead, he was now perpendicular to the oncoming cops. Quickly, he turned in the seat, reached to the rear of the tractor, and released the pin that held the coupling mechanism.

At that instant, the laws of physics became a powerful ally. Recognizing what was about to happen, the driver on the right slammed on the brakes while violently cutting to his right to avoid the loose string of carts now only a few feet from his front bumper. The abrupt braking action immediately broke the tires' tenuous adhesion to the wet pavement, and centrifugal force, that phenomenon that tends to impel an object outward from the center of rotation, threw the entire weight of the vehicle to the left, entering a four-wheel drift across the rain-slick surface, an uncontrollable slide stopped only by a collision with the car on its left. On the left side, Lang was unsure which of the two remaining policemen, smoke pouring from screaming brakes, first slammed into the baggage train head-on, lifting two carts off the ground and through the windshield of the remaining cruiser.

All four were out of action for the moment, at least.

Relieved of its train, the tug noticeably picked up speed as Lang made for the terminal. Two more police cars were wailing across the field as he pulled up beside a door and dashed inside.

He was facing a flight of stairs, no doubt to the passenger lounge, where those who fly in private aircraft wait for their planes in comfort unequaled by the most luxurious frequent-flyer facilities of airlines. He had taken a single step when a flash of color caught his attention. On pegs next to the door hung bright green, chartreuse, coveralls, a combination safety and comfort device for ramp workers. He paused long enough to pull on a pair that almost fit. Then he began a leisurely ascent of the stairs, the walk of a man who has nothing to do but pass the time until his shift is over.

In the terminal, uniformed cops poured through the doors, hands on white leather holsters. Wide and fearful eyes of travelers surveyed each other with distrust. It was as though an old and very exclusive club had been invaded by the very people it was organized to keep out. A gently modulated intercom system spoke in several languages, vainly trying to calm passengers whose view of the chase across the field had inspired visions of terrorists everywhere.

Lang followed the *Ausgehen* signs, his assumption that they meant "exit" buttressed by pictures of a bus and a cab. He stepped outside seconds before a line of police took up position just inside the glass doors. He turned a corner and, seeing no one, peeled off the coveralls, wadded them up, and looked for a place to dump them. He didn't have far to look; Germans, it seemed, loved public trash baskets, placing one every few meters rather than risk the horror of litter. He stuffed the clothes in, covered them with newspaper pages, and walked to a taxi stand.

He had always planned on returning to Frankfurt, but he had anticipated a more conventional arrival.

CHAPTER TWELVE

Frankfurt Am Main
Dusseldorf Am Hauptbahnhof Strasse
An hour and a half later

At mid-afternoon, the *bierstube* was filled more with the smell of cooked sausages and sauerkraut than with people. The sole waiter was fussing with tablecloths and napkins. The only other customers were an elderly couple whose fragile appearance was belied by the meal they were finishing: roast pork, red cabbage, and dumplings.

Lang was the only other person in the single room.

Gazing out of the plate-glass window to the building in which he had spent so much of his time with the Agency, he wondered how the square could be so clean and yet appear so grubby. After all, the Hauptbahnhof Platz had been subjected to extreme urban replanning by the U.S. Army and Royal Air Forces and totally rebuilt only sixty years ago. Yet the indelible smudges of coal-burning trains seemed to have been there for centuries. Frankfurt was a city of commerce, banking, and other financial services, not beauty, although the rebuilt Romerberg, the medieval center of town, had a certain charm.

He sipped at the dregs of a beer, still tasting the sharp brown mustard with which he had coated his bratwurst. He had just put down his glass when Gurt came through the door, wheeling her suitcase behind her.

She glanced around the room an instant longer than it took to see him before she sat across the table.

Lang stood, leaned across, and kissed her cheek. "I was beginning to worry."

She rolled her eyes. "Worry? You? You downshut the airport. I had to wait an hour before the U-Bahn began to run again."

Lang eased back into his chair. "I did what?"

"Robbing a man at gunpoint, then hitting a policeman and taking his gun. You managed to wreck four police cars, too."

Lang was uncertain if what he detected in her voice was admiration or the atavistic Teutonic horror of disorder. "Me? What makes you think I had anything to do with it?"

A snort told him she did not consider the question worthy of an answer. "After waiting an hour, you can imagine how crowded the train from the airport was."

As though imposing a penance, she drained the remainder of his beer.

"You could have taken a cab," he suggested helpfully.

Another snort, this one of frustration, as she gave the empty glass a look of regret and set it down. "The length, er, line, er, queue for cabs was forever. I have hunger. Can we eat rather than discuss the problems you caused?"

Gurt signaled to the waiter, who was already openly staring at her. In mere blue jeans and nondescript blouse and jacket, she could have stopped traffic. He appeared at their tableside with considerably more speed than Lang had seen him move before.

"*Tageskart,* menu?"

Lang knew there are few things, including *War and Peace,* thicker than the organized listing of daily specials for both lunch and dinner, as well the standard dishes, each arranged as to appetizers, soups, main courses, and desserts, that is a German *Tageskart.* He often wondered if the war would have turned out differently if the Germans had spent as much time fighting as they had reading menus.

Like most of her countrymen, Gurt perused the pages with the care of an investor checking the closing market reports before ordering exactly what Lang knew she would, the bratwurst.

They waited until the waiter disappeared behind the curtain that screened the kitchen from the dining area before Gurt repeated his question. "How did I know it was you that turned the airport up downside? Maybe a lucky guess. More likely because you left your suitcase with your name tag on it."

Lang winced at the breach of the protocol he knew so well. One does not put the standard name tag on baggage. Such markers decrease considerably the deniability of having been somewhere. Additionally, personal baggage of Agency personnel frequently contained items like a totally plastic, X-ray-proof pistol, component parts of bombs, and other things likely to be frowned upon by officialdom. Identifying the person possessing such things could lead to unnecessary difficulty. He had put the tag on for a brief trip on behalf of the foundation when the Gulfstream had been in the shop for its hundred-hour inspection.

Not only did the damned thing have his name, it had

his address. The German cops were probably already in touch with American authorities.

Swell.

Gurt looked lovingly at the tall glass of beer the waiter sat before her. "Of course, I reported the suitcase stolen."

"Thanks. I didn't have time to."

Gurt took a tentative sip from her glass, closed her eyes, and sighed in delight.

"That beer makes you happier than sex." Lang chuckled.

"I do not have to depend on you for the beer," she retorted.

"And you can enjoy it even when you have a headache."

She put the glass down. "I never have those kind of headaches."

True.

Lang became serious. "Think they believed you?"

"About the beer or the sex?"

He shook his head. "About the baggage being stolen."

She shrugged. "Who knows? I do think it might be wise to cross the Platz there and see if we could get a favor from some friends of mine, see what they might be able to do with the local police."

Very little, in Lang's experience. Germans, like any other nationality, did not accept being an American agent as an excuse for creating bedlam on their soil.

"I suppose they could at least find out if they bought your story."

Thirty minutes later, Gurt and Lang crossed Mosel Strasse to an unimposing four-story stone building. Wet with the continuing drizzle, the rock face seemed somehow ominous, like the facade of a prison. Both Gurt and Lang knew that, as they approached, they were appearing on a series of surveillance cameras concealed in the stone work and behind the small, tinted windows made of explosive-proof plastic, reinforced sufficiently to withstand any projectile smaller than an artillery shell. Well out of sight from below, the roof sprouted a forest of antennae. The venetian blinds on the windows were rubber-lined. When drawn, they prevented window-glass vibrations that, scanned by laser or other listening devices, could betray conversations inside.

The door onto the Platz, also reenforced and explosive-proof, opened onto a small foyer. On one wall was listed the American Trade Attaché and a number of businesses, none of which ever had a customer visit because the companies did not exist. The foyer opened onto another room that housed a counterlike desk manned by a white-haired man in the uniform of a private security company. Had he looked behind the desk, Lang knew he would have seen a shotgun in a rack, a television monitor, and an alarm button on the floor. The wall behind the desk was mirrored with one-way glass, behind which were men in full combat gear.

The guard gave Gurt and Lang a smile that was perfunctory only. "Help you, sir, madam?"

From the lack of accent, he was American, not German.

"Good afternoon to you, too, Allie," Gurt said, holding up a laminated card for him to see.

"Nice to have you back, Ms. Fuchs."

Gurt gave him a smile. "Is Eddie Reavers in?"

Lang remembered the name, if not the face. Reavers had, like him, been in the Intel section, although he had begun in Ops. One of the few agents to survive capture by the Russians, he had spent two years in Lubyanka prison, the KGB's own very special hellhole, before being swapped for a Soviet spy. He had returned a hero. Lang was surprised the man had not retired by now.

The guard looked down, checking what Lang knew was a list of anyone expected that day. "Don't see as you have an appointment."

Gurt's smile radiated sexuality. "We—I don't. Just tell him I'm in town with a friend and I'd like a couple of minutes of his time."

The guard gave her an uncertain look before picking up a phone and mumbling into it.

Hanging up, he reached under the desk and produced two laminated visitor's passes. "Clip these on and go on in." He pointed to her suitcase. " 'Cept that bag. You'll have to leave it here."

Gurt was still holding her own Agency identification. She put it into her purse and took the one being proffered.

Gurt approached the desk, clearly well-versed in the drill. Extending both arms, she placed the thumb of each hand on a screen that was part of the top of the desk.

The door to the left of the desk wheezed open, and Gurt and Lang entered a small room. One person could not carry enough explosives to blast through the concrete-and-steel reinforcement of this antechamber. Two men in fatigues without insignia and a large Labrador retriever were waiting for them. As the dog sniffed, one man ran a metal detector over their bodies while the second kept them covered with an M16A2 assault rifle.

The detector squeaked at Lang's belt line, and he grinned sheepishly. "Sorry. Forgot."

He lifted his jacket to allow the man without the rifle to pull the airport policeman's weapon free. For the first time, he noted it was a Glock 9mm.

The man held the gun up, suspicious. "Anything else slip your mind, like maybe a stick or two of dynamite?"

Gurt gave the guard a glare that could well have singed the paint on the walls. "Perhaps you forget he is with me?"

Both men were instantly apologetic.

"Sorry, Ms. Fuchs."

"Just following orders, Ms. Fuchs."

If Lang remembered correctly, the latter excuse had not played well at Nuremberg. But he said, "It's okay, fellas. You're doing your job. Just be sure that's here when I come back."

Lang and Gurt stepped onto an elevator that had no buttons for floor selection. It was controlled from somewhere outside. The hallway into which they stepped looked pretty much the same as Lang recalled it: gray commercial-grade carpet that he would expect in a thirty-dollar-a-night hotel room, institutional pale-green walls. The same taste with which U.S. government offices worldwide were decorated. Lang suspected that, buried somewhere in the General Services Administration, there was a grandmotherly lady who furnished such places, a lady who was color-blind, found oatmeal too spicy, and lived at yard sales.

Painted metal doors were closed but could not entirely absorb the hum of machinery. The one at the end of the hall opened.

"Ah hope to hell you've come home," a soft voice drawled.

The accent was southern? No, western. Lang put the name with the face, aided by the voice. Eddie "Lone Star" Reavers. He had been near optional retirement age when Lang had left. He must be in his seventies by now. The man had reveled in his Texas origin, keeping the dialect and mannerisms of West Texas years after he had left it for the last time. Regulations required agents, even those not working in public view, to dress conservatively, drawing as little attention as possible. Reavers sported snakeskin cowboy boots and Stetsons. Lang wondered if he had replaced his standard-issue Sig Sauer with a Colt Peacemaker.

He stood as erect as a much younger man, dark eyes glinting like a hawk's. A square jaw and a nose that had been reset none too gently gave him a pugnacious air, a fighter ready to spring from his corner. Most bald heads only made men look old. Reavers's, shiny and bullet-shaped, made him look tougher, an effect like Yul Brynner or Kojak.

Reavers gave Gurt a hug not entirely avuncular. "Welcome back, Sugar. We've sure as hell missed you 'round the old corral."

Lang winced. Geo-ethnic was one thing; dialogue from a B Western movie was another. Had Gurt slept with the guy? It didn't require the Agency's level of intelligence to see he sure wanted to, age notwithstanding.

Gurt endured the embrace a second longer than Lang thought friendship required before slipping by Reavers and into the office.

Lang followed, hand extended. "Lang Reilly. I remember you."

Reavers stepped in front of a desk that definitely was not government issue, motioning Lang to sit. "Shore Ah do. Legend 'round here among us desk cowboys. You're the hombre from Intel went and got Gurt's daddy out from East Berlin, snatched him just like a sidewinder with a rat."

Lang had never thought of himself as a rattlesnake, but he sank down into a leather wing chair, another piece of furniture the government was unlikely to supply. In fact, Reavers's office was the only part of the Agency's station that did not reflect the budget cuts prompted by the fall of the Soviet Empire.

"I don't know whether to say thanks or be insulted."

Reavers kept his hand on Gurt's arm as though she needed help getting into the mate to Lang's chair. "No insult intended." He looked from Gurt to Lang. "Ah see by the drops on your clothes it's still drizzlin' out there."

It was only then Lang noticed the office had no windows. A windowless office meant top security. Reavers was probably Chief of Station. He certainly had the seniority for it.

"Still wet and miserable," Lang agreed.

Reavers slid behind the desk and leaned back in his chair. "You remember: It can be like that for days. Makes me miss home, even in the summer when the devil himself won't come to West Texas because of the heat. Hell, I recall onc't as a kid Ah bet my whole week's allowance that the sidewalk was hot enough to fry an egg."

Gurt bit. "Did you win your bet?"

Delighted to have a straight man, Reavers laughed. "Never knew, Sugar. Time we got the egg to the sidewalk, it was already hard-boiled."

Lang chuckled appreciatively while Gurt, ever literal, thought that one over.

Reavers snapped forward to place both hands on his desk, palms down. "What kin Ah do for you folks? Ah gather Gurt ain't ready to go back to work, and Lang, you're too old to go through the training again."

Corny or not, Lang was beginning to warm to this guy, even if he was as full of bullshit as a cattle pen. "I'm afraid you're right," he said good-naturedly. "I'd never make it through The Farm again. But I could use the experience. I don't know if you remember Don Huff from the old Berlin Station. He retired, was in Spain, and got murdered. His daughter asked me to look into it."

Lang proceeded to tell him what happened.

"Didn't know Huff, but Ah'm damned sorry to hear someone survived duty in Berlin back then only to get shot. But life's not fair, as one of our presidents observed. Only thing he said ever made sense. What kin Ah do for y'all? Sounds like somebody's on your ass."

Gurt leaned forward in her chair, exposing just a smidgen of cleavage above the neckline of her blouse. "We're afraid the Frankfurt police are looking for Lang." She looked at him with the trace of a smile. "He left his baggage behind . . . along with a name tag."

Lang now knew what it had been like when one of his small friends wet his pants in front of the entire second grade.

"That was downright careless," Reavers observed. "Wouldn't last as long as free rice an' beans in El Paso, you did that while you were with us. But you know that. Agin, how kin Ah hep?"

"If they are looking for Lang by name, a driver's license, passport, and a few credit cards in some other name would help," Gurt said.

Reavers slowly shook his head. "Lang, I dunno if you're aware how bad the politicians back home have cut our budget. You'd think the Commies were the only enemies we'll ever have. Hell, even 'lowin' for inflation, the Agency got nearly three times the fundin' twenty years ago we get today. Hardly enough to pay the phone bill, let alone keep track of ever' raghead in Germany wants to become a martyr with a homemade bomb. Hell, I say, one o' them jihadist nut bags wants to join Allah in Paradise, we need to help him along 'fore he takes Americans with him. What we need an' need bad is someone in Washington unnerstan's these A-rabs not gonna rest till the whole Western world's one big Islamic pile o' camel dung. But . . ." Lang was truly astonished when Reavers stood, leading them to the door. "You know my ass'd be in th' crack, Ah git caught providin' false ID.

Hell, Ah git caught, I'll claim Gurt here threatened to shoot me. C'mon downstairs, git your picture took, an' we'll have you fixed up in an hour. An' you can be on your way to . . . ?"

"Heidelberg," Gurt said. "There's a man there Huff worked with."

The Agency man gallantly held the door for Gurt. "Wherever, I jes' hope this damned drizzle stops 'fore I mildew."

CHAPTER THIRTEEN

Heidelberg, Germany (Hauptstrasse)
Haus zum Ritter
That evening

The eighty-four-kilometer drive from Frankfurt had been uneventful. Their newly minted identities showed them to be Mary and Joel Couch of Macon, Georgia. The stamp on the passports showed they had arrived at Frankfurt that very morning. The document was given careless scrutiny by a desk clerk wearing striped pants and a cutaway coat. The Agency-issued credit card was duly imprinted and returned. The only question was whether they wished to reserve a table at the hotel's restaurant for dinner. Lang's response had been an immediate affirmative.

From the windows of their third-floor suite, Lang could see across the empty *marktplatz* to the fourteenth-century church and, beyond, the slow-moving waters of the Nekar reflecting the dull sky of the dying day. Gurt, smoking what Lang hoped was only her first cigarette of the day, was less interested in the view than observing how a home built in 1592 had been converted into a luxury hotel.

She was studying a gilt sconce that had lightbulbs screwed into what had once been candleholders. "You did not even think when asked about dinner. You have eaten here before?"

Lang was leaning to his left in a vain attempt to get a glimpse of the bluff behind the town, the one crowned with the ruins of a castle. "Years ago, the Agency had a research team here, German college professors who had studied the Russkies, figured out what the Commies would do in certain situations. I came about once a month, always stayed here. One of our tame Germans recommended the restaurant. Best sauerbraten in Germany. They use apples."

Gurt made a face at the mention of the traditional dish of marinated beef served with dumplings in a rich brown sauce. "You will go home fat."

He gave her an exaggerated leer, running his eyes from her to the bed. "I'm planning on you keeping me slim."

"You can eat more often than you can love."

He sat on the *Federbett,* the soft eiderdown that served as top sheet and cover on German beds, pulling her with him. "Really? Let's try a predinner workout."

She lay beside him. "Should we not call Herr Blucher? He is the reason we are here, no?"

Lang sighed as the romance of the hotel in the old city evaporated like the morning mist. Gurt's priorities were always in order. They were also frequently a nuisance.

"Okay, okay, I've got his number right here."

He scrolled down the list on his BlackBerry and handed the cell phone to Gurt.

She spoke for a few minutes before asking, "What is this place named?"

"*Haus zum Ritter* on Hauptstrasse. Does he want to come here?"

She shook her head and spoke a few more words, ending with a cheery *auf Wiedersehen,* turned the phone off, and handed it back. "No, ten o'clock tomorrow at the castle."

"The castle, not here? Or his house? He wants plenty of people around, doesn't trust us yet despite Jacob's introduction."

Gurt pushed him back against the comforter. "And your workout?"

Lang ate too much.

"Now I know what a Thanksgiving turkey feels like," he said as they drained the last of their after-dinner schnapps. "Let's take a walk."

Outside, the day's drizzle had washed the skies clean. A myriad of stars hovered just out of reach of the town's lights. Hand in hand, they walked the block over to the church, its Gothic facade gleaming in strategically placed spotlights. A block over, Lauerstrasse fronted the river in the periphery of the town's lights. Swaying gently at their moorings, two glass-canopied tour boats, each a hundred or so feet long, rocked gently at their moorings.

"Do you have with you the gun you took from the policemen at the Frankfurt airport?"

Gurt's question was so out of place in the peace of the night, Lang thought he had misunderstood.

"Huh?"

"The gun, the one from the airport, you have it with you?"

Instinctively, Lang's hand went to small of his back to

touch the hard metal of the Glock he had jammed into his belt. "Yeah, but why?"

Gurt laughed, the sound of a woman enjoying an amorous evening. She nuzzled Lang's face as though to give him a kiss. "One, perhaps two, men follow us," she whispered.

The surroundings suddenly became threatening rather than romantic. The darkness, the absence of any other strollers, even the black river, all seemed the perfect spot to kill and escape. His left hand still in hers, leaving his right free to use the gun if necessary, he moved in a seemingly aimless fashion so their backs were against a wall rather than unprotected.

Other than the river's sucking at the pilings along the dock and an occasional automobile a block over, there was no sound. A quick glance around confirmed Lang's impression: an ideal spot for an ambush. The church was between the river and town, shielding the riverside area from the town's lights. Only shops, shuttered for the night, lined the dock. It was unlikely there was another living soul within blocks.

Other than whoever was following them.

Backing deeper into the doubly dark shadow, Lang took the Glock from his belt and released the clip. By touch, he counted the shells in the magazine before pushing it back into the grip with a resounding click.

The sound of a clip being loaded into an automatic pistol is both unmistakable and authoritative. In the quiet night, it also carried farther than would ordinarily be the case.

Almost instantly, a blurred figure stepped into an area where a small stream of the town's glow leaked onto the cobblestones beside the river.

He held both hands high. "Don't shoot, Mr. Reilly. It's me, Franz Blucher."

Wordlessly, Lang handed the Glock to Gurt and walked away at an angle to avoid her line of fire toward the stranger. "Stay where you are, Herr Blucher," he said. "And keep your hands where I can see them."

Franz Blucher was a smallish, elderly man in worn tweed pants, a sweater missing one elbow, and unruly hair that caught just enough illumination to form a halo around the man's head.

It took Lang only a few seconds to ascertain that he was unarmed. *Sprechen Sie Englese?*

He asked mainly as a courtesy, Blucher having already spoken in English. Lang was unable to remember the last time he encountered a German, at least a West German, who did not speak English far better than Lang spoke their language.

"I speak English reasonably well," the old man said, pulling a pair of wireless spectacles from the pocket of his sweater and giving Lang a stare. "You *are* Mr. Reilly, are you not?"

The English had a trace of upper-class British in it.

"Just as you are Franz Blucher."

Blucher nodded slowly, probably remembering a time when showing one's papers was common. He fumbled in a hip pocket and produced a worn passport.

With it in his hand, Lang walked closer to the light flowing around the corner of the church. He still couldn't read it.

He handed it back to Blucher. "I'm Lang Reilly, all right. And this," he motioned to where Gurt was emerging from the shadows, "is Gurt Fuchs. You spoke to her on the phone earlier this evening."

Blucher held up the glasses again, surveying Gurt. "Yes, yes, I did."

Lang slid his hands into his pockets and shook his

head. "Sneaking up on somebody in the dark might not be good for your health, Herr Blucher."

Apparently satisfied with what he saw, Blucher returned the eyeglasses to a pocket. "I apologize. Frau Fuchs . . ."

"Fraulein," Gurt corrected.

"Fraulein Fuchs told me where you are staying. I decided not to wait until tomorrow and called the hotel, who said you were at dinner. By the time I got there, the man in the restaurant said you had just left. I was trying to catch up."

Lang and Gurt started walking back toward the hotel, the old man between them. Blucher kept looking over his shoulder, his head turning in short, nervous jerks. He reminded Lang of a mouse deciding whether to leave the security of its hole.

"You are expecting someone else, Herr Blucher?" he asked.

Blucher shook his head emphatically. "Expecting? No. I worry there may be someone else, though. The same someone who killed your friend Donald Huff."

"And that would be . . . ?"

The old man drew his sweater closer around him, although the night was warm. "I do not know his—or their—name, but you can be sure it is someone who did not want Huff's book published."

Lang caught himself looking over his own shoulder. Paranoia was contagious. "I'd say they have accomplished that goal, so why . . . ?"

Blucher stopped, looking up into Lang's face. "They do not wish their secret told."

Lang was glad the hotel was now in view. "What secret?"

"I am not sure, but it has to do with something in Huff's research, something I was helping him with."

Gurt broke her silence. "Herr Blucher, we can have a drink at the bar and discuss—"

He shook his head again. "No, too dark."

The *vom Ritter*'s bar and restaurant were unusually dark, even given the murky atmosphere preferred by eating and dining establishments. Ancient polished wood and tiny, weak tabletop lamps gave the appearance more of a cave than a room.

"Our room, then," Gurt suggested. "We have a suite, an area where we can sit and talk."

Minutes later, the three were seated around a low table, a room-service carafe of coffee and three cups in front of them.

"Exactly what was Don's book about?" Lang asked, pouring.

Blucher held up a hand to decline the sugar Gurt offered. "War criminals, German war criminals."

"And you were helping him research?"

The old German made a sound that could have been a mirthless laugh. "Research? I had little need to research. I knew most of them."

"You mean like Himmler, Goring?" Lang asked.

Blucher shook his head. "No, no. The ones never punished."

"And you knew them?" Lang was fascinated.

"Oh, not well. I was only seven or eight when the war ended. It was my father. He worked for a newspaper taken over by Herr Goebbels's propaganda ministry. He interviewed a number of these men for the radio or newspaper. Often they would come by our apartment in Berlin for an initial discussion. My father said I should meet them, someday they would be famous."

Prescient if not exactly on target.

The professor stared at something only he could see and continued, "It was these 'famous' men that was the end of my father. He was drafted into the *Volksturm,* the army of boys and old men who were to defend Berlin from the Russians there at the last. He deserted to make sure my mother, brother, and I got safely out of the city, to go west toward the Allies. For this he was hung from a lamppost by order of one of these 'famous' men."

"Why would these men go unpunished?" Gurt wanted to know.

"Because they were useful. What would you say should be done with a man who employed slave labor to build a weapons system to kill hundreds, if not thousands, of civilians, including women and children?"

"I would have thought he would have been in the dock at Nuremberg," Lang said.

"Wernher von Braun, the founder of your aerospace program? His were the V-1 and V-2 rockets that struck London. He used Jews, Poles, anyone from the camps as workers until they dropped from exhaustion and starvation. Yet he was too valuable to pros . . . er . . ."

"Prosecute," Lang supplied, his coffee cup frozen halfway between the table and his mouth. "You are telling me this is the same von Braun who was responsible for the U.S.'s space program?"

The old man's head bobbed. "It was a race between the Russians' German scientists and your German scientists as to who would reach the moon first. Von Braun surrendered to American troops. Others of his group were not so fortunate. They fell into the hands of the Communists."

Lang set his cup down untouched. "There were others?"

Once again, an emphatic nod. "Many. Your intelligence organization . . ."

"OSS," Lang suggested.

"The OSS and its successor slipped a number of Nazis

out of Germany, those they thought might be helpful in spying or revealing Russian spies. There was even a name for the operation—Operation Paper Clip."

The sheer banality made Lang smile for a second. "And you think it is these old Nazis who don't want the information Don had to get out?"

"It cannot be," Gurt interjected. "Whoever they were, eighty or ninety would be their age now. Don Huff was not over run by a wheelchair or clubbed with a crutch."

Blucher took a long sip from his cup and set it back down. "There was such an organization, *Die Spinne*, the spider, that aided escapes from Germany. People like Bormann, Hitler's personal secretary, and Mengele, who conducted medical experiments on live inmates of the camps. Many also escaped on Vatican passports."

Lang glanced at Gurt, remembering her reference to the same organization. "But you don't think . . . ?"

"I don't think some Nazi organization killed your friend, no. As Fraulein Fuchs says, the old men are either dead or nearly so. There is perhaps other information your friend was about to reveal, perhaps without even knowing it."

Not much help, Lang thought. "What about you— what's your connection to all this? I mean, I know what you said about your father, but how did you and Don hook up?"

Blucher slumped as though someone had placed a weight on his shoulders. He stared straight ahead. "After the war, I finished school, went to university right here in Heidelberg. I became interested in history and got a doctorate in it." He smiled sadly. "I almost didn't receive my degree. I wrote my dissertation on the war criminals who escaped justice, not exactly a popular subject. In fact, I think had the administration not feared the world would learn they had in essence censored

such a work, they would not have awarded my Ph.D."
He turned to give Lang a painful look. "The Germans
have national amnesia where the war is concerned. It is
not a popular subject, nor was I a popular professor.
Fortunately, I was invited to teach at Cambridge in England, where I spent the rest of my academic career.

"By the time I retired, most of the faculty and all of the
students I had known here were gone. My wife died a
year after our return, and I feared I was to die of bore-
dom. Then, somehow, your friend found a copy of my
dissertation. He called and asked if I was interested in
helping with his book. I was tired of gardening and the
other activities of the old, so I agreed. We e-mailed each
other and talked on the phone almost every day. Every
day until . . . until he was killed."

All three were quiet, their coffee getting cold as each
thought.

Lang stood. "I've got some pictures I'd like you to
see." He went to the bedroom and returned with a number of prints. "I had these made from a CD that Don's
killer didn't get. Take a look and see if you recognize
anyone."

Blucher produced the glasses again, placing them
firmly on his nose and deliberately hooking the frame
around his ears. Through the lenses, Lang could see his
eyes widen. "Skorzeny!"

"Who?"

"The man Jessica said her father was writing of,"
Gurt reminded him. "Otto Skorzeny."

Blucher held the picture up, the one of the man in uniform standing in front of the Vatican. "That's him, Otto
Skorzeny."

Lang settled back into his chair. "Tell us about him."

Blucher put the picture down and unhooked the spectacles from his ears before he spoke. "Austrian, college edu-

cated, got that scar in a *Schmisse,* student duel. Passionately pro-Hitler, SS, sometimes called Hitler's commando. He was the one who flew gliders onto a mountaintop to rescue Mussolini without a shot being fired. Organized the parachute drop onto Cypress that took the British completely by surprise. It was Skorzeny that Hitler sent to Montsegur . . ."

"Where?" Lang asked, the word faintly familiar.

"The place in the Languedoc in France. It was on one of Don's cards, too," Gurt said.

Lang had the feeling he was getting somewhere, but he had no idea where. "Excuse me. Please continue."

Blucher nodded. "Montsegur. It was the last holdout of the Cathars, a here . . . here . . ."

"Heretical sect," Lang said, remembering his adventure in the region last year with something less than fondness.

"Yes, heretics," the professor continued. "They were victims of one of the Crusades declared by the Pope in the early thirteenth century. Slaughtered to a man. Question was, what was their heresy? Were they like the Gnostics, who believed Christ rose from the dead spiritually rather than in body? Or was their problem that they had something the Pope wanted or did not want known? With Hitler's obsession with things of a supernatural nature—he was continually searching for the Holy Grail, for instance—he sent Skorzeny to the remnants of the old fortress and cave—"

"Cave?" Lang asked, instantly annoyed with himself for interrupting.

He wasn't the only one. Gurt produced and lit a cigarette in retaliation.

"Yes, a cave." The old man held up another photo, this one showing Skorzeny in lederhosen. "This one may have been taken there. See the wall behind him with what could be carving on it? Odd. Skorzeny did not allow himself to be photographed very often. A very secretive man. Almost as though he knew he would be one of the people the Allies would come looking for."

"Why?" Lang wanted to know. "He sounds more like a hero than a criminal."

"I suppose the line can be, er, slender," Blucher said. "In 1944, Hitler sent Skorzeny to seize the Citadel of Budapest. The Russians were preparing to invade Hungary, and the Hungarians had been allies of the Germans. Now they wanted to make a separate peace. Hitler couldn't have a Russian ally on his doorstep, so he sent Skorzeny to capture Admiral Miklos Horthy, Hungary's leader, and the whole Hungarian cabinet. With just a few SS troops, Skorzeny overthrew the legitimate government of the country, replacing it with a puppet one."

"Impressive," Lang said, thinking of too many similarities. The old switch-governments trick had been pulled off more than once by his former employers. "But criminal in the context of war?"

"Perhaps, perhaps not," the professor conceded. "In December of 1944 in the Ardennes—the Bulge, I think you Americans called the battle—Skorzeny rounded up several hundred idiomatic-American-speaking Germans, dressed them in U.S. army uniforms, and infiltrated American lines."

"They would have been shot as spies," Lang said. "But hardly criminal."

The professor smiled weakly. "You would have been right had not Skorzeny's men taken over a hundred prisoners, bound them, and shot them in the back, a crime even greater than the theft of every bit of art or treasure he found in Hungary."

"So," Lang wanted to know, "why wasn't he tried for that?"

The old man gave a shrug. "After the war, he disappeared, simply ceased to exist. A few years later, he resurfaced in Spain, under Franco's protection, helped reorganize his army."

Lang got up to look over the professor's shoulder. Once again he had a feeling of déjà vu, a sense of having seen that face before the photographs. "If the Allies knew he was there, why not force Franco to give him up? I'm sure we had extradition treaties with Spain."

Blucher grinned slightly. "You speak like a lawyer."

"I am a lawyer."

The old man gave Gurt a wink. "I am lost. I have entrusted myself to a lawyer."

Lawyer-bashing, now an international sport.

Blucher stood. "Why Skorzeny was not taken from Spain is a good question, Herr Reilly. I have some material at home you will find most interesting. It is getting late. Perhaps we can still meet at the castle tomorrow? I'll bring it then."

"Why not just meet here again?" Gurt asked. "This suite is more secure than the ruins of a castle."

"True," Blucher admitted, "but in daylight, I feel safer surrounded with people."

"Let me call you a cab," Lang volunteered, reaching for the room's phone. "Write down your address so I can give it to the driver."

Blucher complied without protest. In a few minutes, he was gone.

Lang looked at Gurt, puzzled. "If it's not some Nazi group, skinheads, or something, who cares if there's a book published about people who've been dead for years?"

Gurt stubbed out her cigarette. "Perhaps no one. Perhaps it is other information the book contains, as the old man suggests."

"But what?"

She was reaching behind herself to unbutton her blouse, a move that thrust her breasts forward. Lang watched, spellbound, before he realized she had asked a question.

"I suppose we'll know tomorrow."

Gurt folded the blouse neatly and stepped out of her skirt. Although he had seen the performance nightly, it held his undivided attention.

"It is most unattractive to stare like that. I feel like a hamburger Grumps is drooling over."

"I gave up drooling last week. Besides, if you didn't want me to watch, you'd go into the bathroom."

"Who has said I did not want you to watch?"

Just as Lang was drifting off, Gurt asked, "Are you asleep?"

"Not now."

"Do you really think some organization, *Die Spinne*, or something like it, is what is against us?"

"What we're up against? Possible. No one, not even old men, want to go to jail or be deported, like I said. And you can bet, old or not, there are really wealthy former Nazis, rich enough to hire assassins by the bushel."

It was not a comforting thought.

CHAPTER FOURTEEN

Heidelberg, Germany (Hauptstrasse)
Haus zum Ritter
The next morning

Along with the breakfast of rolls, jelly, cheese, and sausage slices, the tray brought to their room included the day's *Frankfurt Allegemeine Zeitung.* Gurt unfolded it while Lang poured coffee.

"Mein Gott!" she gasped.

Lang didn't notice that he had spilled boiling coffee on himself as he gaped at a front page with his picture on it and a caption that translated as "Airport fugitive identified as American lawyer, businessman."

Gurt's head swiveled around the room as though someone might be watching this very moment. "How did they get the picture?"

"Shit!" Lang jumped out of bed, using a linen napkin to dab at the hot coffee he had dumped in his lap. He took the paper and stared at the grainy photograph. "Could have been taken by a security camera."

"Not unless it is custom for you to pose and smile in airports," Gurt observed. "You also look younger."

"Don't let jealousy cloud your judgment," Lang said, still staring at the newspaper. "I'd swear that's the service photo from my Agency file."

Gurt knelt on the bed to look over his shoulder. "Possible. Remember, someone managed to chop into—"

"Hack into."

"Hack into the Agency's files and get your picture last year in London."

"How would the Frankfurt cops even know the Agency had a picture of me?"

Gurt thought for a moment. "That police detective in Atlanta, the black man who does not like you very much . . ."

"Rouse? He loves me like a brother. We just put on a show for your benefit."

She shook her head. "For one time, be serious. From this picture you could be recognized. Rouse knows you with the Agency worked, no?"

"He knows from last year that my government service wasn't with the Navy like I told him, yes."

Gurt nodded. "Since the Frankfurt police have your name and address because you furnished to them on your luggage, it might be normal to contact the Atlanta Police."

A way of making certain the matter was either permanently misplaced or mishandled, Lang thought. But he said, "And so?"

"This man Rouse, he would tell them you were with the Agency . . ."

"If he knew it, and I'm not sure he does."

Unperturbed, Gurt rushed on. "So the Frankfurt police would demand a picture for the paper to identify you."

Lang was feeling a little calmer after seeing his face on the front page of a major paper. If you weren't a celebrity or politician, that ranked right up there with finding a *60 Minutes* news crew waiting for you at your office in forecasting you were not likely to have a good day.

"I suppose that would be possible," he admitted, "but you know as well as I do, the Agency won't even confirm someone worked for them, let alone give out their file picture."

Deflated, Gurt nodded. "You have right, of course. But how?"

Lang brought the paper to within inches of his face. "Could be a drawing, if the cop has that good a memory. I mean, he only got a second's glimpse before he hit my elbow with his face and I was outta there. Let's hope the picture is too blurry to make a good ID. When we finish with Blucher this morning, maybe you can ask Reavers to do us another favor and change the picture on my passport to include a mustache or something."

"Me?" Gurt placed her fingers on her chest. "Why do not you ask?"

"It wasn't my blouse he was trying to look down yesterday."

An hour later, Gurt and Lang climbed the winding path up to the castle that stood guard over the city. Little more than a ruin since a lightning-induced fire in the early eighteenth century, it had been the ancestral home of the Wittlebach line of German kings and Holy Roman Electors since the thirteenth century. Consequently, an amalgam of Romanesque, Gothic, Renaissance, and German mannerist towers, crenellation, and buttresses combined in an architectural smorgasbord. Below, the red-roofed buildings of the town clustered around the church like chicks around a hen.

The pair found a seat under the shade of an oak that might have been as old as the courtyard it adorned. They watched a horde of Japanese tourists, led by an umbrella-wielding guide, explore and photograph. A much less organized group of schoolchildren, more interested in the holiday from class than any history lesson, clambered over ruins of walls as they chattered gaily.

Lang looked at his watch. "Ten-thirty. Blucher's late."

Gurt was unconcerned. "He is an old man. It will be an effort to make the climb up here."

By eleven, not even Blucher's age seemed a plausible excuse. Gurt phoned his home from her BlackBerry, getting only a recording.

Lang stood, dusting off his pants. "You stay here, call if he shows." He pulled out his wallet and extracted a slip of paper. "I've got his address here from last night. I'll look for him there."

The professor lived in a neighborhood of semidetached, tile-roofed, two-story homes with flowers in boxes at each window. The absence of trees told him the subdivision was relatively new. At the number Lang was looking for, an old but shiny VW Beetle was parked in a driveway bordered by a manicured lawn.

He parked the rental car and rang the bell beside the door. Two more rings produced no result, so Lang rapped his knuckles against the oak and the door swung open.

Lang peered inside, a queasy feeling stirring in his stomach. Even in this quiet neighborhood, he doubted people left front doors unlocked and unlatched.

"Herr *Doktor* Blucher?" Lang called from the doorway. "Is anyone home?"

Only silence answered him.

Lang gently pushed the door wide and went in.

The front door entered directly onto a small living room inhabited by undistinguished furniture and an upright piano. To Lang's right was a fireplace outlined in a mantel of some dark wood. To his left, the room opened into a dining/kitchen area. Everything Lang had seen so far had an impersonal, antiseptic look about it, as though he were seeing a furnished model home.

The Herr *Doktor* either spent no time here or was first cousin to the Tidy Bowl Lady.

A door in the kitchen opened onto a tiny yard where freshly turned rows of dirt indicated the beginning of a vegetable garden, as did a compost pile beside the house. A wooden fence might keep out rabbits but wasn't high enough to give privacy from the second stories of the adjacent houses.

Lang went back inside and called the professor's name again, with the same result.

Afraid of what he was likely to find, Lang started up the stairs.

The staircase bisected a short hallway. Lang moved silently toward the larger of two rooms, one at each end. The bedroom was as neat as the living room and as unremarkable. A partially open closet door showed an array of outdated but pressed suits. Along the floor, shoes marched in precise ranks.

The total quiet of the house was unnerving. No floorboards creaked, no utilities hummed. In fact, he hadn't even heard the ticking of a clock. It was as if the building existed in some sort of universe of its own.

Lang turned and went down the hall, passing the bath, also neat and sparkling clean.

The other room was used as an office, from what Lang could see from the hallway. One wall was completely lined with books. As he gently pushed the door open, he saw a table used as a desk. A computer screen, papers, and open books covered its surface. It was the closest thing to disorder he had seen so far. He pushed the door wide. Papers covered the floor, blanketing a hooked rug. File folders spilled their guts across shelves, two chairs, and every other available space.

Lang pushed the door completely open and found the professor.

Sprawled into a corner behind the door, Blucher stared at the ceiling with lifeless eyes, his spectacles still in his hand. His face was twisted into an expression of abject horror, as though he had been fully aware of what was about to happen.

Although certain the man was dead, Lang stepped over the outstretched legs, crouched, and put his hand on the head, moving it forward. If there was any question as to survival of the victim, it was answered by the small red hole just at the juncture of skull and spine. The faint odor of cordite and burned hair, as well as the bluish marks around the wound, told Lang the gun's muzzle had been only inches from its target. An execution-style killing with a small caliber that would easily take a silencer.

The same thing with Don Huff.

And for the same reason.

From the coagulation of the small amount of blood and the lack of warmth of the body, Lang guessed Blucher had been dead for some time, perhaps since last night. He wished he could remember the lecture at The Farm. How long does it take for rigor mortis to set in? How long to disappear?

What did it matter? he told himself. Dead is dead.

The important thing was whatever the deceased had intended to show him. Was it still here? Lang looked around the devastation in the room. Someone had certainly been looking for something.

He stood, uncertain where to begin.

"Herr *Doktor* Blucher?"

The call came from downstairs.

A glance from the window showed a police car parked behind his. No doubt some well-meaning neighbor had noticed the open door and summoned the authorities.

With his picture in the paper as a fugitive, his presence at a murder scene would cause the police to draw unfortunate inferences, no matter that the forensics would show the man had been dead hours before Lang's arrival. If necessary, he would explain later. Right now, he needed to disappear.

A quick look confirmed his initial impression: There was only the one staircase, the one that would take him into the living room, where he could hear the investigating cops walking about.

Suppressing the urgency he felt, he walked slowly to the window away from the street, careful to make no sound. It took a second or two to figure out how the window latch worked before he slid it open. Ten or twelve feet below was the compost pile.

Lang was thankful he was not on a farm, where such a pile would contain things a great deal more rank than rotting grass clippings and the remains of last year's vegetable plants. Climbing through the screenless window, he held on to the sill with one hand while pulling the window as close to shut as he could. Not perfect, but at least the police's attention would not immediately be called to a gaping open window in the murder room. If he was lucky, they wouldn't notice it at all.

They would find his prints if they thought to dust a second-story window. It couldn't be helped.

He let go, and the pile of mounded vegetation broke his short fall. Dusting himself off, he looked up into a face staring openmouthed from a neighboring second-floor window. Shrieks of alarm followed him as he dashed for the fence's gate.

The police were coming out of the front door as Lang rounded the corner.

He pointed to his right. *"Schnell! Er hat da gelaufen!"* Quick! He ran that way!

Lang was relying on the theory that any command, if shouted with sufficient authority, would be obeyed by Germans. He was only partially correct. One cop dashed off in the direction Lang had indicated. The other blocked Lang from the street and his car, his eyes narrowing. Lang was certain he was comparing the man in front of him to the picture he had seen in the morning paper.

Reaching for his weapon, the police officer asked in English, "Who are you and what were you doing in the Herr Professor's house?"

Lang had been made as an American. He apparently growled when he should have spit.

Forgetting his linguistic shortcomings, Lang had the Glock in his hand and pointed at the German's head before the officer could open the flap of his holster. "Hold it right there. Reach your left hand across your body, take the gun by its butt, and let's see how far you can throw it."

Evidently not liking what he saw in the American's eyes, the cop did as he was told.

"Smart man! Now, the same with your radio."

The radio followed the gun in an arc over the fence behind Lang.

Giving quick glances in the direction in which the other officer had gone, Lang marched his prisoner to the police car, disabling the unit's radio before using the unfortunate man's handcuffs to secure him firmly to the steering wheel. A short search revealed the hood latch, enabling Lang to reach into the engine compartment and remove the distributor cap, which he tossed after the radio and gun.

Lang then departed in the opposite direction than that in which the other cop had gone.

On his way back to the hotel, he stopped at an apothecary, designated by a sign bearing a mortar and pestle. Inside, he purchased hair dye, cotton balls, an orthopedic corset, and a pair of premade eyeglasses. A few doors down the street, he finished replacing the clothes in his abandoned suitcase with ill-fitting, German-made jeans designed for no cowboy he had ever seen and Italian knit shirts. He was careful in his selection of sandals and the black socks European men insist on wearing with them.

Anyone looking for Langford Reilly, American, would see a blond man with jowls, slightly obese, wearing normal European leisure clothes. He would no longer resemble the picture on his passport, but that would not be a problem until he departed Europe. The Common Market had essentially abolished borders between its members.

On the way back to the car, three police vehicles wailed past, headed in the general direction of Blucher's house. Lang guessed a very embarrassed cop was trying to explain things to his superiors.

He was in the bathroom, applying the hair coloring, when Gurt got back to the hotel.

Noting his purchases spread out on the bed, she said, "Things did not go well at the Herr Professor's?"

Lang was looking at her reflection behind his in the mirror. "Keep your day job; you have no future as a comic."

Her puzzled expression drew an explanation. "Blucher's dead, killed the same way Don was. The police showed up while I was in the house. I left one of them handcuffed to the steering wheel of his cruiser."

Gurt did not seem particularly surprised. Getting in trouble with the police was becoming a habit of Lang's. "And the others?"

"One. He went chasing off somewhere."

She nodded, slowly digesting the news, before groping into her massive purse and producing a pack of cigarettes.

Turning from the mirror, he frowned as she lit it. "Those things will eventually kill you."

She ejected a stream of blue smoke. "Not if you get us shot by the police first."

Touché.

She glanced around for an ashtray, found one, and deposited the spent match. "Did you find anything at the professor's house besides the police?"

"Somebody had pretty thoroughly tossed it, papers scattered all over the place. Gestapo showed up before I had time to really look through any of it."

She sat on the edge of the bed, the hand without the cigarette in it twisting the small glass ashtray around and around. "I suppose we will be leaving Heidelberg soon."

He turned back to the mirror to inspect the dye job. "Shortly. As in 'shortly before the cops can get my picture spread even wider than the newspaper.' "

"And we go where? They will be looking at every airport."

Satisfied, Lang reached for the hotel's hair dryer. Before turning it on, he said, "How 'bout a nice drive— say, to Montsegur?"

She stubbed out her cigarette and raised her voice to be heard above the whine of the dryer. "Why Montsegur?"

He turned to face her, his hair multidirectional. "If we can find out what this guy Skorzeny was looking for, we may learn why someone wants us dead and who that someone might be."

CHAPTER FIFTEEN

Berlin (Wilhelmstrasse)
The Reich Chancellery
March 1944

Adolph Hitler usually worked standing up behind the massive marble desk. Today he was not only on his feet but pacing, waiting for the news that would arrive any moment. Plans for the defense of the French coast, crucial orders for the movement of troops, could wait just as he, the most powerful man in Europe, possibly the world, had waited.

Although he was expecting it, the knock at the door of his office made him jump.

An immaculately clad SS *Feldwerbel,* sergeant, stood in the doorway, arm outstretched in salute. Well over six feet, his blond hair and blue eyes could have been taken from a recruitment poster had the SS needed to seek members. *"Mein Fuhrer!"* he almost shouted, eyes locked onto a spot several feet above Hitler's head, *"Reichs-fuhrer* Himmler!"

Small by comparison, Heinrich Himmler entered, giving the same salute as the sergeant withdrew, quietly shutting the door. The light from the windows reflected from Himmler's glasses, making it impossible for Hitler to see the man's eyes. He was dressed in the black dress uniform of the SS: pressed jodhpurs stuffed into jackboots that gleamed with polish, a blouse resplendent with party, rather than military, decorations. The most feared man in Germany, Himmler commanded both Gestapo and SS as well as the latter's own intelligence agency, the *Sicherheitsdienst,* or SD. It was in connection with this latter function that Himmler had come today.

"Well?" Hitler asked, too eager to observe the pleasantries with which he normally greeted old comrades from the early Nazi party. "What have you found?"

Unfazed by the unusual brusqueness, Himmler smiled. "Good news, *Mein Führer!* The priest Kaas has confirmed the rumors."

Hitler looked puzzled. "Kaas?"

"The Vatican priest, the one whose family lives in Munich. He has confirmed the discovery made while excavating for the last Pope's tomb."

Hitler's eyes took on that faraway look Himmler knew so well. "Excellent! All we have to do is verify it for ourselves. That whining Pope in the Vatican will be silenced!"

Himmler was unsure exactly what difference papal pronouncements could possibly make. After all, the total army at the Vatican's command, Swiss Guards, numbered only a hundred or so, but he knew better than to question Germany's leader. Hitler was, after all, following the advice of his astrologer, the infallible prophet who had advised action in the Rheinland, Austria, and Czechoslovakia when the generals had wavered.

Hitler had a fascination for religion and the occult. Himmler winced when he thought how much had been spent to obtain the spear of Longinus, supposedly the spear that had pierced Christ's side but actually a very ordinary piece of ancient military hardware that looked suspiciously contemporary. Hitler had thought nothing of the expense and risk of sending a team to British-controlled Palestine in a fruitless search for the Ark of the Covenant. He had had four truckloads of what looked like pure junk removed from a cave in south-western France, a cave Himmler understood had served as the last refuge of some medieval group of heretics. Only the threat of a cross-Channel invasion had delayed a further expedition to southwestern France, where Hitler was convinced the Holy Grail was hidden.

But then, who was Himmler to question the mind that had defied first the political geniuses of Germany by becoming Chancellor perfectly legally, and then the best military minds by the bloodless annexation of what was rightfully Germany's? If *Der Führer* said the Pope needed to be cowed into silence, so be it.

"Imagine, Himmler," Hitler continued, "no longer having to be concerned about that damned Dago meddling with world opinion." He glanced around the room as though he anticipated seeing someone or something not there before. "In fact, Himmler, I have additional plans for the Pope."

Himmler recognized the onslaught of one of Hitler's famous monologues that frequently went on for hours. Feeling only slightly disloyal, Himmler tuned him out and began to make mental plans to accomplish his *Führer's* wishes.

". . . And you have just such a man," Hitler finished.

Uncertain if he had been standing there an hour or only a few minutes, Himmler came back to the real world. "Who would that be, *Mein Führer*?"

He was not surprised at the answer.

It was then Himmler had one of his few original ideas, an inspiration so brilliant he could not keep it to himself. "*Mein Führer,* why bother? Would it not make more sense to simply take this potentially bothersome Pope prisoner, do so secretly? That would shut him up. We could also ransom him off for the considerable treasure of the Catholic Church."

Himmler could see from the flare in Hitler's blue eyes that his plan was recognized as potentially brilliant.

"Say nothing of this," Hitler said slowly. "Let us keep it to ourselves while I consider it. First, though, let us see about obtaining this new discovery from under the Vatican."

The door had hardly closed behind Himmler when Hitler picked up the phone on his desk. "Get me General Wolff, SS commander in Rome."

CHAPTER SIXTEEN

Southwestern France
Montsegur
The present

How the hell had Skorzeny gotten up there? From where Lang stood, the south face of the hill went straight up, crowned by what could have been a pile of scree or the ruins of some sort of building. Two of the other sides, east and west, were even steeper. The north of the hill, Lang guessed, could have been conquered by experienced climbers hammering pitons into the few crevices in the white rock. That was it, he decided. The Germans had made a technical climb up the north face, then rappelled down to the cave's mouth.

"You will not be climbing that," Gurt said from the car, where she had retreated after one glance at the slopes.

"There is nothing left there, anyway," added Guillaume, the guide they had hired for the day. Montsegur was not exactly on the maps tourists bought. "Half the cave collapsed a few years ago, anyway."

Alternating his gaze between the hillside and the rock-strewn ground, Lang began to circle the incline. "Maybe so, but I still need to get up there."

Guillaume sighed with a Galic shrug that conveyed his frustration with people who did not understand. Americans never admitted something was impossible; they just went ahead and did it. In this case, ascent of Mont-segur was not only impossible but pointless. A number of nearby mountains had as good or better views of the tortured landscape of the Languedoc, with the Pyrenees little more than a blue dream in the west. Some of these views came along with small restaurants where the food was passably good and, if one was a local, you were not cheated on the wine.

Guillaume had mentioned this both to the tall German woman who had the sense to sit in the car out of the sun and to the taller American who did not. But nothing would dissuade him from *this* specific hill. His hand went to his pocket, as though assuring himself it would be available for the euros he had been promised. That was another characteristic of Americans, his favorite: They paid without haggling over the price.

Suddenly, the American was gone, vanished as suddenly as if he had evaporated.

Guillaume moved toward the place he had last seen him. Having a man disappear like that was frightening, almost as frightening as the chance Guillaume would not be paid if he didn't reappear.

Then he was there again, seeming to step right out of the rock of the mountainside.

"Gurt," Lang called, "come take a look at this!"

Gurt's height made her look as though she were un-folding as she got out of the car and walked over.

"Look." Lang was pointing.

"It looks like a small hole to me," Gurt said, careful not to slip on loose rocks.

"A hole, yes," Lang said. "But notice the edges."

Gurt reached an exploratory hand out to run along the sides of the opening. "They are smooth, as if they were carved."

Lang sank to his knees and began to pull rocks away from the orifice. Within minutes, a symmetrically arched aperture about four feet high was visible.

Still kneeling, Lang crept forward. "This isn't natural, either. There's some sort of path inside."

And for the second time he disappeared, returning with a grin on his face. "Stairs. Leading to the top, I'll bet."

"Now we know how Skorzeny got up there," Gurt observed.

Lang stood, dusting himself off. "Not this way. There's rubble, stones, dust piled up inside." He turned to Guillaume, who was showing renewed interest. "You said part of the cave collapsed a few years back. Do you remember when?"

Guillaume frowned. Part of the roof of a cave, visible from the road but of no use to anyone except this American, falls in. Rocks fall down mountains, sometimes blocking the road; some days it rains, others it does not. Who keeps track of such things? It is difficult enough to decide if temperature and rainfall have combined to produce good vintages and rich clover that, by way of the cows, will be converted to cheese.

But the American wanted to know, and the American would decide the question of whether there would be a gratuity above the price agreed upon.

Guillaume screwed up his face in thought. "It was

shortly after Easter the year my sister's first child was born."

Lang waited, hoping for a date of somewhat more general recognition.

"Two, no, three years ago," Guillaume said, now nodding. "We made much rain." He spread his arms as though precipitation came in armloads. "The Aud flooded and much mud washed onto the road from the hills. I was driving past one day and noticed I could see sky where before there had been only the top of the cave."

"The same thing that caused mud slides caused water to fill the tunnel inside that mountain," Lang said, "washing away the rocks and junk that covered the entrance that leads to the top."

"You hope," Gurt said. "Part of the tunnel could also have washed away. If that is actually a tunnel."

Lang was bending over, looking inside again. "Has to be. Place was besieged for over a year, if I remember from the last time I was in the area. The Cathars had to have a way to get supplies and water up there. If there had been an outside way to the top, the king's army would have found it long before a year."

"They also would have found that entrance," Gurt said.

"It was probably pretty well hidden behind rocks and vegetation. Even if the entrance was found, no more than one man at a time could have gotten through, and the stairs wind counterclockwise so that only a defender at the top could use his right hand, his sword arm."

Lang looked from Gurt to Guillaume and back again. "Well?"

Gurt squatted, duck-walking into the tunnel.

Lang followed, pausing only long enough to ask Guillaume, "Coming?"

Guillaume shook his head. It was a long way to the top, if the stairs were sufficiently intact to be usable.

Inside, a gray light filtered down a narrow, round shaft no more than three feet across. Carved into the wall were steps, each no more than a foot long and perhaps ten inches wide. They ended in rubble around the first turn. It took Lang only a couple of minutes to realize a slip in the dimness was likely to be fatal.

He stopped. "Let's go back down. I'd feel safer with a couple of flashlights and rope."

Gurt was backing down the stairs uncertainly. "Rope?"

"Tie ourselves together so if one slips, the other can arrest the fall."

"Or fall, too."

Gurt, the optimist.

Although he missed his wife, Fabian, Guillaume was glad she had chosen this particular week to visit her sister in Rochefort. Now there was no need to tell her how much money the American had paid him this afternoon and he could enjoy as much of it as he wanted. Or all of it, for that matter.

That was why he had made an unaccustomed trip to the town's bistro to let someone else prepare his dinner while he drank wine and shared local gossip in the cool of sunset. Moving inside the restaurant, he was wondering how much of the American's money he should put aside to buy a gift for Fabian, if any. Although only about half of the place's eight tables were occupied, a man he had never seen before motioned him over, indicating he should have a seat.

"You are Guillaume Lerat?" the man asked in French marred only by an accent Guillaume had never heard before.

A quick look at the stranger's clothes also told Guillaume that the man was not local. No one around here

could afford American-made jeans. Guillaume nodded
and gave the man a smile, fueled partially from the wine
he had consumed and partially from the prospect of another well-paying customer.

"You are a licensed guide for this area."

It was a statement, not a question.

Guillaume nodded again. "Yes."

Not quite true. Being a licensed guide required the
payment of an annual fee, one much more expensive
than simply having a commercial driver's permit. But
then, who could distinguish between a professional guide
who drove his customers around the area and a driver
who simply pointed out the sights as he drove? Only
governments could make such distinctions.

Instead of asking about specific locations, the man
glanced furtively around the room before laying his hand
on the table. Beneath his palm was a stack of euros. No
matter how hard he stared, the man's hand prevented
Guillaume from ascertaining exactly how much money
he was seeing.

"You had customers today?" the man asked.

Guillaume was trying, with little success, not to appear overly focused on the bills on the table. *"Oui."*

The man thumbed the currency, letting Guillaume
see the thickness of the stack. "Who were they?"

Guillaume's eyes flicked to the man's before returning to the money. "Information, like anything else, has
its price."

The man across the table twisted his lips into what
might have been intended to be a smile. It reminded
Guillaume of a dead shark he had once seen washed up
on the beach. He used one hand to slip a bill from the
pile. "I agree. Who were your customers today?"

Guillaume pursed his lips, trying to feign indifference

even as he slipped the money into his pocket. "A man, an American, and a woman. I think she was German."

He had the distinct impression the stranger was not surprised.

He dealt another bill. "Where did they go?"

"They were interested in the ruins of old castles and fortresses."

This time there was no move to hand over more money. "I know *where* they went. I want to know what in particular interested them, where was their attention?"

For an instant, Guillaume considered the possibility of holding out for more money. A look at the stranger's face told him that might be both unwise and unhealthy. He told him about Montsegur.

Guillaume's dinner, *demi poule en vin blanc*, half a chicken roasted with vegetables in white wine sauce, arrived as the stranger stood up, pushing the remainder of the euros across the table. "I paid you to remember. This is to forget—forget you ever saw me."

For the first time in his life, Guillaume was oblivious to food and a bottle of wine in front of him. Hardly noticing the savory aroma, he watched the man's back as he walked across the square and disappeared into the deepening shadows. Minutes ago, Guillaume had been ravenous. His appetite had somehow disappeared.

CHAPTER SEVENTEEN

Southwestern France
Montsegur
The next morning

Lang had insisted on spending the night in Lyon, where
they had taken up the earlier part of the evening shopping for equipment: several lengths of nylon rope, flashlights, heavy work boots, and a grappling hook, the sort
mountaineers might use. He then visited a camera shop.
It was only when he backed out of the parking space on
the town square that he remembered he had made similar purchases at both stores the year previous, only to
leave them on a hillside.

That, as they say, was another story.

Before the sun was up, they were on their way back to
the same hill they had visited the day before.

Gurt climbed out of the car, a large, comfortable Mercedes with such little power, Lang was certain that was
the reason the class and number were not on the trunk,

as was customary with other models of the marque. The factory was ashamed of the thing.

Gurt yawned and drained the dregs of cold coffee from a paper cup. "This has been here how long? Seven, eight hundred years?"

Lang was unloading the trunk. "The ruins? Yeah, I guess so."

She wadded the cup with a crunching sound and tossed it into the rubbish bag hanging from the glove box. "Then why so early do we come?"

Lang shut the lid with a soft thump. "I'd just as soon finish whatever we're gonna do before anyone knows we're here."

Gurt followed him into the entrance they had found. She squatted as he tied the rope around his waist and stuck a flashlight in his belt. Climbing the first two steps, he swung the hook on a rope, tossing it upward. He was rewarded with the dull clunk of metal on stone as the hook fell back.

Two more attempts and he gave up. "Shaft's too narrow; I can't swing the rope with enough velocity to get to the top."

Gurt tied one end of rope to her belt. "We climb, then."

Lang shook his head. "*I* climb. If I fall, I want to be sure there's someone to drive me to the nearest hospital."

"If you fall from there, a hospital you will not need," she observed.

Lang tried to ignore the truth in her observation as he sat so that his back was against one wall and his feet against the opposite. Using hands and feet pressed against the stone, he began to work his way upward and then stopped, reaching to the back of his belt.

He pulled out the Glock, holding it where she could

see it. "I need to get rid of all the weight I can. Take this."

She caught it neatly, stuffing it into the back of her pants. She watched until he was nearly indistinguishable in the shadows above her head, playing out rope as he climbed. Soon she could mark his progress only by the grunts and exhalations of breath echoing down the shaft. Finally, it was quiet.

"Lang?"

There was a tug on the rope. "Gimme a minute. There! I've secured the rope to a boulder. Now I can pull you up."

Although she knew he could not see, she shook her head. "A pull I do not need. I went through the same training as you and am even younger than you. I can climb myself."

There was a properly abashed silence from above as she began.

The top of the shaft opened onto what Lang guessed had been the courtyard. The destruction of the Cathars' redoubt had been complete: Cut stones were strewn in a semicircle, few of which still rested on another. The keep's tower had presented more of a problem, probably because of the attackers' impatience with tearing it down starting at the top. Instead, it looked as though it had been split lengthwise. Behind the courtyard yawned the mouth of a cave, not particularly deep, but as tall as Lang guessed the keep had been, located so that, once encircled by the outer wall, the defenders of this hill would have had a fortress assailable from only one direction.

As their guide had said yesterday, part of the top of the hill had fallen in, leaving the center of the cavern open to the sky and filling the interior with rubble of white stone. Anything that had been under the collapsing part of the cave's roof was going to remain there.

Without spoken agreement, Gurt and Lang separated, each slowly walking along the inner perimeter of the wall and into the shadowy darkness of the cave. Since the collapse, the white stone sides had become streaked, crumbling under the relentless force of the elements. Vines had managed to take root in what appeared to be solid rock. If this was the cave shown in the photograph on Blucher's CD, any inscriptions on its walls were going to be difficult to find. In another year or two, exfoliation would obliterate them forever.

Lang swept his light from the top of the cave downward and across the rubble-strewn floor. Twice he stopped, thinking the beam had picked up what he was looking for, only to find that the natural fissures in the walls could briefly assume the appearance of human-made letters just as rocks on the floor took on the look of handmade objects. If Skorzeny had filled four truckloads from this cave, either he was taking largely geological specimens or the cave had deteriorated greatly in the last sixty years.

Problem was, which was it?

"Lang, here!" Gurt's voice had the tinge of an echo.

Impatiently, Lang picked his way around piles of debris to where she stood, her light steady on a section of wall no more than four or five feet above the floor. There was no doubt he was looking at man-made letters over holes carved into the stone.

"Is like a bee, bee . . ." Gurt was pointing to rows of evenly spaced holes cut into the rock.

"Honeycomb," Lang supplied, forgetting the inscription for a moment as he inserted a fist into one of the holes.

It was about two feet deep and perhaps ten inches across.

Gurt looked puzzled. "A rack for wine?"

Lang shook his head. "Wine would have been some-where underground to keep it as cool as possible. This would have been a library."

"For books?"

"For scrolls, I think."

"They did not have books?"

Lang nodded absently. "Of course they did. You've seen those beautifully illuminated Bibles. But in ancient times, libraries, like the one at Alexandria, would have had racks like these where scrolls could be stored in clay tubes."

The mystery of what Skorzeny may have needed trucks to haul away may have been answered, but that raised an even more perplexing question, one Lang voiced.

"Problem is, why would Cathars in the thirteenth century be writing on loose parchment when the rest of Europe had started using bindings?"

Gurt pointed to the carved letters. "There the expla-nation may be."

He reached out and touched some sort of growth that obscured part of the inscription. "We're gonna have to cut this away."

Gurt grabbed several sprigs and started to pull before Lang could grab her arm. "Cut it, not pull it loose. Shal-low as those roots are, they have to be widespread. Yank them hard enough and the face of the rock will crumble."

Nodding her understanding, she handed him her flash-light and took a small knife from her pocket. Where had she gotten it? He had never seen it before and, harmless enough, it was not something that would have cleared air-port security. Whatever its source, it sliced cleanly through each branch and root. In minutes, the wall in front of Lang was clear of vegetation.

Lang stepped back, the better to play his flashlight across the lines of letters. His first impression was of precision. This inscription was not some ancient graffiti scratched into rock but the measured characters of a professional mason. Time, moisture, and other natural forces had effectively erased several letters, their former presence noted only by blank spaces.

IMPERATORIULIANACCUSAT (——) REBILLISREXUS
IUDEAIUMIUBITREGI (——)UNUSDEISEPELIT

"Julian, Emperor . . . ," he read aloud.

Gurt followed the flashlight's beam with interest. "Who?"

Without looking away, Lang said, "Julian. Roman emperor in the late fourth century. In Christian writing, he's always referred to as 'Julian the Apostate.' He was the first non-Christian emperor since Constantine, the last pagan, reinstituted the persecution of the followers of Christ."

Gurt looked closer, playing her own light along the lines. "This was here cut by a Roman emperor?"

Absorbed by the antiquity of what he was reading for the second time, Lang shook his head. "Most likely at his order." He pointed to a word. " 'IUBIT,' he commands. I doubt Julian ever came here after he took the throne. Before then, he was governor of this part of Gaul. He wasn't emperor long. An inscription attributed to him is rare."

"How do we know it wasn't actually written here by the Cathars? Anyone could have, er, forged such writing. It could be a forgery. Then what?"

"Send it to Dan Rather."

"Who?"

"Never mind."

Lang frowned. Either he was misreading the Latin or something was wrong.

A light breeze hummed across the opening above while he ran his fingers along the words.

"What does it say?" Gurt asked.

"I'm not sure. I can't tell, for instance, whether this word, *accusat,* is missing the ending. It's chipped off. I can't tell if someone is making an accusation, made an accusation, or of whom. Likewise, the word *regi.* It has something to do with a palace, a feminine, first-declension noun. But without the last two or three letters, I can only guess if whatever Julian's talking about *belongs* to the palace, is *in* the palace, and so forth."

Gurt understood that the endings of nouns denoted not only the gender of the thing in question but also case—nominative, genitive, dative, or accusative. Although frequently dropped in conversation, German still had endings that indicated whether the thing possessed was being subjected to or was simply mentioned. The few remaining equivalents in English were like the " 's" added to denote possession—that is, the dog's bone or the "s" or "es" to create the plural.

"Is Latin like German in that the whole sentence has to be read before you can put the words into the order that makes sense in English?" Gurt asked.

"No," Lang responded, too occupied to engage in a discussion of linguistics.

In German sentences containing more than a single clause, the verbs were frequently stacked at the end so that the reader had to pair them up and determine what made the most sense. This, of course, in addition to infinitives that were not only split but permanently rent asunder. A German would to the railroad station quickly go, for example.

"There's not enough light to read all of this in context," Lang finally said, putting down his flashlight. "If you'll move your beam slowly, I'll copy down the words and then we can photograph them."

It took Lang about ten minutes to carefully transcribe the inscription, underlining letters that were too worn or chipped to positively identify. He then used the camera he had purchased the previous night to take two shots directly in front of the carving before moving to each side, letting the small flash attachment cast shadows that would make the words more legible.

He was stepping up to take close-ups when he and Gurt exchanged puzzled looks, unsure if the other heard the sound that seemed to be getting closer, the beating *whup-whup* of a small, non-turbine-powered helicopter. What, Lang wondered, would be so pressing in this rural community as to justify a chopper?

The answer came when the sound became stationary directly overhead. As one, both looked up to the jagged section of sky that showed through the now-open cave roof. Lang recognized the aircraft hovering like a huge insect as one of the smaller Sikorsky models available for personal transportation worldwide. From the angle at which Lang was looking, he could not see the identifying letters or numbers.

"Who . . . ?"

Lang's question was cut short as a man, his face masked by goggles, leaned out of the open doorway of the 'copter and dropped something. For only a millisecond, the object was silhouetted against the sky, but that was long enough.

Lang shoved Gurt into one of the natural niches in the wall, shallow but better than nothing. The second he heard an impact nearby, he sprung. He had less than five seconds, considerably less if the man in the aircraft above had enough experience to count off two or three so the weapon would explode on impact. Lang saw the

plastic cylinder perhaps eight or nine inches on the cave
floor not a foot away. In a single motion, Lang scooped
it up and underhanded it toward the opening of the cave
mouth. He watched it describe a gentle parabola before
he threw himself flat, ignoring the sharp edges of rock.

He never knew whether he hit the floor of the cave before the ground shook with an explosion that, even from
outside the cave, sent rock fragments buzzing through
the air like angry bees.

Instantly on his feet, he raced to where Gurt was
shaking her head, attempting to clear her ears of the
concussion. "What in . . . ?"

He propelled her toward the opening. "Later."

No time to explain that he had instantly recognized
the object launched from the overhead chopper as an
"offensive" hand grenade as distinguishable from the
more familiar fragmentation "pineapple" that was basically unchanged since World War Two. The grenade the
unknown people overhead had chosen had the same
"pin"-activated fuse with the same delay, but contained
high explosives in a plastic wrapper rather than cast iron
intended to shatter. The choice of such a weapon revealed a plan: to use the MkIIA1 offensive grenade's
content to collapse the cave, burying him and Gurt alive
if they were not already dead from the shrapnel-like
chips of rock. Either way, they would never be found.

Her hand in his, they sprinted across the courtyard.
Behind them, a muffled explosion told them the men
above had no intention of giving up.

The malignant shadow of the helicopter beat them to
the shaft, its patient hovering an announcement that
there was no escape. Lang glanced around. To try descending through the narrow hole would be suicidal.
Even if a near miss failed to collapse the tunnel, its tight
confines would make it impossible to avoid the rock

shards. Between their escape route and the cave was open ground littered with the evenly carved stones that had been the wall. There was not so much as a tree or bush to provide shelter.

The helicopter's passenger leaned out again, lobbing another grenade, and Lang threw Gurt to the ground, partially covering her with his own body. The following explosion seemed to jar even his teeth, but he was thankful he was still alive. The cordite-tainted air was welcomed as he forced breath back into lungs the concussion had emptied.

Almost before the shower of dirt and rock splinters settled, Gurt pushed him aside and sprang to her feet, a sure target for the stone chips with which the next grenade would fill the air. Lang snatched at an ankle, missed, and stumbled to his feet in pursuit.

His legs refused to obey his commands, moving at a pace that seemed almost leisurely. But then, everything seemed sluggish, to take on the dreamlike quality of a film in slow motion.

As gracefully as any ballerina, Gurt spun as she drew the Glock from her belt, making it an extension of her outstretched arms to point upward. The man in the helicopter used both hands also, one to hold the grenade, the other to pull the pin. As he extended his arm to drop high explosives directly onto Gurt, two shots came, so close as to be indistinguishable.

The man leaning out of the chopper stood erect, his mouth forming a perfect O, as though he was astonished either at the two holes centered neatly above his eyes or the fact that the hand grenade was still in his hand. Then he disappeared from the doorway.

Lang screamed a warning, knowing what was about to happen.

For what seemed forever, nothing did.

Then the helicopter dissolved into a fiery orange ball that reached all the way to the ground. The force of the explosion knocked Lang onto his back. The last thing he remembered before everything went dark was the transformation of flame in the sky to a greasy, roiling black cloud.

Lang reckoned he had been unconscious only a few seconds. He sat up and looked around. The blast had knocked him flat and out of the hailstorm of flying debris. Unidentifiable pieces of metal, still smoking, surrounded him. Shakily, he got to his feet and realized that not all the wreckage was inorganic. Bile rose in his throat as he stepped over the charred remains of a human hand, wedding ring still attached.

"Gurt!"

There was no answer.

Trying to swallow both nausea and growing panic, he forced himself to make an orderly search of concentric circles. After a couple of minutes, hope flickered like a candle in a breeze. After twenty, it died.

Explosions can do weird things, he told himself. Stories of victims of World War II's bombing of London were replete with women dashing into the streets after a direct hit, unharmed other than the fact that their clothing had been completely blown off, of men finding themselves buried under rubble blocks away from where they had been when the bomb had hit.

No doubt true, but there was no Gurt, bomb-denuded or otherwise.

Despair became fear—fear he would find her, or, worse, some grisly part of her. The thought finally overcame his resistance to the urge. He knelt and vomited his breakfast.

He staggered to his feet, swaying like a drunk as his empty stomach continued to cramp and convulse. His view of the cave and of the surrounding white hills blurred with tears. He had never felt so alone as on this hilltop an ocean away from home. Not even when Dawn died. At least then he had had ample time to prepare. Gurt had been snatched away in an instant.

He lifted his chin, looking into a sky so innocently blue it was hard to believe that, just minutes before, it had been filled with death. He forced his mounting grief aside for the moment, thinking as he had been trained to do so many years ago.

Even as remote as this area was, someone had most likely heard the series of explosions, possibly seen the fireball of the helicopter. He must assume the authorities were on their way. With only fragments, it would take months to even establish the number of people who had perished here, if in fact it could be ascertained at all by time-consuming comparisons of DNA. Unless that DNA had been previously recorded, it would serve only to number the dead, not identify them.

Lang moved mechanically, straining to keep his mind concentrated on the tasks at hand. He stooped to retrieve the camera from where it had fallen when the blast had knocked him down. Surprisingly, it was unbroken. Using the rope still in place, he descended through the shaft. Unlocking the car's trunk, he took out Gurt's purse. His control momentarily slipped as a rogue memory of how he had teased her about its size interrupted the routine and tears wet his cheeks. Checking the bag's contents to make certain it contained nothing of significance, he returned it to the trunk. Sliding into the front seat, he opened the glove box, pocketing only Gurt's passport. No need to involve her now.

The rented car would be traced to Joel Couch. His passport and the few human remains on the mountain should make Lang Reilly officially dead at least until

DNA proved otherwise. That should keep the Frankfurt Police, if not all of Interpol, quiet for the time being.

Joel Couch would seek revenge.

He took a final look at the hilltop, from which smoke was still rising. Fists clenched, he spoke aloud through gritted teeth. "You bastards, you fucking bastards! No matter who you are, this world is too small for both of us, and I don't plan on leaving."

He took some small comfort from the fact that the threat was not idle. He had tracked the killers of his sister and nephew, and, if necessary, he would end his days in pursuit of whoever was responsible for Gurt.

His hand involuntarily went to the pocket where he had put the paper with the Latin phrases on it. He'd get them this time, too. At least now he had a starting point.

Pocketing the car keys, he turned his back on the Mercedes and began to trudge along the narrow country road.

He had gone less than a mile before a pair of police cars, sirens wailing, blurred past, headed in the direction from which he had come. Minutes later, he hitched a ride in a tractor-towed wagon dusty with remains of winter wheat. Turning his back to the machine's driver, he released the tight grip on his emotions and sobbed.

CHAPTER EIGHTEEN

Frankfurt am Main
141 Mosel Strasse
The next day

Reavers put both hands flat on the desk and stared at them. "Gurt dead? You sure?"

Lang nodded wearily. "There wasn't enough left to ID anybody without DNA."

Reavers glanced up without moving his head, a move that made his eyes look even more like those of a raptor. "But you searched anyway?"

Lang knew it wasn't his fault, but he couldn't shake the feeling there had been something he could have done. "Other than the cave, there wasn't any place to hide. If she'd been there, I would have seen her."

"And you're going to continue to try to find the sum'bitches who killed Huff." It was not a question. "God knows them cheap bastards in Washington aren't going to give us the budget to do it. Just once, I'd like to think the security of the United States and our agents is worth more than funding some turnip museum in Iowa."

"Damn right I am. When I know that, I'll know who's responsible for Gurt."

"Tell me again what I can do."

Lang shrugged, the trivial nature of his requests overshadowed by Gurt's death. "I'd like to keep the Couch identity, maybe acquire one other, preferably a citizen of an EU country. As for the credit cards, I can guarantee payment—"

The CIA chief of station made a dismissive gesture. "Forgit paying the credit cards, pard'nuh. Budget cutbacks or not, we don' chintz when it comes to trackin' down people who hurt our people, you remember?"

Lang remembered the Agency of the eighties probably destroying countless forests with the paperwork required to justify any remotely unusual expense in anticipation of periodic congressional inquiries. Apparently, there really had been a peace dividend after all.

Or politicians occupied with other matters.

" 'Xactly how you plannin' on finding whoever you're lookin' for?"

Lang sat back in his chair and shrugged. "There was an inscription on the cave wall, something about an indictment and the palace of the sole God."

"You plannin' on trackin' a bunch o' killers from some sorta religious claptrap?"

Lang sighed deeply, all too aware of the task ahead. "That carving dates back to the fourth century; they would have been there when Skorzeny looted whatever was there. He must have seen the same words."

"So?"

"I can read them, know what the words say. I need to figure out what they *mean*. I'd guess the Germans did. If

I follow wherever they lead, maybe I'll find out who wants me not to."

Reavers picked a pen from a cup on his desk, working it through his fingers like a magician about to perform a trick. "You're guessing the sum'bitches killed Huff an' Gurt are tryin' to protect some religious secret sixteen hundred years old?"

"It's the only lead I've got."

Lang felt no need to point out he had nearly been killed a year ago by people trying to keep an even older secret. "It's either that or some organization trying to prevent identifying old Nazis."

The Agency man returned the pen to the cup and gave Lang pretty much the same look he might have given someone seriously delusional. "I don' see it, but okay." He opened a drawer and fumbled through it. "One more thing . . ." He slid a square object across the desktop. "Take it."

Lang picked it up. "A BlackBerry? Thanks, I already have one."

"With built-in scrambling and a global positioning system? You set you'sef a three-digit code, you press it, an' we know not only the caca has hit the ole ventilating device but 'xactly where it struck. They're special made for us."

Lang dropped it into his pocket. "It would be your ass, the Agency finds out you let me have this."

Reavers leaned back in his chair, grinning. "Or the passports, or the ID. Hell, at my age, gittin' fired ain't much threat. Tell ya, pard'nuh, best I can, I'm committed to findin' whoever killed that li'l gal."

Lang could only imagine how Gurt would react to being referred to in the familiar diminutive. "I appreciate you getting involved."

" 'Involved'? Hell, I'm committed."

Lang stood, thinking the conversation at an end. "Involved, committed. I value any help you can give."

Reavers stood also, extending a hand. "Y'know the difference between 'involved' an' 'committed'?"

Lang had a feeling he was going to learn.

"Ever' mornin' I have *Speck und Ei,* bacon and eggs. The chicken's involved, but the pig, he's committed."

The Lone Star State's very own Jay Leno.

CHAPTER NINETEEN

Frankfurt am Main
Dusseldorf Am Hauptbahnhof Strasse
That evening

Lang lay on the bed, staring at the abstract designs of the cracks in the ceiling without seeing them. He didn't notice the pulsating colors that came through the room's only window from neon signs outside advertising sex shops, pornographic movies, and cheap restaurants. If asked, it would have been doubtful if he could have named the cheap railroad hotel in which he was spending the night.

He was far too lost in his own self-pity.

First his wife, Dawn, then his sister and nephew. Now Gurt. All snatched away, exited from his life as if his existence were some cosmic revolving door turning in a single direction. Though neither religious nor superstitious, he waited for the other preordained shoe to fall.

Gurt. Her blond hair swirled around her face like a

halo as she spun around to display the dress she had just
bought. He smelled the musk of their lovemaking and
felt the comforting warmth of her body next to his.
Without realizing it, he smiled at some of her more egre-
gious grammatical or idiomatic faux pas. The thrust and
parry of their conversations, the smell of her cooking.

Gone.

Gone forever.

He wondered if the pain would have been greater or
less had she agreed to marry him.

The same, he supposed.

If he ever needed consolation, it was now. He held his
watch up, squinting to see the face. Just past five in the
afternoon in Atlanta. Getting out of bed, he crossed the
room to the electrical outlet and his BlackBerry, plugged
into the current converter to charge. He called up the directory as he recrossed the room and punched the call
button.

Two rings later, a man's voice answered as clearly as
though speaking from across the room instead of an
ocean.

"Francis?"

The voice warmed with pleasure. "Is this my favorite
heretic?"

Lang felt better already. "Francis, I've got some bad
news."

He related what had happened since Huff's death,
omitting only references to the Agency. He went into
detail describing what had happened at Montsegur.

"You're sure she's dead?"

Anger flashed through him like a lightning bolt and
was gone just as quickly. The second time in a few hours
somebody had asked. What did they think, that he just
assumed Gurt had died and abandoned her?

"I'm sure I couldn't find her on that hilltop, Francis.

I mean, the biggest human thing I saw was a severed hand, which, by the way, wasn't hers."

There was such a long silence, Lang was beginning to think the connection was broken.

Then: "What are you going to do?"

Lang was sure of only one thing. "Find whoever is responsible."

There was concern in Francis's reply. "Isn't that something best left to the police?"

Lang swallowed a sharp retort and made himself speak slowly. "I can't exactly walk into some French cop shop and announce I was there when three or more people were killed. By the time the Froggies finished their investigations, they'd be sure to turn up the fact that I'm wanted by at least the Frankfurt Polizei, if not in Heidelberg, too."

"Lang, acting out of revenge may not be wise."

"Francis, I know you're in the mercy and forgiveness business, but I have no intention of turning the other cheek right now."

Another pause.

"Lang, you know I'll help any way I can. I loved Gurt, too. I'll be praying for her soul."

"Better you should pray for whoever I find killed her."

"That carving on the cave wall—what do you make of it?"

Lang knew he was being manipulated, steered away from the subject of Gurt. "Not sure. In fact, why don't you write it down? I'd appreciate your thoughts."

He read it, careful to spell out noun endings.

"Got it," Francis said. "Doesn't make a lot of sense, translates as something like 'Julian, Emperor, orders that the accusation against Jews' king be interred in the palace of the sole god.' Without the endings, can't be sure. Sure you haven't screwed up the declensions again?"

The old familiar sparring made Lang think he might get through his grief somehow. *"Decamo bona verba."*

"I never said you didn't speak good words, it's mixing a classical language with the Southern accent that makes your diction difficult. You speak . . ." This time Lang was aware he was smiling. The priest was capable of miracles. ". . . *ore rotundo,* as Horace described gifted orators." He turned serious. "What about the *solus dei* and the Jews' king?"

"Christ, of course, was mocked at his crucifixion by being called 'king of the Jews,' but the phrase could refer to some actual Old Testament king like David or Solomon. Likewise, the 'sole god' could very well refer to the one God of Jews, Muslims, and Christians."

Lang was thinking as he stretched out on the bed. "That presents something of a problem: Julian repealed Constantine's laws granting Christians the right to worship. He hated them, felt they were diverting Rome from its heritage of pantheism."

"What else can you tell me about the man?"

"Like all literate Romans, he loved riddles, and I have a feeling we may have one here. What is the palace of the sole god?"

"Could be in the Christian concept of heaven," Francis speculated.

"But how do you bury someone in heaven? I think there's something more literal there."

"We can figure it out over a dinner at Manuel's."

Lang was suddenly homesick for the first time he could remember. The thought of overcooked food and an atmosphere of pseudo-intellectualism had never been so appealing. He knew what he was going to do.

"Reserve us a booth for night after next. I'm coming home."

CHAPTER TWENTY

Atlanta, Georgia
Lindberg MARTA Station
Two days later

His mind told Lang it was time to go to bed, but the sun was still bright as he stepped from the train. He could have taken a cab, but Atlanta's rapid rail, though not particularly rapid, made the run from the airport in less time than a taxi, was cleaner, and obviated the necessity of speaking Swahili, Tutsi or whatever other African dialect was native to the driver. Lang supposed the city's Cab Bureau, in Atlanta's tradition of Civil Rights Mecca, felt requiring English of its licensees to be discriminatory.

At the top of the escalator, he found one hack driver who at least seemed to comprehend "Peachtree Road" and got in the back.

Lang was not expecting a reception, certainly not one from the SWAT team.

As the cab turned into the condominium's circular

drive, a police car pulled in behind it while a van blocked the other end. The concierge and Lang's neighbors gawked in awe as ten helmeted men clad in body armor, wearing an assortment of windbreakers denoting police, FBI, and U.S. Marshal's Service, and pointing Mac 10 machine guns advanced on the terrified cabdriver as though Osama bin Laden were the passenger. Lang took a quick look from the rear window in time to see a thin black man in a suit climb out of an unmarked third car.

He immediately understood: The Federal Republic of Germany had officially translated its displeasure at the airport incident into an extradition request.

Hands raised, he stepped from the cab. "A pleasure to see you again, Detective."

Rouse grinned maliciously, motioning to the armed men. "Pleasure's all mine, believe me, Mr. Reilly. This time you ain' gonna wiseass yo' way outta trouble. Us Keystone Kops been holding an international want on you, jes' waitin' fo' you to come home. Sho nuff, heah you come, struttin' through the airport like you owned the place."

Lang kicked himself in his mental rear end. As soon as he had presented his passport to Immigration, he had removed his disguise of eyeglasses, jowls made with cotton balls, and a stuffed corset that added twenty or thirty pounds to his appearance. The blond hair alone wasn't enough to fool the surveillance cameras.

Two of the policemen roughly spun Lang around, pulling his arms behind him and snapping on the cuffs.

Reilly gave the black detective a smile he certainly didn't feel as he was quickly patted down. "I'll always have you to thank for the lovely trip to Germany I'm about to take."

Rouse bobbed his head. "You most certainly welcome, Mr. Reilly. City gonna be a lot more peaceful, you gone."

One of the cops held the contents of Lang's pockets. "He's clean. Keys, wallet, two BlackBerrys."

Rouse looked incredulous. "*Two* of them expensive phones, Mr. Reilly?"

"Every lawyer has two so he can talk out of both sides of his mouth. Can you get your bullyboys here to pay the cab for me?"

"Why, sho'. Take your bag inside and have the man put it yo' 'partment, too."

Lang had a small ray of gratitude, thanks to himself for putting the Couch passport into his suitcase when he removed his disguise. Traveling under a false passport would have earned him weeks, if not months, fending off questions from the State Department, the Transportation Safety Administration, and an alphabet soup of other bureaus, agencies, and administrations he had never heard of.

The inside of the police car smelled of Lysol and vomit.

On Garnett Street, just south of downtown, was the jail, or in the parlance of current political correctness, the City of Atlanta Pretrial Detention Center. The name was misleading. Not only were local miscreants confined there, but the federal government leased space to temporarily house a few of its involuntary guests. A modern curved facade of red brick faced a neighborhood of weary concrete-block buildings, enlivened only by flashing neon that proclaimed "City Bonding Co.", "ABC Bonds," or, surprisingly original, "Born Free Bonding."

The outside of the edifice was the only thing that looked new. Inside, linoleum tiles were unevenly worn, walls displayed tiresomely similar graffiti, and the smell of disinfectant was strong enough to bring tears to

Lang's eyes. He was not surprised that the two officers did not even have to use keys to gain entrance to the supposedly secure areas. The locks had long ago been destroyed by inmates, perhaps the same ones who had knocked out half the glass outside the barred windows. A former governor might well have had this place in mind when he commented that what the penal system needed was a better class of prisoner.

After being probed and prodded in a strip search, Lang exchanged his cordovan loafers for paper shower slippers. Slacks and polo shirt were duly tagged and he was issued a bright orange, beltless jumpsuit at least two sizes too large before being shackled hand and foot and taken up in an elevator that had the odor of human sweat.

"Hey," he said to one of two guards. "I get a phone call, right?"

The man, a tall and muscular black, never took his eyes off the elevator's control panel. "You gits all the phone calls you want. There's a pay phone in the rec room, and you gits four hours a day watchin' TV, playin' chess or checkers, or readin' magazines."

"A regular social club," the other man sneered.

"Pay phone?" Lang asked. "They took all my change, along with everything else in my pockets."

The big black man was still intent on the panel. "I'd say that there's a real shame."

Both men chuckled over what sounded like an old, familiar joke.

Although he had been here many times to visit clients, Lang had only seen the spacious if featureless visiting rooms where lawyers were allowed unrestricted access to their clients. He had never seen the tiered cell blocks, four-story stacks of cages abutted by narrow catwalks. He also had never been aware of the noise, an endless hubbub of screams, shouts, and curses that seemed to be amplified in the confined space.

He was being escorted between his guards. The one in front, the one with the shaved scalp, stopped and examined a ring of keys on his belt. Lang looked at the door to the cell, noting that the locking mechanism consisted of a conventional lock that could be opened with a key, or an electric sensor that probably would allow all doors on this particular block to open or lock simultaneously.

With a muffled click, the bolt slid back and one of Lang's jailers stooped to unlock the leg irons while the other watched from a position too distant for a surprise attack. Legs free, the handcuffs were removed and he was shoved into the cell to the accompanying clang of slamming steel bars.

The space was about ten by ten feet. Against one wall was a double-decker bunk. Two cotton-tick mattresses lay on the floor against the other. A steel basin and seatless toilette completed the furnishings. At the point the rear wall met the ceiling, a slit window admitted weak sunlight filtered by years of accumulated dirt and grime.

In years past, Lang had read of regular escapes from the jail, more unscheduled departures than your average Holiday Inn. However men had gotten out, it hadn't been from these cells. One by convincing a guard he was somebody else, another by simply putting down his mop and broom and walking out of an unsecured area. Lax security, complacent guards, and general staff incompetence, not the physical plant, had been at fault.

Lang guessed he wasn't going to be here long enough to find the seams in the system.

Sitting on the lower bunk, he stared at the far wall, seeing not cracked and chipped plaster but a mountaintop in southwestern France, a fireball that had been a helicopter and then smoldering rubble.

Gurt.

Gone.

Not possible.

His reverie was interrupted by an electronic buzz and the clang of doors opening in unison. Lang looked up to see three men, one white, the other two black, paused outside his cell. Also in orange jumpsuits, they waited until the door was fully opened before, as one, they stepped across the threshold.

Unsure of the appropriate protocol, Lang stood.

The larger of the two black men, like Lang's guard, had a shaved head. He was well over six feet, his biceps filled the loose sleeves of his jumpsuit, and Lang guessed he was well over two hundred and fifty pounds. Scowling, he regarded Lang with curiosity, the way a buyer might examine a horse. " 'Nother whitebread," he finally said to no one in particular.

Lang held out a hand. "Name's Lang Reilly."

The black man glared at the hand as though it held something offensive. "Name's whatever I say it is, an' don' you forget it."

Lang had always heard there was a "boss" for every cell, and he guessed he'd just met this one's.

The other black man, somewhat smaller than the other and clearly older, took Lang's hand. "Mine's Johnson, Eddie Johnson. Don' study Leroy there too much. He jus' come in an hour or two ago. Me an' Wilbur," he indicated the white man, "we shared this here room for a coupla months."

Wilbur was small, with the face and eyes of a rodent. Juglike ears added to the illusion. He sported a reddish bruise under one eye, and Lang could see dried blood on one lip along with swelling. He guessed someone had given Wilbur a bad morning.

Lang had a candidate.

"Honky," Leroy growled, pointing. "You were sittin' on *my* bed."

"My bed, actually," Wilbur said before being cowed by a glare from Leroy.

Lang looked the big black straight in the eyes, an act he had heard amounted to a challenge in prison. He spoke gently, a smile flickering around his lips. "You been here just a few hours longer than I have, friend. Doesn't seem you have much in the way of seniority."

If there was going to be trouble, Lang wanted it now, not sometime when his back was turned or he was asleep.

"Don' matter how long I been here, white boy," Leroy rumbled. "I be the meanest muther here, I make th' rules."

As if by unspoken signal, Wilbur and Eddie Johnson bounded to the farthest point in the cell, the upper bunk. If Lang had had doubts about what was going to happen, their anxious faces confirmed it.

Had he not anticipated it, Leroy's swing could have taken Lang's head off. Instead, Lang ducked to his right, keeping equal weight on both feet. As he had learned so many years ago, not even a trained prizefighter can deliver a roundhouse blow without shifting his balance dangerously when he puts his weight behind his punch. Before Leroy could recover, Lang pivoted on his left foot so that all his poundage was on his right to give force to a stroke with cupped fingers, swung upward immediately below his opponent's rib cage, an impact calculated to temporarily collapse the lung in addition to a jolt of paralyzing pain.

Leroy hit the floor like a side of beef dropped from its meat hook, writhing as he tried to suck in air and expel it with a low moan at the same time.

Lang was vaguely aware that the constant racket from

outside the cell had increased, a sound that would soon summon the guards. Lang wanted this finished right now.

Standing above the man on the floor, Lang bent his knees and dropped, aiming to use his weight combined with gravity to crush the trachea with his shinbones. He was surprised when Leroy rolled away with the quickness of a much smaller man and Lang hit unforgiving concrete.

Both antagonists made it to their feet at the same time.

Lang glanced quickly around the cell. There wasn't room to stay more than a few inches out of his opponent's grasp, and the disparity in their size would make any clinch fatal to Lang.

Warily, he moved from side to side, awaiting Leroy's next attack.

Or, better, the arrival of the guards. Time was on his side now. The roar from those cells who had a view into his was getting deafening. How could his keepers not hear?

A trickle of blood bubbled on Leroy's lips as he still tried to regain full lung capacity, but there was no disability in his eyes nor question as to his intent as he glared across the few feet that separated the two. Then he bobbed his head as though having made a decision. A hand went inside the jumpsuit and returned with a flash of metal. A knife. No crudely made prison shank, the black man held a stiletto, its long blade reflecting evilly from the overhead lights.

If Leroy had just come in that morning, how the hell would someone have had the time to smuggle him a weapon?

There wasn't time for academic speculation. The large black man held the blade away from his body, cutting edge up. Crouched in a stance that enabled movement in any direction, his eyes searched Lang's, waiting for the first flicker that would indicate what his intended victim was going to do. Unlike a gun, success with a knife depends on reaction to an opponent's move. Aggressive slashing and jabbing is more likely to lead to a struggle for the weapon than the intended result.

In other words, Lang realized, he was facing a professional.

Seconds expanded indefinitely as Lang felt a trickle of icy sweat course down the side of his face. Neither man wanted to make the first move.

Fine with Lang. Sooner or later, a guard would show up and disarm Leroy.

With the Atlanta Department of Corrections, it was likely to be later.

If ever.

Leroy must have realized the same thing. He began a slow shift from side to side, an attempt to force Lang to commit himself. Instead, Lang shot a glance toward the bunk, bending knees as though to move. Leroy shifted his weight, not a lunge but a subtle move that would require perhaps a quarter of a second to return to a direction-neutral stance.

It was enough.

Lang threw himself toward the wall opposite the bunk. Rolling as he hit the floor, his fingers caught the edge of one of the mattresses, wrapping it around his body like a jelly roll.

As Leroy struck, knife aimed at Lang's midsection, Lang unwound the padding, leaving nothing but cotton and stuffing to take the impact of the steel. Lang jerked the remaining end of the mattress, snatching both blade and attacker's hand upward, for an instant exposing the entire lower body.

In the fraction of a second before Leroy could recover, Lang put his entire soul, body, and weight into a

kick to the other man's left knee. He was rewarded with
the sound of crunching patella and tearing tendon, followed by a scream of pain that drowned out the noise of
the cell block. The knife was a comet of light as it spun
through the air.

Lang had it in his hand before Leroy could grasp his
shattered joint. The larger man lay on his side, embracing what was left of his knee. Once certain Leroy was no
longer a threat, Lang propped the knife up on the floor,
leaning against the bunk, before stamping his foot down
on it. The steel snapped in half.

Lang was stuffing both pieces into Leroy's pocketless
prison suit when he looked up to see a guard working
the lock of the cell's door. Behind him three others
stood, truncheons in hand.

"What's going on here?" demanded the man with the
keys in hand.

"Leroy here was demonstrating the lotus position and
seems to have twisted his knee somehow," Lang said.
"I'm afraid he might have hurt himself."

The guard didn't even bother expressing skepticism.
"Yeah, sure. Fighting gets you time in isolation," he said,
pushing Lang against the wall while one of his companions twisted Lang's arms behind his back so the first
could snap on the cuffs. "You'll have plenty of time to
think things over."

Two of the guards marched Lang toward the elevator
while a third used the radio on his belt to call for a
stretcher for Leroy.

Lang had no idea how long he had been in the eight-by-
eight cell. Here the door was solid steel and there was no
window, so night and day were the same. His stomach's
complaints told him he had not eaten in a long time.

When he heard footsteps stop outside his cell, he expected to see a food tray slide through the door's slot. Instead, there was the snick of a bolt being drawn and the door swung back. Standing in front of it was Detective Rouse.

Lang rolled off the single cot and stood. "What a pleasure, Detective, to see you again today. I would invite you in, but as you can see, I'm a little short of places for company to sit."

Rouse glared back before snapping at the guard at his side, "G'wan, unlock that door."

To Lang he said, "N'mine the smart-assin', jus' come on out. You're bein' turned loose."

Lang could not suppress a sudden intake of breath. "And to whom do I owe my most sincere thanks?"

"The Frankfurt, Germany, Police, Mr. Reilly. You gotta be the luckiest man alive. We e-mailed 'em we had you, and they e-mailed us back th' man you assaulted—"

"Allegedly assaulted," Lang corrected as he stepped out of the cell.

"Yeah, yeah." To describe Rouse as annoyed would be like describing Death Valley in July as warm. "The Germans couldn't find the guy. Seems he gave them a false address."

Why wasn't Lang surprised? "And the cop who supposedly was a witness?"

Rouse took Lang by the elbow, steering him toward the elevators. "Germans got their problems jus' like we got ours. Citizen doesn't have a beef, why go to the trouble? Not like either us or them got a shortage of work to do."

At the elevator bank, Rouse pushed the Down button. "Oh yeah, Frankfurt police asked what I could do to see 'bout the cost of repairs to two cars, replacin' two others."

The door hissed open and Lang, Rouse, and the guard stepped inside.

"So," Lang asked, "what did you tell 'em you could do?"

"Not more than ask politely, Mr. Reilly. I figger that's a civil matter, an' I don' even want to hear how you tore up four police cars."

The elevator came to a stop on the floor Lang recognized as the location of booking.

"Tell 'em to send me a bill, Detective. I'll see that it gets paid."

He left Rouse staring in disbelief as he went to get the return of his personal property.

He was leaning on the counter that divided the room, counting his cash and inspecting the items that had been returned to him, when he caught the eye of the woman on the other side. Blond hair from a cheap bottle, she was exhibiting middle-age spread rampant. Her rump was fighting what might be a winning battle against the seams of her uniform pants. Buttons on her blouse strained against breasts of Wagnerian proportions.

"One of my cellmates, guy name of Leroy, got hurt a few hours ago. Can you tell me if he's okay?"

She eyed him with the suspicion of one in a business where the customer is always wrong.

Lang gave her his most engaging smile. "He was just booked in this morning."

She moved to a point across the counter, running a hand around the edge of frizzy hair. "Y'remember the cell number?"

Lang gave it to her and she moved to a computer, where she began to slowly click the keyboard.

"What'd you say his name was?"

"I only got his first—Leroy."

She shook her head, an effect of a lion shaking a scruffy mane. "Ain' no Leroy nobody in that cell. Fact is, ain' no Leroy been booked in today." She gave him a smile, a glimpse of tobacco-yellowed teeth. "But then, the day ain' over."

Lang felt a chill that had nothing to do with the room's temperature. "You sure?"

She nodded, again with leonine effect. "I make mistakes, but this ain' one of 'em."

Lang knew the answer, but he had to ask. "If no such person was booked in here today, how'd he get in the same cell I was?"

She shook her head. "Ast the head jailer. I jus' work here."

CHAPTER TWENTY-ONE

Atlanta, Georgia
Manuel's Tavern
The next evening

Lang and Francis found a booth, scarred with fraternity symbols, names, and dates clumsily carved into wood long yellowed by a half-century of human touch. Lang had not expected the food to improve in his absence. He was not disappointed. He also was not disappointed that the place was noisy, cluttered with five decades of political memorabilia, and filled with Emory grad students.

He felt he had come home.

"What's good?" he had asked a waiter in a T-shirt, soiled apron, jeans, and sneakers.

"The beer. Anything else, an' you better try McDonald's."

Same straight line, same punch line.

"I don't suppose the salmon is fresh," Francis asked.

"Father, I ain't lyin' to a priest," the young man said.

"If Darwin's right, that fish been outta water long enough to grow legs."

Both Lang and Francis ordered burgers, the most difficult thing on the menu to screw up.

Francis passed a plastic basket of fries, its paper liner translucent with grease. *"Cuius est divisio, alterius est electio."* One divides; the other selects.

Lang dumped about half on his plate, glumly noting that those on the bottom were well charred. "I should have chosen the half that weren't burned to ashes."

Francis regarded the red in the center of the burger he had ordered well done. "Neither of us come here for the food."

"I didn't come as a penance, either," Lang growled.

"No," Francis agreed, "but where else in Atlanta can we eat, drink, and try to unscramble that inscription without the waiter trying to turn the table?"

Like European establishments, a single beer would entitle the customer to remain at the table no matter how many people were waiting. Manuel Maloof, the original proprietor, had never believed in rushing his patrons through pitchers of beer, meals, or anything else.

Dinner, such as it was, was eaten with little conversation. Neither man wanted to be the first to mention the absence of Gurt, who had insisted on joining them here several times. Twice Lang glanced up from his meal, half expecting to see her returning from the restroom.

Finally, he shoved the plate away, half the burger remaining, and passed a copy of the Montsegur inscription to Francis. "Here are the actual words. See what you can make out of them."

Francis also had no problem leaving the rest of his meal uneaten. Gurt had apparently been at his elbow, too. He was relieved not to have to continue the charade of two old friends dining together as though nothing had changed.

He fished in a pocket, producing a pair of glasses, which he meticulously fastened around his ears. "First, tell me a little about the Emperor Julian—specifically, why he'd have an inscription carved on a wall in France."

Lang reached out to pick a fry from his plate, more to have something to do with his hands than renewed interest. "Like I said, last pagan emperor of Rome, hated the Christian religion, which had become acceptable, thought it dissed Roman culture. Before becoming emperor, he was governor of that part of Gaul."

Francis nodded, looking at Lang rather than the paper on the table before him. "Coincidence the carving was at the last stand of the Cathars?"

"Don't think so." Lang reached for another fry, thought better of it, and returned his hands to his lap. "As you know, the Cathars were heretics, the object of, what, the Fourth Crusade?"

Francis nodded. "Thirteenth century, 1208, current events to you, but yeah. The Cathars questioned, if not denied, Christ's human birth or death, held him to be an angelic figure. They didn't particularly care where they worshiped, so a cave would have done fine, particularly one they could fortify. Innocent III, the Pope, got Simon de Montfort, father of the one in English history, to besiege the place for almost four years."

Lang leaned forward, his mind fastening on a single object. "And the Merovingian kings?"

"My, but you are wandering far afield from ancient history tonight. Now you've jumped back to the fifth to seventh centuries. The kings of that dynasty ruled southwestern France, claimed they were both the physical and spiritual heirs of Christ since His family fled there from what's now Palestine after the crucifixion. A couple of interesting characteristics: They were friendly to Jews, unlike any other European monarchs of that time, and believed their hair was the source of their strength."

"Like Sampson."

"Interestingly, yes. Sampson was a Nazarite, just as many people think Christ was. Jesus, the Nazarite, mistranslated to 'Jesus of Nazareth.' As for the Merovingians, unsubstantiated rumors still surface occasionally of both lateral and lineal descendants."

"Rumors the Church finds discomforting," Lang interjected.

Francis's eyebrows rose as a smile crept across his face. "Food for the apostate mind. Like yours."

It was an old subject, one the two friends had debated often but one that served no real purpose tonight, save one.

"Let's agree that the Languedoc area of France seems to have spawned more than its share of heretics, religious wars, and legends concerning Christ."

"No argument about that."

Lang was eyeing the french fries again when the waiter picked his plate up. "Done?"

"Lang nodded. "Yeah, thanks."

The young man surveyed the amount of food left on each plate. "Told you guys you should consider McDonald's."

"Veritas nihil veretur nisi abscondi," Francis said.

"It's not the truth I fear, it's the tip," the waiter said.

Where else but at Manuel's?

Lang watched the retreating back of their server. "So where were we?"

"Somewhere in the turbulent history of the Languedoc."

"Oh yeah. I think the place, the main room at Montsegur, was a library, maybe a repository for early Christian writings the Cathars somehow had managed to salvage, maybe even something the survivors of Christ's family brought with them. Something Christian, anyway, since it drew Julian's attention. In addition to hating Christians, he was a prankster. He would have loved to embarrass the early Church in some way. Next, let's speculate the Cathars found this library or whatever it was, made a church out of it."

"And a fortress," Francis interrupted. "What you say makes sense. When Montsegur was besieged, the Cathars finally surrendered on the basis they wouldn't have to come down from the place for another couple of days. Perhaps time to secrete whatever they had, like the library."

"The library Hitler would have loved to possess," Lang said, signalling for a refill of the pitcher of beer. "You know he had a passion for the supernatural or religious. Apparently, Skorzeny found something, truckloads of something."

The same waiter substituted a full pitcher for the empty one.

Francis filled his glass and stretched out into the corner of the booth, putting his feet up on the bench. "Okay, so much for the *why* of what you're looking for. Let's take a look at this inscription. I make it to be something like 'The Emperor Julian accuses—' "

"*Accusatem* is a noun, not a verb," Lang pointed out, making no effort to conceal his glee at his friend's mistake.

"Knew that—just wanted to see if you're on your toes. Problem is, we don't really know if we're dealing with a verb or noun. The ending's missing."

"It's in the wrong place for the verb."

"Only if we're dealing with prose."

"You think this is poetry?"

"Could be one of the seven meters of lyric verse, yes." Francis smiled. "Perhaps you've forgotten that there are seven classic meters, or feet, of Latin lyric verse, anapest, or short-short-long."

"Which this isn't."

"And dactyl, or long-short-short . . ." Francis looked at Lang with a mocking grin. "Surely you were aware of the structure of Latin poetry."

"Don't you guys have to take a vow of humility or something?"

Francis reached across the table to fill Lang's glass. "Okay, okay, so it probably isn't poetry." He put the pitcher down and examined the paper again. "We've got a clear verb with *ibit*—someone, third person, commands."

Lang sipped from his glass. "Good bet it's the emperor. They tend to command a lot."

"Problem is, what? He commands an accusation? He could make his own."

"A synonym would be indictment. Suppose he orders the physical indictment, the writing be . . . what?"

Francis adjusted his glasses as though the move would make the language intelligible. "Only other verb is *sepelit,* bury or entomb."

Lang was staring at his copy, beer forgotten. "Orders the indictment be entombed? Makes no sense. Let's take the easy part, *rexis iudeaium,* clearly 'king of the Jews.' "

Both men looked up, meeting the other's eyes.

"Christ?" Lang asked. "Wasn't that what they put on the cross, a sarcastic title given a condemned man?"

"True, but I'm not so sure it was totally sarcastic," Francis said. "In fact, why don't you take a look at that?"

"How?"

"Friend of mine, professor of Judaic studies at Emory."

Lang's glass stopped en route to his mouth. "Emory?

Thought that was a Methodist school. They got Judaic studies?"

"Apparently so. Leb Greenberg and I speak on the same program occasionally. One of those ecumenical things where a Jew, a Catholic, and a Protestant speak on some of the same agendas about freedom of worship and how Americans tolerate all faiths. We had a Muslim imam, a Shiite. He quit when we wanted to add a Sunni."

So much for the feel-good of freedom of religion.

"So," Lang asked, his glass resuming its journey, "what can Professor Greenberg tell us?"

Francis was contemplating his glass, clearly estimating if there was enough beer in the pitcher to fill it. "I'd like a background on this 'King of the Jews' thing from a non-Christian view. It might help us correctly translate Julian's inscription."

Still turning over the existence of a department of Judaica at a Methodist school, Lang asked, "Any reason you can't ask?"

Deciding a compromise was in order, Francis poured the pitcher's contents evenly into both glasses. "I think so. Although Leb and I get along fine, I think he'd be a lot more candid about a Jew's historical point of view with you than with me. I'm a priest; you're half heathen anyway."

"Nicest thing you've ever said," Lang was motioning for the check, "conceding I'm only part heathen."

"Don't let it go to your head."

Lang lost the flip of the coin for the tab, an act that had become merely ceremonial. Francis always won. Lang suspected the priest had special help.

Outside, Francis stopped to admire Lang's new car, its black paint glistening under the streetlights. "A Mercedes? I thought you like those little German toys, Porsches. This one even has a backseat."

Lang had not told him of the need to acquire new wheels, a car not quite so conspicuous as the destroyed Porsche, a highly visible, unique-sounding turbo cabriolet. There must have been hundreds of Mercedes just like this one in his neighborhood.

"CLK convertible." He opened the door and inserted the key. "Watch."

Pushing a button made part of the trunk flip open as the windows automatically receded into the doors. The top lurched upward and stopped.

"Pretty clever," Francis observed. "Now, what do you do to make it go all the way down?"

Lang pushed the button again. No response.

"Good question."

Both men stared at the car as though expecting it to solve the problem itself. At the price still visible on the sticker, not a totally unrealistic expectation.

"There's a MARTA station a couple of blocks away," Francis finally volunteered. "You can't very well drive it with the top sticking straight up."

"Why do I get the feeling buying the extra warranty was a good investment?" Lang muttered. "Help me manually raise this thing in case it rains."

The top wouldn't go up, either. They left the car there, an expensive steel-and-chrome box with an open lid.

CHAPTER TWENTY-TWO

DeKalb County, Georgia
Emory University
Two days later

Lang parked the Mercedes between an SUV with fraternity Greek letters on the rear windshield and a Toyota
with a bumper sticker that proclaimed, "Harvard: The
Emory of the North." He was facing a quadrangle of
leafy oaks. Two marble-sided, red-tile-roofed buildings
on each side, one at each end. He checked his written
directions and his watch. He had taken a circuitous
route to ensure that no one had followed, but he was a
few minutes early and it looked like he was in the right
place.

Curious as to the existence of a Judaic studies program at a Methodist school, he had called up a catalog
on the Internet, learning that the institution also had a
Holocaust studies program. Searching further, he had
pieced together an interesting history.

In the late 1950s, Emory's college had been a small and relatively obscure institution, serving basically as a minor league training ground for the university's regionally prestigious medical school. Liberal arts degrees were frequent consolation prizes given to disappointed doctor-aspirants.

A little-known professor of theology, Tom Altizer, changed that perception. He announced his theory that God was dead. Not departed, not disinterested, but dead, deceased, gone to wherever the Lord of Heaven might go.

Members of the Theology School faculty tripped over their academic gowns in a stampede to have the university's lawyers review Altizer's tenure contract.

Somehow the national media got wind of the story, slanting it to show the diversity of thought possible even at a small Southern, church-operated school.

Altizer became the most famous name associated with Emory since a man named Holiday, a nineteenth-century grad of what was to become the Dental School, went West for his tuberculosis, and teamed up with the Earp brothers at a dusty corral in Tombstone, Arizona.

Overnight, Emory became a touchstone of Southern academic liberalism. Students from other regions of the country began applying, particularly those who could afford the Ivy League schools but whose grades could not gain admittance. Some actually came to study something other than premed. Many were Jewish. Forgetting Altizer's heresy, the university added courses in women's, black, Latin American, and Asian studies, embracing all diversity of thought.

As long as it was politically correct diversity of thought.

Lang had also read the professor's curriculum vitae. Son of Dutch Jews, he had spent part of his childhood in a series of Nazi death camps. After the war, he had immigrated to Israel, where he studied Hebrew history

at several universities and gained a scholarship to Ox-
ford. There he had completed his postgraduate work in
Judaic-Christian thought and taught, before moving to
Atlanta to be with his married daughter and a number of
grandchildren. He had published several books, the titles of which were in Yiddish or Hebrew and unintelligible to Lang. Many of his articles, however, had English
titles, although Lang had heard of few of the publica-
tions and assumed they were journals largely serving
those who must submit to the academic imperative of
publish or perish.

Another look at his watch told Lang he would be right
on time. Opening the car door, he withdrew the ignition
key. Immediately, the car's theft alarm squawked, a wail
Lang was certain would filter into every classroom on
campus. Reinserting the key did no good, nor did crank-
ing the engine.

Defeated, he looked around to make sure no one
could identify the perpetrator of such a racket and slunk
away like a thief in the night.

Leb Greenberg was a small man with a strong hand-
shake and brown eyes that sparkled as though he had a
joke he was about to share. Other than the yarmulke
from under which sprigs of gray hair sprouted, he could
have been anyone's favorite grandparent.

"Thank you for seeing me, Professor," Lang said as
he stepped across the threshold of a small office.

"Leb, please," he said, indicating Lang should sit in
one of two uncomfortable-looking chairs arranged in
front of a desk. "All day, it's Professor Greenberg this,
Doctor Greenberg that, usually complaints about grades.
Let us skip the honorifics, shall we?"

Lang recognized a British accent, one without the
dropped h's, the voice of the upper class. He often won-

dered why everyone who had lived in England, no matter how briefly, adopted that enunciation.

Greenberg sat behind a desk empty of clutter other than a cup and saucer and a stack of papers Lang guessed was a manuscript. "Francis tells me you're interested in a specific bit of ancient Jewish history as it might relate to Christianity. Wouldn't say exactly what."

He glanced down at the cup. "Oh dear, forgive me. I was just having tea. Might I pour you a cuppa?"

He lifted an electric coffeemaker from behind the desk. "Sure, thanks."

Agency training. Sharing a meal, a beverage, increased whatever bonding might take place. Defectors from Communist regimes had been more likely to share information with debriefers who joined them in eating and drinking.

The professor produced another cup and saucer, one not matching his own. "I'm afraid you'll have to settle for concentrated lemon juice, no milk, no sugar."

"That's fine, thank you."

Lang watched his cup fill with a liquid as dark as coffee and took an experimental sip. He fought back a gasp. The stuff was tart enough to make his teeth itch.

"Specially blended for me," Greenberg said proudly. "I get it through a merchant in Beirut."

Lang had never previously viewed Lebanon as a terrorist country.

Licking his lips in pleasure, Leb sat back in his chair, arms behind his head. "What can I do for you, Lang?"

Somehow mollify the taste of this tea that was sour enough to pucker his mouth like a green persimmon. But Lang said, "Francis and I were looking at a Latin inscription, fourth century. It referred to a 'king of the Jews,' the title put on Christ's cross. I always thought it was derisive. Francis wasn't so sure, said you might have some historical thoughts on the matter."

Leb was silent for so long, Lang thought perhaps he didn't hear. Although the professor was looking straight at him, Lang was certain he saw something else.

Finally, he sat up, his hands cupping his tea as though to keep it warm. "I think you can understand the problem here. We Jews have a very different perception of the Christ and of the Gospels of your New Testament. That difference frequently leads to misunderstandings. For two millennia it led to the shedding of blood. Ours."

Lang put his cup on the desk. "Leb, I'm seeking history, not a religious argument."

The Jew smiled. "In many ways, that's unfortunate. We Jews dearly love to argue points of religion and law among ourselves." He grew serious. "Exactly what is it you think I might know?"

"King of the Jews. Was Jesus a king or was he simply being mocked?"

Leb offered the coffeepot to Lang, who declined a refill, before concentrating on refilling his own cup. "I can give you historical fact. You have to supply your own spiritual significance."

"Fair enough."

Leb held his cup in both hands, gently blowing across the top. "Let's start with Judea of the first century. It wasn't the pastoral place the Gospels might lead you to believe. Instead, it was a defeated country, seething with an undercurrent of nationalism. Most Jews of the day were less than fond of the occupying Romans. Think France 1940 to 1944.

"There were basically three political groups: The Sadducees, the wealthy landowning class who profited from Roman occupation, somewhat like the *collaboteurs* in France during World War Two. Then there were the

Pharisees, priests and those who stuck to the strictest
Jewish law. Then we have the Zealots, those who intended to restore the Promised Land to its intended
inhabitants. You may recall these folks fomented the rebellion that resulted in Rome leveling the temple and
sacking Jerusalem in seventy or seventy-one C.E., only
thirty, thirty-five years after Christ's death."

"The siege of Masada?"

"Yes, that was the last battle, the Little Big Horn of ancient Israel." Leb took a long sip, his eyes fastened on
something Lang couldn't see. "Except the nine hundred–
plus Zealots killed themselves rather than surrender.
Anyway, at the birth of Christ, many Jews were looking
for a man from God, a man to deliver them from foreign
rule just as the Maccabees had a hundred years before
and Moses centuries earlier."

"A messiah," Lang volunteered.

Leb nodded slowly. "Perhaps. But remember, Lang,
messiah simply means 'one anointed' in Hebrew. The
Greek word *christos* means the same."

The professor took another sip, placed his cup on the
desk, and continued, still gazing at something Lang was
sure was far away. "Your Gospels tell us Christ was of
the House of David. That would be the royal family, the
equivalent of the English Windsors."

There was a pause.

"A potential king born in a stable?" Lang asked.

Leb shook his head slowly, not moving his eyes. "A
stable, perhaps. Luke says so, but Matthew tells us Christ
was born an aristocrat in the family home in Bethlehem.
In fact, he also tells us Christ was of royal blood, a direct
descendant of Solomon and David. Pretty heady stuff, a
legitimate contender to the throne of a united Jewish
State.

"Luke has the birth attended by poor shepherds,

Matthew by kings from afar. John and Mark are silent on the subject. But then, your Gospels weren't contemporaneous accounts. They were written anywhere from sixty years after the crucifixion to nearly a century later, probably taken from other accounts. Hardly an assurance of accuracy.

"At any rate, no one tells us much about Christ's early life other than a single account of a young man arguing with elders in the temple. When we next see Christ, he is at a wedding in Cana, a very fancy wedding where so much wine is consumed, more has to be brought in. Or created. The first miracle."

Leb inspected Lang's barely touched tea. "Don't like it?"

"I was so interested in what you were saying, I forgot about it."

The professor smiled. "Perhaps you are a capable lawyer, Lang, but a very poor liar."

"Okay, so it's a little . . . unusual."

Leb poured the contents of Lang's cup into his own. "An acquired taste. Now, we were talking about . . . ?"

"The wedding at Cana."

"Oh yes. Not only is there copious amounts of wine, but Christ and the hostess order servants about. Unlikely someone would presume to command another's domestics, so we could conclude it was Christ's wedding and a rather big affair at that, not the marriage of peasant stock but of aristocracy.

"I also think it's worth remembering that Matthew's Christ 'comes not to bring peace but with a sword.' "

Lang sat up in his chair. "I hadn't realized the Gospels were so different."

Leb snorted. " 'Different'? They're in irreconcilable conflict! I can imagine the reason why the early Christian church chose those four diverse versions of the life of Christ."

"And that would be?"

"Because the others available were either more diverse or mentioned something the Church didn't want known."

"Any idea what?" Lang was fairly certain the man had a very clear idea.

Leb held up a conspiratorial finger, a professor in the midst of a lecture. "Let's continue and see if we can't reach the same conclusions together.

"We know Christ spent a great deal of time traveling with supporters and lecturing to crowds. I submit the Gospels' version of what he had to say is less than accurate."

He held up a hand to stop Lang's question. "Let's move on to the end of his ministry, to that Passover where he was charged as a criminal and crucified. First, as you as a scholar of ancient history know, crucifixion was punishment reserved for subversives, enemies of the State."

"But wasn't a thief crucified next to Christ?"

"So we're told. But I submit, the Gospels were written for a Greco-Roman audience, not Jews. Even back then, the stubbornness of Jews in their religion was a given. Facts were changed so it appeared the Jews were responsible for the death of the Messiah, a fiction from which we Jews have suffered for two millennia. Who might or might not have died next to Christ is mere speculation with a strong editorial slant. Witness: The council of Jewish elders, the Sanhedrin, supposedly originally condemned Christ on that Friday night. In other words, the most respected Jews in Jerusalem broke *Sabbat* by meeting after sunset on a Friday in flagrant violation of Jewish law. Not only that, those men had the absolute power to condemn a man to death by stoning.

"In short, had the Jews wanted Christ dead, they were perfectly capable of executing Him themselves.

"Further, as you no doubt know, someone who had earned Roman enmity wasn't usually buried but left to rot on his cross as a reminder to others who might harbor seditious thoughts."

Lang sat still, considering what he had just heard. "So, Leb, it's your guess that Christ's message wasn't all peace and love?"

The professor shrugged apologetically. "I have no hard facts, of course, but I can make the following surmises if I may . . ."

"Please."

"First, Christ was of royal blood, if not the direct heir to the throne of all the Jews. Second, he came along when the Roman province of Judea was seething with a rebellion barely under the surface, one that, in fact, broke out shortly after his death. Third, his message was sufficiently disturbing to the colonial powers that he was tried for treason and executed, his actual title on the cross. Finally, his followers saw an opportunity to press their leader into the Messianic mold, thereby aggrandizing themselves. No matter what evidence finally surfaced, the Church wasn't going to back down: Christ was the long-promised son of God who ruled through His Holy Church. To admit he was basically a revolutionary was unthinkable. Think more Lenin than Gandhi. The early Church fathers cocked us a snook."

Lang was certain he misunderstood. "Cocked us a . . . ?"

"Snook. Cocked a snook. I'm sorry. British idiom. You would say pulled the wool over our eyes."

The barrier of a common language.

Lang considered this and what might have been contained in the library at Montsegur. "But there's no evidence of any of this."

Leb shook his head wearily at an argument he had heard many times. "Of course not. If there ever had been, it would have long been destroyed. For that matter, there's no contemporaneous record of Christ, either."

Indictment.

King of the Jews.

Rebel.

"An absence of proof," the professor added, "is not proof of absence."

Lang smiled. "How very Zen."

Leb nodded. "The university also has a curriculum in Buddhist studies."

CHAPTER TWENTY-THREE

Atlanta, Georgia
Rectory, Church of the Immaculate Conception
Two hours later

Lang was drinking his second cup of coffee in hopes of cleansing his palate of the professor's tea. Outside Francis's office, the Mercedes's theft alarm was again howling, unstoppable but at least muted by the thick brick walls. He had just finished summarizing his meeting with Dr. Greenberg.

Francis took a legal pad from a drawer in his green metal, government-issue-type desk and began to copy the inscription. "Okay, let's put the English over each Latin word."

Lang watched.

Imperator	Emperor (nominative case)
Iulian	Julian (nominative case)
accusat—	accusation/indictment (case unknown)

rebillis	rebel (genitive case)
rexus	king (genitive case)
iudeaium	Jews (genitive case)
iubit	commands (first person singular, present tense)
regi—	palace (case unknown)
unus	one (genitive case)
dEI	god (genitive case)
sepelit	buried/entombed (third person passive?)

The priest reversed the pad and held it up. "Allowing for the fact the Romans had no articles, *a, an,* or *the,* I make it to be 'The Emperor Julian commands or orders.' "

Lang nodded. "Yeah, but orders what? Without the ending, I'm not sure if he's ordering someone be indicted or something be done with the physical indictment."

Francis drew a line between two of the words. "If he's ordering someone, presumably the King of the Jews, to be indicted, he's three centuries late. Let's assume the inscription is supposed to make some sort of sense."

Lang leaned forward. "Okay. What's being done in/to/with the palace? Without the ending, we don't know."

Francis used a Bic pen as a pointer. "I think we can assume the palace doesn't possess something, leaving the nominative, dative, objective, or ablative cases. There's no verb that could apply; palaces don't order, nor are they entombed. That would leave . . ."

There was a knock at the door and a woman's steel-gray-haired head popped around the corner like a jack-in-the-box. "Father, you have only five minutes before Eventide service." She saw Lang. "Oh, pardon me. I didn't know you had company."

She disappeared behind the door.

Francis stood, smiling. "Mrs. Pratt. Been the Church

secretary forever. If she didn't know you were in here, it's the first thing she's missed since Sherman left this as the only building in town he didn't torch. I've got souls to save. We'll have to finish this later."

Outside, the Mercedes's theft alarm had quit for the moment.

CHAPTER TWENTY-FOUR

Lang sat at the breakfast bar that divided living area from the condo's kitchen. In front of him were spread half a dozen pages from a yellow legal pad, each covered with variations of the inscription.

"Emperor Julian orders the King of the Jews indicted at the palace of the sole god?"

That left an extra verb.

". . . The King of the Jews entombed and indicted at the palace of the one god?"

That made no sense. As Francis had noted, three hundred years too late.

The cogs of the mind, like any other wheels, turned better when oiled, and what better lubricant than a little application of single-malt scotch? Lang got down from the bar stool and went over to the Thomas Elfe secretary, one of the few pieces that had survived Charleston's premier cabinetmaker and even fewer that had made the cut when Lang moved after Dawn died. The bottom served as a repository for Lang's better liquors.

As he straightened up, he noticed Grumps's eyes following his movements. This was the first day since Lang had returned from France that the dog had not conducted a room-by-room search for Gurt. Apparently aware that she wasn't coming back, the dog had become listless, even uninterested in his food.

Well, if not *un*interested, *less* interested. He still cleaned the bowl; it just took him longer.

Maybe he could use a little company.

Lang returned to the bar and used the remote to turn on the television in hopes that the sound of a feminine voice might perk Grumps up, even if it was electronically generated. Filling a glass with ice, he poured two fingers of amber liquid and sat back down at the bar.

". . . Now is the time, America, before it is too late."

Lang glanced into the face of Harold Straight. His blue eyes were as hard as diamond chips and there was something mesmerizing about him that made disbelief difficult.

"If we allow the mutinationalists, the one-worlders, to continue their plan to eradicate our individuality . . ."

Lang stared a long time at the face, watching until the thirty-second ad dissolved to strains of "God Bless America." Not only was the man spellbinding, he was . . .

What?

As an employee of the Agency, a memory for faces had been a basic survival tool, an ability created by hours spent viewing hundreds of photographs, of which only one or two were repetitive but in different settings. The students of the school had to identify not only the faces seen before but the background as well. The woman in a hat standing outside a movie theater, a man's profile in a car now looking full face. The woman without a hat in front of a blur. The man quarter view outside a store, now wearing a baseball cap.

Lang had seen Straight somewhere.

But where?

Lang shook his head. Unlikely. Straight had been governor of one of those states where there are only two seasons, July and winter, some ice-bound part of mid-America that Lang had never visited. Minnesota, Wisconsin, somewhere. Some rogue neuron's spark plugs misfiring along its dendrite somewhere in the brain, the same malfunction that makes our memory certain we have been somewhere before when we know we have not.

Lang took a sip of scotch and returned to the puzzle of Julian's inscription, oblivious to the television.

Harold Straight wouldn't go away.

More pressing matters finally prevailed. He reached for the phone on the wall over the counter and punched in a number.

Francis answered.

Without introduction, Lang said, "Okay, I've given you every chance to figure this thing out so as not to embarrass you."

"Embarrass me. What does it say?"

"Emperor Julian orders that the indictment of the King of the Jews be interred in the palace of the one god."

There was an audible sigh. "That's gibberish."

"No, that's jealousy that you didn't properly translate. Every other preposition, *to, of, by,* et cetera, simply doesn't work. *In* does."

"But why would you inter an indictment?" the priest wanted to know.

"Ask your pal Greenberg. If he was right and Christ

was as much revolutionary as prophet, making such a charge would certainly have humiliated the early church he so hated. Would make a brawler out of the Prince of Peace. I gotta think Julian would have gotten some yuks outta that."

"Okay," Francis said slowly, "but burying it doesn't seem a way to have the word get around. If putting the church down was your man Julian's gig, burying such a document makes no sense."

Both men were quiet for a moment before Lang said, "That would depend on how and where it was buried."

"Which brings us to the palace of the one god," Francis said.

Lang picked up his glass and took a generous swallow before asking, "Any ideas where that might be?"

"The temple at Jerusalem comes to mind," Francis's disembodied voice said. "Trouble is, the temple was leveled long before Julian came along."

"What about the Vatican?" Lang asked. "Constantine built a papal palace there before Julian came to power."

There was a brief silence. Lang visualized Francis rubbing his chin in thought. Then: "Could be."

"But where? I mean, Constantine's palace, or what was left of it, was allowed to fall into near ruin, then rebuilt in the sixteenth and seventeenth centuries. The indictment, if there really was one, wouldn't be something the church would display in the papal museum. It probably crumbled to dust a thousand years ago."

Francis said, "If so, somebody's going to a lot of trouble for dust. Were I you, I'd consider searching whatever part of the present Vatican predates the reconstruction."

Lang had never considered that possibility. "You know more about the Papal State than I do."

There was an audible sigh. "Okay. Make yourself comfortable while I instruct the ignorant heathen.

"Being an ancient-history freak, I'm sure you know the Romans liked to build their circuses at the bottom of inclines. Originally, the Vatican was just the name of one of the city's seven hills, like the Aventina, Laterail, Esquiline, and so forth. The Circus Maximus was at the foot of another. The slope provided natural grandstands for the thousands who turned out for chariot races. This particular circus, the Vatican, was well outside the ancient city's walls and was in a swampy marsh, complete with snakes and malaria until it became a place of entertainment. Since the land was unusable for most purposes, the hill was used to build tombs, a use that continued even after the Circus was built."

"Fascinating, but *Quicade praecipie esto brevis.*"

"Hush or I'll send you to the principal's office. The Apostle Peter was brought to Rome, Nero's Circus located at the base of Vatican Hill, for public execution. You may recall he insisted on being crucified upside down, the honor of dying like Christ being too great for him. The Romans accommodated his request.

"Legend has it that Peter was buried among the scattered tombs on the hillside, and that years later when the Emperor Constantine made Christianity Rome's official religion, he built the first papal palace on the place Peter was supposedly buried.

"Within fifty years of Peter's death, the area became a necropolis, a city of tombs for the dead. A number of the tombs became the outside wall of the original Pope's palace, unmovable without bringing down the entire structure.

"If your guy Julian was as big a joker as you say, what better laugh than to have something potentially embarrassing to the Church actually buried, or entombed, in a support wall?"

The remainder of Lang's scotch sat at his elbow, untouched. "This necropolis—is it open to the public? Dawn and I spent an entire day at the Vatican and I don't recall it. Is it in that lower level where the Popes are buried?"

"Below that, I think. The necropolis is open, but only by reservation with the Vatican Archaeological Office."

"Use your influence—see how soon you can get me in."

"I understand all admittance is by guided tour. You're not going to have a chance to explore on your own."

Lang grinned. "You take care of getting me in. I'll take care of any unauthorized exploration. If I can find the indictment, whatever it is, I may find out why somebody is willing to kill to keep me from it. I'll see how quick I can get to Rome."

The room was featureless. Only a door marked the four gray walls. Brilliant overhead lights sanitized shadows from the corners. The only furnishings were a metal desk and office chair, the latter filled by the room's sole occupant, a man intent on a series of monitors.

A sequence of letters marched across one screen, an electronic transcript of the words coming through the man's headset at the same time: "I may find out why somebody is willing to kill . . ."

Without looking away from the procession of words, he picked up the receiver of a surprisingly ordinary-looking phone. "He's planning on going, all right."

"All as planned," came the reply.

CHAPTER TWENTY-FIVE

Law Offices of Langford Reilly
229 Peachtree Street
The next morning

Lang sat, his back to his desk, facing the window with a view of the street below, a view of which he was unaware at the moment. Instead, he saw a face, the face he had dreamed of last night. Or, at least, he thought he'd dreamed it.

Either way, he had awakened as suddenly as a cork's pop from a champagne bottle. He had jerked to a sitting position in bed, uncertain exactly what had roused him so abruptly. Then he remembered the question in his mind earlier that evening. His subconscious had evidently retained the query, resolving it suddenly, like a flash, remembering where you left the car keys or an errand temporarily forgotten.

But the answer at best made no sense, and at worse

was downright insane. Still, Lang had trusted even less rational impulses and been thankful for it.

Scowling at his inability to simply forget the matter, Lang reached for the phone and dialed a number from memory.

"Yeah?" The answer was characteristically abrupt.

"Charlie?" Lang asked. "You doing anything in the next day or two?"

Charlie Clough. Disbarred lawyer, thrice divorced, total failure in everything. Except getting information that most people assumed didn't exist. Shortly after the State Bar of Georgia had seen fit to remove Attorney Charles M. Clough from its rolls, Charlie had visited nearly every criminal lawyer in the Atlanta area, seeking work as an investigator. More from sympathy than expectation, Lang had given Charlie the task of locating a witness in an upcoming trial who had successfully evaded service of a subpoena. Predictably, the county sheriff's department had given up after one halfhearted attempt. They were, after all, far too underpaid and overworked to do anything not related to raising pay and lowering hours. The firm Lang normally used to locate reluctant witnesses spent a week and an inordinate amount of his client's money before coming up empty.

Charlie found the man, followed his car, and handed him the subpoena at a stoplight.

"Of course I'm doing something," Charlie growled. "You think I'm some rich lawyer, can afford to sit around on my ass?"

And what an ass. At over three hundred pounds, Charlie had his suits made specially, probably by Omar the Tent-Maker. Airlines insisted he buy two seats, an added expense since he refused to fly any way but first class.

"I got a job for you. Airfare, expenses, a grand a day."

"I gotta kill who?"

"Not that difficult. I want some public records examined."

Charlie was instantly skeptical. "Public records? Most states, you can call 'em up on your computer."

Lang nodded to the unseen Charlie. "That's the point. I have reason to believe the public part of these records may have been altered. I want you to sniff around, take a look at the actual hard copies, see if there's anything suspicious."

There was a sigh. "Lemme get something to write on. Okay, shoot."

Lang told him.

"You nuts? You think I can find anything hasn't already been looked at, examined, and generally gone over?"

"A grand a day, Charlie."

"Can't get on it till next week," the investigator said crossly.

"That's fine."

It was only after he hung up that Lang realized Charlie hadn't even asked to whom he was speaking.

Lang had come to the office an hour sooner than usual to make sure he arrived before Sara, his secretary, ostensibly to see what needed to be handled before he left. The earliness of his arrival was confirmed by the fact that the daily phalanx of aggressive panhandlers were still asleep in doorways, in bus stop booths, and on park benches. The city evidently believed the streets, doorways, and parks belonged equally to all, but those who slept, drank, and relieved themselves there were more equal than others.

Gratified he had succeeded in arriving before Sara, Lang reached into his center desk drawer. His fingers fumbled until there was a click and the false back came out in his hand. Reaching back into the drawer, Lang removed what could have passed for an ordinary cell phone. He had taken the device, along with the Sig Sauer, when he left the Agency. The IACD, intra-agency communicating device, was actually a radio using the Agency's exclusive satellite to reach, with the push of a single button, the person represented by a three-letter identifier no matter where on the globe their location. All conversations were automatically scrambled and sorted out on the other end. Although ordinary by today's rapidly changing technology, the thing had been a marvel fifteen years ago. It still had the advantage of allowing Lang to reach old comrades direct.

He called up three letters on the screen, punched, and waited, listening to the whisper and crackle of low-space orbit.

There were three clicks and then: "Lang Reilly! Goddamn if I thought I'd ever hear from you again!"

" 'Lo, George," Lang said, a smile spreading across his face. "I figured if anyone had kept anything as outdated as an IACD, it'd be you."

"Outdated my ass! Thing's still very much in use, although I doubt yours has the updates, night or day picture-transmitting capability, GPS, all the bells and whistles."

Lang thought of the BlackBerry-like device Eddie Reavers had given him. Didn't it have GPS? "So, George, where they got you stationed now?"

Even the tinny quality of the sound of the receiver couldn't take the jolly out of George's voice. "Classified, Lang, you know that. I tell ya, I gotta kill ya. Besides, you didn't call just to locate me on some map of the Agency's unrelenting fight against terrorism, tyranny, injustice, overtime, and low salaries. What's up?"

Lang's grin widened. George Hemphill's assignment

to Frankfurt had overlapped Lang's. George had been only partially successful in concealing an uncanny linguistic ability with almost supernatural instincts behind the facade of a perpetual college sophomore. From mere inflections in languages Lang had barely heard of, let alone spoken, George had predicted coups and assassinations. It had been this ability that had saved him from the trouble caused by his love of whoopy cushions and electronics placed in inappropriate places.

Like wiring and amplifying the women's restroom.

"I got a favor to ask, George."

"If you want help crashing the next White House ball, forget it."

Lang became serious. "Remember Don Huff?"

"Older guy. Was in Ops, wasn't he? I seem to remember something about him saving your sorry ass at Checkpoint Charlie back in the bad old days."

"He was murdered. So was Gurt Fuchs."

There was a long pause. "Gurt, the Kraut goddess who looked like she might have stepped off a German travel poster?"

"The same."

Another pause. "Lang," he said, the exuberance gone from his tone, "talk around the water cooler was that Gurt left the Rome station to, er, well, she had taken a leave of absence to be with you. Your new *nom de guerre* was 'the lucky bastard.' Can't tell you how sorry I am."

"Thanks."

"Any ideas?"

"That's why I need a favor, George. Information, actually."

"I'll see what I can do."

Lang told him what he wanted.

Still another pause. "That may take a while. I mean, shit, you want me to go back to the beginning of time, maybe further. Hell, maybe even before everything was computerized."

Lang had barely gotten the IACD back into its compartment when Sara came in with a stack of file folders. "Take a look and see what needs handling before you leave."

CHAPTER TWENTY-SIX

Washington, D.C.
National Archives (Pennsylvania Avenue)
That afternoon

Departing the United States from Washington had a double advantage: Once again, a familiar face on the Dulles–Rome leg would reveal any tail. Second, answerless questions buzzed around Lang's mind like aimless bees in search of the hive. He might answer a few here before departing in the morning. A quick call to the office of one of Georgia's senators and a reminder of the size of the nonprofit he headed produced the required documents allowing him into the nation's record room.

Passing the line of tourists waiting to see the glass-encased Declaration of Independence and slipping around the line for the movie theater, he found the desk he was looking for. Behind it, a matronly woman, her steely hair tied in a bun, examined his nonacademic credentials, her displeasure obvious. With the reluctance peculiar to a bureaucrat forced to do her job, she handed him a plastic visitor's badge and directed him to the third floor. She seemed slightly mollified by giving him an admonition that the records he sought were largely unindexed.

He found shelves of boxes, each containing batches of randomly arranged documents stuffed into containers in no particular sequence. The authors of those documents, the Germans, would have been horrified at the total lack of order in which their handiwork was stored. The cargo manifest and schedule of each train, the requisition of each liter of petrol, all crammed together. At no time in history had such complete records of a nation fallen into enemy hands as had the minutiae of the Third Reich. And nowhere in history had such records simply been packed up, willy-nilly, their total disorder untouched for over sixty years.

Well, perhaps there was some order, after all. A faded placard at the end of each row bore a year, and some a location, Italy, France, and so on.

When had the German army supplanted the Fascists in defense of the Italian boot? Lang selected two boxes from the Italy 1943–44 shelf and carried them to the nearest table, where a small sign instructed him not to attempt to return boxes to shelves. That would be done by Archives staff.

The Archives' very own public works program.

The smell of musty paper tickled his nose. Fortunately, most of the documents were typed rather than in the old German script Hitler had resurrected and decreed to be used in handwritten papers, one of several less-than-successful efforts to take Germany back to its glory days.

Like the eighteenth century under Frederick the Great.

For the first hour, Lang glanced through mind-numbing orders for train movements, distribution of food rations, and repairs to vehicles, the minutiae of Kesselring's army. He was tempted to read the dispatches but abandoned the idea. If he was going to find anything related to what he wanted, he had no time for the blame shifting that is the correspondence of an army in retreat.

Shoving the boxes aside, he replaced them with two more. It was halfway through the last Italy 1944 that he found it: an aged copy of a letter on unique letterhead. Instead of the usual spread-winged eagle with a circled swastika in its claws, this bird was a two-thirds profile, also spread-winged. In one talon it held a pair of lighting bolts, the crooked cross in the other. A motto circled the figure: *Meine Ehre Ist Treu.* My truth is honor, slogan of the SS.

Lang pulled his chair closer to the lamp to read the faded ink of a teletype flimsy. It translated as:

```
          8 May 1944
      URGENT & TOP SECRET


Sturmbahnführer Otto Skorzeny
Via Rasslia 29
Rome


Herr Sturmbahnführer!


You are hereby specifically relieved
of duties imposed upon you by orders
effective 1 April 1944. You are to
report Berlin immediately for
reassignment by most expeditious
means available, aircraft included.
Prior departure Rome, all documents
```

```
concerning previous orders to be
destroyed, repeat, destroyed.
```

```
                    Heil Hitler!
                    H. Himmler
```

Since he was looking at an order that had come by
telegraph, there was no actual signature. Still, an order
direct from Himmler was an order from Hitler himself,
an order confirming that Skorzeny *had* been in Rome. It
was a possibility, if not a good guess, that he had been
searching the necropolis for Julian's joke on the Christians. Whatever Skorzeny had been doing there, it
wasn't as important to Hitler in the late spring of '44 as
having him somewhere else.

But where?

According to Professor Blucher, Skorzeny had been in
Montsegur soon after the fall of France in 1940. Shortly
thereafter, he'd led a parachute attack on . . . Cyprus?
He'd been around to rescue Mussolini in 1943, been in
Rome in the spring of '44. When did Rome fall to the Allies? Same day as Normandy, June 6, 1944. That would
explain one reason Skorzeny was ordered out. That must
have been before he went to oust what government? Oh
yeah, Hungary. No doubt the reassignment in Himmler's order. By winter of 1944–45, he'd been at the Bulge
in Belgium.

Otto Skorzeny, man about Europe.

Rescue a dictator here, take over a government there,
no big secrets. Except what he might have found at
Montsegur. And Blucher hadn't mentioned what he was
doing in Rome. Even so, how did the actions of a fervent
Nazi sixty years ago relate to Don's death? The only
answer Lang could see was that Skorzeny had found

something, a long-buried secret that someone would kill to keep that way.

He looked at his watch. Ten till five. The archives would close in a few minutes. He had discovered all he was going to about Skorzeny and his secret today. He stood, stretched, and read again the sign forbidding return of boxes to shelves.

Tomorrow, he'd be on a flight for Italy. Tonight, he was headed to Kincade's for some Chesapeake oysters and, hopefully, soft-shell crabs. Anticipation turned sour as he recalled he'd be dining alone. Gurt had loved soft-shells.

He remembered the first time. It had been, what, Chops, one of Atlanta's more expensive steak and sea-food houses? She had looked at the crab, including claws and shell, and then back at him.

"This is a *Vitzen*, joke, no?"

"The crab certainly doesn't think so," he'd replied.

She looked at him suspiciously. "It is a treat. You go first."

"With pleasure." He had severed a claw, the tastiest part, dipped it in heavy tartar sauce, and popped it into his mouth.

Gurt watched carefully, fully expecting him to try to spit it out. Or perhaps some sort of magic trick where he hadn't really put it in his mouth at all.

He put down his fork.

She was still staring.

"You ate it," she finally said.

In response, he cut into the body and took another bite.

She needed no further coaxing. They ordered an extra serving, to eat between the two of them.

Lang's eyes were wet as he exited the building.

CHAPTER TWENTY-SEVEN

Rome
The Vatican
April 1944

Pope Pius XII faced a problem unique to both him and his two hundred and sixty-one predecessors.

He sighed as he sat behind his desk, the one in the office with a view of St. Peter's Square. Bernini's gently curving colonnades usually gave him a sense of serenity. Today the view was marred by armed German soldiers standing in a crescent exactly one step outside the border of the Holy City. According to Kesselring, the German commander of Italy, they were there for the Pope's protection. Pius knew better; they were his jailers. Worse, they demanded the papers of every person leaving or entering the Vatican. And things got no better. General Wolff, SS commandant of Rome, had let slip, intentionally or not, the fact that kidnapping the Pope for the Vatican's riches was an option being considered in Berlin.

Pius cared little for his own safety, but the secret that had been unearthed below the Vatican was his responsibility. If the inscription was correct, its existence presented a painful dilemma. On one hand, it proved Jesus Christ had walked this earth, potentially silencing two thousand years of skeptics. On the other, the picture of Christ it painted was far different from the humble carpenter's son from Galilee.

He could perhaps eradicate the inscription and remove the relics that both validated the Gospels and made them liars. But where would he put such documents? Certainly not in the secret papal library that was anything but secret to the inner core of church scholarship. He would have to pray for guidance from above.

In the meantime, he must do nothing to force the Germans to act, do nothing although future generations could well revile his failure to condemn Hitler, the Nazis, and the barbarism Europe had not seen in a thousand years. The history of his papacy, even what would be perceived as his legacy, was irrelevant. The Church would survive him. It might not survive what was below the Vatican.

He had hoped he would be revered as the Pope who found the first contemporaneous documentation of Christ's existence. Now he was faced with being seen as collaborator with the Germans.

He had prayed such proof might be found by excavation, that Constantine had left some evidence, some relic of Our Lord, and those prayers had been cruelly answered. What was he to do? Did the Germans know exactly what had been found? If so, Pius despaired of the Church being able to keep the find, let alone its secret.

There was nothing he could do, really, other than pray for guidance from above. Pray and do nothing to provoke the Germans into action.

An ornate Louis XVI clock beside the window indicated that there were a few minutes left before the scheduled meeting. The Pope picked up a stack of papers and began to refresh his memory with a chronology that would not have been conceivable even a year ago.

The Allies had landed in Sicily last July. A few days later, the first bombs had fallen on Rome, damaging a rail staging area in the St. Lorenzo District as well as a medical school and a church. Pius, the first Roman Pope in over two hundred years, had reacted with shock and anger, as had his fellow Romans.

He had proposed that Rome be made an open city, one neither defended nor attacked. After all, the Eternal City should be spared the destruction bombs had created in London and Berlin. It was the last time he had spoken out.

There was a gentle knock at the door. Without waiting for a reply, Fra Sebastiani, Pius's personal assistant, appeared with a tray bearing espresso and four small cups. He set the tray on a table in front of the desk and withdrew. Years of service had acquainted him with His Holiness's moods, and one look at the pontiff's face told him conversation was neither wanted nor needed.

Getting up, Pius filled a cup and returned to his desk and the dismal scenario in front of him.

After the bombing, Pius had spent hours of the night in the lower levels of the Vatican, praying for peace, for Rome. And he had prayed for . . . He closed his eyes. God had seen fit to grant the latter prayer, the cause of Pius's present distress.

Within days of the air raid, Mussolini had been arrested at his weekly visit with the king. Six weeks later, Eisenhower, the Allied Commander, had announced the capitulation of the Fascist government, and two days after that, the Allies landed on the Italian peninsula.

The Germans had occupied Rome, filling the vacuum left by the collapse of Mussolini's government and the flight of King Victor Emanual. Shortly thereafter, over a thousand Jews had been arrested in the ghetto barely a mile from the Vatican. The only remaining true descendants of ancient Rome had been trucked off to the railway for deportation, many of the vehicles actually stopping long enough for guards and drivers to snap photographs of St. Peter's.

Pius had said nothing publicly. He could not. The fate of the Jews was deplorable, unthinkable, but to provoke the planned kidnapping and certain discovery of what the archaeologists had uncovered by opposition would be even worse.

Occasional bombing of Rome continued despite the prior Fascist boast that not even a swallow could fly over the city without permission. The Germans parked their tanks and trucks in the most historic piazzas, their anti-aircraft weapons on the roofs of many of the four hundred–plus churches. They also raided one of the Vatican's extraterritorial properties, a monastery, taking prisoner several Jews as well as men evading the orders for conscriptive labor.

Pius, outraged, sent a mild protest to the German ambassador. His reply was that the Italian Fascists had committed the sacrilege, a fiction the Pope was forced to swallow. He forbade the future use of Church properties for sanctuary to persons evading the Germans, although he suspected his orders were widely ignored.

In March, an SS police company was ambushed in the Via Rasella. Thirty-two Germans died along with two Italian civilians. Within twenty-four hours, by direct order of Hitler, three hundred twenty Italian men and boys were taken to the Ardeatine Caves outside Rome and shot, five at a time.

The papal newspaper, widely read as the only non-Fascist source of news, prepared an editorial expressing outrage. Pius changed it to blame the resistance for their attack on the occupiers. It was a bitter cup from which to drink, but the Pope could not risk provocation of the Germans. Not now, not with . . .

Another knock at the door, this time the meeting. Cardinals Rossi, Pizzardo, and Canali, the Pontifical Commission for the Vatican City State, the entity charged with the security of the Vatican. Pius extended his hand for the kissing of the papal ring. He was still unsure exactly where to begin, but at least he would no longer have to bear the secret alone.

CHAPTER TWENTY-EIGHT

Nimes, France
L'Hôpital de Nimes
A week earlier

She had no idea how long she had been here, but this morning was the first she had awakened aware fhat she was, in fact, here.

In the days (or weeks or months) previous, she had roused to the sound of her own screams more often than not, screams provoked by the same, unchanging dream. It was so real, she thought she must have experienced it rather than dreamed it.

That, of course, was impossible.

The sun, a brilliant orange light in a cloudless sky, exploded, hurling her out into space like one of those jets of solar gas she remembered seeing somewhere. She seemed to hang motionless in space for a long time before she began to fall, her velocity increasing as she saw an inhospitable earth rushing up to meet her at an impossible speed.

That's when she began to scream, both in the dream and in real life.

Sometimes she thought maybe at least part of the dream was real, the falling to earth part.

Her earliest memory was of aching all over and being partially covered by bits of jagged rock that could have come from another planet, for all she knew. And she didn't know much. For instance, she had no idea where she had come from, what her name was, nor why she was lying on a hillside covered with stone fragments.

At first she had thought her face was bleeding heavily. Putting a hand to her brow, she touched something both wet and furry. That's when she realized her eyes were shut. Opening them, she looked right into a shaggy face with big brown eyes. A dog was caressing her forehead with a very wet tongue, a not entirely unpleasant sensation. And not a totally unfamiliar one, either, although she could not remember when a dog had last licked her face.

As her eyes began to focus, she saw a man—a boy, actually—peering at her with a worried expression. He had said something to her, but she could not hear. The only sound her ears perceived was a soft whisper like gentle rain falling through heavy foliage.

She touched her ear with the one hand free of rubble. This time it wasn't the dog's licking making the side of her face wet. The hand came back dripping crimson. From some place she could not remember, she knew facial wounds, even superficial ones, bled heavily. Still, she wasn't exactly comforted by the knowledge.

Superficial or not, she felt no pain other than the ache all over her body.

Gathering her strength, she stood, her legs as shaky

as a newborn colt's. The dog ran in a circle around her, its mouth opening in what she supposed was a bark. The boy/man extended a hand, and she reached for it.

Then her world went dark.

Her next memory was staring at white walls seamlessly blending into white ceiling. It had been disorienting, not knowing how she had gotten here, where she was, or how long she had been here. She glanced down at a hand resting on a starched sheet. An IV needle was taped in place. From the smudges of old adhesive, she gathered the needle had been replaced several times. Without moving her head, her eyes traced the tube to a bag half full of transparent fluid hanging on a chrome stand.

From the visual clues, she guessed she was in some sort of hospital, although she had no idea how she knew this.

She had had no life before the sun exploded.

Through vibrations of the floor or some other means, she sensed someone else in the room.

Fully conscious of the effort, she refocused her line of sight from the IV bag and stand to the foot of her bed. The doctor was there again. At least, she guessed he was a physician. He was definitely a man in white—white shirt with white lab coat, topped by unruly shocks of white hair.

He looked up, noting her attention, and flashed white teeth at her, saying something she could not hear.

She knew what was coming and neither looked forward to nor feared it. After flipping the pages of her chart at the foot of her bed (how did she know what he was looking at?), he pulled back the covers, took the arm with the IV in it, and half-pulled, half-lifted her to a standing position on the floor. The tiles felt cool and soothing. With one hand on the IV stand and the other resting lightly, if protectively, around her waist, he led her out into the hall.

After she had gone about halfway toward the end, the doctor surrendered her to a nurse before standing in front of her, smiling. He pointed to his ear, then to hers, before making a circle with thumb and forefinger, the universal OK sign.

But her ears weren't OK. She could not hear. Perhaps he meant she soon would be OK. She hoped so. Not just because being deaf was a decided disadvantage. Without hearing, she had so much trouble speaking that she had all but abandoned the effort.

She could communicate by writing on the notepads they gave her. Unfortunately, she couldn't convey the very information the doctor and nurses wanted most: her name, where she came from, and so on. She had no such data to give them.

Somehow, again from that reservoir of knowledge that seemed to have no source, she knew that it was likely at least most of her memory would return, although she had no idea when. Until then, she would have to be patient, let the cuts, bruises, and aches heal, and hope she would know who she was before much longer.

CHAPTER TWENTY-NINE

Flumicino, Italy
Leonardo da Vinci International Airport
The present

Bleary-eyed from lack of sleep, Lang trudged down the concourse, cursing whoever had designed the airport so that nothing was near anything else. One of the newer passenger terminals in Europe, customs and immigration were nowhere near flights arriving from non–European Union countries, the flights that would need those services. Likewise, the train station connected to Rome was far closer to domestic arrivals, those passengers most likely to have left cars at the airport.

The Byzantine mind was alive and well in Italy.

In a rare moment of self-assessment, he realized he was simply in a foul mood, the result of plain bad luck combined with his own decisions.

First, he had decided to use the Couch identity provided by Reavers. No point in having his own name on a passenger manifest, readily available to anyone who knew how to hack into the airline's less-than-secure computer, or the charge appear on his own credit card, equally accessible. Let Reavers get "committed" by picking up the ticket.

Of course, the fictional Mr. Couch was not a frequent flyer and therefore was beneath the minimal notice given platinum, gold, or silver flyers. Ineligible to use the limited facilities of the preferred customer lounge, Mr. Couch had experienced the endless security lines reserved for nonprivileged passengers before spending an hour or so sharing the gate area with screaming children, blaring but unintelligible announcements, and overpriced fast food.

He had also been treated to passengers bellowing things like *"Dallas,* not *Dulles!"* or *"Tampa,* not *Tempe!"* into cell phones—a response to the airline's mechanized-voice reservation system that made it difficult if not impossible to speak to a human being.

Good goes around, but nobody at the airline wanted to talk about it.

The fact that it had been his decision to keep a low profile by entrusting himself to the uncaring hands of Atlanta's dominant carrier rather than arrive by Gulfstream did nothing to diminish his temper.

Even before arriving at the airport for the Washington leg, he had had signals that this was not going to be an enjoyable experience.

Since the Porsche's destruction, Lang had let Park Place's attendants park and retrieve the Mercedes, both from an assumption that another potential assassin would see the futility of a second car bomb and because he simply didn't care how the young men treated what he viewed as simple transportation.

This particular morning, the Mercedes had chosen not to respond to the electronic device that unlocked the car. His call to the dealership, one of several owned by the same company, had left him with the impression that the service department viewed his continuing problems as somehow his fault rather than designer-induced over-sophistication.

Mercedes-Benz CLK: the revenge of the Third Reich.

It had been no surprise that the Dulles–Rome flight had been delayed three hours for a mechanical problem the pilot described as "a minor glitch." The tone of the man's voice said it was no surprise to him, either.

Time to spare, go by air.

Forgetting life's sharper points for the moment, Lang set down his single bag to buy a cup of espresso at the coffee bar in the rail terminal. A large, barnlike structure with a glass roof, the airport station contained a few shops and four tracks, all of which went to Termini, Rome, departing at approximately twenty-minute intervals. The only question was whether to take express or local. Lang took the first departure.

Staring out of the window at the weed-covered switching yards and intermediate stations, Lang wondered how many times he had taken this ride. Shortly before leaving the Agency, he had brought Dawn here. Her first trip outside the United States, she had taken delight in even the dreary scenery that surrounds most rail right-of-ways. Before arrival at the final stop, she had become radiant at the sight of the first antiquity, a bland section of ancient brick that had been part of the city's wall.

Lang had always heard Rome was a city of churches, but he had never realized how many. Dawn had insisted on seeing the places of worship of the Jesuits, the Dominicans, and the Capuchins. They visited churches boasting sculpture by Michelangelo and Bernini and paintings by Caravaggio and Raphael. Before the first morning was over, Madonnas, martyred saints, and incidents from the Gospels melded into a religious blur. Never had Lang been so thankful for the three- to four-hour afternoon period when museums, businesses, and especially churches were *chuiso,* closed.

But he had never let Dawn know, feeding on her delight like a starving man presented with a banquet.

Only last year, he had been on this very same train, unknowingly about to revive a relationship with Gurt dormant since he had met Dawn. He and Gurt had made wild love in a small pension in the Trastevere District, ridden her motorcycle into the countryside, and hidden in an Agency safe house just across from the Villa Borghese, Rome's largest park.

Now Gurt, like Dawn, was gone.

He could take no vengeance against the cancer that had stolen his wife, but he could, and, by God, would, make those responsible for Gurt pay. Only the apprehensive look on the face of the woman seated facing him made him aware that his teeth were grinding. At the same time, he noticed the pain of fingernails digging into the heel of each hand.

An hour later, he was unpacking at the Hotel Hassler, a slightly past-its-prime, very American-style hotel at the head of the Spanish Steps. It was the sort of place Couch might stay, particularly if he was on business and, like most Americans, more than willing to compromise quality for the certainty he would not be confronted by people speaking only the native tongue.

Lang had requested a room on the side facing away from the steps, fully aware that those flights of marble constituted the place for younger tourists to congregate, play loud music, smoke, and photograph one another.

Finished unpacking the small bag, he stepped into the hall, looking both ways. He saw a maid's linen trolley but no maid. Bending over to shield what he was doing, he pulled a hair from his head, ran a saliva-moistened finger along it, and stuck it to the top of the doorknob. Once dry, that hair would fall at the slightest touch. Unlikely the telltale would be needed, since no one in Rome knew who Mr. Couch really was, but old habits died hard.

He checked his watch. If he didn't dally, he would make it on time.

A little over a mile away was a cartoonlike carving of an elephant with an obelisk on its back. The monks of the monastery that had become the church Santa Maria sopra Minerva had commissioned Bernini to grace the small square in front with the animal and then proceeded to insist the original plan was unstable, unsuitable, and overpriced. Not lacking a sense of humor, the sculptor had adorned the supposed symbol of wisdom and piety with a trunk of serpentine proportions and ears that could well have been the inspiration for Dumbo.

That had been the thought for centuries, anyway.

Then, in the recent past, excavation for enlargement of the Vatican's underground parking lot had uncovered a large beast first thought to be the remains of some sort of dinosaur. Quick research of the vast papal library had revealed that the king of Portugal had made a gift to one of the several Pope Leos of an albino dwarf elephant. The pontiff named the beast Hano, and elephant and man shared such an affection that the little pachyderm followed his master everywhere, including papal masses.

Lang never passed this way without a smile.

Just behind the piazza was a small store that sold ecclesiastical vestments and paraphernalia. Before entering, Lang debated: a simple black shirt with clerical collar, or full cassock, perhaps with biretta, the three-ridged square hat favored by many European priests? He chose the latter along with a simple ebony-beaded rosary. He was tempted to include a Bible printed in Italian but decided keeping his hands free might prove a better choice.

In a half hour, he was on his way. The shopkeeper had asked not a single question nor requested any documentation of Lang's ordination into the Church. He did, however, carefully examine and count each euro with which Lang paid.

Lang was uncertain exactly what this said about the clergy.

Package under his arm, Lang stopped at a favorite pizzeria just off the Piazza Della Rotunda. There were only two tables, both outside on the street. Both were filled with chatting American college students. He took his square of anchovy, pepper, and onion to enjoy while sitting on the edge of a fountain and looking at the Pantheon, Rome's oldest structure still in use. His pleasure, if not his sense of history, was undiminished by the presence of a McDonald's on the very same piazza.

The Pantheon was erected by the Emperor Hadrian a hundred years before Constantine, a temple for not one but all the gods. Every emperor after him erased his predecessor's name from over the door and carved his own. When Rome became Christian, the building became a church. Michelangelo studied that dome to learn how to do one for the new St. Peter's. In the eighteenth century, Bernini was hired to put bell towers on each side. The people ridiculed them, called them "donkey's ears." They came down. The hole in the center of the dome allowed sunlight into an otherwise windowless single room.

The massive bronze doors, the symmetry of the round building, as well as its antiquity had always had a salutary effect on Lang. He could feel the anger associated with the trip melt away like smoke in a breeze. Thankful Rome's fountains flowed with potable water, he cupped his hands to drink and washed the last of the fish taste away before using the thin square of paper that had served as a plate to wash his hands.

He took his time, wandering familiar streets, many of which were too narrow to admit sunlight for more than a few minutes a day. Far too confined for automotive traffic, scooters buzzed by unfazed. Lang was careful to back up to a wall as each Vespa passed, fully aware that the little machines provided a great getaway from purse- or parcel-snatching. He also remembered an attempted stabbing by a killer on a similar contraption.

He was not going to be distracted by his love for the Eternal City.

Back at the hotel, he stood at the front desk, awaiting his room key. He happened to notice a newspaper with block headlines taking up the top fold. Below was a vaguely familiar face, a slightly chubby man in an expensive suit.

Lang held the paper up for the clerk to see. "Who's this?"

The young man didn't have to look up from his computer screen. "The prime minister. He is about to be indicted for taking pay, er, pay . . ."

"Bribes?" Lang supplied, reaching for the key a young woman was handing him.

"Bribes, yes."

Lang couldn't recall the man's name, but he recalled him as being, if not one of the richest men in Italy, a conservative (at least by European standards) and a mainstay in a country that changed governments more regularly than its men changed their shirts.

The telltale was as he had left it.

Without taking off his clothes, Lang stretched out on the bed and was asleep before he was aware of being drowsy.

Chapter Thirty

Refreshed and his body clock now on the same time as Europe's, Lang untied the string that bound the paper-wrapped package. A few minutes later, he surveyed his image in the bathroom mirror. He looked as much a priest as any he had seen. He took the stairs to the ground floor to minimize being noticed. The Hassler was not a hotel within the budget of an ordinary priest.

Thirty minutes later, he was in St. Peter's Square.

Among the usual throng of visitors, two men were more interested in the priest striding past the fountain than in the architectural splendor that surrounded them.

"Sure that's him?" one asked.

"No way to be mistaken," the other said.

"We cap him here?"

The second man, obviously in charge, shook his head. "Too much of a crowd. We'd start a panic. Better we wait, make it look like a robbery."

"Of a priest?"

"They'll find him, they'll find out soon enough who he is. He walked here. He'll walk back. Be patient."

As Francis had instructed, Lang veered to the left, approaching a Swiss Guard on duty where a small avenue separated the Bernini Colonnade from the basilica itself. As though to repel a medieval attack, the purple-and-gold-costumed guard lowered his halberd to block Lang's progress. From the determination on the young man's face, there was little doubt he would use the weapon if necessary.

Reaching into a pocket, Lang produced the pass from the Scavia Archeolgia that had been faxed at Francis's request.

The Guard gave the paper the briefest of scans and pointed as he spoke in accentless English, "First door on the right. Show this to the man behind the counter."

Lang did as he was told, entering a small room filled with nine or ten priests, including one standing behind a ticket booth–like fixture.

"Okay, listen up," the man in the booth said in tones that came somewhere from midwestern America. "In a few minutes, a couple of our Jesuit brethren are going to take you through the necropolis. Stay with the group. We'd hate for you to get separated and locked up with an unknown number of heathen souls."

There was a murmur of chuckles.

"And watch out crossing over the street out there." He pointed as a small truck whizzed by. "You get hit and nobody's gonna stop to administer final rites."

Subdued laughter.

The various priests returned to the process of informally introducing themselves. Lang hadn't counted on this and hoped none were from Atlanta.

His anxiety was relieved when two more came through the single door, their guides.

"A few preliminaries," the older one said, also an American, although Lang couldn't exactly place the accent. "As most of you know, the Vatican was originally no more than one of ancient Rome's seven hills . . ."

Lang's mind drifted as facts he already knew were repeated.

His attention snapped back as one priest led the way outside and to a glass door that led into a small vestibule, while the second made sure there were no stragglers by following the group. The lead priest pushed a series of buttons on the wall. Lang memorized the sequence. A door opened with a whisper that indicated it also served as some sort of airlock.

"The temperature and humidity are carefully maintained," the leader said over his shoulder, as though answering an unasked question. "You'll see why in a moment."

From an invisible ceiling, soft lights illuminated a narrow cobblestone road between brick buildings that, at first glance, could have lined any ancient city street. Closer examination revealed that the structures even had windows and doors. The insides were decorated with sculptures and wall paintings of scenes from mythology and nature. A bird, easily identifiable as some sort of partridge, sat on a pine bough, depicted in tones fresh enough to have been applied yesterday. Lang marveled that something so ancient could be so well preserved. Another room was done in glittering mosaics, a picture of Apollo in his golden sun chariot being pulled across the sky by two white horses in midcanter. Almost every tiny tile was just as the artist had placed it.

"Most of these mausoleums were buried for nearly two thousand years," the guide/priest said. "That's why they are so well preserved."

The road climbed more steeply the farther they went. At irregular intervals, another door would open and close with a ghostly sigh.

"They certainly buried their dead in style," someone observed, speaking in a whisper, much the same as one might do in church.

"The families came to visit on certain days," the lecture continued. "See the hole in the roof there? For food and drink. The Romans believed the deceased's spirit could be maintained by pouring nourishment into the sarcophagus or cremation urn."

Lang stopped, nearly causing a collision with the priest trailing behind the group. He surveyed the incline and looked up and down a street that had not seen the sun in almost two millennia. It was as though he had entered another world, as indeed he had. It took little imagination to see toga-clad Romans walking this street. At several points there had been gaps between tombs. Intersecting paths? Lang was certain the necropolis had more than one avenue. In fact, finding the right one was going to be a problem.

Mistaking his hesitancy for fatigue, the following priest came up behind him. "We're almost at the top."

Unnoticed, the ceiling had become visible and was getting lower with each step.

"That's the floor of the Vatican?" Lang asked.

"Almost directly under the main altar, yes."

They trudged upward in silence until the street came to an end a few feet short of the union of ground and roof. Overhead, a pane of glass or some other transparent material admitted a thin light.

Their guide pointed. "We are under the main altar."

Lang had never suffered from claustrophobia, but the thought of bring confined under the millions of tons of basilica directly above his head gave him pause. He hoped whoever had excavated this necropolis had known what the hell they were doing.

This time the guide pointed to a confined area shaped like a box directly under the light filtering down. "There!"

Lang and the other visitors looked closer. The poor light flickered and danced on a shiny surface. Finally, he made out a transparent container of some sort, not much larger than a cigar box. The glass or plastic sat in a silver holder.

"The bones of St. Peter," the guide whispered in awe. "They were discovered in the forties when Pius XII allowed excavation of the necropolis you've just seen."

"How do we know the bones are Peter's?"

Lang couldn't see the source of the question, but he was not the only one surprised by it. This was, after all, a group dedicated to faith, not historical skepticism.

The lead priest was unfazed, fielding the question as smoothly as a shortstop would a ground ball. Perhaps he had heard the same query from audiences of a more secular nature. "At first, the church had only the legend to go by, that is, that Constantine built his church on Peter's gravesite. We know from old drawings the first basilica had the Trophy of Gaius, a two-story chapel with a trapdoor into the tombs below. One of the walls of that chapel, the graffiti wall, is still there, covered with Latin names, prayers, and the like, carved into the plaster along with the phrase 'Peter is here.' A Roman named Gaius wrote of Pope Zephirinus in the third century, who boasted of 'the trophies of the Apostle' being entombed here.

"When Julius II was removing what amounted to the ruins of Constantine's basilica to build the new one, bones were found under the main altar, wrapped in tatters of purple cloth, a sign of royalty. Those very bones are the ones you see. In 1968, Pope Paul VI had them placed in transparent reliquaries, one of which you see here."

"And the others?"

"Underneath."

The same doubter spoke again, perhaps emboldened by the darkness. "All you've got is bone fragments, some rags, somebody's carving on a wall, and a legend."

"Not quite. When the bones were encased as you see them, a team of forensic archaeologists examined them. There were no foot bones."

"So?"

"The feet of a crucifixion victim were nailed to the cross. Once he was dead, the body was left to rot unless there was some reason to take the body down, like freeing up space at the Circus of Nero. Removing the nail to take the body down was too much trouble. The Romans simply cut the feet off. The bones were from someone who, most likely, had been crucified."

The thought of a number of Renaissance paintings depicting Christ's ascension came to Lang's mind. None of them showed Him footless.

The tour guide shone a pencil beam of light onto an inscription. "The Church's official position is in the Latin inscription on the silver. It means 'From the bones that, discovered under the Vatican arch-basilica, are believed to be those of the blessed Apostle Peter.' "

Sounded like equivocation to Lang. He understood covering your bets.

"We'll leave by way of the Vatican grotto," the lead priest announced.

A final door wheezed open and they stood in a large, low-ceilinged room. Squares were formed by groups of sarcophagi, each with the effigy of the former Pope it contained. Minutes later, the group emerged into sunlight. From where he stood, Lang could see the entrance to the necropolis.

He made a mental list of what he was going to need.

CHAPTER THIRTY-ONE

Nimes, France
L'Hôpital de Nimes
At the same time

The doctor in white came into her room, a big smile on his face. Instead of helping her out of bed for her usual afternoon stroll around the ward, he turned on the television secured to the wall opposite her bed by a bracket. Curiously, she watched a man appear, his lips moving silently as a crawler slid across the bottom of the screen. She recognized the format as a news program, even though she had no idea when she had ever watched such a broadcast.

It went on a full minute before she realized the sound she heard was no longer that in her head but the voice from the man on the television. Her hearing had returned as suddenly as it had gone.

She squinted at the screen. For some reason, she knew

two things: The man was asking anyone who could identify her to call the Nimes prefecture of police, but he was
asking it in a language that was not hers. What her own
tongue might be, she still did not know.

Suddenly, her own face was staring back at her with a
confused and perplexed look. She had no memory of
the picture being made but accepted as fact that many
things may have taken place during the periods she
could not force her memory to divulge. From the same
source as the often-unrelated snippets of fact she knew,
she realized her likeness was being shown in hopes
someone might recognize her.

The thought frightened her. For reasons lost in the
black void of her recollection, identification equaled danger. She had no idea why this was true, only that it was.
As the doctor watched her image on the screen, her eyes
roamed for a weapon, coming to rest on the curtain that
separated her bed from the other in the room. Folded back
against the wall, it hung from a rail attached to the ceiling so it could be pulled to afford either patient privacy
had she a roommate.

As soon as her face faded from the screen, the doctor
stretched up to turn the set off and helped her out of
bed for her afternoon walk. She submitted meekly, still
thinking about the rail.

It was only then she thought to say in the same language as the TV broadcast, "I can hear again."

The doctor's glee was genuine, even though he was as
puzzled at the sudden return of the auditory sense as
was she. He insisted that both he and the chief resident,
a young man with wispy blond hair, examine her ears.
He used his cell phone to order a number of tests for the
next day.

With a low bow that, in his long white coat, reminded
her of a goose ducking its head, the resident said,

"Madame, though I don't know who you are, I do know you are well enough to join us in the physicians' dining hall instead of having your supper brought to you."

Holding the split in her hospital gown closed with one hand, she gave the best rendition of a curtsy she could. "If you can find me a robe, I would be delighted."

And she would be. Delighted for company at a time she felt she was in danger, although she didn't understand exactly from whom or why. She was also delighted for a respite from the sorry fare that appeared on her tray at every meal, food tasteless and colorless, if nourishing.

National borders were no protection against hospital food.

The physicians' dining hall had more title than substance. A battered table with six chairs filled a small interior room. From the smells and the clatter of pots and pans, she guessed it adjoined the kitchen. Dr. Philipe—the name of the doctor with white hair, she had just learned—the resident, and two others sat before paper place mats and tin utensils. One of the men was giving a dissertation on the woes of the liver of a certain Mdme. Madesclair, a lengthy and not exactly appetizing discussion that she listened to simply because hearing was like a new experience.

". . . It is, of course, problematic if the nodes are malign, since . . ."

An orderly entered from the direction of the kitchen carrying a tray on which was a carafe of red wine and a number of glasses. The room went silent as he set it down and departed. Dr. Philipe, as senior doctor present, poured a small sample into a glass, twirled it, sniffed, and finally tasted it.

Mdme. Madesclair and her liver were temporarily forgotten.

"A second growth, once again," the doctor announced.

There were general groans.

"We can afford better ourselves," the resident stated.

"Who, then, will share his private collection for the good of the group?" asked one of the doctors she did not know.

Silence greeted the suggestion before the conversation returned to Mdme. Madesclair's problems.

"Is surgery an option?" the youngest asked.

This time, she tuned the conversation out until she became suddenly aware one of the physicians was speaking to her. "Can you give us the earliest memory you have?"

Dr. Philipe said, "This is Dr. Rogé, our psychiatrist. He asked that you join us in an informal setting as soon as your hearing returned." He gazed around the table with a smile. "There are few more informal settings than this one."

Everyone chuckled.

"And do not concern yourself that he stares at you. He does that to all pretty girls, patients or not."

More merriment.

"The earliest," she repeated, pushing against the blank wall that was her memory. "Perhaps the hillside where I was found."

"You speak with a slight accent. Are you aware of . . ."

The same man from the kitchen entered again, this time with a savory roast on a platter.

"Lamb," observed the resident.

"With rosemary," added the other young doctor.

"Let us hope it is rare," wished Dr. Philipe.

The state of her memory was as forgotten as Mdme. Madesclair's liver. The conversation turned to lamb. Was it better roasted on an open spit? How did it compare to that done in a certain brasserie in Paris?

Once again, her mind ceased to register the words.

Instead, it conjured up a vision of Napoleon sitting at a table in front of his tent at Waterloo. He was watching a column of dust that could mean the Prussians would arrive in time to join Wellington. But he was discussing the relative merits of whole- versus skimmed-milk brie.

She smiled. That person, that special person always had a joke about the French. If she could only remember . . .

An hour later, a nurse saw her safely returned to her room.

She looked around. She was certain the closet door had been closed. Perhaps housekeeping had been looking for something?

She didn't think so.

Again, the sense of undefined danger.

She allowed the nurse to help her up and into the bed and pretended to sleep until she heard the squeak of the other woman's rubber soles on the tile fade out into the hall. Throwing the sheets aside, she got out of her own and climbed into the other bed, standing uncertainly on protesting springs. It took only a moment or two to unscrew the rail—actually, a section of round pipe over which hangers were fitted.

Unlike most of her actions, she understood the urgency of what she was doing. That was why she had only fiddled with her wineglass at dinner instead of drinking from it. She did not want to have to fight against her own urge to sleep plus the effect of the alcohol.

Besides, it was only a second growth.

CHAPTER THIRTY-TWO

Rome
Ponte San Angelo
A few minutes later

As Lang started over the sluggish green Tiber, the Vatican was on his right, its dome a dark silhouette against a fiery setting sun. Closed to vehicular traffic, the bridge was a prime location for African street vendors of everything from knockoff designer purses to primitive carvings with enormous breasts or penises. Behind him, the massive Castel Sant' Angelo contemplated centuries past in which its circular wall had enclosed the mausoleum of the Emperor Hadrian, papal refuge, fortress, palace, and prison. The center of the bridge was an ideal place for tourists to have their pictures made with a choice of impressive backgrounds.

A group of Japanese were taking turns immortalizing themselves on film in front of monuments to a history as

foreign to them as No or Kabuki theater was to western-
ers. It was when they parted like a human Red Sea to let
Lang pass that he saw the man.

On one level, Lang had been examining and discard-
ing methods of getting into the necropolis unobserved.
On another, years of training made him alert to his surroundings, so much so that his jaw was beginning to
ache from the smiles he had felt compelled to return
from Italians obligated to at least nod to a priest. When
the Japanese tourists had stood aside, he became suddenly aware of two things: Approaching directly in his
path was a young man with studs in his lips, eyebrows,
nostrils, and ears, more apertures than your average
clarinet. He not only wore a denim jacket, superfluous
in the warmth of the day, but both hands were in the
pockets instead of swinging freely as a normal stroller
would do.

Second, the afternoon sun cast shadows from the
right rear, and one of them was closing quickly.

Lang recognized the maneuver: Two or more opera-
tives approach the subject from opposite directions in a
confined space where lateral movement is impractical or
impossible. If adept enough at his trade, either or both
would swipe a deadly blade almost quicker than the casual observer would notice. There would be no attention
getting shots. If done properly, the victim would be dead
or mortally wounded before he could cry out. Nothing
would seem out of the ordinary until the prey collapsed
in a pool of his own blood.

Real danger or only perception?

Lang didn't have a lot of time to decide.

Stud Face was less than two steps away, his hands
sliding out of his pockets. Lang caught the briefest reflection of light on metal. He would have to be handled
before his confederate behind Lang could help.

The knife, metal, whatever it was, was in the youth's right hand. Lang feinted to the potential attacker's left. If the guy meant Lang harm, he would have to commit himself by moving to block his intended quarry.

He would also be off balance for a right-handed attack.

The assassin countered Lang's move, a stiletto not entirely concealed by his hand.

Lang dodged back to his own left, at the same time taking a step forward. Stud Face followed, the blade coming up for a mortal slice.

Lang took another step, this one toward his assailant and slamming a foot on the other man's most distant shoe, firmly anchoring him to the spot. At the same time, Lang fastened both his hands on the other's right wrist, pulling down hard and accelerating the move the knife-wielding attacker had initiated. Inertia brought the free foot against Lang's leg, causing the man to stumble forward as Lang snatched down hard on the wrist.

Lang was the beneficiary of unforeseen circumstance. He had planned on the man smashing into the low wall that lined each side of the bridge. Instead, his momentum threw him into the wall waist high. His body jack-knifed and flipped over.

There was a scream and a loud splash.

The herd of Japanese, cameras momentarily forgotten, rushed to the edge to look down. Lang turned, but the man behind was indistinguishable from anyone else on the bridge, all now surging to look down into the Tiber.

No one seemed to have noticed that the man thrashing in the water had been thrown there by a priest.

Before they did, Lang departed as hastily as possible without drawing attention. Many Japanese were taking pictures of the man thrashing in the water below.

It was dark by the time he crossed the Piazza Navona,

Spotlights shone through the fountains with wavering light that made Bernini's sculptures seem to move. The oval was full of the laughter of those dining at tables outside dozens of trattoria. He toyed with the idea of stopping for dinner. A couple of the establishments had been recommended by *Food and Wine* magazine. He decided against it. There was still at least one person out there he had not dealt with, a person who, presumably, wanted to stick a knife into him as much as Stud Face had. Better to dine at his hotel. The food wasn't the greatest, but he wasn't going to get stabbed between the antipasto and the platte primo, either.

The editors of *Food and Wine* magazine probably never had to make that sort of choice.

He walked north on the Via Guistiniani, still making a mental to-do list when a cat arched its back in a doorway. Rome has at least as many felines as people. The animals are all sleek and fat because neighborhoods feed them without regard to ownership, if indeed anyone truly owns a cat. Dogs are welcome in tavernare, trattoria, and café alike, but if the city had an animal as its true symbol, it would be a cat.

Lang stopped to watch it, a tabby that must have weighed twenty pounds, lazily stretch before setting out on a night's prowl.

Then it registered in Lang's mind, something missing. Sound. Something he had heard a moment ago was absent. Footsteps. There had been the sound of footsteps on the pavement behind him. Hardly sinister on a warm Roman evening.

But the footsteps had stopped just as he had.

Paranoia, a survival tool for anyone in Lang's former line of work, took over. After all, has anyone ever been killed by caution?

He walked purposefully, stopping suddenly in the middle of the block while he pretended to examine a doorway. One, two steps from behind. Then no sound. He was being stalked. The back of his neck tingled, as it did every time he anticipated action.

When he had the time to anticipate.

He turned, more a man getting different lighting on the doorway's carvings than an alerted target looking behind. He swallowed hard when he saw no one, his first impression confirmed. A person out for a late-evening stroll would hardly hide in the nest of shadows that darkened windows spawned between blocks. Neither would someone who had any idea how to follow someone. Ducking out of sight would be more likely to alert a subject than being seen, something a professional wouldn't do.

The clumsiness of the effort suggested an amateur, a mugger. What were the chances of an attempted robbery less than an hour after an attempted murder?

Lang's mind went into automatic drive, the lessons of years of experience, a computer pouring forth a printout. Whoever was trailing him would likely act before reaching the Corso del Rinascimento, a couple of blocks ahead. That comparatively wide boulevard would be well lit by streetlights and evening traffic heading to fashionable restaurants.

He could simply throw his wallet onto the street and run for it. The contents would more than sate the appetite of whoever was following. Lang could make it to the lights ahead before his potential assailant checked the extent of his windfall. He could, but he knew he wasn't going to. Lang would be damned if he would knuckle under to a simple street criminal, particularly in Europe, where the odds were small the robber would be carrying a gun. He had seen all the action he wanted for the day, but surrender was too distasteful to contemplate.

Apparently satisfied with his inspection of the doorway, Lang walked leisurely ahead. Attuned to what he was listening for, he could hear steps matching his own. With a slow step, Lang turned a corner into an unnamed, unlit alley and flattened himself against stones still warm from the day's heat. Almost instantly, a form was limned against the alley's entrance. It held something bulky, something that reflected the light behind.

Lang wasn't going to get a better chance. He pushed off from the wall. With all the force he could put behind it, he swung a fist.

"Signor!"

Lang stumbled as he pulled the blow up short. Even in the miserable light he could see the shawl-covered head, the shabby ankle-length skirt. He was facing a female, her eyes wide with terror. A *Zingara,* an old Gypsy woman, a bag full of bottles in her hand.

Its proximity to Eastern Europe makes Italy a prime destination for those perpetual tourists, the Gypsies. They seem to live by begging, rummaging through trash cans, and, many say, stealing. Apparently, the lure of collecting bottles for resale was enough for her to ignore whatever custom usually kept the women off the streets after dark.

Lang leaned against the wall for support. He was trembling with the thought of what had nearly happened. She had a justifiable fear someone would chase her away, a common practice among those Romans who see Gypsies as professional thieves. Of course, the old woman had used the shadows to remain invisible.

She recovered from shock before Lang did. She reached for his hand, mumbling the incantation preparatory to reading his palm, another Gypsy avocation.

He backed away. *"Non no soldi spielioli,* I have no

coins," he said, using one of the Italian phrases he knew, before hurrying down the street.

He heard her wailing behind him, no doubt casting a curse on him, his family, and his genitals. Another Gypsy specialty.

He stopped when he reached the Spanish Steps, well within view of his hotel. Only then did he realize he was trembling. Had he landed the punch he had intended, the old woman's jaw would likely have been broken. Or her head snapped so viciously as to break a neck brittle with age.

The picture of the terror on the old woman's face made his stomach heave. This wasn't the lawyer Dawn had married. Not even the retired agent Gurt knew, although he suspected a little bit of violence would not have disturbed her. What had he become? Since responding to Don Huff's daughter, he had been exposed to more savagery than during all the time he had spent at an agency where murder and mayhem were often tools of the trade.

You asked for it, a voice within himself noted. No one made you go trotting off to Spain. Now you are no closer to Don Huff's killer than you were, and Gurt's dead because you weren't content to practice law and manage the foundation you set up. Why not go home before you succeed in getting yourself killed, too?

He began to climb the steps, unaware he was speaking aloud. "Quit? Maybe. But not until I find who killed Gurt."

By the time he reached the top, he realized he was no longer hungry.

CHAPTER THIRTY-THREE

Nimes, France
L'Hôpital de Nimes
At the same time

Night.

She had taken her evening sleeping pill, holding it under her tongue until the night nurse had had ample time to return to her station before spitting it out into a tissue and dumping it into the trash can by the bed. She fought sleep as she would a mortal enemy, concentrating on staying awake as though her life depended on it, as she believed it did. She was thankful the room was dark now so anyone glancing in the room could not see her open eyes. She doubted she had the strength to remain awake had she had to close them to appear to be lost in slumber.

Before dawn, she would know if her instincts, her experience from a time she could not remember, could be trusted.

Outside her door, the colorless light from the ward's

nursing stand invaded her room with a pattern of shad-ows. She was not sure what she had actually seen when part of those shadows shifted color to a penumbra, not quite dark but not light, either.

She blinked, half certain she had seen nothing but a trick played by a weary optic nerve. She strained, hop-ing to hear some sound, but her ears gave back only the sound of her own heartbeat and the whisper of her breathing, a sound like the static of a radio station that has gone off the air.

Something blocked the demilight from the hall. Only for an instant, but long enough to give it human shape.

Moving as slowly as possible, she edged to the far side of the bed, holding the iron rod under the sheets. She wanted as much space as possible. Whether her newly restored hearing or some sixth sense, she felt a presence moving toward her.

She turned her head sideways so the corner of her eyes, that part most sensitive to motion, could catch movement. Next to her bed, a place in the charcoal-gray darkness became denser, blacker than the rest of the room. There was not enough light to distinguish the outline of any form or substance, only an indefinable point where black became inky black.

She imagined she could feel someone's breath, a faint warm stirring in the air.

She had only a guess and what seemed an atavistic knowledge of what she must do. Grasping the tube of metal at one end, she lunged to a sitting position, putting whatever weight she could into a jabbing, upward thrust. Swinging the rod horizontally might or might not con-nect with the intruder's head, but if she missed, she was unlikely to get the another chance. An upward stroke could catch whoever was next to her bed anywhere. If she got lucky and hit right under the ribs, a ruptured spleen and disabling pain would result, perhaps even a punctured lung.

The impact was so hard it sent a jarring shock all the way to her shoulders. There was a resulting grunt of pain and the sound of a collision with the far wall.

With one hand, she found the switch to the bedside light and was out of bed almost before the darkness dissolved. She was looking straight at a man slumped against the wall. His feet were scrabbling against the tile as he tried to stand. Blood dripped from his chin where a flap of bloody flesh hung like some gory goatee.

The same glance caught the light's reflection from the knife on the floor about halfway between them, the weapon he had dropped when she jabbed him.

He saw it at the same time she did and made a lunge for it.

Before his fingers even touched the handle of the blade, she had a clear shot at his head, shoulders, and back of his neck. The metal rod flashed over her head like the sword of an avenging angel and struck its target between the third or fourth cervical vertebrae and the first thoracic, that spot where the segments of the spinal column are no longer protected by part of the skull nor yet shielded by the shoulders. It is where the entire weight of the skull rests on the neck.

There were two distinct but simultaneous sounds: a thump of flesh being pulverized and a snap like a dry twig being broken. The man was no longer moving.

She kicked the knife into a corner before she stooped and rolled him over on his back.

Eyes stared into eternity from a face that meant nothing to her. She sat on the floor next to him. Methodically, she began to search his pockets, even though she could not have enunciated exactly what she was looking for. She found lint and a few loose threads from the cheap pair of slacks he wore. No wallet, no identification.

For reasons she also could not have explained, she was not surprised. It was as if she had not expected any.

There was an inside pocket in the light windbreaker he had worn over a polo shirt. At the very bottom, she felt something like paper. Pulling it out, she held it up to the light. Some sort of ticket, a bus or subway in . . . The name was difficult to read. She extended her arm fully to get nearer to the lamp.

No use. Whatever had been printed on the stub had been faded into illegibility by washing or dry cleaning.

Still . . .

Uncertain of exactly what she hoped to achieve, she got to her feet and padded over to the closet. When she had been found, she had been wearing hiking boots, jeans, and the tattered remnants of a blouse. She supposed she had had some sort of purse or wallet containing whatever identification she owned. It had never been located, probably destroyed in the explosion.

The jeans, a sturdy American product, albeit stitched in Taiwan, had endured, the only garment she possessed at the moment except for the steel-shanked boots.

She slipped the pants from the hanger and reached into one of the front pockets. Her hand emerged with a crumpled slip of paper. Letting the all-enduring jeans fall to the floor, she held the stub from the dead man up next to the one she had taken from her own pocket.

The same shade of green.

She placed one on top of the other. A perfect match.

For almost a full minute, she stared at the two stubs. They spoke to her of a monotone voice announcing arrivals and departures, of crowds of people, many carrying luggage. Then she was sitting at a table across from a man very special to her. Through plate-glass windows she could see buildings wet with drizzle.

She and the man had been . . . were going to . . .

Seemingly unrelated, she saw the skyline of a city far away, in America. She heard the whine and felt the soft, wet muzzle of a large, ugly dog, an animal whose name was . . . was Grumps? What kind of a name was that? There was a black man, kind face, clerical collar. Most of all, there was that man very special to her and in real danger of which he might be unaware.

How could she . . . ?

Then she remembered, the facts unfolding like cards dealt on a table. She was Gurt Fuchs, an employee of a very unusual organization that had trained her how to do a number of things most women never even dreamed of. Like how to take care of people like the man on the floor. It was as if a dam had burst, unleashing a flood of memories that crowded her mind for space. There were a number of questions she still could not answer. Others had answers that frightened her. Still more told her she must act.

Now.

She pulled the jeans on under her hospital gown. She was, as the very special man . . . Lang, that was his name, Lang, liked to say, history.

But first, the man lying on the floor of her room. She couldn't leave him here to be discovered before she had gotten as far away as possible. Too bad her employer had no service here to clean up messes like corpses. Such assistance had been called . . . ? What? Housekeeping, yes, that was it, housekeeping. In other places, housekeeping crews were specially detailed to sanitize crime scenes.

Well, tonight she would have to do her own housekeeping. Taking a foot in each hand, she dragged him to the side of the bed and gripped the waist of his trousers.

If she could somehow get him into her bed and cover him with a sheet, she wouldn't be missed till morning. She tugged, but the weight was more than she could lift. Removing his belt, she looped it around limp, cold wrists. She walked to the other side of the bed, sat on the floor, and pulled so that at least the arms, head, and shoulders of the corpse now rested on the bed linen and the bed bore part of the load. From there it was a simple matter to boost the feet up.

She helped herself to the man's shirt before covering him with a sheet.

The sole nurse on duty was staring at a small portable TV, one that could quickly be unplugged and hidden under the desk in the unlikely event a doctor should appear at this hour of the night. From the canned laughter, she must have been watching the French version of a sitcom.

Or someone had suggested foie gras was bad for the health.

CHAPTER THIRTY-FOUR

Rome
Hotel Hassler
The next morning

"Mr. Couch!" the desk clerk called across the lobby.

Lang was so intent on what he had to do that morning, he had almost forgotten the name under which he was registered. He stopped just short of the door leading outside and retraced his steps.

Lang noted the morning coat, gray vest, and striped pants. Staff at Italy's better and aspiring hotels dressed like they were attending a wedding. Except the doormen. They dressed as bit players in a Gilbert and Sullivan operetta. He exchanged a euro for an envelope. Inside was a note from an unfamiliar number:

Your package has arrived.

Lang nodded as he wadded the paper and tossed it into one of the brass ashtray stands that populated the lobby. Before his departure, he had told Sara to let him know when a parcel arrived from George Hemphill. She was to go to the UPS store in the lobby of the office building across the street and fax Couch here. He had seen the question in her eyes but declined an explanation. To try to convince someone that he was dealing with an unknown but powerful organization, and that organization might well have the capability to intercept phone calls came too close to a myriad of conspiracy theories. There was no good reason to explain that faxes, like any other telephonic communication, were subject to interception, particularly those transmitted by satellite, as almost all transatlantic calls were these days. If his number was being observed by one of the machines that could easily monitor thousands of calls at once, using computer technology to flag certain preprogrammed words, any call from his office could draw unwanted attention.

Using an unrelated phone number utilized the Achilles' heel of the mass intercepts made possible by RAPTOR: The capability to listen and record almost any conversation or fax existed. The technology to separate the electronic wheat from the mass of chaff did not.

Sara had long accepted what she viewed as Lang's harmless idiosyncrasies. Sending a message to someone she had never heard of in Rome was no more abnormal than overnighting a package to general delivery in the same city. In fact, her message denoted that the parcel had already been sent.

One more item on Lang's list.

As he passed the concierge's desk, he stopped, his attention diverted by a stack of the day's newspapers. Under banner headlines, the same chubby, well-dressed man he had seen yesterday smiled out at the world.

Unable to either read the Italian or resist his curiosity, Lang approached the desk. "Your prime minister . . . ?"

The concierge shrugged, a matter of no consequence. "He has gotten a law requiring bribery to be persecuted . . ."

"Prosecuted?"

"Yes, requiring the crime of bribery to be prosecuted within a year, six months too late to prosecute him."

Italy: If not honest politics, entertaining politics. Louisiana residents should feel right at home.

He walked to the Trastevere District, that area of Rome south of the Tiber that, during the Renaissance, had housed masons, bricklayers, and other laborers as well as a number of the era's most famous. Rafael, it was said, kept a mistress in the rooms over a tavernare there. Long ago, laborers' humble rooms and lofts had been converted to trendy apartments for those who could afford to live in an area now fashionable.

Even so, the locale's more humble origins were still visible, if one knew where to look. An example was a simple doorway between a trattoria and a shop displaying the highest end in women's shoes. A hallway led between the two establishments until it widened into a series of rooms offering tools and equipment for sale. There had been no exterior sign. As is often the case in Rome, the proprietor relied on trade from residents who knew the location of his emporium anyway.

Such logic, Lang thought, would drive American ad agencies into therapy if not bankruptcy.

Lang selected two flashlights, batteries, and a short crowbar.

Paying for his purchases, he walked northeasterly along the Tiber, enjoying the shade of massive plane trees. In front of him, two teenaged girls clad in identical low-rider, epidural jeans giggled as they looked in shop windows. He would eventually arrive at the post office to which Sara should have sent his package, but for the moment, he was enjoying the sights and sounds of the Ghetto, the area occupied by Rome's Jews since antiquity. It had been almost emptied during the German occupation.

World War II.

As he walked, carrying his puchases, he tried to imagine a connection between a Roman emperor's, Julian's, idea of a prank, what an SS officer, Skorzeny, might have found in an ancient fortress and the murder of Don Huff. He rethought the procedure he was following. Find the indictment of Christ, or at least its hiding place, and hope whatever was there would lead him to the truckloads of whatever Skorzeny had removed from Montsegur and hope whatever it was, it pointed to the killer.

The whole thing seemed like some sort of intellectual Raggedy Ann, poorly stitched together with seams fully exposed. Raggedy Ann or Barbie, it was all he had, the only trail to Don's murderer. More important, his only hope of finding whoever was responsible for Gurt.

He stopped in the post office. In Italy, as in most European countries, traditional telephone service is administered by the postal department, possibly accounting for the inefficiency of both. With the advent of cell phones, provided by private carriers, the stuff of legend and jokes at the government's expense were coming to an end. Still, a woman was shouting into a receiver, her hands gesticulating as only the Italians can. Lang would have guessed her weight at a svelte two hundred; and, from the few words Lang caught, that she was expecting money from someone in Naples. From the tone of her voice, Lang would not have bet on her receiving it.

He stood in line before the single window, impatiently

shifting his weight as one postal customer after another exchanged pleasantries and the daily neighborhood gossip with the clerk, a female petite only in comparison with the one on the phone.

In Italy, years of pasta consumption and middle age often combine to produce a condition not adequately described as "middle-age spread."

Holding up the Couch passport, Lang's meager Italian succeeded in having the clerk produce an envelope with Mr. Couch's name on it. Lang turned it over, making sure the small bit of red tape he had asked Sara to affix to the back was there. It had not been opened. He hefted its lightness. He had expected it to be somewhat thicker.

It is common, he supposed, that we imagine important documents to be bulky, weight added by significance.

The woman was still screaming into the phone when he left.

Back at his hotel, Lang emptied his pockets. He may as well stretch out on the bed. He looked at the stuff from his pants: passport, keys, change, his cell phone.

Where . . . ?

The device Reavers had given him—he had forgotten it, leaving it on the dresser. Uneasily, he looked around the room. No, housekeeping hadn't made it here yet. The contraption hadn't been compromised. Not that chambermaids were likely to show a lot of interest in something that resembled a BlackBerry, anyway.

He took off his trousers and lay down on the bed, taking a long moment to examine the envelope. Perhaps it contained answers, perhaps a waste of time.

With a sigh, he opened it.

Two pages, clearly produced by typewriter, not computer. But then, the information would predate the common use of computers. Other than what was written on them, the pages were blank, no headings, no clue as to a return address.

Lang would have been surprised had there been any hint as to the origin of these sheets of paper.

A list of numbers on the left side, a single word on the right, the same word, starting with 24–4–60 and ending with 5–8–74. The word was the same, "Madrid."

CHAPTER THIRTY-FIVE

Rome
Saint Peter's Square
That night

Even at night the square in front of the Vatican was crowded. Lang had relied upon the fact.

Wearing his cassock, he walked purposefully toward the left side of the papal palace, the same place where he had been admitted by the Swiss Guards the day before. This time, though, he had no pass. As he approached, he slowed his pace, looking around until he saw a group of nine or ten priests hurrying toward him.

The square was sufficiently lit for him to see that they were all young, probably students at one of the many schools and colleges for clergy the Vatican operated. From the animated nature of their conversations, he guessed they were returning from a supper at which spirits were not entirely of the holy nature.

He fell into step, laughing gaily when the others did.

In ragged formation, they held up identifications for the guard. Lang extended a copy of his Georgia driver's license, hoping the generous light wasn't quite good enough to distinguish it from a pass.

Without slowing them down or moving his halberd from his shoulder, the guard waved them through.

Once past, Lang kept up with the group only until he was opposite the door that led to the necropolis. Then he slowed his pace and, waiting until a passing automobile speeding into the Vatican grounds could provide a shield, ducked into the shadows. He was certain no one had noticed, but he crouched in darkness for a full five minutes before moving.

He simply watched. It was unlikely there was observation equipment. Who, after all, would want to break into what amounted to a graveyard? Still, there was no reason to hurry and less to take chances. His patience was rewarded when he detected the slightest movement in the dusky dark above the street on the wall opposite the door. Staring as hard as he could, Lang discerned a small camera moving back and forth on its mount. A slow count of the seconds confirmed that the thing swiveled on a regular scan.

Lang waited until the camera was pointing directly at the doorway before he moved. With slow, purposeful steps he reached the wall beside the entrance, his eyes watching as what little light there was reflected from the lens. He could no longer see the camera itself.

When the reflection disappeared, indicating the camera was facing away from him, he moved to the door. He estimated he had about fifteen seconds before he was on somebody's TV screen. He took a deep breath, willing himself to be calm as he mentally counted off the seconds and began to punch in the code he had memorized.

Ten seconds.

As he pressed each number, a green light appeared on a small panel. He supposed his concentration on watching the numbers the priest had used had prevented him from noticing. There was a pause between touching a number and the green light, the time it took for his selection to be compared to the correct sequence.

Five seconds.

He heard the whoosh of escaping air just as he estimated the camera was a second from being directly on the door. Flattening himself against the ground, he held the entrance open, counting until he knew the surveillance camera was pointed the other way.

In an instant, he was up, inside, and had shut the door.

He was surprised by the lights, the same seemingly sourceless illumination that he had seen before. Evidently, the lighting system was activated by the door's opening. Standing perfectly still, he played a flashlight in a hundred-and-eighty-degree arc before turning it upward and across the ceiling, some twenty feet above his head. The constant pressure and consistent air circulation had made the air remarkably clear of particles of dust from the dirt and stone, enabling the beam of his light to search for more cameras.

He turned the light off, and his eyes probed the darkness for any threads of light across his path, infrared, enhanced light, or other electronic streams, which, when interrupted, would set off an alarm. The idea of a motion detector in a cemetery seemed oxymoronic, but, then, someone, probably the *Scavo Archilogica,* had deemed an outside surveillance camera prudent.

Reasonably certain he was unobserved and unhindered, he turned the light back on, this time painting the facades of the tombs he had seen yesterday. If the ancient necropolis was as Francis had described it, there would be more than the single avenue taken by the tour group.

That assumption was joined by another, one Lang had pieced together while walking back to his hotel that afternoon: If the Emperor Julian had wished maximum embarrassment to Christians by use of the indictment, accusation, whatever, he would have picked a preeminent place for it, not some random sepulcher. What more predominant spot than the closest proximity to Peter's grave? If the hypothesis was true, one of these streets in this city of the dead would be crowned by what Lang sought.

But which one?

The flashlight illuminated another mausoleum and then a dark space. Probing the emptiness, Lang saw a gap, an alley, perhaps no more than two feet, between the structure and its neighbor. Extending the arm holding the light into the opening revealed a line of walls extending beyond the flashlight's range. He breathed deeply and squeezed into a stygian darkness pierced only by the narrow column of his flashlight.

Halfway through, he bumped into something solid. A brief examination revealed an acrylic barrier, sealing the tourist route from the rest of the necropolis. Made sense. No point in trying to heat, cool, and pressurize an area not used. A closer look revealed a door, this one unlocked, allowing passage into the rest of the burial ground. A gentle push and it opened, creating a mild breeze of pressure differential.

The alley led him onto another road, one identical to the one he had left in width and slope. Here, though, dirt lay in irregular mounds, studded with bits of plaster, marble shards, and general rubble. The street's surface was rough, fraught with holes where cobblestones had rolled loose. The structures lining the way were dingy,

caked with the dust of millennia. This area had been excavated and abandoned.

Lang began an uphill trek made laborious by the necessity of shining his light on the road surface before
each step. It would be all too easy to snap an ankle by stepping into a hole or tripping over the debris that seemed
to have been randomly scattered. Parts of some of the
mausoleums had crumbled, giving the impression of a
town that had been the center of a battle.

The fact that this area did not have the air-conditioning
or pressure control of the single avenue he had seen was
becoming increasingly obvious. The shirt under the cassock was glued to his back with sweat, and each breath
seemed to include as much dust as air.

The barrier between the part of the necropolis open
to select tourists and this part, the unseen, larger part,
meant that if his supposition about the location of the
indictment was wrong, that it wasn't at the top near St.
Peter's bones, he would have to work his way across the
hill, getting farther and farther removed from the sole
exit into the outside as he moved up and down the
spokes of a wheel.

The thought was less than comforting.

The air seemed to be increasing in humidity. Lang remembered he was climbing above what had once been a
swamp. He had little doubt the fetid springs that had fed
stagnant streams were still here someplace. Sweat was
beginning to run into his eyes.

Discomfort notwithstanding, he was tempted to loi-
ter, to look at some of the sepulchers with particularly
ornate carvings, portrait busts or, occasionally, a fresco
partially visible through the accumulation of grime. Never
again would he have such an opportunity to examine
untouched Roman ruins. He shrugged off the thought.

He would be lucky to find what he was looking for to-night. If he made an exploration out of the task, he would be here a month.

Panting, he stood slightly bent at the crest of the hill. Through the transparent wall, he could see the box that held the reliquary of the saint. To his left was an arched doorway from which the keystone had long fallen. Only the packed dirt that filled the structure held it up.

He stood on tiptoe and used one hand to brush away the grit and dust covering the inscription while the other held the light.

"Teutus Forneas, Centurion . . . ," he read, unaware he was speaking aloud.

The rest of the epitaph had been on the missing stones.

Turning, he focused the flashlight's beam on a square structure with the remains of classical columns framing what had been the doorway. The words on the lintel identified it as the last resting place of an entire family of Greeks who had served and bought their way out of slavery. Judging by the ornateness of the tomb, they could have bought anything else they had desired, including slaves of their own.

Lang sighed in disappointment. If his theory was correct, how many of these streets would he have to climb?

On his way back down, he felt more alone than he had in his entire life. In pitch darkness in a burial ground, his only companions the dead of nearly two thousand years ago.

This was a graveyard he wasn't going to whistle past.

As he started up his next street, Lang froze, his ears straining. He had heard something, a sound out there just beyond the edge of his flashlight's beam. Unlike the one next to the lighted avenue, none of the illumination from the tour route leaked over this far, and the dark was so complete it seemed to swallow his feeble light.

There it was again, the sound of something scrabbling among the rubble, sending small pebbles rolling downhill. He lifted the light above his head for added range and a pair of red dots reflected it, blinked, and disappeared to the accompaniment of angry squeals. Rats, annoyed that their habitat had been invaded for the first time since the excavation back in the thirties or forties. What the hell was there for them to eat where the last morsel of food had been left in the first or second century?

He tried not to think about that or the question of just how bold the rodents might be in defense of their realm. He pushed on up the hill, this slope seemingly more steep than the others.

The first thing he noticed at the top was that he was closer to the box supposedly holding St. Peter's bones than he had been either on the tour or the excursion of the last few minutes. To his right was not a tomb but a wall that seemed to support the ceiling. Lang gazed at it a moment before he realized he was looking at the back of the so-called Graffiti Wall mentioned by yesterday's guide as denoting the tomb of Peter. It had been part of Constantine's original papal palace and a support wall for Constantine's basilica.

Standing with his head against it and leveling the flashlight along it, he discovered more than a few carvings on this side also. Greek letters were almost as numerous as Latin inscriptions. There were also figures Lang did not recognize.

He stepped back to get a more complete view, slipped, and would have tripped over his cassock and fallen had he not been able to break his fall by steadying himself with his free hand against the wall.

Otherwise, he would never have seen it: a piece of stone that didn't exactly match that surrounding it at the bottom of what looked like one of the support columns of the old church. Kneeling, he looked closer. A uniform layer of dust and dirt covered the entire wall. Only at an angle could Lang detect a slight difference in the stone's texture, too. Again using his hand, he brushed as much grit and dust away as possible.

Something had been carved into the stone, a series of letters someone had taken great pains to obliterate. Lang stood and moved to his right and to his left. The angle of the light picked up parts of letters, but not enough to even speculate as to the inscription.

He ran the light up and down the wall again, making certain of his original observation that this had been a support wall, one that could not have been moved. In fact, in early Christian times, technology would not allow weakening of this part of the foundation by cutting into it. Hence the effort to simply erase the words as easily as one emperor removed the name of his predecessor from the Pantheon. Lang sat on his haunches and thought. Most likely he had found Julian's secret, the emperor's prank.

But without being able to read it, how could it lead him anywhere?

Whoever had tried to kill him, had killed Gurt, obviously thought mere knowledge of the existence of this destroyed carving presented a danger to them.

Then he had another thought: Suppose they didn't know the words had been rendered unreadable?

Either way, he was determined to decipher what had been rendered illegible. As he scrambled down the slope, he was making a mental list of equipment. Hadn't Reavers insisted on being committed?

The monitors in the featureless room were dark, their screens a row of blind cylopean eyes. In contrast, an overlay showing a map of Rome was backlighted, a single bright dot moving slowly across the southeast corner.

Taking a specially calibrated ruler from the drawer of the steel desk, the room's sole occupant laid it beside the dot, measuring its movement for several seconds before he picked up a telephone with no dial on it.

"He's leaving now," was all he said.

CHAPTER THIRTY-SIX

Somewhere between Paris and Rome
Eurostar
At the same time

It had been a long time since she had ridden on a train. Not even once during the year she had spent in the United States, where such transportation was largely scorned for any journey longer than across town. Understandable, since American trains were far slower than travel by car, while those in Europe frequently exceeded a hundred and fifty kilometers an hour.

She leaned back in the seat, comfortable even though in third class, and peered out of the window into the night. Except for the few flashes of towns that were only smears of light, the darkness concealed any real sensation of movement other than the gentle rocking of the train itself.

Comfort or not, she would not have chosen to travel by rail had convenience and speed been her only criteria. To fly, one had to present identification, something she lacked. Airport security was far stricter than that of rail terminals, despite the terrorist bombing of the Spanish train a year ago. She needed to travel in anonymity.

That was why she was enduring the man seated next to her, some sort of electronics salesman from Milan. He had made an elaborate display of offering to pay for the cheap sandwiches and bottled water offered by vendors who seemed to board the train at every stop. He had made no secret (and, she suspected, little truth) in recounting the endless successes of his business, the cost of whatever motorcar he owned (she had almost dozed off and missed the marque), and the thrill and excitement of the life he lived.

He had not (and, she suspected, would not) get around to discussing the gold wedding band she guessed he was unable to remove from a pudgy finger.

A poor dye job on barely enough hair to comb over a pink scalp, a cheap, off-the-rack suit, and a cologne that could have been a weapon of mass destruction. He was so intent on her breasts as he spoke, she doubted he could recognize her face.

Antonio—that was the name he gave her, anyway—clearly considered himself to be a gift to women. She considered him to be atonement for some long-forgotten sin. Still, she avoided the temptation to simply turn her back to him or, better yet, get up and move. There were no reserved seats in third class.

Bad as he was, Antonio served a useful function: A woman traveling with a man, even Antonio, was less conspicuous than one alone.

Keeping an attentive smile plastered in place, she simply tuned him out.

Another reason for traveling by rail was the opportunity to do so. She had gone from the hospital to the local rail station and been gratified to find a train due in the next few minutes, one that would take her to Lyon, where she would transfer to one for Paris and then directly to Rome. Pretending to read the posted schedules, she had waited until a man purchased the ticket to Paris. As he had turned from the ticket booth, stuffing his ticket into a billfold, she had backed away and directly into his path. A Frenchman is unlikely to let such an opportunity with a pretty girl escape. While he pretended it was an accident that his hand found its way to her breast, she had helped herself to the wallet in his inside coat pocket.

A fair trade is an honest bargain. Or was it the other way around?

In other circumstances, she might have felt some modicum of guilt for the victim whose pocket she had deftly picked, but she desperately needed to get to Rome. And she could never have lifted the wallet had he not groped her. Perhaps the experience would prevent him from doing the same thing to another woman.

She doubted it. A Froggie who can keep his eyes and hands off an attractive woman is a dead Froggie.

Antonio launched into a new anecdote. Her mind was whirring with images blurred by the speed at which they appeared, somewhat like a film on fast-forward. The helicopter, hovering like a mechanical dragonfly, before exploding in a brilliant flash, the ensuing blackness. A brief moment of consciousness, being unable to move under huge weight that seemed to crush the breath from her. A silence so intense it had a sound of its own.

The facts had come back to her, but in no particular sequence. Until she sorted them out, it seemed equally likely she had gone to Montsegur before, not after, leaving Atlanta or being in Seville. She did know what she had found in the pocket of the man who had intended to kill her, and she knew she must tell Lang.

But how?

She had lost her encoding communication device along with everything else but the clothes on her back. Some of the clothes on her back, she corrected, remembering the shredded blouse. Besides, she had no idea exactly where she could reach him, although she was certain she knew where to find him sooner or later. She could call his office and ask Sara to have Lang contact her. But if what she suspected was true, anything said over any phone connected to Lang was being monitored. She only hoped he recognized the possibility his conversations were not private.

She would simply have to follow the theory she had put together. She only hoped she got there in time.

She also hoped he would figure out he was on the wrong path. Or, as the Americans said, barking up the wrong tree. Why would anyone want to bark up a tree, right or wrong?

CHAPTER THIRTY-SEVEN

Rome
The Vatican
April 28, 1944

At the same time Pius XII was conducting a meeting of the Pontifical Commission for the Vatican City State, Waffen SS *Sturmbahnführer* Otto Skorzeny was pretending to be just one more German taking pictures of St. Peter's Square. Even had it not been for blue eyes the color of glacial ice and the dueling scar that circled his right cheek, the ordinary *Wehrmacht* troops along the border of the Holy City would have shown him even more deference than the black SS uniform merited.

The rugged good looks, the soft Austrian accent did nothing to conceal an air of one who commands as though he were born to lead men into desperate ventures. One of those ventures, the rescue of Il Duce, had resulted in a notoriety that made him uncomfortable. A soldier's place was on the front lines, not the headlines.

Having his name in the papers was even more disquieting. At least he had successfully declined to allow photographs. Anonymity was like virginity: once lost, never regained.

He had had no choice in the matter. His *Führer* had ordered him to make himself available to Herr Goebbels's press corps, and he had followed those orders as would any good soldier. Fortunately, fame was indeed fleeting and the civilian public's brief attention quickly focused elsewhere. Even now, though, months later, a number of the troops called him by name as they saluted.

With invasion of France by the Allies imminent, he had requested a command similar to the one he had had on the Eastern Front until he had been wounded in 1942. Instead, he had been summoned to Hitler's home atop the mountains of Berchtesgaden, where the *Führer* himself had explained the present mission and its importance. Although Skorzeny would have preferred a return to combat, the *Führer* had been very persuasive.

Today Skorzeny was reconnoitering another raid.

Through the viewfinder of the Zeiss camera, he watched the Swiss Guards. Although their medieval pikes and uniforms provided more show than protection, he knew the men were trained in the use of modern weapons and prepared to die defending their employer, the Pope.

He hoped that would not be necessary, although he could not imagine them standing by as the Pope was taken prisoner.

He trained the camera on the area surrounding the obelisk. A souvenir of Rome's conquest of Egypt, it had been brought to Rome in the first century, A.D., although it had been moved to its current location only when the present St. Peter's Basilica was under construction in the sixteenth century. Its previous location and the significance of that spot was, Skorzeny understood, marked by an inset in the paving of what was now a fairly busy roadway between the southern edge of the basilica proper and the beginning of the Bernini colonnades. Two costumed guards were stationed here to prevent the unauthorized from entering the Vatican grounds.

If Skorzeny's information was correct, the subject of his interest was just beyond that entrance.

If it existed. He was uncertain exactly what the enigmatic inscription on the wall at Montsegur had meant. Even when translated by the head of the Classics Department at the University of Berlin, it made little sense and had even less significance. Who cared what crimes had been alleged against the son of a Jewish carpenter two thousand years ago? Non-Jewish, he mentally corrected himself. The Nazi party had done extensive research and produced conclusive evidence that Christ was not a Jew—conclusive for any German who valued his life or liberty, anyway.

Still, who cared?

Der Führer, that's who. Anything dealing with religion or the occult fascinated Hitler. That, of course, was why Skorzeny was here instead of fighting the British and Americans as they battled their way up the Italian boot or helping fortify the French coast.

Kidnapping the Pope was another matter. The Christian world would shriek its protest just as all of Europe had when the *Führer* had marched into the Rhineland, Austria, the Sudeten, and then all of Czechoslovakia. And with about as much effect. In the meantime, His Holiness could be ransomed off for the greatest treasure in the world, the priceless objects of art in the Vatican. After nearly five years of war, Germany's treasury could use the infusion of cash such riches would bring.

And Hitler would have a surfeit of religious artifacts, including whatever that emperor . . . Julian, the Emperor Julian, had hidden.

He let the camera fall loose to hang on the strap around his neck. The information. Intelligence provided by trained military observers was frequently misleading or downright wrong. Here, he was relying on the observations not of a soldier, not even a partisan civilian, but of Ludwig Kaas, the financial secretary to the Reverenda Fabbrica, a mere clerical bureaucrat.

Of course, Kaas had more incentive than most to get his facts straight. The families of his two siblings and his aged mother, all in Germany, to be exact. No one had actually threatened them, not in so many words. But when Hitler and his inner circle had heard the rumors of excavation below the basilica, they searched the voluminous records of the Third Reich until they found someone in the Vatican, someone who might be, shall we say, subject to patriotic persuasion.

Kaas had produced the information sought: entrances, number of guards on duty at any given time, and the location of the object of German interest. The priest had not even asked why the data was requested. Perhaps he knew. More likely, he wanted to make sure he did not. Well, the good father's self-delusion of innocence wasn't going to last much longer. The priest was scheduled to give Skorzeny a tour of the area beneath the basilica tomorrow morning.

After that, there would be no reason to delay the operation.

CHAPTER THIRTY-EIGHT

Rome
Hotel Hassler
The present

When Lang awoke the next morning, he sat up in bed, reviewing what, if anything, he had learned the night before. The inscription on the wall had been obliterated, but by whom? Historical revisionism and political correctness were at least as old as the Caesars. An emperor's name, Julian's inscription, either could have been removed. Unless Lang could manage to read a carving intentionally destroyed, he would never know what, if anything, Skorzeny had found or the motive for whoever had killed Don and Gurt and now had him in their homicidal sights.

But how do you read . . . ?

Inspiration is like a broadcast: free, but you just have to be tuned to the right station.

Hurriedly, he showered and dressed. Checking the

charged status of both his own cell phone and the Black-
Berry Reavers had given him, he slipped both in his
pocket, counted his cash, and decided he needed more
and left the room. A few minutes later, he was walking
briskly toward the rail station. One of the many things
Lang loved about Rome was its mix of history. A block
from the station was the massive Baths of Diocletian,
emperor at the end of the third century and author of the
Roman equivalent of Boston's Big Dig. Except the emperor's huge public bathhouse had actually been completed in a single lifetime. Straddling both modern and
ancient, a seventeenth-century building housed Rome's
archaeological museum, its location forming a triangle
with the baths and rail station.

Lang pulled open the museum's glass doors, entering
a small lobby, and approached the tickct booth.

"Curator?" he asked.

"Five euro," the woman behind the glass said, pointing to a price list in five languages prominently displayed
behind her.

Lang shook his head. "No, no. I'd like to see the curator, not the museum."

"If you no want see museum," she challenged, "why
you here?"

Once again, Lang became aware of how efficient the
barrier of language could be. He spoke little more than
memorized phrases of Italian, and her English was little better. "It's too much money," "May I have red wine,"
or "Where is the men's room?" wasn't going to be of
much use.

"Can I help you, sir?"

A young man in a white shirt, tie, and neatly pressed
pants had appeared like a genie at Lang's elbow.

"You can if you speak English," Lang said hopefully.

"Of course. What is it you wish?"

Lang grinned. "Your English is very good. Where did you learn it?"

The young man smiled back, a dazzle of white teeth. "P.S. 41 in the Bronx, where I live. I'm visiting my grandparents here, working at the museum, hoping to improve my Italian." He extended his hand. "Enrico Savelli."

Lang shook, almost blurting out a name that wasn't going to match his passport. "Joel Couch. I wanted to see the curator."

Savelli's face screwed up into a question. "He's in the field for the next few days. Might I ask why you want to see him?"

Lang thought fast. "I'm writing an article for the newspaper I work for, an article on forensics in archaeology. Stuff like being able to read old and nearly obliterated inscriptions, ancient manuscripts, stuff like that. Maybe as a fellow American you could arrange . . . ."

Lang had long ago observed that Americans who had nothing in common in their native country took it as a debt of honor to help their fellow citizens abroad. Read a menu you can't decipher? No problem. Give you directions to the embassy? Why don't you let me walk you there? Had your wallet lifted? Here's a few euro to get you to the American Express office. It was a positive facet of the us-against-them syndrome.

Savelli stuffed his hands in his pockets. "Wish you had called or written—"

"Actually, I'm here on vacation, just thought of finding out how one of the world's primo archaeological outfits does it. But if you can't, you can't." Lang turned as though to head for the door.

"Tell you what," Savelli said. "Curator's at Herculaneum, supervising a new dig along what was the waterfront. . . . You are familiar with the city?"

"Destroyed in the same eruption of Vesuvius as Pompeii, about A.D. seventy-nine."

Savelli gave that flash of a smile again, glad to be talking to a reasonably knowledgeable countryman, not one of those American tourists who view Italy as a combination Olive Garden Restaurant and Armani outlet store. "I can call. It's about a three-hour train ride to Naples and a fifty-euro cab trip to the site, if you bargain well. Ask for Dr. Rossi."

Lang did a quick calculation: It would take at least an hour to get to either of Rome's airports, and how long would he have to wait for the next flight to Naples? As is so often the case in Europe, the train was preferable to air travel.

He reached in his pocket and peeled off several bills. "For your trouble."

The mistake became instantly apparent as Savelli frowned and shook his head. "I am not the concierge at your hotel, Mr. Couch."

Lang feigned surprise. "Not for you, of course. A contribution to this museum in payment for your efforts."

It was as if the sun had come out from behind storm clouds. "*Grazie.* A moment and I will write you a receipt."

Lang left considering a common conundrum: Where was the line between a favor and a service for which a gratuity was expected? Like most Americans, he tended to err toward the latter rather than the former.

Whatever the art of tipping, there was something not quite right about the young man leaning against the adjacent building as he talked on a cell phone and smoked.

There was nothing unusual about anything. Italians are perhaps the most accomplished loungers in the world. Generally, they prop themselves against brick, stucco, or stone with equal insouciance, seeming perfectly comfortable in contorted poses that would send the average

American to a chiropractor. Smoking also is common, fear of cancer, heart or respiratory ailments apparently viewed as less than manly. The preferred method being to let the cigarette dangle from the lower lip or be used in the hand as a short pointer to emphasize the gesticulation for which the nationality is famous. Even more ubiquitous than cigarettes are cell phones. An Italian, or at least a Roman, is somehow not complete unless his phone is held to one ear while he manually expresses himself to his unseeing correspondent with gestures. Sometimes this takes place while driving an automobile or motor scooter, frequently with very exciting results.

All of this being true, there was still something about the way the fellow detached himself from the wall, his eyes following Lang, something Lang would have described as not quite passing the smell test. He stopped, ostensibly pantomiming some point while Lang slipped Mr. Couch's credit card into a teller machine. The man had positioned himself where he would not be obvious in watching.

Lang could almost feel his antennae rise and quiver. It had been years since the course in surveillance detection, but its lessons were unforgotten.

Lang dawdled at a news kiosk and his companion actually walked half a block ahead, constantly turning as he continued his animated conversation. The man was following, but not so obviously as to remove all doubt. Lang took a quick survey of his surroundings. There was no handy alley to draw in his tail where Lang might turn on him. Besides, the area was heavily patrolled by the *Polizia,* a measure to discourage the pickpockets preying on arrivals at the train station. Assaulting someone who had actually done nothing would certainly draw their attention.

Lang took his time at the newsstand. Was he being

followed by more than one? Didn't look like it. He could lose the man, simply duck into a store and head for a rear entrance. But if he failed, his shadow would know he had been spotted. Better to keep the follower obvious.

At the station, Lang was certain the man could see the rail ticket he bought was to Naples. The stalker did not board the train.

Lang was confident he was going to meet someone else in three hours or so. He only hoped he could spot him.

CHAPTER THIRTY-NINE

Herculaneum
Four hours later

Like any tourist who had ever been subjected to the legal thievery of Italian cabdrivers, Lang had haggled over the fare before getting into the shiny Mercedes. Now the meter showed an extra seventeen euros. The driver, who had spoken good if broken English at the Naples depot, was suddenly unable to remember a word of the language and was reduced to violent head-shaking and Italian invective as Lang tendered the amount agreed upon. The stopped cab was blocking half the narrow street, and the cars behind were expressing displeasure at the delay.

None of this was a first-time experience for Lang. He used the time to survey the surroundings. On the way from the train, Naples's traffic had been far too dense to discern if he had been followed. As a suburb of the city, his destination consisted largely of mid-rise apartments, small shops, and crowded sidewalks. The few strollers who had gathered to watch the altercation would provide perfect cover for anyone who was now following.

Conceding defeat, Lang parted with the euro notes. This time there was no question as to the appropriateness of a tip. Unless he could have handed over a live hand grenade.

The spectators dispersed, but at least one lingered long enough to watch Lang enter through stone portals that led to a path.

The trail ran along a ridge. On the left side was dense vegetation, on the other a yawning hole that grew in size as he descended. Suddenly, he was looking down at a small town, one in which, other than roofs, the buildings, streets, and public spaces were perfectly preserved. He could make out one, two villas whose timeless Mediterranean features are seen today wherever warm sun meets cerulean sea.

Herculaneum had been a seaside resort, the site of vacation homes for wealthy Romans. Unlike Pompeii, Herculaneum had not been smothered in a cloud of fiery volcanic ash. Instead, a single blast of superheated, possibly toxic gas had extinguished every form of life within seconds but, other than charring exposed wooden fittings, had done little damage to the actual buildings, leaving them to be preserved by successive coats of mud that slid with millennia of rain from the surrounding hills. Many of the frescoed walls and elaborate mosaic tiled floors had survived, the colors of their designs as vibrant as the year in which they were last used. For years, archaeologists had marveled at the lack of loss of life, assuming the inhabitants had fled in private ships. Only in mid–twentieth century had the former waterfront been excavated, now several hundred yards inland.

The boathouses, evidently used as a refuge pending embarkation, had held enough skeletons to satisfy the most gruesome imagination.

The walk took a sharp right turn, ending at a small building housing both ticket office and a restaurant with outdoor tables overlooking the ruins. From the concrete pad surrounding the structure, Lang could see what had been a seawall. Along the wall, several tents had been erected. He guessed that was the site of the present dig. Indeed, that was the only place left for archaeological exploration.

Two or three hundred yards the other way, the direction from which he had come, a steep hill crowned with apartment buildings stood. Sheets, shirts, underwear, anything that had been laundered that morning flew from the clotheslines between rails of balconies as proudly as pennants from the yardarm of a man-o'-war. The paradox of a cheap checkered tablecloth flapping over the villa of a long-gone, wealthy Roman had a message, Lang supposed, even if he couldn't verbalize it.

What was certain was that the expense of shoring up dozens, if not hundreds, of people's homes made digging in this direction impractical if not impossible.

He stepped inside the building and bought a ticket. Outside, a flock of guides waited on tourists who simply weren't there. Lang supposed the crowded streets at the top of the hill and lack of visible parking sent the big tour buses to Pompeii, a much larger if less preserved ruin that could accommodate thousands of sightseers daily. Two hundred people would clog the few narrow streets so far exposed here.

Climbing down the steps, he followed the seawall until he was opposite the place canvas covered the base. Standing with a piece of stone in one hand and a magnifying glass in the other was Indiana Jones. Or at least his Italian counterpart. Tall, with a broad-brimmed hat, military-style khakis, and knee boots, he was intent on whatever he was inspecting.

"Dr. Rossi?"

Indiana turned and looked up with eyes that had become myopic from close scrutiny of too many antiquities. The face was tanned and prematurely lined from exposure to the sun. A queue of white hair protruded like a tail from under the hat. There was nothing defective about the smile as bright as young Savelli's.

"Mr. Couch?" He shifted the glass from one hand to the other, put both it and the stone down, and extended a hand. "Enrico must have called even as you were leaving the museum. It is not every day we are honored by an American newspaperman."

The accent was more British than Italian.

In spite of a twinge of guilt at the deception, Lang produced a small tape recorder, setting it down on a stone that might have served as a bollard for Roman galleys. "I'm particularly interested in forensics, the tools you use to read old and obliterated inscriptions or ancient and faded texts."

The archaeologist nodded. "There is no magic in that, Mr. Couch." He picked up the stone he had been holding. "Note the indentations on this. I suspect it was some sort of a marker, perhaps what we today would call a slip number for someone's private watercraft. Centuries of abrasion in the sand of the beach have worn it nearly smooth."

Even through the magnifying glass Dr. Rossi held, Lang could see only faint indentations and grooves.

He stood back. "You have something that will enable you to read that?"

The Italian crossed the small enclosure to lower the

flap of canvas. With the light breeze shut out, sweat instantly began to prickle Lang's neck. The archaeologist reached into a box and produced a contraption that resembled a hair dryer.

"Please forgive the heat, but it is necessary to exclude as much light as possible. This is an ultraviolet scanner." He held it so the beam would run along the surface of the stone before he turned it on. "There!"

Like a magician's trick, the faint grooves became readable: "XXI."

"Twenty-one?" Lang asked skeptically, still unsure what he was seeing.

"Twenty-one," Dr. Rossi confirmed. "What we don't know is if that is a slip number, the number of a boathouse, or part of a larger inscription. This business is full of puzzles."

He seemed more elated than overcome by the prospect.

"That light," Lang asked. "How does it work?"

Rossi put down the stone and opened the flap. The air rushing in was warm and moist but refreshing, like opening the kitchen door after broiling a roast.

"When a stone or any hard substance is engraved, by hand or machine, the groove frequently goes deeper than the human eye can see, albeit very narrow. The ultraviolet simply picks up and casts shadows from the otherwise invisible grooves. This one was fairly easy. Had we not been able to read it, I would next have used this."

He produced a camera with a very short, wide lens.

"Thirty-five millimeter with a huge macro lens and ultraviolet filter. We would have put the rock on the table there, turned on the klieg lights, and photographed it."

"Like trying to read the numbers filed off a firearm," Lang suggested.

"At least in your television crime dramas, yes."

He put the camera down and picked up its twin. "This

one has the same lens but with an infrared filter. When we come across writing on parchment, papyrus, any form of material that would have required some form of ink, we use this. Often the pigment has long ago faded but it leaves a residue, one this camera can pick up. In fact, the Oxyrhynus Papyri, found in the nineteenth century in what amounted to ancient garbage dumps, have yielded parts of Aristophanes' plays long lost, early parts of the Gospels, all sorts of things tossed onto the rubbish heap from the second century B.C. to the seventh A.D. With this camera, we can actually read what the original discoverers could not."

Lang braced himself for the full duration of an academic lecture. He was surprised when Dr. Rossi came up short.

"I digress from your question. You might want to remember 'Oxyrhynus Papyri' if you have any questions about how this sort of equipment is being used. I'm sure there's an Internet site."

He spelled the words for the benefit of the empty tape recorder and lifted his watch to inches in front of his face.

"Oh my. It's past time to stop work for the afternoon recess. The men will be complaining. Do you have labor unions like that in America, Mr. Couch?"

Lang started to suggest the doctor ask any out-of-work airline employee. Instead, he said noncommittally, "We certainly have them. Doctor, you've been most helpful."

They were stepping out from under the canvas.

"Could I perhaps persuade you to stay for tea? Or perhaps something a little cooler?" the archaeologist asked.

Lang was about to reply when something streaked across the corner of his eye. A flash of a reflection, the early-afternoon sun dancing off of glass. A small, polished piece of glass.

"Shit!"

Lang threw himself to the ground, an arm extended to knock down the Italian. Tiny fragments of rock stung his cheek a millisecond before he heard the flat crack of a rifle.

Dragging the doctor behind him, he rolled under the canvas, which would screen them both.

The man outside the Rome museum on the cell phone, no doubt a call to a confederate in Naples. A tail in traffic so thick it was impossible to detect. The man who had watched him enter the path to the ruins.

And enough time to get a rifleman with a telescopic sight in place in one of hundreds of apartments facing the ancient town.

Dr. Rossi was breathlessly speaking into a cell phone. Lang heard the word *polizia* more than once.

A burly workman, dirt caked to his hairy bare chest, took the doctor by the arm, helping him to stand on none-too-steady legs. Even without understanding the words, Lang knew the archaeologist was assuring his workers he was OK.

He turned to Lang, a nervous grimace twitching at the corners of his mouth. "You think it's safe now?"

Lang nodded. "Whoever it was, he's long gone. Trying another shot's too risky now that we know the area where it came from."

The doctor made a show of brushing himself off and said with forced humor, "I knew the crew expected me to observe the midday recess, but they could have simply asked."

The police arrived in force, made a detailed if futile search of the apartments, and interviewed everyone in sight, including the horde of guides. The few visitors had been evicted for the afternoon closure before the shot had been fired.

As far as Lang could tell, the local cops were pretty sure Rossi had been the intended victim. There had been a rumor that the apartments were to make way for complete excavation, a possibility a number of the inhabitants opposed vociferously without inquiring into its actual existence.

Only one policeman, Lang guessed the only English speaker, paid him any heed at all. After taking his name, address, and residence in Italy, the man asked, "The doctor says you shoved him out of the way. He would be dead had it not been for you. How you know someone gonna shoot?"

Lang shrugged modestly. "The doctor is mistaken. I heard the shot and hit the ground, pulling him with me."

The cop eyed him suspiciously.

Lang gilded the lily. "I was in the Gulf War. I know what a rifle shot sounds like, and getting down is still instinct."

Now that he was a war hero, the policeman seemed satisfied and wandered off to question the workmen.

CHAPTER FORTY

Rome
The Hotel Hassler
That evening

The train ride back to Rome had provided an opportunity for thought, more so than Lang would have preferred. He was fairly certain he knew the actual mechanics of getting a sniper in place, but he had no more idea as to the reason than before. Whoever was trying to kill him seemed to be intensifying the effort the closer he came to whatever secret the Emperor Julian had left and Skorzeny may have attempted to solve.

What possible relationship was there between a fourth-century pagan Roman and a twentieth-century SS officer?

The answer kept coming back the same: None.

Except both may have discovered a document that contradicted the conventional view of Christ.

OK, come around on another tack: Don Huff had been killed because of his work, a book on unpunished war criminals, Nazis. As Franz Blucher had pointed out, it was unlikely an ever-decreasing number of old men could or would form a consortium to keep a secret over sixty years old, but such an organization had been put together sixty years ago. What if it still existed with new members?

Instead, Lang was inclined toward the theory that Skorzeny, either at Montsegur or Rome, led to a larger, older mystery, one of such theological significance that some group was willing to keep on killing to prevent its solution. To the ordinary person, such a hypothesis might rank right up there with UFO cover-ups and JFK conspiracies. But Lang wasn't ordinary, at least not in that sense. Only a year before, he had uncovered what could, arguably, be called the oldest and greatest conspiracy of all time. He had also confronted one of the world's richest and most powerful entities, a name unknown to even the most sophisticated.

Religious intrigue existed, and there were undoubtedly secrets some groups would kill to keep.

Then there was Skorzeny himself, the brilliant and rarely photographed Austrian. What, if anything, did the information Hemphill had provided have to do with the necropolis? Although Lang had found proof positive, the Himmler order, that the elusive Skorzeny had, in fact, been in Rome, had he had time to explore the secret of the necropolis before returning to Berlin? Likely. Huff's pictures showed him in front of the Vatican.

And after Berlin . . . ? The capture of the Hungarian prime minister, according to Blucher.

The takeover of the Hungarian government. Where . . . ? Had he read something about the subject? Possibly, although modern history was of little interest to him. There was something just outside Lang's mental reach, as

ephemeral as a dream and just as likely to disappear into
the mist of uncertain memory.

Oh, well, the most certain way to retrieve a scrap of
recollection was to put it out of conscious thought, let
the old subconscious drill for it until it suddenly gushed
to the mind's surface like oil from a newly discovered well.

Once back in Rome, Lang sat in his room, staring at
the BlackBerry-like device Reavers had given him. Its
function was similar to that of the intra-agency communicating device he had used to contact Hemphill but, apparently, more sophisticated. He pushed the three letter
identifier for the Frankfurt chief of station.

"Howdy, pard'nuh!" Reavers's Texas twang came
through the device as clearly as though the man were
sharing the room. "What can Ah do fer ya?"

Lang got up and stood at the window, watching the
congregation of young loafers on the Spanish Steps. "I
need some fairly sophisticated equipment. You insisted
on being committed to tracking down whoever killed
Don and Gurt."

"As intent as a coyote diggin' after a prairie dog.
Whatta ya need?"

Lang recited Dr. Rossi's list. "A fluoroscope, the sort
of thing used to read serial numbers filed off guns. An
infrared scope as well as a thirty-five millimeter camera
with macro lens and both ultraviolet and infrared filters."

"Great Sam Houston, whaddaya find, another collection of Dead Sea Scrolls?"

"*Might* find," Lang corrected. "I don't have unlimited
access to the place I may need to use all that stuff. I'm
hoping one more trip will do it. I don't want to need
something and not have it."

"God forbid any of us not have what we need. You remember the safe house cross the street from that church,
has all the skulls and bones arranged in patterns?"

Lang didn't have to think. "The Capuchin's Santa Maria della Concezione on the Via Veneto? There used be a couple of rooms on the third floor directly across the street."

"That's the one. Go to the church day after tomorrow, look in the side chapel, the one with a picture of that faggy-looking guy . . ."

"St. Michael?"

"Yeah, the one puttin' his foot on the head of the bald guy crawlin' outta a hole that's on fire. Has a sword in one hand."

"St. Michael slaying the devil coming out of hell," Lang supplied.

"Devil, hell. Could be some beaner tunnelin' under the border at Juarez, all I care. You know the place?"

A good spy was one who could become invisible. Like evading congressionally mandated annual ethnic, cultural, and racial sensitivity seminars.

"I know the picture. It was a specially commissioned altarpiece . . ."

"Okay, n'mind the art lecture. On one o' them benches in front of the chapel, there'll be a package. Your stuff'll be in it."

A number of the male kids on the steps were turning to watch a fat girl in a very short skirt make her way upward. From the attention being paid a woman who resembled Miss Piggy, Lang guessed she was wearing thong underwear. Or none at all. "Wouldn't it be just as easy to deliver the stuff to the concierge at my hotel?"

"Just as easy, pard'nuh, but not as secure. See, we can watch, make sure you're the one gets the package. Gotta go."

The line went dead. Except there was no line, only air. Lang shook his head slowly. Agency motto: Never do openly what you can do covertly.

He returned to the room's only chair, a worn club up-
holstered in what had once been grass green. Now the
lawn had wilted somewhat.

As he knew it would, the shadow of recall on the train
took on full substance. Something he had read . . . A
newspaper story about Budapest? The details were still
fuzzy around the edges.

He got up and left the room.

The man behind the desk in the lobby directed him to
the hotel's business center with a look of bewilderment.
Work after business hours? The actions of Americans
were truly incomprehensible.

Lang sat in one of four cubicles containing computers
and studied the keyboard. There were a few language
keys, umlauts, acutes, inverted question mark, and the
like that he recognized as peculiar to several European
dialects, German, French, Spanish. Everything else looked
ordinary. Turning the machine on, he followed the multi-
language instructions on entering his room number,
which served as his password. After two attempts, he
managed to bring up the *Atlanta Journal-Constitution*
index for the past twenty-four months. Not exactly the
Times, but if he had read it in a newspaper, it would have
been the one in Atlanta. During the baseball season, the
Atlanta paper was, understandably, the only one with
full coverage of the Braves. As long as he had the paper,
Lang occasionally read news articles that caught his interest. It was the faint recollection of one of these he was
looking for.

He tried the word "Hungary" and got over a hundred
references. Too broad. He tried "Hungary" and "1944."
Thirty-two articles. Better, but still too many.

What was the gist of the article?

He tried "Hungary," "1945," and "train."

A single article, a feature in the Weekend section, a hodgepodge of stories that might be of interest but not necessarily current news, everything from scientific discoveries of dubious application to human interest. In short, a journalistic landfill.

> *Budapest (AP) Hungarian authorities have joined Jewish advocates in their demand the Austrian government return art objects allegedly taken by the occupying Nazis from Jews being sent to death camps. The articles, paintings, sculptures, even jewelry, were loaded onto a train as Russian troops approached in late 1944.*
>
> *Austrian officials note the same train was loaded with much of that country's own art objects for the same reason.*
>
> *The train, intercepted by the Allies within days of the end of hostilities in Europe, was never completely inventoried and an unknown part of its cargo was used to furnish the headquarters of the occupying army and subsequently disappeared.*
>
> *Descendants and relatives of Holocaust victims claim Austria is making no effort to differentiate between objects from that country and those stolen from Jewish families.*
>
> *Hungary, originally one of the Axis Powers, was prepared to surrender separately to Russia when a German-backed coup replaced the government with one friendly to the Nazis.*

Lang reread the article. Nothing to connect Skorzeny with any of it. He had been involved in the "coup" described by the article but had been in Belgium in December '44 and January '45, the Battle of the Bulge. Was it possible he had gone *back* to Hungary? Either way, how had the inscription at the Vatican's necropolis figured in?

In forty-eight hours, he might have his first solid answer.

CHAPTER FORTY-ONE

Lake Red Cloud, Minnesota
Mugwanee County Courthouse
The next morning

Charlie Clough used a wrinkled handkerchief to wipe the sweat from his face. Only fifty-five degrees outside, but the effort of hauling his three hundred pounds-plus across the square was real effort. So far, though, things were working out better than he had anticipated. First-class ticket to . . . where? Sioux City, South Dakota. Or was it North Dakota? Charlie was fairly certain he didn't really believe North Dakota existed anyplace but on maps, so it must have been South Dakota. He had gotten a real rental car, not one of those fuckin' compacts he could hardly get into. The drive had taken about three hours, including one stop for gas and two more for snacks.

He'd been lucky, arriving at the Holiday Inn, the town's only accommodation, just before the dining room closed for dinner. According to the desk clerk, he'd gotten the very last super-king-sized bed. Good thing. A queen simply wasn't big enough. His arms draped over the side. Charlie figured the world was configured to fit the little people, folks who barely tipped the scales at two-fifty. Some even less. It was tough making your way in a universe where you were already super-sized.

This morning, he had pretty well decimated the break-fast buffet before driving the mile or so into town. Town was too big; village was a better word. All tricked up like some fuckin' Alpine hamlet, even though the highest ground he'd seen so far was a speed bump across from the school.

He slapped at an insistent buzzing. Fuckin' mosqui-toes! He'd suffered from gnats in South Georgia, every kind of biting insect in Florida, but he'd never known mosquitoes grew this large. These babies could stand flatfooted in the road and fuck a turkey!

The inside of the courthouse looked like something out of an installment of *In the Heat of the Night*. Only thing missing was that actor, Carroll O'Connor, same one who played Archie Bunker. He took the stairs down to where a sign indicated he would find records.

After an hour, he hadn't even come close to what he was looking for. Puffing with exertion, he climbed back up the stairs to the clerk's office and went in.

A red-cheeked young woman put down her copy of *People* magazine and came up to the desk where Charlie stood, again mopping his face.

"Th' records," he said in response to her polite in-quiry. "I can't seem to find any records, births, deaths, before 1950."

She looked at him quizzically. "Those are on comput-ers, the ones in the record room."

He shook his head. "I know, but I want to see the actual records, the physical pieces of paper."

She looked at him again, this time as though he wasn't quite right in the head, potentially dangerous. "Those are archived, sir. They're not here."

Charlie looked around, found a secretary's chair, and eased his bulk onto it gingerly. He had been standing for an hour down in the fuckin' record room, and now he was standing here, jawing with this nitwit who seemed not to understand the difference between electronic copies and the real thing. His feet hurt. They weren't made to hold up as much weight as he put on them.

"Where are they?"

She pointed as though the documents were just across the room. "Follow Main Street to the city-limit sign, take your first left. There's a warehouse where we keep the archives."

He stood, turning to go. "Thanks."

"Sir! Wait a minute. That warehouse isn't open all the time. I'll call to see when you can get in."

Swell.

Well, at least he could take time for an early lunch at the café he had seen across the square.

"Thanks. I'll be back in a few minutes."

Forty minutes later, Charlie paid the tab and walked out onto the sidewalk. He'd had better chow, but he'd had worse, too. A lot worse. At the corner, he looked both ways before stepping into the street toward the square. He was no more than a few paces from the curb when he heard the growl of a large engine. He looked up straight into the grille of the biggest fuckin' truck he had ever seen.

His last thought was that there wasn't going to be time to stop.

CHAPTER FORTY-TWO

Rome
Santa Maria della Concezione, Via Veneto 27
The next afternoon

Lang had intentionally waited until the church was about to close for the midday siesta. The narthex was empty, and the nave and single aisle were empty except for an older woman in a nun's habit whose lips moved in what Lang supposed was prayer as she ticked off the beads of her rosary. Voices from the apse and transept behind the altar told him that a smattering of tourists had paid to see the macabre crypt displays of bones for which the church was noted. Arranged in rosette patterns, bones of equal or different sizes were displayed in varying designs featuring femurs, ribs, vertebrae, and other skeletal parts Lang could not identify.

Art is truly in the eye of the beholder. Some beholders, anyway.

The chapel of St. Michael was little more than a small

room to his right just inside the nave. There was room for only three rows of five uncomfortable-looking wooden chairs each. The side chapel was empty of worshipers, but a brown paper shopping bag occupied a corner seat on the right front. If someone was watching, they were either invisible or the Agency had exempted the nun from its already liberal retirement age.

He picked up the bag and left.

It was when he was about to descend the twin staircase to the street that he saw her: a young Gypsy woman squatting just at the foot of the steps. When Lang had entered less than two or three minutes earlier, there had been a wrinkled crone crying out in the most pitiful tones imaginable. Entrances to churches were prime real estate in the begging business, spots not to be given up without a fight. Yet the old woman was gone, replaced. Stranger still, the bowl in front of the newcomer had a number of coins already in it. She had either seeded the dish or was one of the city's more accomplished beggars, a mendicant whose attention was fixed on the front of the church, not passersby. Her clothes, though far from fashionable, were neat and clean, not the soiled and torn attire he was used to seeing. Unless he was seriously mistaken, her fingernails were evenly trimmed and polished.

He dug into a pocket and dropped a handful of change into her bowl. She was watching him, not the money. A dead giveaway.

"Grazie, signor," she said.

Bending over so he could not be heard by other pedestrians, Lang replied in English. "Spend it on nail polish remover."

CHAPTER FORTY-THREE

Rome
Hotel Hassler
That evening

Lang had spent a good part of the afternoon acquainting himself with the contents of the package. He had learned the fluoroscope could make badly worn numbers and letters on old coins spring into legible relief. The infrared brought alive old floral patterns of painted-over wallpaper perhaps best left forgotten.

The camera was digital. It had the advantage of being able to call up the pictures he had taken instantly and the disadvantage of his lack of knowledge of how to make it do that. After thirty or so frustrated minutes, he left his room in search of a photography store, finding one within a few blocks. With far more patience than Lang would have exhibited under similar circumstances, the English-speaking store clerk used the same type and model to demonstrate the simplicity of bringing up pictures for review.

The problem was that, for Lang, nothing digital was simple. Under Sara's tutelage, he had mastered the use of his office computer for composing letters and legal documents. It was when it came time to send them off into cyberspace that his worst fears became realities. A brief that had required a week to compose was devoured by malign electronics in a nanosecond. His machine mocked him with reminders of his own ineptness with messages like "Unable to send due to incomplete address" or "Account number incorrect" the few times he had tried to pay bills or buy an airline ticket online. Instruction manuals were useless. Written with the clear assumption the reader understood bytes, hard drives, and other arcana, the printed material served only to reinforce Lang's sense of being very alone in a cyber-shrunken world.

He viewed with sad nostalgia the days when you simply put whatever you were going to send into a real envelope, licked a stamp, and sent it on its way without fear of incomplete addresses, balky if not downright malevolent electronics, and temperamental delivery systems. He never understood how anyone could master the esoteric series of keystrokes (or, in the case of the camera, buttons pushed) necessary to achieve one task rather than another.

It was, then, with the closest attention, that he watched the clerk demonstrate the use of the camera, limiting the lecture to turning it on and off, and displaying pictures.

He was reasonably confident he could figure out how to plug the charging mechanism in.

Back in his room, he waited for sunset, in Rome a distinct event that turns the cold marble monuments to gold and gives buildings' ocher a glow as though lighted from within. Tonight, he was less interested in colors than the job ahead. Donning the cassock, he filled an old-fashioned leather briefcase with equipment he had both purchased a few days earlier and had received from Reavers.

A few minutes later, he was just one more priest scurrying along the streets and alleys of Rome in a hurry to keep an appointment at the Vatican. He was, though, the only one that night who was actually rushing to make sure he could find a group with whom he could blend in. He was also the only one whose business was with a pagan emperor dead nearly two thousand years.

Before reaching the Tiber, his cell phone buzzed twice and went dead, the signal prearranged with Sara.

Distrustful of the security of his own, it took Lang only minutes to find a bank of pay phones. He was all too aware of RAPTOR, the satellite system shared by the United States, Great Britain, Canada, Australia, and New Zealand that intercepted any telephonic communication the world over. The idea had been brilliant in its conception if faulty in its execution. The English-speaking nations had the ability to listen in but no means of ascertaining which conversations were of interest. The solution had been to program the system to flag conversations including certain key words.

Although Lang was certain any transatlantic chat with his secretary would be buried under thousands of other dialogues, he knew no system was immune to hacking or interception. Whoever had tried to kill him could, possibly, somehow sort through the surfeit of information and retrieve his words. Using a pay phone simply ensured that his anonymous enemy could not rely on a simple interception device. Unless, of course, his office line had also been invaded.

He punched in the code for the United States, area

code, and the office number. After a series of the squeals and squeaks frequently accompanying international calls, Sara answered.

"Lang," she said, her voice quavering. "Charlie Clough is dead."

It took an instant to sink in. "Charlie? How?"

"I only know what I saw in the paper this morning, but he was in a place up north . . ." Pause as she reached for the newspaper. "Red Cloud Lake, Minnesota. Says he was there on business, killed by a hit-and-run eighteen-wheeler. Lang, he was such a nice man . . ."

He wasn't, but Lang murmured the usual meaningless words of comfort before hanging up.

One final time, it seemed Charlie had found what he was looking for. Unfortunately, Lang had only the vaguest idea what.

Chapter Forty-four

Rome
St. Peter's Square
Twenty minutes later

This time Lang merged with an Italian boys choir he gathered were to perform at evensong at one of the Vatican's numerous chapels, perhaps for the Holy Father himself. Shepherded by two dour nuns and several priests, the noisy group passed by the Swiss Guard with little more than a cheery *buona sera* and a wave of credentials. Once again, Lang's Georgia driver's license passed muster. The shadows that were devouring the square by now provided ample cover for Lang to fall to the rear of the boisterous procession and, finally, drop off just before the door guarded by the television camera.

For a full five minutes he observed, making certain nothing had been altered. A change in timing of the camera, of the combination lock, anything, could mean his previous visit had been discovered and additional security measures taken, precautions of which he would be unaware.

Cars whizzed by, the sensation of speed increased by the narrow confines of the road between basilica and the colonnades, but fast enough to be dangerous to the unwary crossing the road. He stepped deeper into the shadows to avoid headlights. The timing of the surveillance cameras was identical. Minimizing exposure to both the light provided by streetlights and by passing motorists, he stepped in front of the door, risking playing the beam of his flashlight over the locking mechanism. It seemed the same. The doorframe bore no indications of the work necessary to install alarms.

He took a deep breath, as though about to dive into bottomless water, and punched in the series of numbers.

CHAPTER FORTY-FIVE

Rome
St. Peter's Square
April 30, 1944

Sturmbahnführer Otto Skorzeny crossed St. Peter's
Square with purposeful strides. Behind him eight SS
troops, Schmiesser machine guns slung across their
chests, marched as though on parade. At the rear of the
small procession, two *Wehrmacht* privates carried a
wooden box larger than even a coffin. Skorzeny watched
the Swiss Guard as they watched him. Hopefully, the
young men in medieval costume would not be fool-
hardy. The SS man had seen more than enough slaugh-
ter of young men.

As the black-clad detachment reached the point where
the colonnade joined the basilica, two Swiss Guards
crossed halberds, barring the path.

Thankful most Swiss spoke at least a form of German, Skorzeny snapped to attention and saluted. *"Am*

Morgen, meinen Herren! We have business inside. Please be good fellows and let us pass without trouble."

One of the young men—Skorzeny would have bet he was under twenty—spoke. "You have the proper authorization?"

The German officer sighed. "My authorization, lad, is in those machine guns you see. Now, please let us pass."

There was no fear, no indecision in the boy's eyes, only hatred. It was the same look Skorzeny had seen in Russian partisans as they stood in front of open graves waiting to be shot.

Skorzeny sighed and gave the order. As one, eight machine guns were unslung. With a single click, eight bolts were cocked. He both admired and was saddened by the complete lack of reaction by the Swiss Guards. Bravery transcends nationality. It is a commodity to be treasured, not wasted.

An older Swiss Guard, perhaps twenty-five, stepped out of the shadows and conducted a conversation in Swisse Deutsch, the dialect of the German-speaking Swiss cantons. Skorzeny only got about half of it. The two younger guards lowered their weapons and took two steps backward, resentment twisting the corners of their mouths.

"That's good fellows," Skorzeny said, motioning to two of his men. "Now, if you'll just stack those axes and come along, all will be fine."

Leaving a single man to watch over the disarmed and unhappy Swiss Guards, the Germans entered through an unmarked side door of the basilica. Skorzeny produced a flashlight from his uniform, as did each of the SS men.

Now came the tricky part, the SS commander thought. He had to remember exactly the tour the priest Kaas had given him yesterday. Opening an unmarked door, Skorzeny was greeted by darkness, an absence of light so complete as to suggest light did not exist. A breeze of cool air drifted over the men, bringing the dusty smell of crushed rock and damp earth.

Ignoring the reluctance he sensed in the men, Skorzeny stepped into the night.

At first, the beam of his flashlight revealed little but clouds of dust motes, swirling like miniature cosmos in some dark universe of their own. As his eyes adjusted to the gloom even his light could not entirely dispel, he saw what resembled a narrow street edged with the dim forms of houses. The way sloped gently upward.

"Careful," he warned his men. "The way is littered with rubble, so step carefully."

For a few minutes the small troupe walked up the slight incline, edging around mounds of clay, rock, and soil. Out of the gloom appeared empty doors and windows, some with just the hint of inscriptions. Others showed dirt-clouded paintings of animals and humans. Between many of the structures were mounds of unexcavated earth. At last they stopped in front of a large circular area ringed with mounds of loose dirt. Picks and shovels were neatly stacked. A rope with buckets attached stretched off into the darkness, a means of removing rubble. They had reached the site of present excavations.

Skorzeny directed the beam of his flashlight upward to a point where it reflected from dull stone overhead, the floor of the Vatican's basement or grotto. Part of the hill they had been climbing actually touched the stone overhead. A small hole had been dug into otherwise undisturbed earth.

That was the place the priest had pointed out to him yesterday. Motioning to the two men carrying the box to follow, he started up the side of the hill, surprised at how firm the surface was. But then, why shouldn't it be? This part of the hill hadn't been touched since the present papal palace was completed over three hundred years ago.

He turned to make sure the men with the box were close at hand before he turned the light into the shallow hole in front of him. At first, all he saw was stone, part of the foundation of the massive building overhead. He played the light back and forth, discerning regularly placed vertical stone piers, each about four feet wide and caked with the soil in which they had been embedded. Closer inspection revealed a slight discoloration at the base of one. Skorzeny stooped to bring the full power of his light to bear. Sure enough, the part of this one column was a slightly different color than the rest of the pillar.

Reaching into a pocket, he produced a whisk brush and began to remove the obscuring dirt. Within minutes, he could see an almost invisible line forming a rectangle where a section of the base of the support had been replaced. There were traces of lettering on the new part, letters that had been chiseled away.

He had no real interest in the characters. He had seen enough at Montsegur to have a good idea what they said.

Using his light to motion to the two *Wehrmacht* soldiers, he ordered them to open the box and bring him the tools in it. In moments, he was supervising two men rocking crowbars back and forth in an effort to wedge them between the original and newer stone. He noticed several of his SS detachment nervously glancing at the floor above, as if anticipating the collapse of the entire Vatican upon their heads. That might have been a problem with the old basilica. Although Pope Julius II had planned to preserve Constantine's papal palace when he began rebuilding the Vatican in 1506, he and more than a century of successors had been forced to abandon the idea. The only part of the original St. Peter's was down here, support columns that no longer were weight-bearing.

In ten minutes, both bars were firmly inserted into the tight space between old and replacement stone. Another few minutes of heaving and prying were rewarded by the sound of stone grinding upon stone.

Squatting, Skorzeny futilely tugged at the smooth surface as if his hands alone could move it. Finally, there was enough space for him to insert the hand with the flashlight and squint down its beam in much the same manner he would have sighted along the sights of a rifle.

At first, he thought he was looking at some sort of wall made of clay. Then he noted the reddish material was round. He pulled back, allowing himself a more comprehensive view. He was almost touching a large vessel of some sort, a jug or vase.

Stepping farther back, he stood. "I want that rock pried fully open," he commanded. "The sooner we can get to whatever is in there, the sooner we can get out of here."

The encouragement may have been the reason that, five minutes later, two men were removing a large, vase-like object. Skorzeny recognized it as an amphora, a large container, usually of Greek origin, with two handles, one on either side of its slender neck. This one was the size of a man, at least of a man in Julian's time.

Skorzeny waited until the two men had removed as much dust and grime as possible before he inspected their find. A seal was still in place, and he thought he could make out an inscription in the centuries-hardened wax. Walking slowly around the huge vessel, hands behind his back, he tried to make a decision. Should he open it here and now?

Probably not, he concluded. There was some small chance the thing was filled only with its normal contents, olive oil or wine, but he considered that unlikely. There would be little point in storing the mundane in this very special place. More likely, the jug held something else, something that needed to be sealed off from air and light. Like some sort of documents. And it was, of course, documents that the Montsegur inscription had seemed to indicate had been removed to the . . . What was the wording the Latin professor had used? Palace of the One God?

Whatever the contents, there was no point in risking them here. Let the container be opened in a place where others would take the blame if damage was done. *Der Führer* would be delighted if Skorzeny's assumption were correct, if . . .

"Herr *Sturmbahnführer?*" One of the men was bending over, peering into the space from which the amphora had been removed. "There appears to be another."

On hands and knees, Skorzeny scrambled to the opening, taking in the remaining contents. Sure enough, a second container, identical to the first, was clearly visible now that the other one had been removed.

This presented a problem: The box the two regular army men had carried in was barely large enough to hold the first. Orders mandated discretion, and carrying a man-sized, ancient Greek amphora out of the Vatican was not going to be accomplished without notice. He might as well leave with the drum and bugle corps so beloved by the party playing "The Horst Wessel Song."

Machts nichts; didn't really matter. In a day or so, a week at most, Pius XII would be in German custody as hostage for *all* Vatican treasure, including the remaining clay jar.

CHAPTER FORTY-SIX

Vatican City
Below St. Peter's Basilica
The present

This time, Lang had known what to expect. He spread a plastic sheet on the dirt before kneeling in front of the altered column. He switched on the fluoroscope and, once again, was astounded by how quickly the purple light made obliterated letters jump into view.

"*Accusatio . . . rebellis . . .*" Pretty much the same diatribe as he had seen at Montsegur, except . . . He moved the light slightly. Except supposedly the very indictment itself was contained inside.

What did that have to do with whatever Skorzeny had wanted?

He was about to find out. Standing, he took two steps back, playing the flashlight over the column. He could see now that the spot he had noted earlier was only the bottom part of a larger segment. A section almost five by three feet had been cut out of the pillar and replaced, presumably to hide something inside. Taking the short crowbar from underneath his cassock, he was surprised at how easily it fitted between the new and old stone. Almost as if someone had pried it open since Julian had sealed it sixteen centuries ago. Maybe someone had, someone like Skorzeny.

On second thought, there wasn't a lot of "maybe" to it. The picture on Don Huff's CD showed the German in front of the Vatican. Unlikely he had come here as a mere tourist.

What if there was nothing here, what if whatever clue he was seeking was gone? What if . . . ?

The last question went unfinished as he put the iron bar down, turned off his flashlight, and listened. He was greeted by overpowering silence, an absence of sound that is a sound within itself, just as white, an absence of color, is itself a color.

What had he heard? He was unsure. Another rat, scurrying about what had been his ancestors' exclusive domain? No, something more substantial than that.

But what?

He counted off a full minute, then another and another. Could he have simply overheard part of a tour of the necropolis on the other side of the plexiglass? Possible, but he thought he remembered a sign announcing that the office through which those excursions began closed for the day at six.

He recalled the old Gypsy woman he had almost struck in the darkness of an alley, the one who had sought no more than a few euros. The paranoia that became the constant companion of all Agency personnel had almost cost that crone dearly. Could the same thing be happening again?

He looked around the inky darkness. Alone, in the

permanent midnight of an ancient burial ground, by stealth rather than by right. Anxiety could not find a more fertile breeding ground.

Besides, who would be here at night?

No one but the spirits of Romans dead for millennia.

And they didn't employ magical curses for those without coins to give them.

Probably didn't pick pockets, either.

Switching the light back on, he returned to prying the stone loose from the base of the pillar. With the gravelly crunch of grit grinding grit, the rock fell out of its socket. Lang bent down, spraying the hole with light.

He had stayed in cheap hotels that had smaller closets.

But never one that came with a large amphora.

The Greek jar loomed out of the shadows with a suddenness that startled him. He reached for it before freezing in midgrasp. He stepped back, surveying the entire opening. In front of the vessel he was looking at was an impression in the dirt, a circle that could have been made by a similar container.

But if so, where was it?

If Skorzeny had found the two of them, why would he take only one?

Only one way available to answer the questions that kept bubbling up in his mind: See what's inside.

He tipped the jar over slightly to examine its gracefully slender neck and rimmed top. Sealed with wax, wax bearing some sort of insignia. The imperial crest of Julian? He rocked it back and forth. Were it not for the fact the thing was sealed, its lack of weight would have made him guess it empty. But people did not close up empty containers.

Perhaps the contents had drained out or evaporated. He rolled the jar in a rough circle, finding no cracks or holes. Whatever had been put in there was still there.

He laid the large urn on its side and fished under his cassock for a pocketknife, which he found and opened. The wax had had a long time to dry and crack. It yielded quickly, giving off an odor of dust, long-dead mold, and faint rot. If Lang had ever wondered how eternity smelled, he now knew. Shining the light into a darkness even more intense than that around him, Lang saw something wrapped in what looked like a shroud, a roll of old, dusty linen. He stuck the light between his teeth, leaving one hand free to prevent the amphora from rolling down the slope and the other to reach inside.

It was like touching cobwebs. He saw, rather than felt, the cloth dissolve at his fingertips. Light still in his mouth, he stood and lifted the bottom of the jar, gently shaking its contents onto the ground.

The whitish cloth looked as though it were melting as it touched the dirt. Underneath was more robust material, a scroll still wrapped around two wooden sticks, the sort of thing large enough to be seen in the hands of an official by a multitude gathered to hear some ancient proclamation. The part exposed to light was written on what Lang guessed was vellum or parchment. Large patches were missing, holes that consumed whole sentences. Still, Lang knew he was lucky. Other documents of like age, the Dead Sea Scrolls, the Oxyrhynchus Papyri, had been discovered sealed in jars but had been in fifty thousand or more crumbs that scholars had been piecing together for half a century. Wary of touching a manuscript so old, he leaned down on hands and knees to see what he might have found. The text was in Latin, Hebrew, and a script he did not recognize, most likely Aramaic, the pastoral tongue common to the peoples of the Middle East at the time of Christ.

He started to put the scroll back into the jar, then

stopped. He knew he should do whatever seemed necessary to preserve such an ancient and possibly historically
significant writing, the only known contemporaneous
evidence Christ had even existed. He was aware that,
should his harming of it become known, he would be ex-
coriated by academic, archaeologist, and historian alike.

On the other hand, he neither knew nor associated
with any of the above.

And the contents of this jar might well give him a clue
as to Gurt's killer.

A no-brainer.

He separated the two rolls and began to read the tattered paragraphs.

What he saw was surprisingly similar to the abstruse
phraseology of the indictments returned against his own
clients. No wonder the lexicon of the law was founded in
Latin.

The Romans had perfected legal obfuscation long before modern lawyers.

The part of the scroll he was looking at charged the
reus, defendant, with publicly encouraging the people
retinere, to withhold, legally due taxes by equivocating
or questioning what was actually due Caesar. Another
accused of attempting to foment, *fovet,* distrust of Rome's
ability to fairly distribute food by pretending there was a
shortage of fish and loaves when in fact an ample supply
was at hand, as evidenced by what remained. Refusing
to recognize the divinity of Caesar, insisting on exclu-
sively worshiping the god of the Hebrews.

Lang could have spent the rest of the night reading of
the offenses against Rome, all of which would have been
treason, all of which would have carried a sentence of
death by crucifixion.

He sat down hard. Not only was he looking at the only
surviving simultaneous record of Christ's existence, he

was seeing a Christ quite different from the man portrayed in the Gospels. Leb Greenberg, the Emory professor, had been right: More Lenin than Gandhi. He was also right that the Gospels perpetrated perhaps the greatest historical revision known by blaming the Jews for the death of an enemy of Rome. This was definitely not something the Church would want known.

He could understand why the modern-day Catholic Church would go a long way to make sure the words in front of him never saw light. In fact, he was surprised the scroll had been left here instead of either destroyed or removed to those very secret archives available to few besides the Pope himself. Another look at the columns gave him a possible answer: Until the excavation was done here, no one could have gotten to the amphora even had its existence been known. By the time the dig was under way, it would have been difficult to tell what was actual support and what was simply a part of the original supplanted St. Peter's Basilica.

The Church, had it known of Julian's prank, his secret, would have thought it safe from discovery.

Had the Vatican known of the inscription at Montsegur?

No way to know.

The medieval Church, the Inquisition, would have suppressed any trace of Julian's secret along with any who even mentioned it. But today? Would they kill to quell knowledge of it? The Church had, after all, survived Galileo, Luther, and Darwin.

Even Dan Brown.

The parchment could well explain why Pius had remained silent, apparently indifferent to Nazi atrocities, maybe even explain why so many Nazis escaped to South America on papal passports issued for fear of revelation of Julian's secret. But today? Things were very different than in the thirties and forties. Advocates of abortion, stem-cell research, gay rights, and other causes opposed by the Church weren't assassinated.

And there were probably those socially conscious souls who would even see Christ the revolutionary more appealing than Christ the submissive. The Church might even gain converts, or at least attract a larger audience.

It had, after all, been playing the same feature for two thousand years.

But if not the Church . . . ?

What had Franz Blucher called the organization that had helped escaping Nazis? *Die Spinne,* the spider.

But old Nazis would hardly be interested in shattering Church dogma; they would want to protect their kind.

Like Skorzeny.

But Skorzeny was dead, wasn't he?

Lang stared for a moment into the darkness. Julian, Skorzeny and . . .

It was like a mental meteor shower, brain neurons firing synapses at each other, the Gunfight at the Cerebral Corral. Phrases, faces, places blurring into a realization Lang knew he had unconsciously possessed long before now. He had been an idiot to concentrate so hard on discovering new facts that he had paid little attention to the ones he had.

Ah'm damned sorry to hear someone survived duty in Berlin back then only to get shot.

No one had told Reavers Don Huff had been shot. In fact, the close, all-but-prohibitive regulation of firearms in most European countries made murder by gunshot unlikely. Unless administered by the police or some form of government agency.

Any government.

An attack in a jail shared by federal prisoners. And by a prisoner of whom there was no record.

A trainload of treasure that had largely disappeared.

Operation Paper Clip.

A politician's face on television, familiar but unre-membered. Because there was no scar. A politician who had reentered the United States on a regular basis from Madrid.

Or somewhere in Spain.

A politician whose plan to strengthen American poli-tics presumably included strengthening the intel com-munity.

Assassins who appeared, knowing he would be on a bridge.

A sniper at Herculaeneum.

How could he have overlooked so much?

Again reaching into his cassock, he took out the com-munication device Reavers had given him, checking to make sure it was switched off. In fact, he couldn't re-member ever turning it on.

He hadn't needed to.

He slammed the contraption against a stone pillar. He was gratified to see it shatter, not surprised a small red eye winked, an LED, light-emitting device, indicating it was operative no matter off or on.

The nature of all cellular phones operating from satel-lites made them traceable by GPS, but only when in use.

Reavers's gadget had GPS, all right, but not only when actually communicating with satellites. Not only had the identity Reavers furnished him with given advance no-tice of his travel plans, every move he had made had been tracked to within fifty feet or less.

Lang stood shakily, trembling with rage. Not only had he been deceived, his stupidity in pursuing secrets of early Christianity had cost Gurt her life. He couldn't bring her back, but he could sure get even for her. He could . . .

The top of the slope was suddenly flooded with light,

as if the sun had risen on the Vatican hill for the first time in nearly two thousand years. Shielding his eyes, Lang turned slowly.

"Take it easy, pard'nuh," a familiar drawl ordered. "No need gettin' shot this late in th' game."

Lang let his arms drop, demonstrating he had no weapon. Thirty feet away and at the edge of the glare Reavers stood. From the snakeskin boots to the belt buckle the size of a hubcap to the ten-gallon hat, he looked the part of the cowboy. But no Colt Peacemaker .44.

Instead, a Sig Sauer P 229 9mm in his right hand.

That was contemporary Agency.

Just like the one sitting uselessly in Lang's bedside table back in Atlanta.

Lang thought there were at least two more men, each carrying something heavier than a side arm. He could not be certain, because the light was too bright, intentionally so.

"So you were tracking me all along," he said lamely. "No doubt Gurt, too."

"No doubt."

Play for time, that had been drilled into him from his earliest training. When faced with capture or worse, talk, keep your enemy occupied. Sing "Dixie" and tap-dance if necessary. Of course, Reavers had the same training. Lang was betting the man's ego would make him ignore it while he savored his victory.

Lang slowly lowered his hands and tried not to be obvious as he cut his eyes right and left looking for a possible weapon.

There was a long silence before Lang spoke. "What is it you want, Reavers?"

The chief of station shifted his weight as though leaning on something Lang couldn't see. "I think you know, pard'nuh."

Lang's foot touched something hard. A quick glance down showed him the short crowbar at his feet. "Maybe you want what's in this amphora. It could cause the modern Church a lot of grief if someone made its content public."

Reavers frowned, shaking his head. "Don' bullshit me, Lang. You know damn well what I want."

"My silence."

The man leaned even farther toward the invisible prop, grinning, his tone as calm as though he were discussing a roundup just finished. "That's about it, pard'nuh. Sorry."

Lang's foot crept toward the crowbar. "At least let me see if I understand. Tell me if I'm right or wrong. You can do that much."

Reavers nodded amiably. "Shore can. Jus' one caveat: You try somethin' funny, my friends here'll shoot. Even if you got heat from somewhere, you can't get 'em all. So fire away."

He laughed at the double entendre.

"Skorzeny," Lang began, feeling the iron beneath his foot. "He was involved in that train from Budapest in 1945, the one with all the treasure on it, right?"

Again the grin. "One o' th' things always impressed me 'bout you, Lang: You could draw a line from A to Z without botherin' about the rest o' them letters."

Lang's foot began a slow movement back, no more than the nervous shifting of weight a man about to be executed might exhibit. "And he, Skorzeny, helped himself to part of the treasure, a treasure he had known about since he deposed the independent government of Hungary virtually by himself."

"So far, you're battin' a thousand. Hell, why do need me? You already know the answers."

"Not quite. Indulge me. In 1945 the Agency, then OSS, decided they would bring some Nazis to the US, those that might be helpful, like Von Braun. Skorzeny was one of them because he knew where the rest of the train's treasure was and he sure as hell wasn't going to tell anyone while he was awaiting sentence from some war crimes tribunal."

Reavers shifted again, becoming tired of the game. "You're guessing."

"True, I am. But I'm right, aren't I?"

"Go ahead," Reavers said noncommittally. "I'm listening."

"I'd bet Skorzeny never told you and someone decided to send him back."

Reavers nodded. " 'Cept you couldn't jus' put him on a plane or ship and deport him. Wasn't that easy."

Lang began to scratch. "This damn priest's robe's gettin' hot. Mind if I take it off?"

Reavers gestured with his pistol. "Take off whatever you like, 'cept I see a weapon, you're dead meat."

"Thanks."

As he slipped the cassock over his head, Lang stooped to lay it on the ground. With the hand away from Reavers, the one in the dark, he picked up the crowbar. Now he was armed. What use the tool was going to be against automatic weapons was unclear.

Stall.

"So, the Agency made arrangements to ship him off to the only Fascist country left, Franco's Spain. But there was one very serious, unanticipated problem."

For the first time, Reavers appeared interested. "And that would be?"

"While he was in the States, Skorzeny fathered a son. Having been born there, you couldn't just bundle off a U.S. citizen, even one a few months old. I'd guess his mother was making threats, too."

"Bitch!" Reavers spat. "Never met her, came on board

long after she had a fatal auto accident, but I unnerstan'
she was a real pain in the ass, always askin' for more
money."

Lang was trying to look into the lights, ascertain exactly where they were. "That wasn't the only problem.
The kid, Skorzeny's son, knew damn well who he was,
insisted on visiting his father in Spain almost every year
from 1960, when he would have been fifteen or so, until
Skorzeny died in 1974. In case you're interested, the tip-
off was 1974. The visits ended the year Skorzeny died."

Reavers was not amused. "You couldn't know that
about where the kid went, not unless you knew . . ."

Lang was guessing now, putting odd pieces together
to gain precious time. "That Harold Straight is Skorzeny's illegitimate son? Look at the man, Reavers! Add
a scar down his right cheek and he couldn't belong to
anyone else. You guys created a whole identity for him
but you left the Immigration and Naturalization records
of his frequent travels to Spain. Seemed a little peculiar
that in all the rhetoric of his he never mentioned foreign
travel. You invented an identity for him, too. Problem
was, it wasn't secure enough. The media, even his political opponents, ran their background checks on computers, I bet. First time someone wants to see the actual
records, birth certificate, maybe, school records, et cetera,
you have him killed. That was a huge red flag, Reavers."

Reavers nodded again. Was that sweat beginning to
glisten on his face? "Yeah, 'bout the time of Skorzeny's
death, I was the new boy on the block, trying to cover up
Paper Clip. We knew there'd be a public howl, always is,
we do somethin' isn't 'xactly Goody Two Shoes. My
predecessor had some of our best forgers fiddle the local
paperwork up there in Minnesota. 'Course, anyone who
knows documents is likely gonna spot a fake sooner or
later but we figger'd the newsies, they'd take a quick

look an go away. Fact is, by '74 we'd gotten all the goody outta all those Krauts and congressional committees were beginin' to ask embarassin' questions. We didn't want no more honey, just wanted the bees off'n us. By that time the Skorzeny kid was a big deal in state politics, sure-fire to make it to Washington in some capacity. His old man, Skorzeny, was sort of a mystery man, few if any photos lying around to compare to Straight. That's why we had to take care of Huff. Pity."

"Yeah, shot him in the back of the neck, same way the Russkies executed prisoners at the Lubyanka while you were there. He was getting too close to learning about Skorzeny's son. He wouldn't have let that go, would have kept digging till he found out the boy was very much alive. From there, it's a short step to seeing Straight as your man, the Agency's champ, right?" Lang was almost certain he had located the source of the light; the same two men with automatic weapons were holding powerful torches. Could he get them both at once? No matter, he had to try. "Put Straight in the White House and surprise! The old Cold War level of funding comes back. You've got a rubber stamp for every plot gets hatched out at Langley. Want to blow up Saudi Arabia? Go to it! Sabotage the French economy, rig an election in Turkmenistan? Your man Straight isn't in a position to say no. That's really what all this is about, isn't it, keeping me from finding out the Agency is trying to put its very own stooge in the Oval Office?"

Reavers's amiable manner vanished. "Damn right! An' we'll succeed, 'least America better hope we do. Bunch of mamma's-boy bed wetters runnin' the country, 'fraid of a bunch o' rag-heads we shudda bombed back into the Stone Age right after 9/11. We need Straight like . . ."

"Like Germany needed Hitler in 1933." Lang was coiling his body, getting ready to throw the crowbar.

"Wouldn't do that, I was you," Reavers advised. "Throwin' things like that, somebody's gonna get hurt. More'n likely, you. Be a good boy and drop the crowbar."

Now or never, as the books say. Lang dropped a shoulder, ready to sling the crowbar at the nearest light. If he hit it, the man holding it, or even came close, there was a chance the distraction would give him a split instant to dive for protection behind one of the mounds of dirt, tombs, or columns.

"Hold it!" Reavers shouted, the Sig Sauer coming up.

"No, you hold it!" The voice came from Lang's left, Reavers's right. A very definitely feminine voice. "And moving those lights you should not consider even!"

Lang thought he was seeing some sort of wraith, perhaps one of those Roman spirits he'd thought about minutes ago. But ghosts, particularly those of Romans, probably didn't wear nuns habits as did this one. Tall, her face hidden by the shadow of her wimple, she stood at an angle where she could clearly see Reavers and his two men without being blinded by the light. Lang could see only the top half of her body. The rest was in shadows, giving the impression she was somehow floating in air.

Reavers froze, turning only his head. "Now look, Sister, you got no dog in this fight an' there's no reason for you to get hurt. You jus' mosey on back to where you came from, an' everthing'll be just hunky-dory."

She didn't move. "Down drop your weapons and put hands high. Now!"

It *was* a ghost! Lang knew that voice, that inflection, even the choice of words.

Reavers came to the same conclusion. Or at least a similar one. "Fuchs, the Kraut bitch! That idiot I sent to the hospital . . ."

Reavers complaining how hard it is to get good help.

He spun, raising the Sig Sauer.

It was a big mistake, the last one he would ever make.

From somewhere beneath the floating head, a quick jet of flame leaped into the darkness and there was the sound like someone clearing their throat, a weapon with sound suppressor.

To Lang, everything seemed to move at a sluggish pace, to take on the tempo of a film in slow motion.

Reavers stood on tiptoe and did a graceful pirouette that belied both his size and the fact that he was wearing boots instead of ballet slippers. The anger in his facial expression was replaced by one of astonishment as his eyes crossed at his nose as though trying to see the grayish-red hole between them.

Just as Reavers's knees buckled, Lang was on him, snatching the gun from his limp grasp before diving into the shadows.

Lang crashed into unforgiving masonry.

It went dark.

A darkness of centuries, the gloom of the pre-creation universe, a night so black it could be felt as well as seen.

It also was very, very quiet.

The quiet of the tomb, Lang thought, suppressing a post-traumatic giggle at his own wit.

Seconds, minutes, hours, could have passed before a man spoke. "Okay, we got us a Mexican standoff here. We go out and then you do. Nobody else get hurt."

There was too much of an echo in the enclosed space to be sure as to the source of the voice, but it came from close by.

Lang started to reply, thought better of it, and said nothing. No point in speaking even if the acoustics would make it difficult to trace the sound. There was about as much chance Reavers's clique would simply walk away from the power of having a U.S. president under their control as there was the Agency would agree to be funded solely by the sale of Girl Scout cookies.

"We got a deal?" the man wanted to know.

This time Lang did speak. "Sure. You turn on your light so we can make sure you're leaving."

Pause, then: "Damn thing's broken."

Right.

Lang thought he had an idea as to the general position of the speaker. Reaching into the void with the hand that didn't have Reavers's gun in it, he touched a wall. Feeling his way upward, he came to an opening, one of the many windows that made these tombs look so much like the very houses the deceased had occupied in life. He moved up to his knees and considered his position.

The streets were narrow, with few places to cross onto parallel lanes. The tombs all opened the same way and were closed on the other three sides. It was almost certain, then, that Reavers's men were facing the same way he was. Since he had been at the top of the hill, or near it, the two gunmen had to be slightly below. The problem was, he was unsure of where Gurt was. He could only hope she, also, was on the same street and, therefore, looking out in the same direction.

"We're waiting," came the same voice. "No point in anyone else getting killed."

Lang hoped it was not mere optimism that detected an edge to the tone, one of mounting desperation.

He stuck the Sig Sauer in the waistband of his trousers and crawled around the interior of the tomb, feeling as he went. Halfway up the rear wall, his fingers found a niche. Further exploration discovered a form with irregular features. Sitting in the darkness, Lang used both hands to touch his find. A funeral bust, the head and shoulder of some rich Roman.

Holding the statue in his arms, he crawled back to

where he recalled the entrance was and into the street. Sharp rocks, crumbs of jagged marble, and roughly edged cobblestones bit into his knees and elbows as he crossed to the other side and groped for the top of the structure. Again running his hand along the top edge, he ascertained it was fairly smooth, although he had no way of knowing whether the adjacent downhill sepulchre was taller, shorter, or the same height. His memory told him each mausoleum had its own individual form.

He stood the bust on the wall and retreated back into the tomb.

He was almost certain the two men had been carrying some sort of automatic weapons. It took extraordinary discipline in a firefight to put guns like that on single-round fire. He was counting on the fact that these men would not even think twice about spraying bullets at any target.

He gave the closest thing he knew to a prayer that Gurt was both alert and watching in this direction.

He yelled, "Gurt, go for it!" knowing she would recognize the ruse.

At the same instant, he flicked the flashlight on and off, illuminating the bust. Ordinarily, marble would not be mistaken for flesh and blood. Likely it wouldn't this time, either. But the impenetrable darkness, tense nerves, and the lightninglike flicker that robbed color from whatever it touched might, just might . . .

The reaction was instantaneous. Before Lang regained the shelter of the tomb, two geysers of ragged flame spouted from a tomb almost next to Lang's like laterally held Roman candles. Although large, the necropolis's cover made the sound deafening, a single stream of explosions that beat against Lang's eardrums like fists, beat so hard as to be painful. He could clearly hear the splatter of fragments of stone and plaster as they pelted the outer wall of his sanctuary.

He couldn't duck completely out of sight, though. He had to see . . . See and hold on to the flashlight, which he stuck into his belt.

Before the first long bursts of two automatic weapons had ceased their clatter, a smaller streak of fire came from somewhere across the street. One of the automatics' muzzle flash traced an arc upward and went dark.

One down, one to go.

The shooters had been so close, Lang could smell the acrid stench of burned cordite. He had been lucky the men had been too intent on escape to hear his foray into the street.

His ears ringing from gunfire, Lang now could hear only his own heartbeat, a sound so loud he was surprised the man right down the street couldn't hear it, too.

Lang had marked the source of enemy fire, although the darkness prevented an exact measurement. He guessed fifteen feet, twenty at the most. Reavers's pistol in hand, he began a hands-and-knees approach to a spot in the curtain of black where he estimated his enemy might be.

In a couple of minutes, Lang calculated he was in front of the building that housed the remaining gunman. He held his breath, the better to hear the other man's, but silence alone greeted the effort. He knew he couldn't stay here, exposed in the street. Another burst of gunfire or the sweep of a flashlight would reveal his position.

His outstretched hand touched a number of pebbles. Shifting the gun to his left, he picked up the small stones, rolled them in the palm of his hand for a second, and threw them in the direction of the gunman.

This time the man didn't fire. But he did move, a clear scraping sound as his feet knocked over rocks in the darkness.

Quickly switching hands, Lang fired two shots in the general direction of the sound as he swiftly rolled across the cobblestones.

As anticipated, automatic fire churned the street where Lang had been. A short burst, but enough. Two more flashes of light, from somewhere across the road, a scream that sounded like it came from only a few feet away, and all was silent again, the quiet after the blast of gunfire seeming to have a physical weight of its own.

Lang felt the wall of something, a tomb or other structure, and slowly stood, pressing against the coolness of the stone. He fumbled at his belt and removed the light. Inching along the wall until he felt the opening, he held the Sig Sauer in his right hand, the light in his left. Pointing the gun into the darkness, he pushed the button on the light.

Even in the puny beam given by a shattered lens and cracked bulb, he could see the fight was over. One man stared into eternity with blank eyes; wherever he had been hit, death had been instantaneous, as there was no blood visible. The other sat stiff-legged in a red puddle against the rear wall of the little house, his hands uselessly trying to staunch the flow of crimson from his throat. He didn't look up as Lang stepped over and kicked away the M16 automatic rifle, thankful Reavers had not added nightscopes.

The man gave a final sound, a noise like a gargle, and slumped to his side. No breath was visible.

"You are glad to see me, *Liebchen,* no?" Gurt was right behind him. "Or is that a gun in your pocket?"

The old Mae West line was one of her favorites.

He turned to embrace her. "Frankly, my dear, I couldn't give more of a damn, Rhett Butler notwithstanding. You have no idea . . ."

She gently pushed him away. "Later. Right now, we

must leave this place. Someone could have the gunfire heard."

Lang thought of the pressurized, climate-controlled part of the necropolis open to a limited segment of the population. "Possible, but I'd say the insulation was enough to quiet an A-bomb."

Gurt's eyes flickered around the small area lit by their flashlights. "A-bomb? No one has—"

He put a finger to her lips. "You're right. Later."

She swept the beam of her light over the two dead men. "And these?"

"They're already in a cemetery. What's the point of having them moved to another?"

She turned her head to peer up the slope. "And Reavers?"

"Him, too. Let the Agency figure out where he disappeared."

He went back to the top to retrieve his cassock.

Minutes later, a priest and a tall nun were walking away from St. Peter's Square. There was nothing particularly unusual about either. Unless the careful observer watched them long enough to note that they seemed to touch a great deal more than decorum would require.

And they laughed incessantly.

FORTY-SEVEN

The Amalfi Coast, Ravello
Hotel Palumbo
Two days later

Most of the roads carved into the mountains of Italy's
Amalfi Coast are one and a half car widths wide, a measurement dating back to a time when bicycles were the
norm and tiny, shoebox-sized automobiles navigated
the hairpin turns with a sense of adventure, if not com-
placency. Today, buses crammed with increasing numbers of tourists stretch from the stone walls on the
seaward side of the road to the sheer rock on the other.
Other traffic seeks such nooks and crannies as they can
find until the behemoths squeeze past with a cheery
honk of the horn and a puff of foul-smelling diesel smoke.

The few streets in Ravello are too narrow even for this
accommodation. Anything larger than a compact risks
leaving body parts in front of someone's door.

That was why Lang had chosen this place. There was

nothing remarkable about the old stone buildings along the Via S. Giovanni del Toro other than interesting examples of Moorish influence in the Mediterranean. The sign announcing the hotel was small, evidencing management's hopes that only those aware of its presence would notice; that new, possibly American, clientele would seek the hospitality of the other hotel, the one that catered to American film and TV stars, on the hill on the other side of town.

That, of course, was exactly why Lang had chosen the Palumbo.

Unimpressive if not downright plain from the street, the lobby usually caused first-time visitors (if they could not be encouraged to go elsewhere) to stop, stare, and mutter whatever translated as "My God!" in their native language.

Two stories of glass looked straight across a gorge at the misty cliffs that lined a golden beach hundreds of feet below. In the distance, fishing boats bobbed in cobalt-blue waters like so many gaily colored corks. The staff was quiet, unobtrusive, and usually invisible unless summoned.

Lang had reserved a room just off the lobby with much the same view. He and Gurt lapsed into a routine of early-morning walks, midday swims in the hotel's infinity-edged pool, lunch at one of the town's one or two trattoria, and frantic lovemaking in the afternoons before a nap.

Eschewing the hotel's barrel-vaulted, frescoed dining room, each evening they dined at a small *ristorante* on one of the two narrow streets that forked off the one in front of the church. Like most such establishments, the place was lit like a surgical theater. Lang theorized that Italians liked to make sure they got what they paid for rather than risk less expensive substitution in a dimmer,

more romantically lighted place. Gurt suggested the unfortunate medieval habit of disposing of one's dinner
guests by poison was the source of the custom.

Either way, the place was run by an elderly woman
who commanded her eatery like the captain of a ship.
Each night, shoeless, she circulated among her guests,
demanding an explanation for any remaining scrap.

After the third dinner there, Lang and Gurt were walking up an incline made steeper by the Fiori di Zucca e
Carciofi Fritti he had had along with his Saltimbocca
alla Romana in his stomach.

He stopped on the piazza, a small square with a *gela-
terie* and a seller of dubious antiques on one side, the
church adjoining on the other, and two sides open.
"Okay, how did you know?"

The events in the necropolis had not been discussed,
but had been avoided like an unpleasant subject everyone knows will have to be thrashed out at some point.

Gurt, in the pencil-legged leather pants and peasant
blouse favored by younger Italian women, thought a
moment. Then she took his arm and guided him back
uphill toward the hotel. She told him what had happened, or what she remembered of it, of the hospital and
her memory and hearing loss.

"It was the piece of torn-off ticket . . ."

"Stub," he said, "a ticket stub."

"The ticket stub, then," she said. "It brought it all
back: being in Frankfurt, the Agency. Also, if this man
who tried to kill me had such a ticket from the Frankfurt
U-Bahn, he had been in Frankfurt. If he had come out of
there, the chances were the Agency was somehow mixed
in it. Why would anyone else want me dead? I would
have called to warn you, but my Agency phone was lost
in the explosion. Besides, if the Agency was involved,
they would be listening to any conversation you had."

Lang pulled open the door to the hotel to let her enter. "Good thing. What the bastard gave me wasn't just a secure phone, it was a tracking device."

"And I suppose that if I had called Sara . . ."

"That line was probably bugged."

She looked at him curiously. "Like the roaches we see in Atlanta?"

"It had a listening device. They would have heard anything you said."

He stopped, looking back down the hill. The piazza was obscured by treetops. "What about *Die Spinne,* some organization to protect old Nazis? Did you ever consider that?"

She pulled him forward. "You were the only one who ever saw Nazis on every bed."

"*Under* every bed. You're right. You and Blucher didn't think much of my theory."

This time it was Gurt who stopped. Even in the dim light from the lobby, he could see her exaggerated expression of surprise. "Ach! The dumb woman has right once?"

He grinned good-naturedly. "The dumb woman who saved my ass again."

She winked mischievously. "It is not your ass I wish to save."

They crossed the threshold and started toward their room, in silence for a moment before he asked, "The necropolis under the Vatican—how did you know?"

She thought for a moment, either trying to get the English phraseology right or deciding exactly what to say. By now, they were outside the room.

He put the key in the lock but blocked her entrance. "Well?"

Again the sly smile. "Would you believe women's intuition?"

"No."

She sighed theatrically. "Very well, deprive from me the illus . . . illus . . ."

"Illusion?"

"Illusion of feminine mystery."

He was still holding the door open, standing in her path. "Gurt . . ."

She shook her head. "I heard you tell Reavers how you thought it out, how you had guessed that Skorzeny was one of the Germans the Americans brought over after the war and that man Straight was the son of Skorzeny. If you can pull that hare out of your cap, you tell me how I knew."

Lang stepped back outside to join her in the narrow hall. This wasn't a conversation he wanted overheard. He pulled her inside and shut the door. They sat on the bed.

"Okay. I'd guess it went something like this." He thought for a second, arranging his suppositions in much the same way he had lined up theorems in high school geometry. "You knew I was trying to track down whatever Skorzeny took from Montsegur. The only clue we had before that helicopter showed up was Julian's inscription, the one about the palace of the single god."

She ruffled his hair with her fingers. "So far, so bad. Just before the helicopter flew over us, you were talking about Julian and a palace of some sort."

He shrugged. "Okay, so tell me."

"You will not like what you hear."

"I can stand it."

This time it was Gurt who shrugged. " 'Palace of the one god.' What could that be but the Vatican?"

It took a moment to sink in. "Palace of the sole god and you immediately knew what Julian meant?"

"I was there, was I not?"

He nodded slowly, absorbed by what she was saying. "It took Francis and me a while to be certain that was what was meant. You figured it out in minutes."

She grinned, fishing in her bag for a cigarette. Just before she lit it, she chuckled. "I told you you would not like it. I called a friend in the Rome station."

"A friend posted with the Agency? You knew the lines would be secure."

"Exactly. I asked this friend where Reavers was because I knew if what I had guessed was true, he would be trying to kill you, too."

Lang stared at her with uncomprehending eyes. "Asked where he was? You know that's need-to-know only."

"As I said, I asked a friend."

"A former lover, you mean."

"I said you would not like this. You have no reason to be, er, angry. We were through before you came to Rome last year."

What she said made irritatingly good sense. Lang had no possible reason to care what Gurt had done since they had broken up before he married Dawn ten years ago.

That, however, did absolutely nothing to stop more than a twinge of jealousy.

Lang pretended he was only interested in how she had found him. "So you found out Reavers was in Rome. Then?"

"I got the nun's dress and hung down . . ."

"Hung around."

"Stayed around the Rome station."

"You were conducting surveillance of the Agency's Rome station and nobody noticed?"

"I was stationed in Rome, remember? I knew what was covered by cameras and what was not. Besides, I convinced a nice man to rent me a room just down the street for only a few days."

The green-eyed monster stirred again. "A nice man?"

She shook her head impatiently. "A nice man who must have been at least seventy. Do you want to interrogate me, or shall I complete?"

Lang's curiosity outweighed any irrational jealousy. "Go on."

"So, when I saw Reavers come out, I followed him."

Lang was incredulous. "You managed to follow a station chief?"

"No one is as cautious as we were in the old days. Reavers has been around so long, he probably forgets women now work there."

It had taken a threat of congressional intervention to bring that about, if Lang remembered correctly.

"Anyway, while I was observing him, he was observing what I took to be a priest, you. I didn't contact you because I might have been watched myself. I was also afraid to call your hotel. I just waited until I saw Reavers and his men follow you into the bottom of the Vatican."

Lang nodded, digesting the information. Then: "The gun—how did you get that?"

"I told you, I had a friend in the Frankfurt office."

Must be some kind of a friend to violate a couple of dozen regs concerning firearms as well as information, Lang thought sourly. If the bastard didn't get summarily fired, he would have spent the rest of his career counting printer cartridges in some place infected with rats smaller only than the scorpions. But he said, "I guess I owe you a 'Thank you.' "

She stood, unzipping her blouse. "It is late and you have had hours since this afternoon to recover. You owe me more than 'Thank you.' "

*   *   *

It was early the next afternoon when reality stuck its ugly head into paradise. Sara's daily call warned of decisions that had to be made for the foundation and clients who were getting restless at the unavailability of their lawyer.

It was time to go home.

"We can fly Naples–Paris–Atlanta," Lang said, taking the phone from his ear. "Or we can drive to Rome and fly direct."

Gurt gave her head a slight shake, a gesture that always implied something negative. "I will be staying in Rome."

Lang forgot the airline reservationist on the other end of the line as well as the per-minute profit the hotel was making. "You're what?"

She took the receiver from him and hung it up with one hand while she caressed his cheek with the other. "It is something I cannot do, *Liebchen*. I cannot live on your char . . . er, char . . ."

"Charity."

"Your charity forever."

"But you're not," he protested. "You have a job teaching . . ."

She waved a dismissive hand. "And after what I have done for the last fifteen years or so, you think teaching rich kids to mangle the German language is going to fascinate me?"

Lang had known her long enough to know she was slow to make up her mind and implacable once she had. He had thought he had lost her once, and now he was about to lose her for real.

He turned and went into the bathroom to collect his toilette articles so she could not see the misery he knew was on his face. "I wish you well. I'll miss you."

When he returned from the bathroom, she was gone.

EPILOGUE

Berlin
May of the same year

Jochim Stern, Ph.D., was puzzled. He had been summoned from his archaeology class at the university to examine some very interesting pottery shards. Interesting because of their location, not quality. One would expect such things to be unearthed every time Rome worked on its underground metro or Cairo began a new sewer line. In fact, the Herr *Doktor* had consulted with a number of cities with classical Greco-Roman pasts.

But Berlin?

As far as he knew, neither Greek nor Roman had ever set foot in the area that was Germany's historical capital. In fact, the Germanic tribes had served up one of Rome's few defeats, routing Augustus Caesar's army at Teutoburg Forest in the first century. As a result, Rome had turned elsewhere for conquest and trade.

That being so, what about these pieces of pottery he was holding in his hands as he squatted in the raw dirt?

No doubt they were ancient in origin, highly likely part of a Greek-style amphora. A large one, the sort of vessel used to store wine or oil.

The Herr *Doktor* looked up from the excavation of a new U-Bahn line. This was the area where Hitler had had his bunker, wasn't it? Hard to be sure. In their fury, the Russians had not only demolished whatever was left of the *Führer*'s redoubt and everything in it, filling it in, they had made a sort of park surrounding the place so that it was difficult if not impossible to ascertain exactly where Hitler's last hours had been spent. Probably the only green space the Russians had contributed to East Berlin, and now far too valuable to the expanding city to leave untouched.

So, what was a Greek or Roman urn doing here?

As far as Stern knew, Hitler had never been particularly interested in ancient history, but the shards were at the same layer of digging at which workers had found Nazi uniform buttons, fragments of what had been furniture, and the like, all of which confirmed that the pieces of the amphora were placed here at the time of the war.

He placed the shards in a large plastic food bag and stood. Like many mysteries surrounding World War II, this one wasn't going to be solved anytime soon. Just as well. That period of German history was best forgotten.

At least by the Germans.

Atlanta, Georgia
Park Place, 2660 Peachtree Road
July

Grumps was less than great company. Alternate snores and burps from his corner of the tiny kitchen announced he had ravished his evening meal and, as usual, fallen sound asleep.

Lang looked up at the bar that separated the kitchen and living areas. "It's your companionship and good looks, fella. That's the only reason I keep you around."

His attention returned to the evening news, today consisting almost entirely of the unanticipated withdrawal from the race for his party's nomination for president by one of the leading candidates, Harold Straight. With tearful countenance, the former aspirant for the nation's highest office had announced that "family matters" would need his exclusive attention for the next several years, necessitating not only an end to his present quest but a termination of all political activity. Based firmly on a total lack of facts, the talking heads interviewed one another, eliciting speculation ranging from AIDS to alcoholism, to the possibility of a scandalous divorce, to possible criminal prosecution for offenses unnamed.

Liberal politicians and the press hailed the event as demonstrating what-was-right-with-America, a theme unheard from the left since Newt Gingrich had declined to run for reelection to Congress. The right wing received far less media attention, as usual, but it was clear that the viciousness of partisan politics had, in their view, defeated a just cause.

Lang smiled with the satisfaction of true knowledge.

It was, however, his only satisfaction. In the two months since his return from Europe, he had buried himself in work, micromanaging the foundation to the extent that several of his top employees were seeking positions elsewhere. Sara had simply refused to come to work for several days, asserting he was unfit for association with human beings. Only pleas of the longevity of their relationship, promises of a real vacation at the end of the summer, and an assurance he would reduce his caseload had lured her back to the office.

He had, however, had time to read of Rome during the German occupation and the sparse literature available concerning Otto Skorzeny. Although none of the books actually connected the two, Lang knew from the Huff CD that the SS officer had been there. Supposition had answered at least one question: Why had Skorzeny taken only the one amphora and not come back for the second? Time, pure and simple. By the end of April 1944, Allied troops had broken out of the German encirclement of the invasion beaches and were heading for Rome as fast as artillery and trucks could be supplied. Skorzeny had skedaddled, no doubt with the first container, the mark of which was still visible in the dirt when Lang arrived sixty-plus years later.

That raised an even more interesting query: What was in it?

Lang would have to live without even a guess. He would have enjoyed swapping theories with Gurt. Another reason to miss her.

His return without Gurt had somehow been communicated throughout the building by a system he suspected akin to blood in shark-infested waters. Almost nightly, his doorbell rang and one or more of the building's single women presented him with a casserole, an entrée or something else edible, almost all of which had clearly come from one of the caterers nearby. After all, cooking was work, and few of these women would admit to being forced into such drudgery.

Lang had remained steadfast in his declinations of invitations to dinners and cocktail parties.

He knew the single women in this building, the Wet Cats, were as predatory as any animal in the jungle and even more desperate to find someone to rescue them from the alternative of having to support themselves. Wealthy and single, he was a wildebeest in lion territory.

Even in his placid marriage to Dawn, he had learned that men were preservationists, women restorationists. A man saw the woman he loved and took her as is, not wishing (or noticing) so much as a change in hairstyle. A woman took a man as a work in progress, a project to be molded and shaped to her specifications. That "aromatic tobacco" would become "that stinking cigar" overnight, and his "comfortable favorite chair" a "ratty embarrassment."

And so on.

Lang wanted none of it.

Dinners with Francis, shared Cubanos, probably this small, easily maintained condo, and Grumps were likely to become no more than vapors of memory if he gave in to the onslaught of single women who were desperate to eliminate the specter of necessary employment.

He knew self-sufficient women—lawyers, doctors, and the like—but he never seemed able to meet them unless they were already taken. In fact, there was a federal prosecutor, a petite redhead, he'd almost asked out before she appeared in court with a diamond of blinding quality and a size that skirted vulgarity. He told himself he was disappointed, but he knew what he felt was relief.

He was not particularly surprised, then, when the doorbell chimed just as he thought he had reached a decision as to which Healthy Choice dinner to nuke in the microwave. Another ready-to-eat something, delivered with a hopeful smile by another woman looking for a male life-support system.

Grumps, long used to the parade, normally favored the applicants with little more than a single open eye before returning to his twenty-three-hour-a-day nap. This time, Lang could have sworn the mutt leapt into the air without touching the floor. Barking furiously, the dog nearly took Lang's feet out from under him in his rush to the door, where he stood on stubby hind legs while using the front two to frantically scratch the paint from the wood surface.

No doubt some woman had decided to seek intercession by Grumps and was delivering a bag of treats.

"Traitor!" Lang snorted at the frenzied animal.

He had barely cracked the door when Grumps used his head as a wedge to pry it wide and disappeared into the hall to dance wildly around Gurt's feet.

She put down a small suitcase to kneel and croon to the excited dog.

Lang simply stood there until she looked up.

"Langford, close your mouth. It is most unattractive hanging open."

"Grumps wrote and asked you to come back," he suggested with a grin.

She nodded toward the suitcase, both hands still on Grumps. "You are not a gentleman? You would have me my own luggage carry?"

Still not sure he wasn't hallucinating, Lang reached out for the bag. "You came back to get something?"

She stood, brushing long black dog hairs from a pair of hip-huggers. "That could be said."

"What?"

She made a show of running salacious eyes over his body. "That is for you to discover."

He simply couldn't stand it any longer. Neither could she. They met just beside the door in an embrace that showed little chance of ending soon despite plaintive barking.

Finally inside, they stood on the small balcony overlooking the city.

"Gurt, have you decided . . . ?"

She turned, putting a finger across his lips. "I decided I would rather teach rich kids to mangle German with you than track potential terrorists across Europe."

"Does that mean . . . ?"

"It means just what I said, *nichts andres*. You must be satisfied with that."

And he was.

THE PEGASUS SECRET
GREGG LOOMIS

What started as a suspicious explosion in a picturesque Parisian neighborhood could end in revelations that would shatter the beliefs of millions. American lawyer Lang Reilly is determined to find the real cause of the blast that killed his sister. But his investigation will lead him into the darkest corners of history and religion. And it may cost him his life.

Lang's search for the truth begins with a painting his sister bought just before she died. Could there be something about the painting itself that made someone want to kill her? Every mysterious step of the way, Lang unearths still more questions, more hidden secrets and more danger, until finally he arrives at the heart of a centuries-old secret order that will stop at nothing to protect what is theirs.

ANDREW COBURN

ON THE LOOSE

By the time he was twelve years old, young Bobby Sawhill had killed two people, brutally and with no remorse. He was tried as a juvenile and sentenced to a youth detention center, where he refused counseling. All he seems to care about is bodybuilding, getting bigger. Stronger. Soon he'll be twenty-one. He'll be released—and then Bobby's coming home. Home to a small town that will live in fear, certain that Bobby will kill again, unable to do anything but wait for him to strike.

WILLIAM P. WOOD

BROKEN TRUST

Superior Court Judge Timothy Nash thinks the brutal murder trial in his court will be like many he's presided over before. That is, until Nash is tapped as point man in a federal sting operation against the most powerful and dangerous of prey: corrupt judges. Risking his reputation and his life, Nash digs deep and uncovers a devastating plot of betrayal. The closer he gets to the truth, the more desperate the judges become—until they fight back with all the power at their command. It's all coming to a head as the murder trial nears its verdict, a verdict that could spell death for not only the defendant but also for Nash himself.
